JOSEPHUS AND THE EMPEROR

ALSO BY LION FEUCHTWÁNGER

LION
FEUCHTWANGER

=

JOSEPHUS AND
THE EMPEROR

=

Translated by Caroline Oram

THE VIKING PRESS
NEW YORK · MCMXLII

JOSEPHUS AND THE EMPEROR

Translated from the German manuscript entitled
Der Tag wird kommen

Printed in U. S. A. by American Book–Stratford Press
Published on the same day in the Dominion of Canada
by The Macmillan Company of Canada Limited
First published in February 1942

CONTENTS

JOSEPHUS AND THE EMPEROR

DOMITIAN

I

No, JOSEPH could hardly let stand what he had written there. Once again he read over his sentences about Saul, King of the Hebrews: how he had resolutely gone forth to battle, although it had been made known to him that he would meet his death and lead his people to destruction. "Thus did Saul," he had written, "and by this act he gave proof that those who strive for eternal fame should do likewise." No, they should not do likewise. Just at this moment he must not write that. His countrymen were prone as it was, in these last decades since the fall of their nation and their Temple, to attempt some new, foolish, warlike undertaking. That secret society which wished to hasten the coming of that day, the Zealots, was continually winning new adherents and new influence. However much the sombre courage of this King Saul appealed to him, he must follow his reason, not his emotions; he must not present this king to his Jews as a hero worthy of emulation.

Flavius Josephus, Roman Knight of the second rank, the great writer whose bust had been placed in the library of the Temple of Peace, or rather Doctor Joseph Ben Matthias, priest of the first rank of Jerusalem, threw aside his stylus, paced up and down, finally seated himself in a corner of his study. There he sat in the half-darkness, the oil lamp picking out only the desk with the few books and scrolls which were lying on it, and the golden writing-tablets which the dead Emperor Titus had once given him. Shivering—for no fire had headway against the damp cold of this early December

3

—with an absent stare, Joseph gazed at the dully gleaming gold.

Strange that he had written those enthusiastic sentences about Saul's foolish bravery. Had his heart run away with him yet once again? Would it still not be content, that fifty-year-old heart, with the spirit of quiet contemplation which alone should find expression in his great book?

At least it happened more and more rarely now that his stylus or his pen ran away with him. He had achieved that equanimity which his great work demanded, his *Universal History of the Jews*. He had renounced the hurly-burly; he did not long for the wild life which lay behind him. He had in his time thrown himself with burning enthusiasm into the great war of his people, had taken part in it on the side of the Jews and on the side of the Romans, as politician and soldier, had looked more deeply into the events of the war than the great majority of his contemporaries; had participated in the great episodes, in the intimate circle of the first and second Flavian Emperors, as actor and sufferer, as Roman, Jew, and citizen of the world; had finally written the classical account of that Jewish War; had been honoured as few others, and abased and vilified as few others. Now he was tired of the successes and defeats; the violent activity had come to seem shallow to him; he had recognized that his mission and his strength lay in contemplation. Not to create history had he been appointed by God and before mankind, but to order and perpetuate the history of his people, to seek out its meaning, to present its participants as admirable or warning examples. For that he was here, and he was content.

Was he content? The beautiful and unwise passage about King Saul did not bear witness to it. He was almost fifty, but he had not yet found that much-desired equanimity.

He had done everything to achieve it. Through no kind of

striving for external success had he let himself be distracted from his task. During all these four years none of his work had reached the public. While Vespasian and Titus had maintained a cordial attitude toward him, he had not raised a finger to get access to the suspicious Domitian, the present Emperor. No, in the quiet, withdrawn Joseph of this last period, there was nothing of that earlier, violent, active man.

The sentences about the sombre courage of King Saul, which he had written there, were beautiful and carried one away, and the Zealots would read them with enthusiasm. But, alas, that was exactly what they should not do. They should become practised not in enthusiasm, but in reasonableness, in sly patience. They should resign themselves, and not for a second time foolishly take up arms against the Romans.

Why indeed had those beautiful and accursed sentences about King Saul come to his pen on this particular day? He had already known why while he was writing the words; he had not wanted to know it, but now he could no longer hide his own knowledge from himself. It had happened because yesterday he had met Paulus, his boy, the sixteen-year-old, the son of his divorced wife. Joseph had not wanted to take notice of that meeting, had not wanted to admit to himself that the young man who had ridden past him there was his Paulus. He had commanded himself not to gaze after the boy, but his heart had given a leap, and he had known: it was Paulus.

A little groan came from the mouth of the man sitting in the semi-darkness. How he had fought in his time for this son of his, Paulus, the half-foreigner, the son of the Greek woman; how many heavy sins he had taken upon himself for his sake. Yet the boy had uprooted everything that he had attempted, with so much shy perseverance, to implant in him, and now he had only scorn for him, the father, the Jew.

Joseph thought of the ghastly hour when he had had to march under the yoke of the victor, under the Arch of Titus; he thought of how at that time, for a fraction of a second, the face of his son Paulus had appeared to him. Among the many thousands of jeering faces in that dark hour, that pale brown, thin, hostile face would never leave his mind, was seared into his heart. It was nothing else than the memory of that face, self-defence against that face, which had guided his pen when he wrote those sentences about Saul, King of the Jews.

For, alas, to go into battle, even if it led to sure defeat, how easy that was compared to the burden which he had taken upon himself in those days. It was heart-rending, degrading, to have to show admiration for the insolent conqueror because one knew that such self-abasement was the only service which one could render to one's people.

Later, in a hundred years or in a thousand, people would be aware of that. But today, on this ninth of Kislev of the year 3847 after the creation of the world, it was poor comfort that those coming so long after would one day admire him. In his ears there was no ring of that fame, in his heart only the memory of that shouting from a hundred thousand mouths: "Villain! Traitor! Dog!" and above it, soundless and yet louder than all the other voices, the voice of his son Paulus: "My father the villain, my father the dog."

Because he had wanted to defend himself against that voice —that was why he had written the sentences about the sombre courage of Saul. Sweet and exhilarating it was to write them. Sweet and exhilarating it was to let oneself be carried away heedlessly by his courage. But devilishly hard it was, heavily oppressive, to remain deaf to the temptation and to hear nothing but the calm, the by no means intoxicating, voice of reason.

There he crouched, a man not yet old, and the room, dim

except for the desk lighted by the oil lamp, was full of the deeds undone for which he yearned. For the self-possession of which he made so much, this calm of his in the midst of noisy, glittering Rome, bursting with exploits, was artificial, was forced, was a fraud. To make a great noise, to thirst for deeds—that was something. To recount the story of King Saul so as to make the youth of his nation exult with him and go to their death filled with enthusiasm as in those days when he, young and foolish, had swept them off their feet by his book on the Maccabees—that was something. To write the history of Saul and David and the kings and the Maccabean rulers so as to make his son Paulus feel: "My father is a man and a hero"—that was something. But the sanction of his own reason, the admiration of the next generations, the later world —that was nothing but an echo and a vapour.

He must not think that. He must chase away those faces which lurked here for him in the dark. He clapped his hands for his servant, ordered: "Light, light." All the lamps and candles had to be lighted. He felt with relief as the room became bright that he actually became himself again. Now he could follow reason, his true goddess.

He sat down at his desk once more, pulled himself forcibly together. "So that it does not appear," he wrote, "that I intend to praise King Saul more than his due, I shall now continue with my actual narrative." And he continued, told his story, objectively, in measured words.

He might have been working thus for an hour when his servant announced to him that a stranger had arrived who refused to be turned away, a Doctor Justus of Tiberias.

Joseph had seen his great literary rival rarely in the last years, and almost never alone. It could hardly be a good sign that Justus should look him up at such an unaccustomed hour.

The man's greyish-yellow face, as he now entered the room, bringing dampness and cold with him, seemed to Joseph to have become even harder, more withered, more furrowed than he remembered it. Justus's head, aged, worn out, painfully held erect, sat upon a terrifyingly thin neck. Joseph, although he was waiting anxiously for what the other would say to him, mechanically directed his gaze to the stump of that left arm which they had had to amputate when Joseph had brought him down from the crucifix. By doing so he had got himself a severe monitor from that cross, who with cruelly sure gaze saw through him to every rotten spot, a man of whom Joseph was afraid and yet whom he could not do without.

"And what do you want, Justus?" he asked point-blank after a few sentences. "I want to give you some urgent advice," Justus answered. "Watch carefully in the next weeks what you say and to whom. Also think over whether perhaps you've been saying things lately which ill-wishers could interpret to your disadvantage, and consider how such comments might be invalidated. There are people in the circle of the Emperor who do not wish you well, and you yourself are said to receive persons at your house now and then whose loyalty to the State is questionable." "Can one not communicate with people," asked Joseph, "who are Roman citizens and who have never been suspect to any officials?" Justus grimaced with his thin lips. "One could," he answered, "in times of peace. But now it's better to look over everybody carefully—not merely whether there was once something against him, but also whether some time in the future there might not be something against him."

"You think that the peace in the East—?" Joseph did not finish his sentence.

"I think the peace in the East has once again come to an end," answered Justus. "The Dacians have crossed the Danube and have invaded the territory of the Empire. The announcement comes from the Palatine."

Joseph had risen to his feet. He had difficulty concealing from the other how greatly the news upset him. The new war that now came rolling onward, this war in the East, could have unforeseen consequences for him and for Judæa. If the Eastern legions were involved in a struggle, if one could count on the intervention of the Parthians, would not then the Zealots break into violence? Would they not attempt that hopeless revolt?

And there, only an hour ago, he had been praising King Saul, the man who, envisaging a sure defeat, yet went forth into battle. He was an even greater fool and criminal, for all his fifty years, than formerly at thirty.

"Justus, what can we do?" he said directly out of his deep anxiety, his voice hoarse with excitement.

"Come now, Joseph, after all you know that better than I," answered Justus, and he jeered: "There are seventy-seven who have the ear of the world, and you are one of them. You must let yourself be heard. You must draw up a clear manifesto which advises against all rash steps. The simpler the better. You can do it, you know. You're an expert in the language of the common man, you're an expert in big and cheap words." His sharp voice sounded especially unpleasant, his thin lips twisted, and again there was the provoking titter which exasperated Joseph's nerves.

Yet Joseph did not enter into the other's spirit of derision.

"How can you possibly make way with words against such a strong feeling?" he asked. "I myself want to go to Judæa"— it burst from him—"to take part in this uprising, in any capacity, to go under in this uprising."

"That I believe," jeered Justus; "that would just suit you. When a stronger man hits one, one simply hits back and provokes him until he strikes one dead. But if the Zealots have an excuse, you have none. You are not so stupid." And as Joseph stared in front of him, helplessly, grimly, Justus added: "Write the manifesto. You have much to make up for."

When Justus had left, Joseph sat down to follow his advice. It took, he wrote, much more courage to control ourselves and to desist from the uprising than to initiate it. For the time being, even if the war broke out in the East, the business of us, the Jews, was to build up further the Kingdom of the Law and of Tradition and to dedicate our whole strength to this task. We must leave it to God and governing reason to create the conditions under which this Kingdom of Law and Tradition, the Jerusalem of the Spirit, might also receive its visible frame and foundation, the Jerusalem of Stone. The day had not yet come. But a premature, armed undertaking would only postpone the day which we were all earnestly awaiting.

He wrote. He tried to saturate himself with enthusiasm for reason to the point where her water would taste like wine, to the point where the attitude which he preached would no longer seem to him the affair of his reason but the affair of his heart. Twice the servant had to renew the candles and the oil in the lamps before Joseph was satisfied with his conception.

The following evening four guests arrived at the dwelling of Joseph. There was present the furniture dealer Caius Barzaarone, President of the Agrippine Ward, representative of Roman Jewry, a temperate, reasonable man, whose name stood in good repute in Judæa as well. There was present also John of Gishala, formerly a leader in the Jewish War, a sly and a bold man. Now he was settled in Rome as a dealer in land; his business undertakings spread over the whole Empire; but in Judæa today, in the minds of the Zealots, the memory of his activity during the war was still alive. There was present as a third Justus of Tiberias. There was present finally Claudius Reginus, the Emperor's Minister of Finance, born of a Jewish mother and never, moreover, making any bones about the fact that he favoured the cause of the Jews, the man who published Joseph's books and who had helped him in all his troubles.

Under the suspicious Emperor Domitian all meetings had to bear a harmless appearance in order not to look like a conspiracy; for there were in almost every house spies of the Chief of Police Norbanus. So for the moment the gentlemen, while they ate their dinner, carried on incidental conversation about the events of the day. Naturally one talked about the war. "At heart," was the opinion of John of Gishala, and his brown, good-humoured, crafty face smiled cheerfully, a little secretively, "at heart the Emperor is not warlike for a Flavian." Claudius Reginus turned to him, lying there sloppily, his heavy eyes looking out sleepily and mockingly from under his bulging forehead. He knew that the Emperor could not do without him, and that therefore he could now and then permit himself some maliciously humorous frankness. Today too he gave no consideration to the servants waiting on table. "No, warlike D.D.D. is not," he answered John; D.D.D. was what they called the Emperor after the initials of his title and his name: *Dominus ac Deus Domitianus,* the Lord and God Domitian. "Only, unfortunately he thinks that the triumphal cloak of Jupiter is not unbecoming to him, and that costume is a trifle costly. I can't do a triumph under twelve million, quite aside from the expenses of the war."

Finally Joseph, ending the meal, was able to dismiss the servants, and they came to the point. The first to express his opinion was Caius Barzaarone. He scarcely believed, the jovial gentleman with the sly eyes explained, that they, the Roman Jews, were necessarily endangered by the coming war. Of course they must, in this difficult period, keep quiet and avoid being conspicuous. He had already arranged prayer services for the Emperor and for the victory of his eagles in his Agrippine Ward, and naturally the other synagogues would follow suit.

It was a vague, unsatisfying speech. So Barzaarone might talk in the association of furniture dealers of which he was head, or at best in front of the council members of his ward; but when he spoke here, to them, there was really no point in shutting one's eyes to the danger.

John of Gishala accordingly shook his brown, broad head. Unfortunately—he gave his opinion with good-humoured irony—the whole of Jewry was not so virtuous and sensible as the well-disciplined Agrippine Ward. There were, for example, as was certainly not unknown to the honourable Caius Barzaarone, the Zealots.

These Zealots, Justus stated in his dry manner, would, annoyingly, be able to refer to many a statement by the Grand Doctor Gamaliel. The Grand Doctor Gamaliel, president of the University and Council of Jabne, was, moreover, the acknowledged leader of the whole of Jewry. For all his moderation, Justus went on, the Grand Doctor had been forced, unless he wanted to let the Zealots take all the wind out of his sails, always to stir up anew the hope of the early re-establishment of the Kingdom and the Temple, and sometimes also to use stronger words. This the fanatics would now recall. "The Grand Doctor will not have an easy time of it," he concluded.

"Let's not fool ourselves, gentlemen," John of Gishala summed up in his inconsiderate way. "It is as good as certain that the Zealots will break into violence."

At heart they had all known that; yet it gave them a little start when John stated it so matter-of-factly. Joseph eyed this John: his body, not tall but broad and strong, his brown, good-natured face with the short moustache, his flat nose, his grey, mischievous eyes. Yes, John was the true Galilean peasant, he knew his Judæa from the inside, he had been the most popular among the instigators and leaders of the Jewish War, and however deeply Joseph rebelled against his whole manner he could not deny that the man's patriotism came from the depths of his being. "We here in Rome," John of Gishala said, explaining the decisiveness with which he had spoken, "can hardly imagine how the war in the East must be stirring the people of Judæa. We here experience with our own bodies, so to say, the might of the Roman Empire; it is constantly around us, the feeling of that power has gone over into our blood and prevents any thought of resistance. But if I," he mused aloud, and his face took on a thoughtful, concentrated, painfully longing expression, "if I were sitting not here in Rome, but in Judæa, and there heard about a defeat of the Romans, then I couldn't answer for myself. I know of course with mathematical certainty that such a defeat would make no difference in the outcome of the war; they have made me feel with my own body where such an uprising leads. I'm not young any more, either. And yet I myself am torn to get up and go, to break into violence. I tell you the Zealots won't stand still."

John's words moved the others. "What can we do to disenchant them?" Justus interrupted the silence. He spoke with cold, almost offensive sharpness; yet the earnestness of his thinking, the integrity of his judgment, had gained him respect; and that he had taken part in the Jewish War, that he had hung upon the cross for Jerusalem, proved that it was not cowardice when he so scornfully rejected a new warlike undertaking.

"Perhaps," suggested Caius Barzaarone carefully, "one could persuade the Emperor to withdraw the poll-tax. One would have to make him believe that it was advisable in such critical times to spare the feelings of the Jewish population. Perhaps our Claudius Reginus would put in a word for us there." Among all the anti-Semitic measures the decreeing of this poll-tax had indeed aroused the most resentment. Not only was it a bitter, derisive reminder to the Jews of their downfall that the Romans collected for the maintenance of the Temple of Jupiter Capitoline the double drachma which formerly every Jew had to pay as a tax to the Temple in Jerusalem, but the entry of the tax on the lists of Jews, its public posting and its collection, were undertaken in a brutal and defamatory manner.

"It takes some courage in these days," said Claudius Reginus after a short silence, "to show that one sympathizes with you. Nevertheless, I might perhaps get up that boldness and convey our Caius Barzaarone's suggestion to the Emperor. But don't you think that D.D.D., if he should really give up the double drachma, would demand an enormous compensation for it? He would at best decree a special tax as compensation which would be less painful to your feelings but all the more so for your purses. I don't know, my good Caius Barzaarone, whether you prefer the continued possession of your furniture factory or the abolition of the Jewish tax. I for my part would rather swallow a few insults and in return keep my money. A rich Jew, even if insulted, still has some power and influence; a poor Jew, even if uninsulted, is nothing at all."

Justus disposed of the platitudes of Claudius Reginus and the impracticable suggestions of Caius Barzaarone with a little wave of his hand. "What we can do," he said, "is damnably little. We can produce words—nothing else. That is paltry, I know. But if the words are very cleverly calculated, perhaps they will work just the same. I have urged Doctor Joseph to draw up a manifesto." All looked at Joseph. He was silent and did not move; he felt, behind Justus's words, an undertone of grating sarcasm. "And have you drawn up a circular?" John finally asked.

Joseph drew the manuscript from the sleeve of his robe and read it aloud. "It's an effective manifesto," said Justus when he had finished, and except for Joseph almost no one detected the scorn in the comment. "It will have little effect on the Zealots," was John's opinion. "Nothing can hold back the Zealots," Justus admitted, "and those associated with the Grand Doctor don't need any warning. But there are people between the two camps, there are people who are wavering, and perhaps they will let us, who live here in Rome and can judge the situation better, control their decision. Some effect the document will have," he insisted. He had spoken almost violently, as if he wanted to persuade not only the others but himself as well. But now he slackened and added gloomily: "And then we have to do something, if only for our own sakes. Aren't you eating your hearts out, squatting there and watching the others rush into misfortune?" He was thinking of how in the old days, before and during the beginning of the war, he had warned them in vain. And in twenty years again, if the same thing repeated itself, he would have to warn them once more, still as deeply convinced that he was stirring nothing but the air. "I think," he urged the others further, "we should put our names to the document and think over whom else we can invite to sign."

The bitter zeal of this man who was usually so reserved touched the hearts of the others. Nevertheless, the furniture dealer Caius Barzaarone shilly-shallied uneasily. "It seems to me," he said, "that it depends less on the number of the signatures than on the fact that those who sign count for something among the younger people in Judæa. What use is it, for example, if the signature of an old furniture dealer stands at the end of this manifesto?" "Perhaps it wouldn't be much use," answered Justus, and his hostility sounded in his words only as an undertone. "But there should be the signatures of unsuspected men on the document, if only to protect the others who sign." "That's true," said Claudius Reginus, putting the fearful Barzaarone in an even tighter spot. "The employees of our Chief of Police Norbanus scent mischief everywhere, and if the manifesto falls into their hands they'll declare that those who signed had knowledge of suspicious activities in Judæa. The more unobjectionable signatures there are on the manifesto, the less danger there will be for each individual." "Don't put up a long struggle, Barzaarone," said John of Gishala, stroking his moustache; "you'll have to give in anyway."

They took counsel as to how one could get the document to Judæa. Not only were there no good boat connexions now in winter, but there were other dangers as well. One could entrust the document only to a reliable man. "I really don't know," said Caius Barzaarone again, "whether the gain which at best we can get out of the circular is in the right proportion to the risk to which we expose ourselves and our community.

For whoever travels to Judæa now, in the winter, under such difficult conditions, must have a tenable explanation to give if he doesn't want to attract the attention of the authorities." But, "You're not going to get out of it, Caius Barzaarone," said mischievous John of Gishala, sticking to his point. "I know a man who has a tenable explanation for travelling to Judæa at this moment, an explanation which also makes sense to the officials. Without doubt land values will fall in Judæa as a result of the war. So it is not unlucky that we have land dealers among us, namely myself. My company has a lot of property in Judæa. It wishes, convinced of the speedy victory of the legions, to make use of the circumstances and to round out its possessions. Is that a tenable explanation? I shall send my agent, the respectable Gorion, to Judæa. Entrust me with the document. It will be conveyed safely."

They signed. Finally, with hesitation, even Caius Barzaarone put his name to Joseph's manifesto.

Three days later the gentlemen learned to their surprise that not Gorion but John of Gishala himself had departed for Judæa.

JOSEPH mounted the stairs to the rooms where Mara lived with the children. It was a cramped, uncomfortable stairway, but everything in his house was cramped, uncomfortable, full of corners. Already at the time when Domitian had evicted him from the beautiful building which the old Emperor had assigned to him as a home, people had wondered that such a distinguished man should select for himself this poor, old-fashioned little house in a highly unfashionable suburb. Moreover, since Mara had come to him with little Jalta and had borne him two sons, the house was really not suitable for him any more; but Joseph, sticking obstinately to a forced modesty, had restricted himself to raising it by one story. It stood there, cramped, narrow, ramshackle, in front of it the booths of a few small tradesmen with all kinds of evil-smelling rubbish, no worthy dwelling for a man of his rank and reputation.

Mara had from the beginning not felt at home in this house, in spite of her unassuming character. She wanted to have open sky overhead; to live in a big city between stone walls was in itself against her nature. And here, in these suffocating walls within walls, in the low room with the blackened ceiling, she felt doubly uncomfortable. If she had had her way they would long since have moved back to Judæa onto one of Joseph's estates.

It was now the fifth day since the news of the invasion of the Dacians had become public. Joseph had often been together with Mara in the meantime; he had shared most of his meals with her and had spoken to her a great deal. Nevertheless, there had been almost no mention of the coming border war. Probably Mara did not suspect what reactions the events along the Danube might have in Judæa. But surely she, who was familiar with his being down to the smallest details, felt the inner anxiety behind the mask of his composure.

As he now went upstairs he wondered why he had taken pains so long to hide this anxiety from her. She was the only person to whom he could show himself entirely as he was, without shame. When others had demanded it of him, she had let him send her away, and she had come back to him when he called her again. She was there when he needed her, and when she disturbed him she vanished. To her he could pour out everything: his pride, his doubts, his weaknesses.

He threw back the curtain and entered her chamber. The

low room was stuffed full of all kinds of objects; even from the ceiling hung baskets of foodstuffs and laundry, after the custom in small Judæan towns. The children were gathered around Mara, the girl Jalta and the two little sons, Matthias and Daniel.

Joseph was glad to leave his daughter and sons to Mara; he did not feel much at ease with children. Yet today as always he gazed with a kind of moved wonder at Matthias, the third of his sons and yet really the eldest, for Simeon was dead and Paulus more than dead for him. But on this son of his, Matthias, Joseph pinned new hopes and wishes. Clearly there were features of the father in the little fellow, clearly features of the mother, but the mixture resulted in something completely new, something of great promise, and Joseph hoped that in this Matthias he would be able to fulfil himself, that he would attain what he himself had not been able to attain: to be a Jew and at the same time a Greek, a citizen of the world.

There, then, sat his wife, working at a piece of clothing with her serving woman and telling the children a story. Joseph motioned to her not to let herself be disturbed. So she chattered on, and Joseph saw that it was a pious, somewhat foolish fairy-tale. It was about the river whose speech is understood by those who have the real fear of God; the river advised them what to do and what not to do. It was a beautiful river, and it flowed in a beautiful country, in their homeland Israel, and one day she would go there with the children, and, if the children were good, the river would talk to them too and would give them counsel.

Joseph watched Mara while she told the story. She had filled out at thirty-two and was already a little past her bloom. There was nothing left any longer of the moonlike radiance of her first youth; now there was no longer any danger that a Roman would insolently demand her for his bed as once old Vespasian had done. Yet for Joseph she was still what she had formerly been, for him the egg-shaped oval of her face remained delicate and clear, for him her low forehead gleamed as in the past.

Mara's face had lighted up when she saw him coming. She had noticed during all the last days that something was weighing on him, and had waited for him to speak to her. Usually he spoke Greek to her, but when he felt close to her and it was a subject of some importance, he would speak Aramaic, the tongue of their home. Now she waited in suspense, after she had sent the children away, to see in which language he would address her.

And, behold, he spoke Aramaic. He was no longer the man of yesterday; his face was furrowed, his beard no longer carefully curled and frizzed; he was a man of fifty; one could see that he had experienced much. Also he had done her much wrong, and she had never completely got over it. Yet in spite of all that, for her there still went out from him that radiance which used to shine around him, and she was filled with great pride that he spoke to her.

He spoke to her of the meeting with the others and of his anxiety about the uprising. He poured himself out to her completely; yes, only now it became really quite clear to him, while he talked to her, just what Judæa's new danger stirred up in him. He had a violent life behind him, peaks and valleys; he had thought that now he had peace and could lose himself in his books, and that a quiet evening was beginning for him. Instead, new trials and bitternesses were approaching. The uprising in Judæa, senseless as it was, would break out, Joseph would fight against it, and he would once again have to take slander and disgrace upon himself because he was suppressing his feelings for the sake of reason.

Mara had already heard him sing that evil tune before. But just as before she had unconditionally granted that he was right, because he was wise and she was unwise, so now her heart rose up in opposition to him. Why, when he felt as the others did, should he act differently? Would it not be better for them all if he were less wise? He was a very great man, this Doctor and Master Joseph, her husband, and she was proud of him, but sometimes, and so also now, she thought how much nicer it would be if he were less great. "Your burden weighs on me as if it were my own," she said, and then, while her back rounded itself and grew slack, she added softly: "Land of Israel, my poor Land of Israel."

"Land of Israel," she said, in Aramaic. Joseph understood her, and he envied her. He had his citizenship of the world, but he was split apart. She, on the other hand, was all one. She was rooted in the earth of Judæa, she belonged to Judæa, under the sky of Judæa and with its people, and Joseph knew that when many times she had urged him in her quiet way to return there she had been right and he had been wrong to refuse it to her.

He thought of the many artful arguments which he had built up to give foundation to his refusal. In Judæa, he had explained, the closeness of things would blur his vision and he would let himself be carried away by the passion of the others; there he would not be able to do his work with the objectivity which was the prerequisite of success. Yet both of them knew that this was an excuse. All the reasons which were supposed to be keeping him in Rome were excuses. He would have been able to write this book in Judæa rather better than here; it would have become more Jewish in the good sense. And perhaps she was right also that it would be better for the children to grow up on a country estate in Judæa under the open sky than here in the narrow streets of the city of Rome.

This last point was, however, very doubtful; for if his little Matthias was to become what Joseph had planned, he had to stay in Rome.

In any case he remained obstinate and turned a deaf ear to Mara's silent pleas. He had decided on a secluded life, but he did not want to do without the consciousness of the bustle of the city of Rome roundabout him. To live in the provinces would have cramped him; in Rome, even if he locked himself into his room, he was comforted by the thought that he had only to take a few hundred steps to stand on the Capitoline, where beat the heart of the world.

In his inmost being, however, he felt an uneasiness, yes, a very faint feeling of guilt, about keeping Mara in Rome. "Poor Land of Israel," he took up Mara's sigh, and, "It is going to be a winter full of troubles," he concluded.

AT SUPPER, in front of his wife Dorion and in front of his step-son Paulus, Annius Bassus, Domitian's Minister of War, let himself go. In front of these two he could talk, and the fact that Paulus's teacher, the Greek Phineas, was present did not disturb him. Phineas was a freedman; he did not count. True, Annius's relations with his wife and step-son were, for all their intimacy, not unclouded. Sometimes he had the feeling that Dorion considered him insignificant in spite of his extraordinary career; that, in spite of her hatred, she longed to be back with her Flavius Josephus, that disagreeable Jewish intellectual. Certain it was that she did not care much for the boy Junius whom she had borne to Annius, while she admired and spoiled Paulus, her Joseph's son. However, he himself could not resist the charm which Paulus radiated.

Yes, he loved Dorion, and he loved Paulus. And though their affection for him might be less than his for them, they were after all the only ones before whom he could give free expression to his worries, to the consuming anger which his office under the Emperor, misanthropic and hard to fathom, brought with it. At the same time Annius was devoted to Domitian from the bottom of his heart, he respected him; and D.D.D., though no born soldier, had understanding for military affairs. But the Emperor's suspiciousness knew no bounds and frequently forced his advisers to depose able men from the right places and to replace them with less able ones whose only distinction was that they did not inspire any suspicions in the Emperor.

And now again the Dacian expedition was being made difficult from the outset by Domitian's sinister *arrière-pensées*. The obvious course would have been to entrust the high command to Frontinus, who had laid out and carried through the masterly fortifications along the lower Danube. But since the Emperor wished that Frontinus should not consider himself indispensable and become arrogant, he had hit on the unfortunate idea of entrusting the command to Frontinus's rival, General Fuscus, the gallant.

Dorion did not seem greatly interested in these developments; her light green eyes gazed a little absently now at Annius, now simply in front of her. Phineas, too—although to him, the fanatical Greek, the difficulties of managing the Roman Empire might furnish inner satisfaction—seemed to take little part. All the more interested was Paulus. He was now sixteen years old; it was not yet a year since they had solemnly had him robed in the toga of the grown man for the first time. His mother would have been glad to see him enter a Greek university, accompanied by his teacher. But he himself was trying to fight against the attraction for Greek culture which the two had implanted in him; he wanted to be a Roman, nothing but a Roman. For this reason he had attached himself to a friend of Annius's, Colonel Julian, an excellent soldier who had spent his summer leave in Rome. Julian had taken an interest in the boy and had instructed him in military matters; but in the autumn he had had to return to Judæa, to his legion, the Tenth. Paulus would have given anything to accompany him, and it would also have pleased Annius, who was a passionate soldier, to make a real officer of his step-son. Dorion, though, opposed it. Phineas, too, had described to the boy, in his quiet, gentle, and therefore all the more effective way, how brutalizing the soldier's life in the distant province would be for him unless he had saturated himself beforehand with Greek culture, and Paulus finally had to give in. Now, however, since the outbreak of the Dacian disturbance, he had new hope. To learn the officer's trade during a war was a unique opportunity which they could not deny him.

So he listened with passionate interest as Annius spoke about the difficulties of the expedition which they were undertaking. They would really have needed a commander of stature at the Danube, that same Frontinus, not that obstinate gallant, Fuscus. The Dacians were not barbarians any more, their King Diurpan had a right to pride himself as a strategist; our forces there, barely three legions, were inadequate to safeguard the border of almost one thousand kilometres; and the severe winter this year made the defence more difficult, for it gave the attacker the chance to keep driving up new reinforcements across the frozen Danube. In addition, the King of the Dacians, Diurpan, was a skilful politician; he was intriguing all over the East and had good prospects of even bringing off an intervention by the Parthians. In any case they had to count on the fact that certain provinces which bore the domination of Rome only with reluctance would become restless, for example, Syria, and especially that never completely satisfied Judæa.

Dorion's indifference ceased suddenly when Annius explained this. For a long time she had heard nothing of Joseph, the man who more than all others had had a hand in her fate. An uprising in Judæa, that was an event which would force this man Joseph also to rise up out of his present obscurity. Her memories of what she had experienced with him rose confusedly: how he had taken the whipping upon himself in order to be able to divorce his ridiculous Jewish wife and to marry her; how they had utterly submerged and immersed themselves in their love, there in the little house which Titus had left them; how enmity had sprung up between them; how she had fought with him about their son, about this Paulus; how she had seen him in his hour of triumph when they had erected his bust in the Temple of Peace and Rome had hailed him—all that, her wild hatred and her wild love, was within her now, indivisible.

Phineas, too, gave up playing the indifferent listener when Annius began to talk about Judæa, and his large, pale head became flushed. If upheavals really occurred in Judæa, so that it was punished, that barbaric nation, how wonderful that would be. Phineas was not sorry that the superstitious Jews might once again come to feel the fist of Rome. To one man above all he did not grudge it, to this Joseph, his former master. He despised him, this Joseph, everything about him, his foolish fight for Paulus, his generosity and his humility, his superstition, his cheap successes, his miserable Greek, everything, everything. It would be wonderful if they showed this Joseph once again how pitiful his Judæa was, if he was made to feel once again what it meant to suffer slavery.

Into his and Dorion's agitated thoughts and feelings broke the words of Paulus. "That will create certain difficulties for a certain man," said Paulus. They were simple words, but the voice in which he spoke them was so filled with hatred and triumph that Dorion was shocked, and even Annius Bassus glanced up. He too disliked Flavius Josephus; the frank, noisy soldier found the Jew cringing, underhanded. However, if he, the Roman officer who had gone to war against the Jews, sometimes cursed Joseph and made fun of him, it was permissible for him. For Phineas also it was permissible, as Joseph's freedman. But it was not permissible for the two others at this table, not for the wife who had once been married to this Jew, nor for his son. Annius was not only opposed to it from a soldierly sense of propriety; he also felt that Dorion's over-ardent hatred against Joseph sprang from an insecurity in her feelings. True, she made unjust, yes, filthy speeches against him from time to time, but then again, when he came up in conversation, her eyes would veil themselves significantly. Annius would have been glad if his wife and his step-son had completely freed themselves inwardly from that shadowy man, so that they neither hated nor loved him.

Meanwhile Paulus was continuing his tirade. It would be wonderful if Judæa grew indignant and at last furnished an occasion for its own chastisement. What a life it would be if he were allowed to make the trip across, to take part in such a punitive expedition under the leadership of Julian, that good teacher. What a blow that would be for his father, the Jew. "You must let me go over to Judæa!" he blurted out.

Dorion turned her long, thin head toward him, and her sea-coloured eyes above the blunt nose gazed at him thoughtfully. "To Judæa? You to Judæa?" she asked. It sounded like a refusal, yet Paulus felt that she shared his hatred for the Jew, his father. "Yes," he insisted, and his bright eyes looked intensely into his mother's critical ones. "I must go over to

Judæa, now that things are getting under way there. I have to purify myself." They sounded sombre, those passionately blurted-out words, "I must purify myself"; yet even the simple soldier Annius understood what they meant. Paulus was ashamed of his father; he desired to atone for the fact that he was the son of that father.

But now it was enough; Annius did not wish to listen to this godless talk any longer; he interrupted. "I don't like to hear such words from your lips," he said reprovingly.

Paulus noticed that he had gone too far, but he persisted, even if more measuredly. "Colonel Julian simply won't understand," he said, "if I don't go to Judæa now. I don't want to give up Colonel Julian."

Slender and delicate Dorion sat there, relaxed and yet unbending; her mouth, somewhat wide and standing out insolently from her imperious face, smiled a slight, enigmatic smile. Annius, much as he was irritated by this smile, felt how deeply he loved this woman, and for ever. But she, Dorion, looked at her son's teacher. "What do you think about it, Phineas?" she asked.

The man who was otherwise so self-possessed and elegant could hardly conceal his excitement. Nervously he bent and stretched the long fingers of his large, thin, sickly-pale hands; he could not even keep his feet still in their Greek sandals. He was torn by discordant feelings. It pained him that he should lose Paulus for good. He loved the handsome, gifted youth; he had striven so ardently to implant his Greekness in him. He had indeed seen that Paulus was slowly slipping from his grasp, but he would find it hard to recover if Paulus was to become once and for all a Roman, and that could not be avoided if he went to the legion in Judæa. On the other hand, it was a strong comfort to imagine for himself what a blow it would be for that Joseph if his own son, his Paulus, took part in the fight against his people, in the camp of the Romans. In his deep, melodious voice Phineas said: "It would pain me if our Paulus went to Judæa, but I must say in this case I should understand him."

"I too understand him," said the Lady Dorion, and, "I fear, my son Paulus," she went on, "I shan't be able to say no to you much longer."

The journey to Judæa at that time of year was troublesome, even dangerous. Paulus undertook the preparations with eagerness and circumspection. He was boyishly happy; there was nothing in him any more of the incalculable violence, of the fierceness which had so often shocked those about him. Vanished were those Jewish modes of thought and the characteristics which his father had wanted to implant in him. Vanished was the Greekness with which his mother and his teacher had striven so ardently to imbue him. The place around him had conquered, the time around him had conquered: he, the son of the Jew and the Greek, had become completely a Roman.

WITH a stiff, awkward gait the Emperor walked along the cages of his zoo at Albanum. The palace had been planned as a summer residence, but Domitian frequently drove out in the bad time of year as well. He loved this royal seat of his at Albanum more than all his other possessions, and because as a prince he had begun the extensive, sumptuous palace with insufficient means, so now he made every effort to complete it the more magnificently. The artfully designed park stretched out beyond sight; everywhere outbuildings rose from the ground.

Shapeless in felt cape, cap, and fur shoes, the tall man

stalked along the cages, behind him his dwarf Silenus, fat, hideously hairy, deformed. It was a cold, damp day; mist rose from the sea; the landscape, at other times so colourful, lay there pale; even the leaves of the olive trees were without sheen. From time to time the Emperor stopped in front of a cage and looked at the animals with an absent stare.

He was glad that he had decided to leave the Palatine and drive out here. He fancied himself in the wintry, misty landscape. Yesterday detailed dispatches had come in from the border of the Danube: the invasion of the Dacians into the Empire had had worse results than he had thought; one could no longer speak of border incidents—what was being prepared down there now was a war.

He pressed his protruding upper lip against the lower one. Now he would doubtless have to go forth into the field of battle himself. That was not pleasant. He did not like quick, uncomfortable journeys, he did not like to sit on horseback for long periods, and now in winter everything was twice as fatiguing. No, he was no soldier, he was not like his father Vespasian and his brother Titus. They were nothing but soldiers, sergeants-major blown up to gigantic proportions. He still had Titus's braying voice in his ears, and a twinge of revulsion passed over his face. No, he did not care for brilliant victories which, after all, could not be carried further. He strove for gains which endured, that formed securities. He had ensured a few things, in Germany, in Britain. He was the fulfilment of the Flavian dynasty. If he had had the Senate confer the title "Lord and God Domitian" on himself, then it was with right.

He stood now in front of the cage of the she-wolf. She was an exceptionally handsome, strong animal; the Emperor loved this she-wolf, her restlessness, her incalculable wildness, her slyness and strength; he loved this she-wolf as the symbol of the City and the Empire. On tiptoe, with his arms angularly pressed backward, stomach thrust forward, he stood in front of the cage. "The Lord and God, the Emperor Flavius Domitianus Germanicus," he said his name and title out loud to himself, and behind him the dwarf, in the very same position, spoke the words after him before the cage of the she-wolf.

His father and his brother might have won more brilliant victories than he. Yet the important thing was not brilliant victories, but only the final results of a war. There were generals who could win battles but not a war. What he, together with his prudent engineer of fortifications Frontinus, had accomplished in Germany, the erection of the wall against the German invasion, was not brilliant, but it was worth more than ten brilliant victories that led to nothing. The ideas of this Frontinus could never have been understood, let alone carried out, by sergeants-major Vespasian and Titus.

A pity that he could not take Frontinus along to the Danube as Commander-in-Chief. But it would be against his principles. One must let no man become too great, no man too arrogant. The gods did not love arrogance. The God Domitian did not love arrogance.

It was of course deeply regrettable that the Fifteenth Army Corps had been destroyed, but there was a good side to that too. When he examined the situation closely, he saw that it was lucky that the Dacian business had taken this turn and had fanned up a real war. For this war came at the right moment; it would stop up mouths which otherwise one might not have been able to silence so soon. This war would provide for him, the Emperor, the welcome excuse for at last taking certain unpopular measures in domestic policy which, without the war, he would have had to postpone still for years. Now, with the pretext of the war, he could force his stubborn

Senators to make concessions which they would never have
granted him in times of peace.

Abruptly he turned away from the cage before which he
was still standing. He was not going to let himself be tempted
to dream any further; his imagination was too prone to go
wandering. He loved method, almost pedantry, in matters of
government. He longed for his writing-desk. He wanted to
make notes, put things in order. "The litter," he commanded
over his shoulder. "The litter," the dwarf passed on the command shrilly, and the Emperor had himself carried back to
the palace. It was a considerable stretch of road. First they
went up through olive terraces, then through an avenue of
plane trees, then past greenhouses, then through zoos and
walks, past pavilions, arbours, grottoes, waterworks of all
kinds. It was a beautiful, large park, the Emperor loved it,
but today he had no eyes for it. "Faster," he imperiously
ordered the litter-bearers; now he wanted to get to his desk.

In his study at last, he gave instructions not to disturb him
under any circumstances, bolted the door, was alone. He
smiled maliciously; he was thinking of the silly rumours which
were current about what he was up to when he locked himself in alone for days. He stabbed flies, they said, cut off legs
of frogs, and the like.

He set to work. Neatly, point by point, he noted down all
that he wanted to get out of his Senate in reference to this
war. To begin with, he would at last realize his favourite old
plan and have the power of censorship transferred to him
for life, censorship, the superintendence of the state economy,
morality, and rights, and with that also the inspection of the
Senate, the authority to exclude members of that body. Up to
now he had assumed this right only every second year. Now,
with the beginning of a war whose duration could not be
foreseen, the Senators could hardly refuse him such a stabili-

zation of his rights. He respected tradition; naturally he was not thinking of changing the constitution which provided for the division of power between Emperor and Senate. He did not want to do away with that division at all: he simply wanted to have the authority himself to exert the necessary control over the co-regent body.

The war offered the welcome opportunity to sharpen the moral laws as well. The ridiculous, conceited, refractory aristocrats of his Senate would of course again make fun of the fact that he forbade others every smallest irregularity, but allowed himself every whim, every "vice." The idiots. How could he, the God, since it was true that he had been ordained by fate to safeguard Roman propriety and morality with an iron hand, how could he know mankind and their vices if he did not himself, like Jupiter, descend to them from time to time?

Carefully he formulated the regulations and laws to be enacted, numbered them, worked out the details, looked conscientiously for an argument for each single point.

Then he set himself to the part of his work which he liked best, the compiling of a list, a list not very long yet weighty with consequences.

About ninety gentlemen sat in the Senate who did not conceal the fact that they were hostile to him. They looked down on him, these gentlemen who traced back their ancestry to the founding of the city and even further beyond that, to the fall of Troy. They called him an upstart. Because his great-great-grandfather was the owner of a banking business and because his grandfather had not won renown, either, they thought that he, Domitian, did not know what true Romanness was. He could show them who was the better Roman, the great-grandson of the little banker or the great-grandsons of the Trojan heroes.

The names of ninety such gentlemen were known to him. Ninety, that was a large number; he could not put so many names on his list; unfortunately only a few of the unpleasant gentlemen could be done away with during his absence. No, he would be careful; he did not like haste. But a few—seven, six, or, say, five—could in any case be put on the list, and the thought that on his return he would not have to see at least these any more would warm his heart when he was far from Rome.

To begin with, provisionally, he wrote down a whole line of names. Then he set himself to the crossing out. It did not come easily to him, and he sighed at the elimination of many a hated name. But he was a conscientious ruler; he would not let himself be swayed by liking or antipathy in his final decisions, but purely by considerations of state policy. Carefully he considered whether this man or that was more dangerous, whether doing away with this man or that would attract more attention, whether the confiscation of this fortune or that might bring in more for the state treasury. Only when the scales balanced perfectly might his personal antipathy make the decision.

Thus he considered one name after another. Regretfully he crossed Helvidius off his list again. Too bad, but it was impossible; for the time being one must spare him, this Helvidius Junior. Helvidius Senior old Vespasian had already done away with in his day. Some time, however, and he hoped it would not be long till then, the moment would be ripe to send the son after the father. Too bad, also, that he could not leave Ælius on the list, the man whose wife he had once taken from him, Lucia, now his Empress. This Ælius had a habit of always calling him, Domitian, just "Vellykins," never anything else—he knew that for certain—because he had the beginning of a protruding belly and because he did not always succeed

in pronouncing the letter "b." Very well, let Ælius call him
Vellykins for a while yet; some time for him too the hour
would come when his jokes would forsake him.

Finally five names remained on the list. Yet even these five
seemed to the Emperor to be too many. He would be content
with four. He would take counsel with Norbanus, his Chief
of Police, before deciding whom he would definitely send
down to Hades.

There, and now he had finished his task, and he was free.
He stood up, stretched, went to the door, unlocked it. He had
worked through his mealtime; they had not dared to disturb
him. Now he wanted to eat. He had summoned almost his
whole court here to Albanum, and half his Senate, almost
everyone whose friend and whose foe he was; he wanted to
put the business of his Empire in order here at Albanum, before he left his capital. Should he provide himself with entertainment? Should he summon one or the other to the table?
He thought of the many who were now arriving here in an
uninterrupted stream; he imagined how they were being consumed with anxious suspense as to what the God Domitian
was deciding about them. He smiled deeply and maliciously.
No, they should remain among themselves, he would leave
them to themselves. They should wait throughout the day,
the night, perhaps still another day, yes, perhaps still another
night, for the God Domitian would consider his decisions
slowly and hurry nothing.

In this his residence at Albanum, Lucia too would perhaps
have arrived by now, Lucia Domitia, his Empress. Domitian's
smile vanished suddenly from his face when he thought of
Lucia. For a long time he had been nothing else to her than
the man Domitian, but then he had had to reveal to her also
the Lord and God Domitian, he had had to put her favourite
Paris out of the way and have her banished by the Senate

for adultery to the island of Pandateria. It was a good thing that three weeks ago he had instructed the Senate and the people to petition him to call back the beloved Empress. And he had then permitted himself to be softened, called Lucia back. Otherwise he would have had to go to the wars without seeing her. Was she here already? If the trip had gone smoothly, she should have arrived by now. He had not wanted to show that he cared to know whether she had arrived; he had given instructions not to disturb him, to announce no one's arrival to him. His heart told him that she was here. Should he inquire after her? Should he ask her to eat with him? No, he remained the ruler, he remained the God Domitian, he restrained himself, he did not inquire after her.

He ate alone, hastily, paying no attention to his food; he devoured it, washed down the mouthfuls with wine. The solitary meal was quickly finished. And what should he do now? With what could he occupy himself to drive away the thought of Lucia?

HE WENT to see the sculptor Basil, whom the Senate had instructed to prepare a colossal statue of the Emperor. For a long time the artist had been asking him to inspect his work.

In silence he gazed at the model. He had been represented on horseback with the insignia of power. It was a noble, heroic, imperial horseman that the sculptor Basil had created. The Emperor had nothing to say against the work, but neither could he feel any liking for it.

The horseman indeed bore his, Domitian's, features, yet at the same time it was just as much any Emperor, not the Emperor Domitian.

"Interesting," he said finally, but in a tone which did not conceal his disappointment. The nimble little sculptor Basil, who had been observing the Emperor's features attentively the whole time, answered: "So you are not satisfied then, Your Majesty? I'm not either. The horse and the trunk of the horseman eat up too much space, there isn't enough left for the head, for the face, for the spiritual element." And as the Emperor was silent, he went on: "It's too bad that the Senate instructed me to represent Your Majesty on horseback. If Your Majesty permits, I shall make the gentlemen a counterproposal. I'm playing with an idea here which seems fascinating to me. I conceive of a colossal statue of the God Mars which bears the features of Your Majesty. Of course I'm not thinking of the traditional Mars with the helmet on his head; the helmet would take away too much of your leonine brow for my taste. What I picture is a Mars in repose. May I show Your Majesty an attempt?" And as the Emperor nodded, he had the other model brought out.

He had represented a man of massive build, but seated, resting in a comfortable position. The god had laid aside his weapons; his relaxed right leg was shoved forward; the knee of the left, pulled up, he clasped carelessly with both hands. The wolf lay at his feet; the woodpecker sat cockily on the discarded shield. The model was obviously in its first phase, but the head was already executed, and this head, yes, this was a head of the kind that appealed to Domitian. The forehead actually had the leonine air of which the artist had spoken; it reminded one of the forehead of the great Alexander. And even the arrangement of the hair, the short curls, gave the head a resemblance to certain well-known heads of Hercules, the supposed ancestor of the Flavians, a resemblance which would cause no slight irritation among some of the gentlemen Senators. The nose stood out slightly aquiline. The flaring nostrils, the half-open mouth, breathed audacity, imperious passion.

"Imagine, Your Majesty," the sculptor elaborated with animation, as his work obviously found favour with the Emperor, "what an effect the statue will have when it is really completed in full scale. If you permit me to execute my project, Your Majesty, this statue will be even more the God Domitian than the God Mars. Because in this case the traditional helmet does not attract the main attention of the onlooker, nor does the massive torso, but every detail is calculated to draw the attention of the onlooker to the face, and it is the expression of the face which raises the god above human measure. This face shall show the world what the title 'Lord and God' is meant to convey."

The Emperor was silent, but he examined his portrait with obvious approval in his protruding, near-sighted eyes. Yes, this was going to be a success. Mars and Domitian, they blended well together, these two. Even the hair, the way he had let the growth spread lightly along the cheek, even this suggestion of side-burns, was suitable to a representation of the God Mars. And the threateningly contracted brow, the eyes full of pride and challenge, the massive neck, these were characteristics of the God Mars and at the same time signs by which everyone must recognize him, Domitian. And in addition that determined chin, the one good feature of his father's head and also, luckily, the only trait which he, Domitian, had inherited from him. He was right, this sculptor Basil: the title which he had had conferred on him, the title "Lord and God," everyone could see in this Mars what it intended to convey. Like this Mars in repose, so would he, Domitian, be, and so he was: in his repose especially sombre, divine, dangerous. That was the way his aristocrats hated him, the way his people loved him, the way his soldiers loved him; and what Vespasian for all his geniality and Titus for all his braying could not achieve—to be a popular figure—he, Domitian, had achieved by that very sombre majesty of his.

"Interesting, very interesting," he acknowledged, but this time in the right tone of voice, and: "You haven't done so badly here, my Basil."

A<small>ND</small> now a long evening lay ahead of the Emperor, and what should he do before going to sleep? When he called up the images of the people whom he had summoned here to Albanum, numerous as they were, he could find none whose company would appeal to him. To one alone his desire turned, but his pride forbade him to call her. So he would rather spend the evening alone; he would find no better company than his own.

He gave instructions to light the whole great banquet hall. He also had the mechanics summoned to work the ingenious machinery of the banquet hall, whose walls could be rolled back and whose roof could be raised until one was under the open sky. The ingenious machinery was formerly intended as a surprise for Lucia. She had not valued it suitably. She did not suitably value many of his presents.

Accompanied only by his dwarf Silenus, the Emperor entered the spacious, brilliantly lighted hall. His imagination filled it with crowds of his guests. He sat there carelessly—involuntarily he had assumed the position of that statue of Mars—and he imagined to himself how his guests, scattered in the many chambers of his palace, were lying there, cowering and waiting, full of fear and suspense. He ordered the hall to be expanded and contracted, toyed with it, ordered the roof raised and lowered. Then for a while he paced up and down, had most of the lights extinguished so that only single parts of the hall still lay in faint light. And he went on pacing up and down in the huge room, his shadow accompanying him gigantically while his dwarf accompanied him in miniature.

Was Lucia really in Albanum?

Abruptly—he still felt fresh and ready for new work—he summoned his Chief of Police Norbanus.

Norbanus had already gone to bed. Most of the ministers were in a quandary, when Domitian summoned them at an unexpected hour, as to how they should appear. On the one hand, the Emperor did not wish to be kept waiting, on the other he felt that his majesty was affronted if one appeared before him otherwise than carefully dressed. Norbanus, however, knew that he was so indispensable to his master and so firmly entrenched in his favour that he contented himself with throwing his official robe over his night-dress.

His not very large but stately form still exhaled the warmth of bed when he appeared before the Emperor. The massive square head on the even more massive square shoulders was not groomed, the firm chin, unshaved as it was, gave an effect of even greater brutality, and the fashionable front curls of the very thick deep-black hair, heavily greased and yet disordered, stuck into his square face in grotesque zig-zag. The Emperor did not take offence at his Chief of Police's carelessness; perhaps he did not even notice it. Rather he became at once familiar. The tall man laid his arm around the shoulders of the much shorter one, led him up and down the dim, spacious hall, spoke to him in a low voice, made suggestions.

He spoke about the fact that one could use the war and his absence to weed out the Senate a little. Once again, this time with Norbanus, he went through the names of his enemies. He was well informed and had a good memory, but Norbanus had in his broad head a supply of many more facts, suspicions, and certainties, pros and cons. Up and down the Emperor walked with him, with his stiff gait, awkwardly, his arm always about his shoulders. Listened, interjected questions, advanced doubts. He had no scruples about letting Norbanus look into his inmost being; he had a profound trust in him, a trust that came from a secret corner of his soul.

Norbanus also of course mentioned Ælius, the first husband of the Empress Lucia, that Senator who had given Domitian the name of Vellykins and whom Domitian would so gladly have left on his list. This Ælius was a jovial fellow. He had loved Lucia, he probably loved her still; he also loved the many other pleasant things with which fortune had blessed him: his titles and honours, his money, his attractive appearance and cheerful personality which won him friends everywhere. But more than all this he loved his wit, and he liked to display it. Under the earlier Flavians his *bons mots* had already caused him unpleasantnesses. Under Domitian, who had taken Lucia away from him, he was doubly endangered and should have guarded his tongue with double care. Instead he declared frivolously that he knew exactly of what illness he should one day have to die: that illness would be a clever witticism. Today too Norbanus reported to the Emperor some new disrespectful jokes of Ælius's. However, in retelling the last one he interrupted himself before he had finished. "Go on," the Emperor urged him. Norbanus hesitated. "Go on," commanded the Emperor. Norbanus hesitated. The Emperor flushed, cursed his chief, screamed, threatened. Finally Norbanus told it. It was a witticism, as polished as it was obscene, about that part of Lucia's body through which Ælius was in a manner of speaking related to the Emperor. Domitian became deathly pale. "You have a good head, Chief of Police Norbanus," he said at last with difficulty. "It's too bad that you have talked yourself and me out of that head." "You commanded me to speak, Your Majesty," said Norbanus. "Just the same," the Emperor answered and suddenly began screaming shrilly, "you shouldn't have allowed yourself to repeat such words, you dog!"

Norbanus, however, was not deeply shaken. And soon the Emperor calmed himself again, and they continued to talk objectively about the candidates for the list. As Domitian himself had already feared, they could hardly finish off more than four of the enemies of the state in his absence; more would have been too risky. In other respects also Norbanus was not entirely in agreement with the Emperor's list, and he insisted stubbornly that they should still postpone the dispatching of the second Senator on the list. Finally the Emperor had to cross two names off his list of five, but in return Norbanus conceded to him one new name, so that at the end four names remained. To these four names Domitian could then at last add the letter M.

This fatal M was, however, the initial letter of the name Messalinus, and this Messalinus was the most sinister man in the city of Rome. Since he, a relative of the poet Catullus, sprang from one of the oldest families, everybody had expected that he would join the opposition party in the Senate. Instead he had bound himself to the Emperor. He was rich; it did not happen for the sake of the set reward that he accused one person or another, friends and relatives as well, of *lèse-majesté*: he did it out of pleasure in destruction. He was blind, this Messalinus, yet no one could better hunt out hidden weaknesses than he, no one could better make captious remarks out of innocent ones, treacherous out of harmless dealings. Whoever had the blind Messalinus on his track was lost; whoever was accused by him was doomed. The Senate numbered six hundred members; their skins had become thick

and hard in this Rome of the Emperor Domitian; they knew
that anyone who wanted to hold his own there would not
get along without a tough conscience. But when the name of
Messalinus came up, even these hard-boiled gentlemen made
a face. The blind man set great store on not being reminded
of his blindness; he had learned to make his way through the
Senate without a guide; he went through the benches to his
place alone and as if seeing. They all had something for which
to repay the evil, dangerous man: the downfall of a relative,
of a friend; all were eager to have him bump against some
obstacle so that he would be reminded of his blindness. Yet
none dared to obey this impluse; they made way for him,
they cleared obstacles from his path.

And so the Emperor finally put the letter M after the four
names.

With that this subject was finished, and actually, Norbanus
thought, D.D.D. could now have calmly let him go back to
bed. But the Emperor continued to keep him there, and Norbanus knew why he did so. D.D.D. would have liked more
than anything to hear about Lucia, would have liked to learn
from him what Lucia had been doing on her island of exile,
Pandateria. But he had lost his chance to find out. In that case
he should not have screamed so at him a moment ago. Now
Norbanus would be careful not to make himself guilty of
any further commissions of lèse-majesté. He would teach his
Emperor, in a gentlemanly way, to control himself.

Domitian was in truth burning with desire to question
Norbanus. But few as were his secrets from the man, he was
embarrassed now that Lucia was the subject, and the question
would not cross his lips. Norbanus for his part continued
slyly and perseveringly to say nothing about it.

Instead of speaking to him about Lucia, he talked to the
Emperor—since the latter would not dismiss him—about all

kinds of social gossip and minor political events. He also told him about the suspicious activity which had been observed since the outbreak of the Dacian disturbance in the house of the writer Flavius Josephus; yes, he could present a copy of the manifesto composed by Joseph. "Interesting," said Domitian, "very interesting. Our Joseph. The great historian. The man who described and perpetuated our Jewish War for posterity, the man in whose hands it lay to apportion glory and disgrace. For the deeds of my deified father and my deified brother he found all kinds of laudatory phrases; of me he took scant notice. So now he's composing ambiguous manifestos. Well, well, think of that."

And he gave Norbanus instructions to observe the man further, but for the time being not to interfere. He would take this Jew Joseph in hand himself, probably even before his departure; for a long time he had felt like having a talk with him again.

Lucia, the Empress, had in fact arrived at Albanum in the late afternoon. She had expected that Domitian would greet her. That he had not done so amused her more than it might have annoyed her.

Now, while she dominated Domitian's interview with Norbanus without their mentioning her name, she was giving a dinner in her intimate circle. Not all of those invited had dared to come; although the Emperor had recalled Lucia, one did not know how he would take it if one had dinner with her. One was never safe from dark surprises; it had happened that the Emperor, when he wanted to ruin someone once and for all, showed him particular friendliness just before the end.

Those who did take part in the Empress's evening meal

devoted themselves to it cheerfully, and Lucia herself was in the best of humours. There was no indication about her of the hardships of exile. Tall, young, exuberant, she sat there, her widely spaced eyes smiling beneath the pure, childlike fore-head, her whole bold, bright face radiating joy. Without em-barrassment she told about Pandateria, the island of exile. Domitian had supposedly assigned that island to her so that the shadows of the royal ladies who had been banished there would terrify her, the shadows of Agrippina, Nero's Octavia, the Augustan Julia. But there he had miscalculated. When-ever she thought of Augustus's Julia, she did not think about her end, but only about her friendship with Silanus and Ovid and about the pleasures which had been the final cause of that end.

She told about the details of her life on the island. There had been seventeen exiles there; the island had about five hun-dred natives. Of course they had had to limit themselves, and it was annoying to see always the same people about one. Soon they knew one another down to the last wrinkle. Living together on a barren rock, with only the boundless ocean roundabout them, made many melancholy, crotchety, led to unpleasant frictions; there were times when they had hated one another so that they would have been glad to devour one another like captive spiders. But there were compensations in being rid of the countless faces of Rome and its eternal socia-bility, and in being left to one's own resources. She had had by no means unpleasant experiences in this communion with herself. And in addition there had been certain sensations of which they in Rome did not dream, for example, the excite-ment when every six weeks or so the boat arrived with letters and bulletins from Rome and all kinds of things which one had ordered for oneself from there. On the whole, she summed up, it had not been a bad time, and when one saw her thus, joyous and tremendously alive, one believed her.

There now remained the question as to how Lucia was to go on living here in Rome, what would be the Emperor's attitude toward her. Without embarrassment they discussed this; and opinions were given with particular frankness by Claudius Reginus, the Senator Junius Marullus, and Lucia's former husband Ælius, whom she had invited to this meal without a moment's hesitation. It was Ælius's opinion that the very next day Lucia would already be able to find out for certain what she had reason to expect for the future from Vellykins. If he wanted to see her first of all alone, that was not a good sign, because then he would want to talk matters over with her. But probably Vellykins would be as much afraid of such a discussion with her as he himself, Ælius, in his day, and would therefore want to postpone this conversation. Indeed he, Ælius, was ready to wager that the Emperor would give a family dinner tomorrow, because he did not want to see Lucia first alone but together with other people.

Lucia, for her part, had obviously no fear of the coming discussion with the Emperor. Without inhibition she called him by his nickname, and in the presence of them all she said to Claudius Reginus: "Later I must have you alone for five minutes, my Reginus, so that you can advise me about what I can reasonably demand of Vellykins before I let myself be conciliated. If he really has become fatter, as they tell me, then he has to pay more."

Like the majority of his guests Domitian did not sleep well that night. He still had not inquired whether Lucia was there, but an inner voice told him with certainty that she was, and now he was sleeping under the same roof with her again.

He regretted having insulted Norbanus. If he had not done

so he would now know what Lucia had been up to on her island of exile, Pandateria. There had been only a few men with whom she had come in contact there, and he could not imagine that any of them would have attracted her. Yet she was incalculable and permitted herself everything. Perhaps after all she had slept with one of those men, perhaps also with one of the fishermen or some other fellow out of the rabble living on the island. Yet no one could tell him that except Norbanus, and his mouth he had idiotically sealed himself.

However, even if he knew exactly what had taken place in Pandateria, if he knew, minute by minute, what she had been doing there, it would not help him much. With a feeling of suspense mixed with uneasiness and longing he awaited the interview which he would have with Lucia tomorrow. He polished up the sentences with which tomorrow he, the generous Domitian, the God, would impress her, the sinner, whom he was taking into his favour again. But he knew in advance that however telling the phrases he found for her, she would only smile, and finally she would laugh her full, deep laugh and answer him something like: "Come, come, Vellykins, now stop that," and whatever he did or said, she had the kind of disposition which made it impossible for him to frighten her. For while the others, the insolent aristocrats, perhaps just because they had sprung from such old families, had become thin-blooded, without strength, in her, Lucia, there lived in truth the exuberance, the vigour, of the old patricians. He hated Lucia for this proud strength of hers, but he needed her, he missed her when she was not there. He told himself that she was the embodiment of the Goddess Rome, and that only for that reason he needed and loved her. But what he needed and loved was simply Lucia the woman, nothing else. He knew he could not go to the wars before he had kissed the small scar under her left breast, and if she allowed him to kiss it, that would be a gift. Alas, one could command her to do nothing—she laughed; among all the living he knew, she was the only one who was not afraid of death. She loved life, she took from the moment everything it could give, but just for that reason she had no fear of death.

T HE Emperor had summoned the most trusted of his ministers for very early the next morning, to a secret meeting of the cabinet. The five gentlemen who gathered in the Chamber of Hermes had not finished their sleep, they would all have preferred to stay in bed longer, but even if it happened that the Emperor let one wait eternally, woe to him who would have dared to be unpunctual himself.

Annius Bassus, in his frank, noisy way, was pouring out to Claudius Reginus his troubles about the imminent military expedition; obviously he wanted Reginus to back him up with the Emperor. On the one hand, he said, D.D.D. did not think it worthy of him, a god, to be economical, so that the upkeep of the court, especially the buildings, devoured money even in his absence; on the other hand, he set store—a trait which he had inherited from his father—on avoiding unbudgeted expenses under any circumstances. As a result, what suffered was the war management. They would not, he feared, put enough troops and materials at the disposal of the generals on the Danubian front, and what was then lacking in forces and supplies the Commander-in-Chief Fuscus—and here was the main danger—would try to make up for by boldness.

"No, our domestic economy isn't simple," Reginus answered, sighing; "you don't have to tell me that, my good Annius. I received this poem here, yesterday, which Court Poet Statius dedicated to me." And grinning all over his untidily shaven, fleshy face, blinking ironically with his heavy, sleepy eyes, he pulled the manuscript out of the sleeve of his official robe; he held the precious poem in his thick fingers and in his high, oily voice read aloud:

" 'To thee alone is entrusted the care of the sanctified treasures of the Emperor, the riches produced by all the peoples, the wealth of the whole world. Whatsoever Iberia hews out of her gold mines, whatsoever glitters within the mountains of Dalmatia, whatsoever is garnered from Libya's harvest, whatsoever is fertilized by the mud of the sun-warmed River Nile, whatsoever pearls are brought to light by the divers of the Eastern Sea, and whatsoever ivory is captured by the hunters along the River Indus: to thee as sole guardian is it entrusted. Watchful art thou, sharp-eyed, and with sure speed dost thou reckon daily what under every sky the armies of the Empire will require, what the feeding of the city, what the temples, the water supply, what the maintenance of the enormous networks of the streets. Ounce for ounce thou knowest the price, the weight, the alloy of every metal, which, glowing within the fire, is transformed into images of the gods, into images of the Emperor, into Roman coin.'

"The man he's talking about here, that's me," explained Claudius Reginus, grinning, and it was really a little ludicrous to compare the slovenly, sceptical, unpretentious gentleman with the exalted verses addressed to him.

The Chamberlain Crispinus walked up and down the small room with nervous steps. The young, elegant Egyptian was, in spite of the early hour, dressed with the utmost care; he must have spent much time on his toilet; as always he smelled of sweet perfumes, like the funeral procession of an aristocrat. The quiet, watchful eyes of Chief of Police Norbanus followed him with visible disapproval. Norbanus could not bear him, the young fop; he felt that he ridiculed his own crudeness. Yet Crispinus was one of the few against whom Norbanus could do nothing. True, the Chief of Police knew many grave particulars about the spendthrift Crispinus's methods of getting money. But the Emperor had an unaccountable preference for the young Egyptian. He saw in him, who was experienced in all his native Alexandria's refinements of vice, the mirror of elegance and breeding. Domitian, the guardian of the severe Roman tradition, did, to be sure, scorn these arts, but Domitian the man was interested in them.

Crispinus, continually pacing up and down, said: "It will be a question again of new, more stringent moral laws. D.D.D. cannot do enough to transform our Rome into a gigantic Sparta." No one answered. Why go over the same matters for the thousandth time? "Perhaps too," said Marullus, with an early-morning yawn, "he has summoned us here just because of a turbot or because of a lobster." He was referring to that malicious joke which the Emperor had afforded himself not long ago, when he had rushed his ministers to Albanum in the middle of the night to ask them how an unusually large turbot which had been presented to him should be prepared.

The eyes of the all-knowing Norbanus, in whose records the dealings and remarks of every individual were set down exactly, were still following Crispinus as he hurried up and down; they were brown eyes, the whites too were brownish, and they reminded one in their quiet, alert attentiveness of the eyes of a watchful dog. "Have you found out something about me again?" the Egyptian finally asked, nervous under that steady gaze. "Yes," Norbanus answered simply. "Your friend Mettius has died." Crispinus halted in the middle of a step and turned his long, thin, finely cut, depraved face toward him; expectation, joy, and anxiety were mingled in it. Old

Mettius was a very rich man; Crispinus had pressed him in intricate ways with tokens of friendship and threats, and the old man had at the last remembered him in his will with large sums. "Your friendship did not agree with him, Crispinus," reported the Chief of Police while now the others also listened. "Mettius slit his veins. Immediately beforehand, by the way, he transferred his entire wealth"—Norbanus laid a slight emphasis on the word "entire"—"entire—to our beloved Lord and God Domitian." Crispinus managed to keep a composed face. "You are always the bringer of good tidings, Norbanus," he said politely.

If the fat inheritance did not fall to himself, then he grudged it least to the Emperor. Ill as Domitian had used them from time to time, all five men in the little room were genuinely his friends. D.D.D., in spite of his sinister peculiarities, fascinated the masses as well as those whom he allowed to approach him more closely.

Claudius Reginus had listened with a little grin. Now he let himself relax again; untidy, sleepy, he squatted on a chair. "They have an easy time of it," he said in an undertone to Junius Marullus, nodding at the three others, "they are young. But you, my dear Marullus, and I, we have achieved something which among the friends of the Emperor has been vouchsafed really only to us: we have both reached an age over fifty."

Norbanus meanwhile had kept Crispinus pinned in a corner. In his quiet, rather menacing way, lowering his rough voice so that the others should not hear his words, he said to him: "I have further good news for you. The Vestal Virgins will attend the games on the Palatine. You will get a chance to see your Cornelia, Crispinus." Crispinus's brownish face turned almost idiotic with consternation. He had several times made a few impudent, covetous remarks about the Vestal

Virgin Cornelia, but only to intimate friends, for the Emperor was severe about his high priestesses and did not like any disrespectful remarks about his Vestal Virgins. Crispinus remembered now exactly what he had said. Even if that Cornelia were sewn into her white robe from top to bottom, he would yet sleep with her, he had boasted. But in what diabolical way had this already reached Norbanus's ears?

At last the gentlemen were asked into the inner study.

The Emperor sat on a raised seat at his desk, gorgeously stiff, clothed in the robe of majesty reserved for him alone, and although the table hid his feet he was wearing the uncomfortable high-soled shoes. It pleased him to be entirely the god: only with a haughty, sacerdotal inclination of the head would he acknowledge the humbly ceremonious greetings of his counsellors, greetings due a god.

All the more, then, did the objectivity with which he conducted the interview contrast with this attitude. Although permeated with the feeling of his godhead, he examined with sound common sense the reasons and objections which his gentlemen advanced.

They dealt first with the proposed law which was to transfer permanently to the Emperor the complete superintendence of morals and the Senate, to reduce the rights of the co-regent body to a formality, to turn absolute monarchy into a reality. They worked out in minutest stylistic detail the arguments with which they intended to support this proposal. After that, they considered how the basic activities of the State at war and at peace might be reconciled. Here it was important in the first place to put large sums at the disposal of the engineer of fortifications, Frontinus, for the continuation of the wall against the German barbarians, and on the other hand to grant high premiums and extra rewards to the troops going to the front. But they could not simply abandon the large-scale building projects in the city and the provinces if they did not want to endanger the prestige of the Emperor. Where, then, could they economize? And where and in what field could they carry through increased taxes without squeezing the subjects too violently? They decided, further, what measures to take toward the insecure provinces, what privileges they should give them or take away. Further, they took counsel at length as to how far they could soften the regulations which were to limit the cultivation of the vineyards in favour of growing grain; they did not want to let this necessary reform become all too popular. They spent a particularly long time, finally, on the proposed moral laws: decrees to govern the increasing emancipation of women, ordinances to limit luxury in clothing, regulations to make possible a more severe censorship of plays. Once again the counsellors had to recognize that it was not by any means hypocrisy when Domitian spoke of his mission as High Priest to re-establish the ancient Roman discipline and tradition by the severest measures. As unscrupulously as he indulged his own unbounded appetites, so deeply was he permeated with his mission to lead his people back to the morality and religious heritage of their ancestors. Roman discipline and Roman might were the same thing; one could not survive without the other; a stern morality was the basis of the imperial might. Stiffly and imperially he sat there, carrying this out, a speaking statue. The deep conviction of his mission shone from him, and the others, although they were not experiencing the drama of the revelation of the God Domitian for the first time, grew almost uneasy before his obsession.

With this exception, however, they discussed all questions expertly, under the expert guidance of the Emperor, and without resentment against one another. Domitian had known how to fuse his counsellors and himself into one organism which thought with a single brain. It became a long session; all yearned for relaxation, but the Emperor grudged himself as well as his counsellors any respite.

And even when he dismissed the exhausted gentlemen, he still detained Norbanus. He would really have done well to rest a little. Before him lay a strenuous family meal—Ælius with his knowledge of human nature had been right: the Emperor wanted to see Lucia first in the circle of the family —and then the feared and hoped-for discussion with Lucia. However, it was just because of this discussion that Domitian still wanted to speak to his Chief of Police. He was after all the only one who could give him material, material against Lucia which would perhaps be useful to him in the big interview. But today too Norbanus remained monosyllabic, and today too the Emperor could not get the question past his lips. He waited for Norbanus to speak of his own accord; it was mean of him not to inform his Emperor, even unasked. But Norbanus had his obstinacy; he did not speak.

With a sigh the Emperor gave up the hope of hearing something about Lucia from him. But since he had him here now, he at least questioned him about Julia. His relation to this niece of his, Julia, was divided and changing. Titus, his brother, had in his day proposed his daughter Julia to him as wife, but Domitian, aiming at that time at becoming his brother's co-regent, had not wanted to let himself be put off in that way. Then, however, he had, partly out of hatred for his brother, partly because he was attracted by Julia's plump, indolently graceful sensuality, made the girl yield to him through force and persuasion. But also after Titus had married Julia to his cousin Sabinus, yes, just for that reason, he had continued his scandalous relations with her. Now Titus was dead, Domitian had no more reason to anger him, yet in the meantime he had become accustomed to blond, indolent, white-skinned Julia. She obviously loved him, and he took refuge in this love when his rage at Lucia's unassailable pride tormented him too fiercely. And his love for Julia varied according to the way in which Lucia was treating him.

Now Julia was pregnant. He had forbidden her some time ago to sleep with her husband Sabinus, his cousin; she swore that the child was his, not Sabinus's, and the man Domitian was indeed glad to believe that, but the Emperor Domitian was suspicious. Or perhaps the Emperor Domitian believed it too, for no one could deceive him, the god, but the human being Domitian was suspicious. He was not embarrassed to discuss these doubts of his with Norbanus. Lucia had borne him a child but it had died at the age of two and the royal physician Valens gave the Emperor no hope of ever expecting heirs from Lucia. It would be magnificent if Julia bore him a child. But who could tell him whether the fruit she bore was really his child? Never would he be able to be quite sure; for if the child had Flavian traits of some kind, these traits might come from herself, from him, or from Sabinus. Who could resolve his doubts?

Norbanus was not only deeply devoted to his master, but sincerely his friend. It would have given him tremendous pleasure if Domitian had had a son who could inherit the throne. "I have reliable people in the house of Prince Sabinus," he explained, "people with good eyes. Not because of Princess Julia, but because of Prince Sabinus. My agents tell me with certainty that the two live together as cousins, not as man and wife." The Emperor fixed his rather protruding eyes on Norbanus in a sad stare. "You want to comfort the Lord and God Domitian," he answered, "because you are a friend of the man Domitian." Norbanus shrugged his broad shoulders impressively and let them fall again. "I'm only reporting," he said, "what reliable people have reported to me."

"At any rate, it is irritating," said Domitian, "that Sabinus exists in this world, that arrogant blockhead. By nature he is nothing but stupid. That he has become so arrogant was Titus's fault. I tell you, Norbanus, my brother Titus was at bottom sentimental, for all his braying. He spoiled Sabinus out of family feeling. It was simply idiotic that he gave him Julia as a wife." "It is not fitting for me," answered Norbanus, "to criticize the God Titus." "I tell you," the Emperor returned impatiently, "he was often an idiot, the God Titus. The arrogance of this Sabinus is really extremely annoying. That arrogance almost borders on high treason already." "He remains scrupulously distant from every political activity," the Chief of Police interposed almost regretfully. "That's just it," said Domitian. "To make up for that he plays the leader to a lot of snobbish intellectuals, all members of the opposition party, of course." "Is that high treason?" Norbanus wondered. "I think it's not enough." "He had his servants wear the white livery which is reserved for the household of the Emperor," Domitian elaborated further. "That's not enough," Norbanus insisted. "He did away with the white livery again as soon as you ordered him to. No, what we have on hand is not enough," he concluded. "But trust Norbanus, my Lord and Master," he encouraged him. "Prince Sabinus is the kind of person who will surely provide something against himself one day. And as soon as that moment is at hand, perhaps on your return from the expedition, my Lord and Master, I shall let you know at once."

IN THE evening the Emperor first of all ate alone, hastily and abundantly, for he wanted to be satisfied so that eating would not distract him from observing the others at the family table. Those others gathered meanwhile in the small, intimately festive Chamber of Minerva. They were Lucia, the two cousins of the Emperor, Sabinus and Clemens, with their wives Julia and Domitilla, as well as Clemens's little twin sons.

The guards clanged their spears to the floor; Domitian entered the room, saw Lucia. Her bold, bright face smiled at him, cheerfully, a little ironically; alas, no, the stay on the desolate island had not subdued her or changed her. He was glad that he was not alone with her.

With his stiff, awkward gait he went toward her and kissed her, the way that he had to kiss all those present according to the ceremonial. It was a short, formal kiss; his lips barely touched her cheeks. Yet beneath his official robes she could feel the violent pounding of his heart. He would have given a province to know whether she had slept with another man there on her island. Why had he not questioned his Norbanus? Was he afraid of the answer?

A wild, almost uncontrollable desire came over him to see the scar under her left breast, to stroke it with gentle fingers. He was in truth a great ruler, he was a Roman, to be able to control himself and turn to the others with a composed face while feeling this tremendous desire.

So he next embraced his cousin Sabinus and kissed him as the custom demanded. A repulsive fellow, this Sabinus, as foolish as arrogant. But Domitian could depend on his Chief of Police. The day would come when he would not have to feel this Sabinus's skin against his own any more.

He turned to Julia. Her pregnancy was not yet noticeable, but everyone there understood the situation. Surely even Lucia has already heard about it, and she too now would be asking herself: "Whose is the child, Vellykins's or that idiot Sabinus's?" The Emperor's whole face as he now approached her, his arms angularly pressed back, his stomach slightly drawn in, was flushed; yet that meant nothing, he flushed easily and all the time. Julia's blue-grey eyes met him, large and inquiring. She had had less to suffer from his whims during these last months, but with her sound, sober understanding she foresaw that this would change once he was together with Lucia again. There she stood then, a true Flavian, of ample stature, thoroughly alive. But did she not make a somewhat vulgar impression if one compared her with Lucia? Domitian kissed her, and her thin, white skin, which a few days ago he had found very dear, was without charm for him.

Now he greeted his younger cousin with an embrace and kiss, Clemens, gentle and lazy Clemens, as he was accustomed to call him jeeringly. For Clemens had never cared for politics; he evinced no sort of ambition; the friendly indolence with which he was completely permeated was an irritation to the Emperor, the guardian of Roman character. Most of the time Clemens spent in the country with his wife Domitilla and his twin sons. There he occupied himself with the pietistic doctrine of a Jewish sect, with the silly teachings of the so-called Minæans or Christians, who promised themselves all kinds of things in the next life, since life on earth did not seem to them worth while. Domitian found this doctrine revolting, weak, womanish, stupid, absolutely unworthy of a Roman. No, by Hercules, he did not like his cousin Clemens either. But in one respect the latter had the advantage over him; for one thing Domitian envied him. That was the twins, the four-year-old Princes Constans and Petronius, the little lions, as Domitian liked to call the soft, supple, healthy little boys. The dynasty had to continue, that was his ardent wish; neither Sabinus nor Clemens was suitable for the throne; what would spring from Julia one did not yet know, so for the time being the twins were all that Domitian could hold to, and in his innermost heart he played with the idea of adopting them. Only for their sakes did he tolerate his cousin Clemens. He, moreover, reciprocated the Emperor's dislike and obviously it was only with reluctance that he suffered the embrace and kiss.

His cousin's wife, Domitilla, who was the last to be greeted with the kiss, provoked and amused the Emperor more. A daughter of his sister who had died young, she too had certain Flavian traits, blond hair and a strong chin. But she was thin, thin in every respect, and sparing in her words as well. True, her light-coloured eyes were expressive, even fanatical. About Domitian she spoke with scorn only as "That One"; even "Vellykins" was too good for him in her opinion, and the Emperor did not need his Norbanus to know that Domitilla saw in him the principle of evil. It was certainly she who fostered in her weak husband his passive hostility, the resilient, quiet softness of his resistance. It was certainly she who drove him into communion with that notorious sect. The Emperor, as he now kissed Domitilla, pressed her more firmly in his arms than the others. He was indifferent to her, but expressly to annoy her he did not content himself with the ceremonial kiss in her case but hugged the reluctant woman long and heartily.

At table he was talkative and in a pleasant mood. To be sure, he did not deny himself the teasing of his cousins, Sabinus and Clemens and Domitilla, in his usual fashion. But he was not offended that Lucia praised him for his abstinence and remarked favourably that his paunch had become only a little bigger. And he urged Julia with earnest solicitude to take care of herself because of her condition, to eat of one course and not another. But above all, he joked with the twins. Gently he stroked their light, soft hair; "my little lions," he said. The Princes liked that very well; obviously they returned their uncle's affection. "The people, the soldiers, and children love me," the Emperor declared with satisfaction. "All whose instincts are unspoiled love me." "Do I have spoiled instincts?" Lucia retorted. And Julia, in a cool and amiable tone, inquired: "Does that mean that you don't love our God Domitian, my dear Lucia, or does it mean that you love him in spite of your spoiled instincts?"

When the meal was ended and the others had left, Domitian felt himself better armed for the talk with Lucia. Yet when they were alone, he could not find any good beginning. Lucia noticed this, and a smile spread over her face. So she began the conversation and thus took its conduct into her own hands. "I should really thank you," she said, "for my banishment. When I found out that you had designated not even Sicily but that desolate Pandateria as my place of exile, I admit I was annoyed, and afraid that it would be pretty boring. Instead, the island became for me an experience which I shouldn't want to have missed. Left to the society of those dozen fellow-exiles and the native proletarian population, I found out that a stay on a desolate island like that does much more for the inner life of its inhabitants than, let's say, a sojourn at Albanum or perhaps on the Palatine." "I'll ask Norbanus in spite of everything," Domitian said morosely to himself, "whether and with whom she was up to something there." "When you condescended," Lucia continued, "to call me back, I was almost sorry. On the other hand, I certainly don't deny that now, after desolate Pandateria, our Albanum gives me pleasure."

"I should have made a severer application of the adultery laws," said Domitian, heavily flushed. "I should have got rid of you, Lucia." "You are moody, my Lord and God," Lucia answered, and the smile did not leave her face. "First you recall me, and then you hurl such crude brutalities at me. And don't you find it rather primitive to propose such bloody solutions to a person right away?" She stepped close to him (she was taller than he), and ran her hand lightly over his thinning hair. "That's in bad taste, Vellykins," she said, "that's no evidence of good breeding. Moreover, I have no fear of death. I think you know that. If I had to die now it wouldn't be too high a price for what I have had out of life." She had known how to get all kinds of pleasures out of her life, Domitian had to admit. And fear of death she really had none; he had tested that. And he believed, also, that she had managed to profit by her banishment. No, he could not tame her; one could not master her. Always anew he was outraged by the boldness of her attitude toward her own deeds, yet always anew this boldness conquered him.

He tried to make himself strong against her. She could be replaced; her absence had shown that. Had not this Julia become more than a bed companion to him in the meantime? And was he not expecting a child from Julia? And had he not made something of his life in her absence also? "I too have accomplished something while you were away, Lucia," he said grimly. "Rome has become more Roman, Rome has become mightier, stronger, and now there is more discipline in Rome." Lucia merely laughed. "Don't laugh, Lucia," he said, and it was a plea and a command. "It is true." And again more softly, almost imploringly: "I did it for your sake, too; I did it for you, Lucia."

Lucia sat there quietly and looked at him. She perceived what was small and ridiculous about him, but she saw also his strength and his gift for ruling. This much she had learned: one had to be a very great man, if such an enormous abundance of power was concentrated in one as in this Domitian of hers, not to lose one's sense of proportion. Ordinary common sense she could not demand of him. She did not demand it. Now and then she even loved him for his obsession that a god spoke and acted in him. It seemed to her a little despicable that he could not bring himself to kill her; at the same time she had often longed for him during her banishment. She gazed at him thoughtfully, with more clouded eyes: she was looking forward to sleeping with him. But she was clear in her own mind; she had to get from him now, beforehand, what she had determined to demand from him. Later, after this, it would be too late, and then she would have to bicker with him for years. She had thought out for herself exactly what she wanted to demand from him, and shrewd Claudius Reginus had agreed with her.

"After so long you should transfer the brick monopoly to me," she said instead of answering. Domitian was sobered. "I speak to you about Rome and love, and you answer me: money," he complained. "During my banishment," she replied, "I learned how important money is. Even on my desolate island I could have made many things easier for myself and the others with money. It was ungracious of you to cut off my sources of income. Am I going to get the brick monopoly, Vellykins?" she said.

He thought of the scar beneath her breast; he was filled with fury and desire. "Be quiet," he commanded her haughtily. "I don't intend to," she persisted; "I'm talking now about the brick monopoly. And you won't get any further before you have given me a clear yes. Don't by any means imagine that you softened me with your Pandateria. You no doubt imagined that I'd think the whole time about the horrible fate of Octavia and Augustus's Julia"—he flushed deeply; that was just what he had intended—"but you were mistaken. And if you send me there again I shan't become any different, either; and just as for me that Julia was a pleasant memory, so later exiles on that island will think of me with envy rather than with horror." Now at last these were intimations which showed Domitian how powerless he was before this woman. He groped for an answer. But before he found one she came back to her demand and stormily pressed him. "Do you think that you alone need glory? If you want to build more magnificently than those before you, I want to have something of that too. Am I going to get the brick monopoly?"

He had to give her the monopoly, and during that night he did not once regret it.

THE ordinances on which the Emperor's cabinet meeting had agreed had to have the approval of the Senate. So they were summed up in four proposals, and a few days after the meeting the Senate was called to consider them.

So there they stood and sat around, the "Conscript Fathers," not having finished their night's sleep, in the white, magnificent, gigantic hall of the Temple of Peace in which the session took place. It was early in the morning; the session was to begin punctually at sunrise, for only between sunrise and sunset could the Senate take counsel, and they had to use the time fully to debate and decide on the four laws.

It was a very cold day; the charcoal braziers could not warm the wide halls. The gentlemen stood around waiting in their purple cloaks and purple-bordered robes, lit up flickeringly by the many torches and the braziers, chatting, coughing, shivering; they stepped on their toes, which were enclosed in the high-soled, uncomfortable, gorgeous shoes, and tried to warm their hands at the containers filled with hot water which they carried in the sleeves of their gala dress.

For most of them it was a fiendish humiliation that they now had to take these little unpleasantnesses upon themselves as well, merely in order to pass, in solemn session, laws which were to deprive them of their power for ever and deliver them up to the caprice of this Domitian, the unboundedly insolent great-grandson of a petty official. Yet even the bravest had not dared to stay away.

Here and there they were carrying on sullen, subdued conversations. "The whole thing is a filthy outrage," Senator Helvidius broke out suddenly, and the gaunt, tall, battered gentleman wanted to leave the hall. With difficulty Publius Cornelius held him back. "I understand, my dear Helvidius," he said, and would not let go the other's sleeve, "that you don't want to have anything to do with this Senate. We'd all prefer to tear off our purple stripes, under this Emperor. But what would you accomplish by making a grand gesture and walking out of here? The Emperor would interpret it as insolent defiance on your part, and you would have to pay for it sooner or later. The fearful, cringing life that we have to lead is no life; how many of us would prefer a dazzling, splendid downfall. But an ostentatious martyrdom is senseless. Be reasonable, my dear Helvidius. It's important that those who love freedom should survive this period. It's important that you should stay alive, even if it is a miserable life." Cornelius was much younger than Helvidius—he was the youngest of the Senators—yet in spite of his youth his face revealed deep, dark furrows. "Instead of his encouraging me," he thought, when he had gently pressed Helvidius back into his place, "I have to soothe him. True, things are easier for me. I'm here to write down what happens under the tyrant. If I weren't always telling myself that, I shouldn't know how to bear this life either."

Finally, a few minutes before sunrise, Domitian arrived. The doors of the building were opened wide, so that the public character of the session should be established, and everyone saw the Emperor in splendour on his raised dais. In purple and gold, enthroned above them, he was determined to hold out in that position until the end of the day's session. He wanted the four laws which were up for debate today, his laws, to be discussed and passed with all possible pomp.

The most important of these laws, the one which granted the Emperor the right of censorship for life, the office of excluding members of the Senate from that body, was third on the day's programme. The exposition of the proposal was made by Senator Junius Marullus, whose name the law was to bear. The elegant old gentleman was having a good day and felt young. He, who had made a fetish of providing himself with so many exotic sensations, tasted to the full the pleasure of paying back to his puritanical colleagues the hostile scorn with which they had often attacked him, the "frivolous, artful libertine." Sitting there solemnly, devoured with rage, the conservative, republican Senators were forced to listen to their colleague Marullus, the great lawyer, demonstrating with seeming objectivity that, to insure the stability of the government, it simply was the duty of the Senate to transfer the censorship to the Emperor for life, and that the survival of the Empire was threatened if they did not grant the Lord and God Domitian this superintendence.

Senator Priscus listened, his hands thrust into the sleeves of his official robe. He blinked at the fluent Marullus out of his small, deep-set eyes; he held stiff his round, completely bald head. Oh, he talked well, this Marullus, he talked very well for a thoroughly infamous cause. How gladly would he, Priscus, himself a man of eloquence, have answered this Marullus; there was much to answer, much that was pertinent, and he would have been able to formulate it magnificently. But he had to keep silent; under this Emperor he was doomed to keep silent. One poor, miserable, comfort still existed for him: he would go out after the sitting and write down what he had to say. Then, some time later, at an opportune moment, he would read it in a careful whisper to a circle of reliable friends,

and if it went over rather well, he would slip the manuscript
into the hands of that insolent Marullus. Sad consolation.

Senator Helvidius, son of that Helvidius whom the Emper-
or's father had ordered put to death, ground his teeth and bit
his lips as he had to listen to Marullus's mean, elegant phrases.
Finally he could not restrain himself any longer. He forgot
Cornelius's warnings, he stood up, the tall, gaunt, battered
gentleman, and in a mighty voice cried out to Marullus: "Insolence! Insolent lie!" Marullus checked his speech, he fixed his
bright, pale grey eyes on the man who had interrupted him; he
even raised his magnifying emerald to his eye. The Emperor
himself, flushing, slowly turned his head toward Helvidius.
But Cornelius had pulled Helvidius back into his seat, and he
sat there and said nothing more.

When Marullus had finished, they went on to the discussion.
The officiating consul called on each Senator by name, in the
order of his seniority, and asked: "What is your opinion?"
Many a man would have been glad to reply at that moment:
"This law is the ruin of the Empire and the world," but no
one gave that answer. Instead each declared obediently: "I
agree with Junius Marullus," and at most the tone of voice
betrayed shame, bitterness, indignation.

Helvidius, during the pause after the vote on this third law,
said to Cornelius: "If from time to time our ancestors were
permitted to experience the greatest measure of liberty, then
we have now experienced the greatest measure of slavery."

In the discussion of the fourth proposal, the last, the new,
more stringent moral law, the Emperor himself spoke. Wherever it was a question of discipline and tradition, he was moved
to speak. And then too he found dignified, powerful, very
Roman phrases in which to express once again his conviction
of the close interrelation of discipline and power. The moral
code, he elaborated, was the foundation of the State; the con-

duct of a person determined his mental attitude, and if one improved a man's conduct when one forced him to behave himself properly, decently, then one also improved his soul and his character. Discipline and morality were the prerequisites of order in every State; the discipline of the citizens was the foundation of imperial rule. Even the Senators of the opposition had to admit that the descendant of the petty official spoke with dignity and very much in the imperial style.

Along the walls of the hall, which was shaped like an ellipse, the statues of the great poets and thinkers stood in solemn rows, among them the bust of the writer Flavius Josephus, the Jew, which the Emperor Titus had had set up there. Slightly turned over one shoulder, held high and haughtily, shimmering strangely, eyeless, full of knowing curiosity, the head of Joseph attended the sitting.

Finally the last law also was discussed and passed, and the officiating consul could dismiss the gathering with the formula: "I shall detain you no longer, Conscript Fathers."

Ten days later, as was the regulation, four bronze tablets in which the wording of the four new laws had been engraved were set up in the state archives, and with that the four laws had been put in force. From that day on, the Imperator Cæsar Domitianus Augustus Germanicus had the authority for life to exclude members of the Senate from that body.

At Joseph's mean-looking house there appeared, to the great astonishment of the neighbours, an imperial courier. He brought to Joseph an invitation to come to the Palatine the next day.

Joseph himself was more surprised than fearful. In the last years the Emperor had at most had an occasional brief word

for him, never anything more. It was strange that he summoned him now, just before his departure, in the midst of the
pressure of business. Did this invitation, or rather summons,
have a connexion with Judæan affairs? Joseph, however, made
an effort on his way to the Palatine to suppress every fear. God
would not permit anything to happen to him before he had
completed his great work, the *Universal History*.

Domitian was wearing the purple mantle over his armour
when Joseph was brought to him: immediately after the interview with the Jew he intended to receive a deputation of his
Senators and generals. So he stood, leaning against a pillar;
his baton, the symbol of power, lay beside him on a small
table. The room was not large; all the more powerful was the
impression made by the figure of the Emperor. Joseph knew
Domitian well, from that time when he had been a nobody,
a good-for-nothing, and when his brother Titus had referred
to him only as the "Sproutling." But now, for Joseph, against
his will, the man before him fused with the many portrait
statues which were set up all around; he was no longer the
"Sproutling," he was Rome.

The Emperor was very cordial. "Come nearer, Josephus," he
urged him. "Nearer still. Come really close." He looked at him
out of his large, near-sighted eyes. "We haven't heard anything
from you for a long time, Josephus," he said. "You've become a
very quiet man. Were you in Rome the whole time? Do you live
only for your literature? And what are you working at? Are
you still writing your history of this period?" And, always
continuing before Joseph could answer, but now with a little,
malicious smile: "Are you going to describe what effects my
measures are having on Judæa?"

Now that he had finished speaking, the Emperor kept his
lips slightly parted, as in most of his statues. Calmly and
thoughtfully Joseph looked him in the face. He knew how

scornfully the father and brother of this man had looked upon him, and Domitian knew that he knew it. This Domitian did have the strong, jutting chin of his father. As a young man he had been a prouder sight than his father and brother, but if one looked at him more closely, he was seen to have little in common with his statues now. If one subtracted the attributes of power, if one imagined him stripped of his power, as just a naked man, what was left? If Rome the gigantic, the mighty, had not stood behind him, what was he but a man of middle age with a thick-lipped mouth, thin legs, an early paunch, and an early bald spot? He was Vellykins. And yet he was also the Imperator Domitianus Germanicus, and armour and purple and baton acquired life only through him.

"I am writing a detailed account of the history of my people," Joseph answered with unruffled politeness. Whenever the Emperor met him he asked the same question and he gave the same answer.

"Of the Jewish people?" Domitian asked smoothly and a little maliciously, and his remark touched Joseph more deeply than he thought. And again, before Joseph could answer, he went on: "It may be that the latest events will have an effect on your Judæa as well. Don't you think so?" "The Imperator Domitian has a deeper understanding of those events than I have," answered Joseph. "Of the events perhaps, but hardly of the people," the Emperor returned, playing with his baton. "You are a difficult people, and there is hardly one Roman who could boast that he really knows you. My Governor Pompeius Longinus is a good man, no mean psychologist, and he reports to me regularly, conscientiously, and thoroughly. And yet—admit it, my Jew—you have a better understanding and a better grasp of what is going on in Judæa."

A flicker of fear touched Joseph after all, even though he

was exerting all his will power. "Yes, Judæa is hard to understand," he contented himself with saying cautiously.

Now Domitian smiled deeply, maliciously, and at length, so
that the other would be conscious of that smile. "Why are you
so reticent with your Emperor, Josephus?" he asked. "You
obviously do know of some proceedings in my province of
Judæa about which my Governor knows nothing. Otherwise
you would hardly have written a certain letter. Do I have to
tell you what kind of letter? Shall I quote passages from it?"

"Since you know the letter, Your Majesty," Joseph answered,
"you know that it contains nothing but an admonition to be
cautious. To advise caution to people who might perhaps be
incautious—that, it seems to me, is in the interest of the Empire and the Emperor."

"That may be," said the Emperor dreamily, still playing
with the general's baton, "but perhaps also it may not be. You
at any rate"—his full lips twisted spitefully—"seem to think it
necessary that someone should arise once again and hail a
Flavian general as the Messiah for these Judæans. Don't you
Jews think the Flavian dynasty is established firmly enough
yet?" The Emperor's large, dark red face was openly hostile.

Joseph himself had flushed. So Domitian thought that that
old episode, when Joseph had hailed Vespasian as the Messiah
at the decisive moment, was a planned, prearranged hoax.
Thought he could be bought, that he was a traitor. But he
must not think about that now; at the moment something
more urgent was at stake. "We believed we were acting in
the interests of the Emperor and the Empire," he declared
again evasively, stubbornly. "A little in the interests of your
Jews too, though, my Jew, and in your own?" asked Domitian.
"Or not? Otherwise, after all, you would have addressed yourselves directly to my officials and generals, warned them, in-

formed them. In similar cases you know how to find them quickly enough. But I can guess what's behind this. You wanted to smooth things over, calm them down, save the guilty from punishment." He gave the table little taps with the baton. "You're great plotters and intriguers, that's common knowledge." His voice broke. Now his face was fiery red. He controlled himself and continued the trend of thought which he had begun before. "The speed," he said smoothly and malevolently, "with which you adapted yourself to my father's game that time showed complete mastery."

It touched Joseph to the quick that Domitian again came back to that hour when he had greeted Vespasian as the Messiah. He had sealed up that event; he did not like to think about it. How much had he believed at the time? How far had he ordered himself to believe? He saw himself plainly as he had stood before Vespasian that day, a prisoner, in chains, probably destined for the cross. He recalled the confused thoughts of that day, how ideas had worked within him, how the prophetic words of the Messianic greeting had burst out of him. He saw again every detail: Vespasian looking him over with his bright, blue, piercing, peasant's eyes; Crown Prince Titus taking down shorthand; Cænis, Vespasian's mistress, suspicious, hostile. He had believed in that moment. But had he not perhaps after all acted a part to save his own life?

However deeply he delved into himself, he could not have said where, in the announcement he had made that day, truth ended and the dream began. And was not the dream a higher truth? There was that story of the Minæans about the Messiah who died on the cross. He, the historian Flavius Josephus, saw the threads, he could unravel the myth, he could point out which details were combined in the figure of this Minæan Messiah. But what had he gained by it? What was left in his grasp but a bit of dead knowledge? And in the last analysis was not this Minæan Messiah, this dreamed-up, legendary Messiah, a better truth perhaps than his merely factual, historical truth? In the same way no one would ever be able to say with certainty how much the Messiah who had once sprung into being inside of him, this Messiah Vespasian, who had after all become a reality later on, how much this dream-Messiah had been from the very beginning a reality for him. He himself could not tell, and the Emperor Domitian, who sat there before him and looked at him jeeringly, most certainly could not.

"What do you have against me, anyway, my Jew?" that same Emperor Domitian now asked further, still in a mild, high-pitched voice. "You served my father and my brother well: do you think I pay worse wages? Do you think I'm niggardly? You would be the first to think so. Because I really do pay well, Flavius Josephus; make a note of that for your historical work. I pay in full, good and bad." Joseph had paled a little, but he looked the Emperor calmly in the face. The latter went up close to Joseph, he moved stiffly in his golden purple, it was as if a gorgeous, walking statue was approaching Joseph. Then cordially, confidingly, the golden and purple man threw his arm around Joseph's shoulders, and talked to him in a persuasive, flattering tone: "If you seriously wanted to serve me, Josephus, you'd have a good chance now. Go to Judæa. Take the uprising in hand, the way you took it in hand once, twenty years ago. Rome is fated to rule, you know that as well as I do. There's no sense in resisting predestination. Give fate your assistance. Assist us, so that we can make our attack at the right time, the way you assisted us before. Assist at the right moment, the way you once did when you recognized the Messiah at the right moment." There was fiendish derision in the softness of those words.

Joseph, deeply humiliated, answered almost mechanically:

"Do you wish, then, that Judæa should break into violence?"
"I do wish it," the Emperor answered in a low voice, very
matter-of-factly; he still had his arm around Joseph's shoulders.
"I wish it in the interests of your Jews too. You know they're
fools, and some time they're going to break out, however
strongly the reasonable ones advise against it. It's better for
everybody if they break out soon. It's better for us to put five
hundred leaders to death now than five hundred leaders and a
hundred thousand followers later on. I wish there to be peace
in Judæa," he finished in a hard and vehement tone.

"Can't that peace be bought some other way than with so
much blood?" Joseph asked in a low voice, painfully.

But at that Domitian stopped pressing him. "I see you don't
love me," he declared. "I see you don't want to do me any
service. You want to write down your old stories for the
greater glory of your people, but for my greater glory you
don't want to lift a finger." He sat down again; he struck the
air lightly with the baton. "You're really very impudent, my
Jew, do you know that? You think that because you can bestow glory and dishonour you can get all kinds of things out
of it for yourself. But who told you that I care so much for that
posterity of yours? Take care, my Jew. Don't get arrogant
because I've shown you magnanimity so often. Rome is mighty
and can afford a lot of magnanimity. But don't forget that
we're keeping an eye on you."

Joseph was not a fearful man, yet his limbs trembled now as
he was carried home in his litter, and his gums were dry. It
was not merely the anticipation of the evil fate which Domitian might perhaps decide to bring upon him. It was also because the Emperor had stirred up in him the memory of that
ambiguous greeting to Vespasian. Had it been genuine, what
he had prophesied at that moment of grave danger to his life,
or had it been an adventurously impudent hoax? He did not

know, he would never know it, and that his prophecy had come true meant nothing at all. On the other hand, it meant nothing either that this Domitian had brazenly and flatly called him a charlatan. Yet his security was gone, and though the fear that Chief of Police Norbanus's agents might come to get him soon disappeared, it took him weeks and months after the conversation with the Emperor to suppress again the memory of that first meeting with Vespasian. Very slowly he grew calm and returned to his work.

ON THE day of his conversation with Joseph, the Emperor ordered the Temple of Janus to be opened as a sign that the Empire was again in a state of war. The heavy gates creaked apart, and the image of the two-faced god was visible, the God of War, the God of Doubt; we know the beginning of things but no man knows the end.

The Romans, however, did not, for the time being, take the Dacian War very seriously. With honest enthusiasm they lined the street along which the Emperor was leaving the city to go forth to the wars: he knew that his Romans wanted him to look representative, dark within his consciousness was the image of the equestrian statue whose model the sculptor Basil had shown him, and he held himself well on horseback.

In his heart he was looking forward to the moment when he would be out of sight and could climb into his litter.

IT WAS difficult to get accurate news from the Dacian theatre of war while the fighting was going on. With the beginning of spring, reports became more frequent; they sounded contradictory. Early in April a dispatch arrived at Rome in which the Emperor gave his Senate an exact account of the progress of the expedition up to that moment. He had, it turned out from this report, together with his Commander-in-Chief, Fuscus, driven the Dacian barbarians out of Roman territory once and for all. Their king, Diurpan, had asked for an armistice. The Emperor had not granted this armistice; on the contrary, in order to revenge this insolent invasion of Roman soil, he had ordered Fuscus to press forward into Dacian territory. At the head of four legions Fuscus had accordingly crossed the Danube and invaded the country of the Dacians. The Emperor himself, after the expedition had advanced so far, was on his way back to Rome.

Even less clear were the reports throughout the winter from Judæa. The authorities announced that there had been "disturbances" there, but the Governor, Pompeius Longinus, had put a speedy end to the mischief with his proven strong hand. The principal Roman Jews, among them Claudius Reginus, had the impression that in Cæsarea, the capital of the Province of Judæa, they were trying to make light of the affair.

All the more were the leading Jews filled with suspense when the land dealer John of Gishala came back from Judæa. They sat together as once before on that anxious evening at Joseph's house, and John made his report. It had gone the way they feared in Judæa. No warning had been of use, the Zealots could not be restrained. They had swept with them a large part of the population; especially in Galilee countless numbers had put on the armband with the battle slogan: "The day will come." But it had soon been clear that the day had by no means yet come, and after a few preliminary victories a horrible reprisal had followed; the Governor had had the long-sought excuse to take action, and he had let loose his legionaries on that part of the population as well which had remained peaceful. "Yes, gentlemen, we're down to locust-beans," he ended grimly, using the expression customary in Judæa to signify the lowest level of degradation.

Then he told them the details. Told of massacres and plundering, of burned-down synagogues, of thousands of crucifixions, of tens of thousands of slaves. "The task which we set ourselves, gentlemen," he summed up, "was as bitter as it was hopeless. You have no idea how it undermines you if you're supposed to shove reasonable arguments under the other fellow's nose all the time, when after all you're really on his side at heart and would like nothing better than to throw your arms around him. They are magnificent youngsters, the Zealots, or rather they were magnificent youngsters. "

The well-to-do, well-fed, carefully dressed Jewish gentlemen in Joseph's study listened to the excited man's report and his bitter complaint. They stared in front of them; their eyes gazed inward and saw that once before they had experienced all that they were now hearing. The most horrible thing about the new collapse was that the Judæans had learned nothing from the suppression of the first uprising, that the younger generation had rushed to its downfall with the same daring, lovable, criminal madness as those of fifteen years ago.

Finally, in his cautious way, the furniture dealer Caius Barzaarone gave expression to the fear which was in them all. "In Judæa," he said, "it's over. I'm asking myself what's going to happen to us here." John tugged at his short moustache with his rough peasant's hand. "During my whole trip," he said, "I kept wondering at the fact that they were letting me go home unharmed. By the way, they actually forced me," he declared grimly, "to earn money. If I didn't want to attract attention I had to occupy myself with my business now and then, and land bargains were just being thrust upon you. You should have been present at one of the auctions where land which had been confiscated or had lost its owner in some other way was being put up for sale. It was grotesque, and terrifying. When I think back about that, when I think back about what happened in Judæa, it just seems incomprehensible to me that I'm sitting in my office and doing business unharmed."

"I too," said Caius Barzaarone, "wake up every day with the feeling: it can't go on like this. Today they will fall upon us. But it's a fact: we're alive, we go around and do business the same as before." "And at the same time," Joseph mused, "they know on the Palatine that I'm the author of that manifesto, and the Emperor threatened me slyly, in·a sinister way. Why don't they bring me up for a hearing? Why don't they bring any of us up for a hearing?"

All looked at Claudius Reginus, as if they expected information from him. The Minister shrugged his shoulders. "The Emperor," he said, "has given orders to await his return. Whether that means something good or bad, nobody knows, probably not even D.D.D. himself."

They sat staring in front of them. It meant waiting, through a grey dawn and a grey day and a grey week and a grey month.

A SHORT time after this meeting John came to see Joseph. Joseph was surprised by the visit. There had been a time when the two men had fought fiercely against each other; then their relations had gradually calmed down, but they had never been on terms of friendship.

"I want to give you some advice, Doctor Joseph," said John. "I'm interested in land deals, as you know, and I made use of my stay in Judæa to poke my nose a little into the management of your estate there. The income from your holdings at Gazara lags far behind the average of similar estates: that's due to the fact that those holdings are situated in a purely Jewish district and the Jews are boycotting your products because they won't forgive you for your conduct during the great war. I'm just stating the case the way it is, and just expressing what everybody who's interested knows. Your poor steward, who's a capable economist by the way, once he gets started never makes an end of bewailing and complaining about this confounded situation. He figured out for me all he could farm out of your holdings if they were situated in a sensible district."

"Well, they just aren't," Joseph said in a negative tone.

"Couldn't something be done about that?" returned John, and a broad, sly smile appeared on his brown, mischievous face, so that the whole of that face, even the flat nose, wrinkled up. "Unfortunately, as I've already told you, a great deal of land and property has come on the market in Judæa as a result of the uprising. For example, there's the Be'er Simlai estate. It's situated near Cæsarea, not far from the Samaritan border, so it's in a district of mixed population. The livestock isn't quite so good as on your holdings at Gazara, but the soil is first rate. The estate bears oil and wine, dates, wheat, pomegranates, nuts, almonds, and figs. You won't easily find another place like it, even in these times, and your steward would shout Hosanna if the Be'er Simlai estate were put into his hands. I've secured an option on it. I offer you the Be'er Simlai estate, Joseph. Take it. You won't get another chance like it before the next Jewish uprising."

That was true. Joseph had made an unlucky choice when Vespasian and Titus had assigned him holdings in Judæa. He had really placed himself in a hornets' nest, and what John was advising, to get rid of his property and move to a district of mixed population, was the obvious course. But why had John made the offer of this Be'er Simlai estate to him rather than to anyone else? The land speculation in Rome had now, after the end of the disturbances, centred with particular fervour on Judæa, and for estates in districts of mixed population there were surely thousands of buyers. Why was John, who had so often been his enemy, doing him such a good turn? "Why are you offering this valuable estate to me in particular?" he asked flatly, and as before there was an undertone of refusal in his question.

John looked him in the eyes, playing the honest fellow. "The government of Cæsarea," he explained, "makes it as good as impossible for Jews, unless they enjoy special protection, to acquire property in districts that are not purely Jewish. If the estates that are situated there now fall altogether into the hands of the Gentiles, then the Jews will have disappeared entirely from certain parts of the country within one year. Whoever has a little Jewishness left in him must make a stand against that. You, Joseph, are a Roman Knight and you have connexions on the Palatine; the government of Cæsarea will hardly put obstacles in your way. On the other hand, I'd rather risk putting the Be'er Simlai estate in your hands than, for example, in Captain Severus's."

"Is that the whole reason?" asked Joseph, still with the same distrust. John laughed good-naturedly. "No," he admitted frankly. "I shan't play hide-and-seek with you any longer. I want to make peace with you honestly, and I want to prove it to you by a good turn. Sometimes you've done me wrong, and sometimes I you. But our hair is getting greyer, we're getting

closer to each other, and these are times when men who have
so much in common would do well to shake hands." And as
Joseph remained silent, he tried to explain further: "We're in
the same boat; we've realized the same things. My whole desire is to go back to Judæa and live there as a peasant culti-
vating olives. I could do it. But I restrain myself and stay here
in Rome and earn an awful lot of money and don't know what
to do with it and am consumed with longing for Judæa. And
I don't go, only because there I shouldn't be able to control
myself, but should keep on stirring things up against the
Romans, and because that would be hopeless and a crime. And
it's just the same with you, Joseph. You long for Judæa and for
a new war in just the same way. We both know it's too late
for that or too early. We both have the same unhappy love for
Judæa and for common sense; we both suffer from our common sense. There's much about you that doesn't appeal to me,
and much about me won't appeal to you, but it seems to me
we're very close to each other."

The writer Joseph looked thoughtfully at the face of the
peasant John. They had waged bitter feuds against each other.
John had considered him a traitor, he had considered John a
fool. Then later, after the war was long past, one had considered the other an idiot because he saw the causes of the war
in the price of oil and wine; the other had considered the first
an idiot because he thought that only the division between
Jehovah and Jupiter had been responsible for the war. Now
the foolish writer and the clever peasant knew that they had
both been right and both wrong, and the price of oil and wine
as well as the division between Jehovah and Jupiter had been
responsible for the war between the Jews and the Romans.
"You are right," Joseph admitted.

"Of course I'm right," John said heatedly, and dogmatically
he added: "Incidentally, this time too it wouldn't have come to

an uprising if the privileged Syrian and Roman agrarians hadn't underbid the prices of the native Jewish population in such a dirty way. Without that, the Zealots couldn't have rushed the country into the uprising. But we won't bring up that old quarrel again," he interrupted himself. "Rather give me your hand and say thank you. Because it really is a good turn if I offer you the Be'er Simlai estate."

Joseph smiled at the rather rude way in which the other offered him his friendship. "You'll see," John went on, "how many problems solve themselves once you're the owner of Be'er Simlai. Of course it's no pleasure to go to Gazara and have the Jews there give you ugly looks. But once you're at home in Be'er Simlai, you'll have an inner excuse to make the trip to Judæa now and again. Only don't in any case let yourself be tempted to live in Judæa. Don't do it, for God's sake. The temptation then to become involved in dangerous undertakings is too great for one of our kind. But to travel there once every two years, especially if one has an inner excuse—I tell you, Joseph, that's a good thing."

Joseph clasped the rough hand in his. "I thank you, my dear John," he said, and in his voice there was that glow which had once won hearts for the young Joseph. "You'll give me two days' time to think it over," he begged. "Good," answered John. "Then I'll send my honest Gorion to you to talk over the details. And write to your steward, Theodore, right away. Gorion will of course try to get something out of it for us; that's quite as it should be. But I'll watch out that he doesn't demand an excessive price of you. And if he does, after all, the money stays among us Jews."

JOSEPH went to Mara. "Listen, Mara my wife," he said, "I have something to tell you. "I'm going to sell my property in Judæa."

Mara became deathly pale. "Don't be startled, my dear," he begged. "I'm going to exchange it for another piece of property, near Cæsarea." "You give up our property among the Jews," she asked, "and make purchases among the heathens?" "Listen carefully," said Joseph. "I was always reluctant to go back to Judæa, and the reasons I gave you were true. But there was a deeper reason also: I didn't want to live between Lydda and Gazara. To live in Rome, to live in a strange country, is bad. But it is worse to live as a stranger in one's homeland. I couldn't have stood living at Gazara and having the Jews regard me as a Roman."

"So we're going back to Judæa?" asked Mara, beaming. "Not now, and not in a year," answered Joseph. "But when I have completed my history, then we shall go back."

JOHN had brought back a book for Joseph which an anonymous author had published in Judæa in the winter of the uprising. "Perhaps you'll find the book a little crude, Joseph," he suggested, "but I like it, perhaps because I'm a little crude myself. People over there were all enormously enthusiastic about this heroic legend. There hasn't been such a success in Judæa since your book on the Maccabees, Doctor Joseph."

Joseph read the book. The tale was improbable, sometimes actually childish, and the short piece had little to do with art. Yet it stirred him; he too was inflamed by the fanaticism of this Book of Judith. How he envied the anonymous author.

He had written not for the sake of honour, and scarcely for the sake of the work itself; he had simply let his burning hate against the oppressor pour forth. "Slay them, the enemy, wheresoever you meet them!" he had cried out. "Do as this Judith did. Cunning, courage, craft, cruelty: every means is justified. Cut off their heads, these loud-mouthed heathens: it is in the service of God. Keep the laws of the Doctors and let fly against the enemy. Whosoever serves God, with him is the right. You will conquer."

It must have been a very young man who wrote this Book of Judith; credulous and naïve he must have been, and his living and dying enviably simple. For certainly he had perished. Certainly he had not stayed at home but had hurled himself against the enemy with the others, and died, his faith on his lips and in his heart. A man who could see things as simply and confidently as that! There is nothing greater than the race of Israel. Its men are brave, its women are beautiful, Judith is the most beautiful woman on earth; not for a moment do she and her author doubt that the general of the Great King will forget the war upon seeing her. No doubt at all has ever gnawed at the author of this book. Everything within him stands firm as a rock; he knows exactly what is right and wrong. What is piety? One obeys the laws of the Doctors. What is heroism? One goes and cuts off the head of the enemy. Every step in every situation is prescribed.

But, none the less, what an overpowering book. This woman Judith, no one will ever forget her return with the severed head and the canopy. Oh, the blessed confidence of that author. "Woe to the nations that rise up against my kindred! The Lord Almighty will take vengeance of them in the Day of Judgment, in putting fire and worms in their flesh; and they shall feel them, and weep for ever."

To be able to write like that! It was not so simple for him,

Joseph. There was that heroic woman from the dim past of his people, Jael, who drove a nail through the temples of the sleeping enemy. That Jael, and the wild, magnificent song of her poetess Deborah, were doubtless the models for this Judith. He too, Joseph, had written about Jael in his historical work. What pains he had taken to remain sober and reasonable, how he had restrained himself and suppressed his enthusiasm. To let oneself go just once, like this young author! Again and again he read the little book; it filled his blood with fire. The uprising had collapsed; this book would endure.

A few days later he met Justus. He too had read the Book of Judith. "What a primitive, bungling piece of work. A nation that gets enthusiastic about such a crazy fairy-tale deserves its Zealots, deserves this Governor Longinus, this Domitian. What a valiant author. How chaste is his Judith: she doesn't even have to sleep with the wicked Holofernes. The author saves her from that; she attains her aim beforehand. How justly, measure for measure, this author's Jehovah rewards the good, punishes the bad. Just imagine, my Joseph, how a real Roman governor or even a real Roman sergeant would behave in Holofernes' place. One of these Judiths comes to him, accompanied by her servant girl who follows her carrying victuals, carefully prepared of course according to the ritualistic regulations of the Doctors so that she won't have to eat any forbidden food in the enemy's camp. She's admitted at once— how could it be otherwise?—because she's so beautiful. Of course a general doesn't get any offers of pretty women; he has to wait around till the Jewess comes. And when she's there he not only forgets the whole war right away, but he gets drunk, just as it's been planned, and doesn't touch this Jewess who's as pious as she is beautiful. He simply lies down and lets her cut off his head. Whereupon the whole lot of legions runs away without any further ado. Oh, yes, that's the way our Zealots imagine the Romans, that's the way they imagine the whole world."

So Justus spoke about the Book of Judith, full of haughty bitterness, full of scornful superiority. Joseph could not deny that his criticism touched the weaknesses of the book, but those very weaknesses were the author's strength; the book was not made worse by them, and for Joseph the picture of Judith, as she brought her people the head of Holofernes, remained grand and noble: "Behold the head of Holofernes, the Chief Captain of the army of Assur, and behold the canopy, wherein he did lie in his drunkenness."

Joseph felt as if he must wash the book and its dead author clean of Justus's jeers, and he went and brought it to Mara, his wife.

Mara read. Her eyes glowed, her body became tense, she became quite young. She recited the song of Judith out loud to herself: "For the mighty one did not fall by the young men, neither did the sons of Titans smite him: but Judith, a simple woman, weakened him with the beauty of her countenance." Alas, how Mara regretted that they were in Rome and not in Judæa.

She simplified the book and told the children the story of Judith. The children played at it. Jalta was Judith, and Matthias was Holofernes, and Jalta got a cabbage out of the basket and crowed triumphantly: "Behold the head of Holofernes, the General of the Assyrians."

Joseph noticed them, and he did not know whether he had not done wrong to have fanned those mischievous fires, even if innocently. But then he smiled, and Mara's enthusiasm warmed his heart.

B UT the Jews of the city were living through grey days and grey weeks. For the Emperor travelled slowly, and the Emperor gave no further instructions; the Emperor let them wait.

No new special ordinances were proclaimed against the Jews of the city of Rome for the moment. Only, the laws against the Jews, which had been laxly enforced up to that time, were administered with the greatest severity. The poll-tax, for example, which the Jews had to deliver as a special payment, was collected with niggling pedantry. Every Jew had to go to the quæstor in person, and hand in those two drach-mas which had formerly been levied for the Temple of Jeru-salem and which now the government had allotted, in a spirit of derision, to the maintenance of the Temple of Jupiter Capitoline.

Otherwise, however, the Jews were not bothered in their daily life, in the performance of their rites and religious serv-ices. From the provinces one heard that here and there the population had tried to make use of the anti-Semitic atmos-phere for pogroms. But the authorities had interfered at once.

Then at last the Emperor arrived in Rome. It was a bright June day, not too hot, and now, together with the soldiers of the guard who loved their generous commander, the Senate and the people greeted the homecoming ruler, who in this expedition had been hailed by his troops as Imperator for the fourteenth time. It became a beautiful, festive early summer for Rome. Rejoicing, brilliant light, was everywhere; the great city which often showed such an angry, sour, sombre face was now bright, good-natured, merry.

But the Jews were under a cloud. For tens of years now they might have been living to a certain degree in safety, even though the destruction of the Temple weighed on them, if it had not been for those unhappy Zealots, who with their mad fanaticism were always plunging the whole of Jewry back into misfortune. The Zealots themselves had had to suffer for it terribly. But what would become of them, the innocent Jews of the city of Rome?

Nothing happened to the Jews in Rome; everything remained quiet. "The Emperor never says a word about you, neither for you nor against you," reported Claudius Reginus to his Jewish friends. "The Emperor never says a word against you," Junius Marullus assured them also. But, "I sense it, I feel it," declared John of Gishala. "Something is brewing. Something is brewing in Domitian's soul. Certainly, my Reginus, and certainly, my Marullus, Domitian isn't talking about the Jews; perhaps he doesn't even know himself yet that something's brewing in his soul. But I, John Ben Levi, peasant of Gishala, who can sense the winter when it comes earlier in the year than usual, I know it."

Tʜᴇ same ship from Judæa had brought to Dorion and Phineas letters from Paulus. Verbosely, with naïve joy, the young officer told how Governor Longinus could not do enough to clean up the country. Excitedly he reported the many little punitive expeditions against the last, dispersed bands of the Zealots.

Phineas and Dorion exchanged their letters. Both gave their heart-felt approval to the chastisement of the insolent Jews, but both were troubled that the refined, slender, elegant Paulus, their Paulus, wrote about the unavoidable horrors with such obvious enjoyment, that he adapted himself so fast to the soldier's life. "He doesn't look on the Jews as human beings," complained Dorion, "but as harmful animals, which are just good enough to be the quarry of sporting hunts. 'Amusing' is what he finds life in Judæa, did you notice that, Phineas? He even uses the Greek word."

"So my teaching was of some use, at least," said Phineas grimly. "No, gratifying the letters are not." He let his large, sickly-pale head sink forward, as if it were too heavy for his lean body; he sat there in dejection, his thin, abnormally long hands hanging down limply.

"We couldn't have held him permanently anyway," said Dorion, making an effort to speak with composure. "He would have slipped from our grasp in any case. For all that, it's still better that he should become a Roman for good than a Jew. And it's a comfort that he, Josephus, has to suffer more from it yet than we." Her drawling voice sounded hard now that she was speaking of her detested, beloved husband. "His Judæa has fallen for ever, and his son has helped to trample it under." She grew animated, she was triumphant.

Phineas looked up. "Has Judæa fallen?" he asked. "Do you think, my dear Dorion, that it was a surprise for Josephus that the Zealots were finished off so quickly? Do you think that Judæa and the Zealots are one and the same thing for him?"

"This letter of Paulus's," said Dorion, "wounds my heart, I admit it. Leave me this one comfort, that Josephus has been hit even harder. What has happened in Judæa must hit him harder than these letters of Paulus do us." Her sea-coloured eyes looked up at Phineas almost fearfully. But, "you are too intelligent, Mistress Dorion," Phineas replied in his deep, musical voice, "to comfort yourself with an illusion. You know perfectly well that Josephus's Judæa has nothing to do with the physical Province of Judæa. The way that Paulus and his comrades are camping in that physical Judæa scarcely pricks Josephus's skin. Believe me, his Judæa is something abstract which can't be reached by fire and sword. He's a madman, the way all Jews are madmen. Only yesterday I was talking with Captain Bæbius again, who in his time took part in the Battle of Sebaste. He confirmed what many others have said before him, he saw it with his own eyes, that the Jews threw away their weapons during that battle. It sounds incredible, and the eye-witnesses themselves were unwilling to believe it for a long while. Because the battle wasn't going badly for the Jews; on the contrary, they had the advantage; the victory was almost in their grasp. They threw away their weapons because their Doctors had forbidden them to fight on their Sabbath, and because that Sabbath was beginning. They simply let themselves be murdered. They're insane, those people. How can you think that what is happening in Judæa now should touch them? And their spokesman and writer is Flavius Josephus."

"What you're talking about, Phineas," said Dorion, "that Battle of Sebaste, that was one occasion. Josephus himself told me about it; he was pale with rage just at the recollection. And it didn't happen a second time; it's ancient history, it's all over." "Perhaps," Phineas admitted, "they really are fighting on their Sabbath now. But their madness has remained; it merely shows itself in a different way. Just look at the Jews here in Rome. Many have climbed high, they're rich, they've been knighted, there are ten thousand ambitious ones among them, the kind that thirst for social recognition. Why, by Zeus, don't those rich Jews go and abjure their Jewishness? They'd only have to sacrifice in front of the image of a Flavian Emperor or some other god and they'd be free of this worst obstacle. Do you know how many of the eighty thousand Jews here in Rome have done so? I'm curious; I inquired about the exact figures. Do you know, Dorion, how many abjured their Jewishness? Seventeen. Out of eighty thousand, seventeen." He stood up; tall and thin he stood there in his light blue robes, his large, very pale head stretched forward, and raised his long, thin hand significantly. "Do you think, Mistress Dorion, that we make people of that type waver when we kill off a few thousand of them? Do you think that we wound our Joseph's heart and vitality when we let loose Paulus and his legion on the Zealots?"

"Our Josephus, you said," Dorion caught up the phrase, "and you're right in that. He is our Josephus. Bound to us by the hate with which we hate him. Life would be poorer if we didn't have that hate of ours." She checked herself. "But why are you telling me all this?" she went on. "Why do you state so clearly and hopelessly that we can't touch him with all our means?"

Phineas stretched his thin body even higher, he raised himself in his silver sandals and came down on his heels again, and in his voice was a barely suppressed, malignant rejoicing. "I have now found the right means," he said, "the only means." "A way in which to overthrow Josephus and his Jews?" asked Dorion; her slender, delicate body stretched itself toward Phineas, her high, thin voice was shrill with excitement. "And what is it, this way?" she asked. Phineas savoured her suspense to the full. Then, with artful dryness, he announced: "One would have to exterminate their God. One would have to exterminate Jehovah."

Dorion considered this keenly. Then, disappointed, she said: "Those are words." Phineas, as if he had not heard this objection, went on explaining: "And there is a sure way to achieve that. Please listen, Mistress Dorion. The Romans have destroyed the nation of the Jews, their army, their police, their Temple, their jurisdiction, their sovereignty; but the religion of the defeated, their 'cultural life,' they have, in their arrogant tolerance, not touched. In particular they have left the Jews a little University, a nest called Jabne, and they have furnished this University, at the request of the Jews, with a few harmless privileges. The Council of Jabne is the supreme authority in religious questions and is allowed to exercise a kind of shadowy justice. Now listen to this, my dear Dorion. If our Roman gentlemen really were the statesmen they think themselves, they would have seen through it from the beginning, seen what's behind this Council of Jabne; they would have trampled this little, harmless University underfoot. Then there wouldn't be any Jabne, then there wouldn't be any Jehovah any more either, there wouldn't be any rebellious Jews any more, and it would be all over with our Josephus, with his Jewishness, with his books and his unbearable pride."

Thoughtfully, mockingly, yet with a mockery which showed that she was willing to learn from her betters, Dorion replied: "You're behaving, my Phineas, as if you were as much at home in the souls of the Jews as in the streets of Rome. Will you explain to me a little more clearly just why Jabne should have such importance?" "That I'll do gladly." Phineas began to instruct her with triumphant calm. "I should never have dared to speak to you with such certainty about my method of overthrowing Josephus and his Jews, if I hadn't found out first what the situation is in regard to this Jabne. I've questioned competent people about it, officials and officers who had been employed in the administration and the army of occupation of Judæa, above all Governor Salvidenus, and I've compared exactly what all these people said. It's like this: this ridiculous University possesses no kind of governmental authority and doesn't strive for it either. It's really nothing but a small, ridiculous school for theologians. But there is no Jew in the whole province who doesn't pay a certain contribution to this University, an exactly stipulated sum, according to his income; there is not one who does not submit to its decisions. Note well, they do this voluntarily. They grant the state authority, under pressure, but they grant their Jabne more authority, voluntarily. They bring their disputes, not only the religious ones but the civil too, not before the courts of the Emperor, but before the Doctors of Jabne, and submit to their decisions. It has happened that the Doctors condemned the accused to death; many such cases have been credibly proved to me. Of course these judgments had no legal validity: they were academic, they were opinions of a theoretical nature, without any binding force. But do you know what the Jews condemned to death did? They died. They actually died. Governor Salvidenus told me about it; Nævius, the Chief Judge, confirmed it; Captain Opiter too. How these Jews died, whether they killed themselves or were killed, that I couldn't find out. But so much is certain: they would merely have had to put themselves under Roman protection and they could have gone on living happily, even quite openly. But they preferred to die."

Dorion was silent. She sat there, rigid, motionless, brown and thin, like one of those early, hard, angular Egyptian portraits. "I tell you, Dorion," Phineas resumed, "this University of Jabne is the fortress of the Jews, a very strong fortress, stronger than were Jerusalem and the Temple, probably the strongest fortress in the world, and its invisible walls are harder to storm than our fortification-engineer Frontinus's most ingenious gateway. The Roman gentlemen don't know it, Governor Longinus doesn't know it, the Emperor doesn't know it. But I, Phineas, know it, because I hate Josephus and his Jews. That tiny, silly University of Jabne with its seventy-one doctors is the centre of the Province of Judæa. From there the Jews are ruled, not from the Governor's palace at Cæsarea. And if three times more we let loose our Paulus on the Jews, and if we kill a hundred thousand of the Zealots, it's no use at all. Judæa lives on; it lives in the University of Jabne."

Dorion had listened tensely. Her mouth, a little wide, which projected insolently from her delicate, imperious face, stood half open almost like an idiot's and revealed her small teeth; her eyes were glued to Phineas's lips. "So you are convinced," she summed up slowly, considering each word, "that the centre of Jewish resistance, the soul of Jewry so to say, is the University of Jabne." The Lady Dorion was fragile in appearance; but now that she was considering this statement, her long, yellowish-brown face with the slanting, high fore-head, the prominent cheek-bones, the blunt, rather wide nose, and the slightly parted lips, seemed hard, pugnacious, even dangerous. "And one can only," she summed up further, "strike at Jewry and Josephus and render them harmless when the University of Jabne has been destroyed." And Phineas said confirmingly, in his deep, musical voice, making an effort to conceal his joyful and malignant excitement behind a dry, indifferent tone: "Destroyed, blotted out, annihilated, crushed underfoot, trampled upon, ground into dust."

"I thank you," said Dorion.

A<small>LL</small> at once, the University of Jabne, of which few in Rome until then had even known the name, became a favourite subject of conversation, and people disputed violently whether the insubordination of the Province of Judæa really was cen-tred in Jabne.

Darkly the whisper of the unthinkable evil which was approaching ran through the whole of Jewry. What Rome seemed to be planning here was worse than what the most fearful of them had thought out; it was of all imaginable horrors the most horrible. Up to then the enemies of the Jews had attacked their bodies, their land, their goods and chattels, their state. They had destroyed the Kingdom of Israel, they had destroyed the Kingdom of Judah, and the Temple of Solomon; Vespasian had destroyed the Second Kingdom, and Titus the Temple of the Maccabees and of Herod. What this third Flavian was planning went deeper; it went against the soul of Jewry, against the Book, against the Law. For the Doctors were the bearers and guardians of the Law. Only the Council of Jabne prevented it from taking flight, from disappearing back into the heavens whence it had come. The Law was the inner bond; a threat to the Council of Jabne was a threat to this Law, to the heart and the essential meaning of Jewry.

But always, up to now, great and clever men had been found who had saved the Law. And so today too all eyes turned to the man who was the head of the Council and the University of Jabne, to Gamaliel, the Grand Doctor.

The Grand Doctor was the envoy of Jehovah on earth, the head of the Jews, not only in the Province of Judæa, but in the whole world. His tasks were hard and manifold. He had to represent his people and the Law before the Romans; he had forcibly to unite the opinions of the Doctors which tended to stray apart; he had, without external means of power, to preserve the authority of the Jewish Law among the masses. His position required energy, tact, swift decisions.

Gamaliel, born and brought up to rule, had taken possession of his inherited honour, that of uncrowned King of Israel, at a very early age; he was now barely forty. He had stood the test of the struggle against Governors Silva, Salvidenus,

Longinus. He had steered the Law between those who wished it to merge with the wisdom of the Greeks and those who wished to let it become part of a cosmopolitan Messianic creed. With shrewd, sharp strokes he had cut off the Law from the ideology of the Hellenists on the one hand, of the Minæans on the other. He had attained the goal which had been the dream of old Jochanan Ben Sakkai, the founder of the Council of Jabne: he had secured the unity of the Jews through a body of ritual Law which he let no one doubt or tamper with. He had replaced the authority of the lost State with the authority of Custom and Law. Grand Doctor Gamaliel was hated by many, loved by a few, respected by all.

He saw at once that the decision about the fate of Jabne and with it of Jewry would not be made by the Governor of Cæsarea, but in Rome, by the Emperor himself. For years Gamaliel had entertained the idea of travelling to Rome and representing the cause of his people before the Emperor. Yet the ritual Law forbade travelling on the Sabbath, and he, the guardian of the ritual Law, could therefore not well undertake a journey which would have forced him to be on the sea on a Sabbath. He thought of laying the question before his Council: whether it might not be permissible in this case, as in battle, to transgress the law of the Sabbath. However, the Doctors, in customary fashion, would have debated it for years. The Grand Doctor, since this was an emergency, did not shrink from their grumbling, despotically took action, appointed certain of his gentlemen to accompany him, and seven of them, which was a sacred number, embarked for Rome.

He made a magnificent arrival in Rome. John of Gishala had selected a palace for him. Here Agrippa, the titular king of the Jews, and Princess Berenice, had received the homage of the Roman aristocracy. Here now the Grand Doctor held court.

From this house in Rome the Jewry of the whole earth was now being ruled. Gamaliel made no noise about himself and his business. He gave no splendid feasts; he behaved graciously, without arrogance. Yet he made a superior, even a kingly impression, and now that he was in Rome it suddenly became clear that the Jewish people, although politically deprived of power, were still a factor in the world. Ministers, Senators, artists, and writers thronged around Gamaliel.

But from Domitian himself nothing was heard. The Grand Doctor had called at the Palatine, as was the custom, and he had asked Chamberlain Crispinus for the permission to express to the Emperor the devotion of the Jews and their profound contrition at the madness of those who had dared to resist his government. "So that's what he wants to do?" asked the Emperor, and smiled. But he made no statement and spoke no further about the Grand Doctor, and neither to his trusted councillors nor to Lucia or Julia or anyone else would he drop a word about Gamaliel or the Council of Jabne.

All the more occupied by the arrival of the Grand Doctor were Prince Clemens and his wife Domitilla.

For among the Minæans of the city of Rome—who, by the way, were now more and more calling themselves no longer Minæans but Christians—Gamaliel's arrival had called forth great excitement. Wherever this man appeared, their leader Jacob of Sekanya explained to his patron the Prince, wherever this Gamaliel appeared he endangered the Christians and their teachings. By sly trickery, in that he had wanted to force them to curse themselves in prayer, he had driven them, who would have been glad to remain Jews, out of the community, and split Jewry into a new Law and an old.

Prince Clemens listened attentively. He was two years older than the Emperor, yet he seemed younger; he lacked the strong chin of the Flavians, and the friendly face with the pale blue eyes and the ash-blond hair had the light colouring of a boy. Domitian liked to make fun of him and called him half-witted. Clemens, however, was merely slow in understanding. Today too he wanted to have explained to him again what was really the difference between the old Jewish Law and that of the Christians, and although he was asking this for the third or fourth time, Jacob of Sekanya explained it to him patiently. "Gamaliel will declare," he said, "that we are no Jews because we think that the Messiah has already appeared, and such a belief is a denial of the principle. But that is not his main reason. His deeper reason is that he wants the Law to be narrow, bleak, and poor, so that it can be completely surveyed. His believers are to be a single, large flock which he can easily govern. Therefore he has imprisoned the Law in a pen, in his ritual Law." One would not have guessed from the appearance of the simple, smooth-shaven man, whom one would commonly have taken for a banker or lawyer, that such questions occupied him almost exclusively. "It isn't as though we rejected this ritual Law," he went on. "What we're agitating against is the claim of the Grand Doctor that his ritual Law contains the whole truth. For it is only a half-truth, and a half-truth which pretends to be the whole is worse than the worst lie. To every true servant of Jehovah it is the highest duty to preach the spirit of Jehovah among all peoples, not merely among the Jews. This, however, Gamaliel suppresses; he doesn't only suppress it, he attacks this principle. When a few years ago your cousin Titus forbade, by the Law of Antistes, the circumcision of non-Jews, we faced the question: should we give up this external sign of Jewishness, circumcision, or our cosmopolitan mission, the dissemination of the Law? The Grand Doctor decided for circumcision, for his ritual Law, for nationalism. But we, the Christians, would rather give up circumcision, and want the whole world to share in Jehovah. The Grand Doctor knows that at bottom we are the better Jews; for God has imbued him with keen understanding and vision. Since he decided for the evil, he hates us and incites you Romans against us. Our proselyting, alone, he declares, is responsible for the eternal dissension between Rome and the Jews."

"But," Prince Clemens objected thoughtfully, "you really do agitate at every street corner to proclaim your faith." "We do," Jacob admitted. "Since the Grand Doctor, out of spiritual greed, wants to have Jehovah for himself and his Jews alone, it is our mission not to let those perish who yearn for the truth. Should I perhaps say to you, Prince Clemens: no, you cannot share in Jehovah; for you the Messiah did not die? Should I conceal the truth from you, just because one of the Emperor's laws forbids you to be circumcised?"

Jacob of Sekanya spoke well; conviction lent fire to his words, quietly as he pronounced them, and the blue-grey, somewhat dry and yet fanatical eyes of Princess Domitilla were glued to his lips. But she was a Flavian and suspicious. "Why," she asked, "if you have the true Jehovah, do the Jews follow the Grand Doctor and not you?" "Among the Jews too," Jacob explained, "more and more are adopting our point of view. They're noticing that the Doctors want to amalgamate Jehovah and the State inseparably, in a way that's forbidden. But the fact that Jehovah has destroyed the State, that He has allowed this last uprising to be broken also, that is proof that He does not want this State, and there are always more of the Jews who don't close their eyes to this proof.

Always more of the Jews are coming over to our side. They no longer want the State, they want only God. And they reject that intricate hypocrisy of the Doctors, who are trying to resurrect the State within the ritual Law. For this ritual Law is nothing but an ingenious disguise, and behind it the old clerical State is hiding."

Domitilla allowed herself to be affected by the conviction with which Jacob spoke, but she hastened to return from the world of the abstract to the immediate, to the Rome of today. So she opened her narrow lips, and declared positively: "So you see in this Grand Doctor your most dangerous opponent?" "Yes," Jacob replied. "What stands between us is the enmity between truth and falsehood. We have the Jehovah of the Prophets, the Jehovah who is the God of the whole world. He has the Jehovah of the Judges and the Kings, of battles and conquests, the remainder of Baal who has always existed in Judæa. Gamaliel is a clever man and has hidden his Baal well. But he serves his Baal, and he hates us, just as the servants of Baal have always persecuted the true servants of Jehovah."

"And you think," Domitilla stuck pedantically to the concrete issue, "this Grand Doctor will use his stay here in Rome to do you harm?" "Certainly he will," answered Jacob. "He will want to save his University of Jabne and his ritual Law by means of throwing suspicion on us. He will make every effort to divert the Emperor's dislike to us. He has always worked with such means. He and his Jews are harmless lambs; we are the agitators. We are the proselytists; we want to lead the Romans away from Jupiter to Jehovah. In Cæsarea, with the Governor, he has often been successful with such arguments: why shouldn't he try it on the Emperor himself?"

"I know him," said Domitilla, "I know That One." Even

now she called her uncle, the Emperor, "That One." "I know That One," said the thin, blond, dryly fanatical young woman. "He'll surely want to shield Jupiter, his Jupiter, Jupiter as he understands him. And surely he intends evil toward Jehovah. He always hesitates a long time before he strikes, and probably it's indifferent to him whether he hits the Grand Doctor and his Jabne or you. He has raised his hand; he will let it fall. It merely depends toward whom his attention is directed."

Clemens had listened to his wife assiduously, a conscientious but a slow pupil. "If I understand you rightly," he reflected, "then we should, if we want to save our Jacob and his doctrine, steer D.D.D.'s attention to the University of Jabne. He should have to strike down the Grand Doctor and his Jabne." The Prince's pale blue eyes had darkened with zeal. Domitilla's gaze also sought Jacob's lips.

But he did not want to have to reproach himself for harbouring revengefulness in his heart. If he took action against Gamaliel, then it must not be out of jealousy but only because he saw no other way of saving his own faith. "I do not hate the Grand Doctor," he said quietly and reflectively. "We hate no one. If we suffer enmity, it is not because we practise enmity. We arouse enmity simply by our existence."

"Then are you or are you not of the opinion," Domitilla persisted, "that the best way to save you is still the suppression of Jabne?" "Unfortunately it seems to be the best way," answered Jacob meditatively.

THE only way by which Domitilla could intervene, to get That One to suppress Jabne, was through Julia.

Julia's relationship with Domitian had undergone changes.

At first things had gone the way Julia had feared: D.D.D.'s attitude toward her had altered after Lucia's return. Lucia had filled him utterly, and he looked upon her, Julia, with critical, hateful eyes. When, before he had gone to war, she had come to him to say good-bye, he had stung her to the quick by his derisive remarks, placid as she was. With a head like hers, he had jeered, one could have no feeling for greatness; doubtless she had slept with that lame ass of a Sabinus; she was carrying Sabinus's child inside her; she had better not get any ideas that he'd ever adopt her brat. Now Julia, however, had really not slept with Sabinus; there was no question that the fruit she bore sprang from Domitian; and his malicious distrust hurt her all the more as it had not been easy for her to look on while her husband Sabinus wasted away beside her in powerlessness and humiliation. It was painful for the habitually placid woman to live alongside the silent and reproachful Sabinus during the whole of the Emperor's absence; day and night she suffered bitterly at the thought that she had not been able to talk D.D.D. out of his childish suspicion; and when finally, shortly before Domitian's return, she brought a dead child into the world, she attributed it to the excitements which the misanthropic Emperor's petty doubts had caused her.

So Domitian had found, on returning from the Dacian War, a changed Julia. She had lost some of her fleshy fullness; her white-skinned, self-possessedly imperious face seemed less indolent, more spiritual. On the other hand, Lucia had received him differently than he had expected. By no means did she see in him the glorious returning conqueror; he had been unable to persuade her that the Dacian War, which was still dragging on, had been a success. It annoyed him that she laughed at him cheerfully and with a superior air; it annoyed him that she saw through all his little weaknesses;

it annoyed him that she took no account of so many things about him of which he was proud; it annoyed him that the privileges which she had tricked out of him for her brick-works brought in much money, while his treasury suffered from the consequences of the war. All this made Domitian look at Julia again with new, friendlier eyes. Now he believed that the child which she had borne had been his child; he believed that his unjust reproaches had brought about the death of the child; he desired her afresh, and that the griev-ing, embittered woman did not meet him with her old, lazy friendliness only heightened his desire.

So Domitilla knew that her sister-in-law and cousin Julia once again had the Emperor's ear. From Jacob, Domitilla had learned that, especially to succeed in a good cause, one must be gentle as a dove and cunning as a serpent. She decided to present the fall of the University of Jabne to Julia in such a way that Julia would have to make its suppression her own cause.

She knew how, cautiously, to establish a connexion between the University of Jabne affair and Domitian's jealousy of Titus. Julia's father Titus had conquered and destroyed Jeru-salem; he was the conqueror of Judæa. But That One be-grudged him that glory. That One was bent on proving to Rome and the world that Titus had not completed his task, the conquest of Judæa, after all, so that a great deal remained for him, Domitian, still to accomplish: the real overthrow of the province. If, for example, That One permitted this ridicu-lous Grand Doctor of the Jews to make such a show and strut about so here in Rome, it was only because he wanted to give new proof to the nation that the Jews now as before were a political power, that Titus had not been able to deal with them, that to put them in order was a mission which the gods had reserved for him, Domitian.

So it was opinions of this sort that cunning Domitilla expressed in front of Julia, and after she had left her, Julia went on spinning out these threads on her own, exactly as Domitilla had wished. It was clear that out of sheer ill-will, just to belittle the memory of her father Titus, Domitian was permitting this High Priest of the Jews to swagger around Rome so boldly. This suggestion of Domitilla's, the suppression of the University of Jabne, wasn't such a bad idea at all. She, Julia, after all that D.D.D. had done to her, had a right to such a visible proof of grace. She would demand that he no longer disparage the memory of her father Titus by artful intrigues. She would demand that he suppress Jabne. Domitilla had achieved her aim: Julia had become the partisan of the Minæans without knowing it.

The next time Domitian summoned her she dressed herself with particular care. Like a tower, in seven tiers of curls, interwoven with jewels, her beautiful, wheat-coloured hair crowned her white face. With a touch of rouge she made her strong, sensual, Flavian lips even redder. Ten times she calculated the effect of every fold of her blue dress. For a long time, advised by her women, she picked and chose among her countless perfumes.

Thus adorned she came to Domitian. She found him good-humoured and receptive. As always of late she avoided intimacies; instead she told him all kinds of society gossip, and incidentally brought the conversation around to the High Priest of the Jews. She found his appearance here scandalous; he was behaving like an independent ruler. He thought his ridiculous University—presumably a sort of village school in which all kinds of superstition were taught—the centre of the world, and since in this snobbish Rome the crazier a belief was the quicker it found adherents, and since no one made a stand against the Jewish priest, matters would yet come to the point where young Romans would go to Jabne to study there.

Julia presented all this with the proper undertone of slight irony. Yet distrustful Domitian suspected his hated cousins behind her. With a crooked smile he answered: "So you wish, my niece Julia, that I should show this Jewish priest who's the master?" "Yes," Julia answered as indifferently as possible, "I think it would be advisable, and it would amuse me." "I hear with pleasure, Niece Julia," the Emperor returned with particular politeness, "that you have the prestige of the Flavian dynasty so at heart. You, and no doubt also yours." And dryly he concluded: "I thank you."

Julia did not yet give up her intention. As he began to loosen her dress and rumple the towering coiffure, so carefully prepared, she once more brought the subject back to the University of Jabne and demanded assurances, promises. He made fun of her for doing so. She for her part called him Vellykins, but she persisted, made herself stiff in his arms, and half in earnest, half jokingly, she refused to yield to him before he had given her his promise. But at that he began to force her, and she, won over by this very brutality, gave in and melted in his powerful grasp.

When she took leave of him, she had behind her a few hours of pleasure. But she had accomplished nothing in the cause of Domitilla and the Minæans. By no word had the Emperor betrayed what he intended to do in the affair of the University of Jabne.

THE intimates of the Emperor also felt that it was finally getting to be time to clear up this matter. The question whether and when the Emperor should receive the Grand Doctor of the Jews came under Chamberlain Crispinus's jurisdiction. He, the Egyptian, had been saturated from youth with a deep aversion to everything Jewish. He had presented to the Emperor the Grand Doctor's request for an audience; with that he had done his duty. It could only be agreeable to him if D.D.D.'s rigid silence gradually made the position of the Grand Doctor ridiculous and untenable.

Finally the friends of the Jews tried to bring up the cause of Gamaliel in cabinet meeting. During a discussion of a question of some Eastern province's cult, Marullus said it seemed to him that on this occasion a clarification of the University of Jabne question was also indicated. Claudius Reginus, with his usual sleepy courage, took up Marullus's suggestion. Was there at all, he wondered, a University of Jabne question? And if such a question was really supposed to have existed, hadn't it been answered by the fact that the Crown had let the High Priest of the Jews stay in Rome so long without summoning him? The fact that in spite of this Jewish High Priest's presence no steps had been taken against the University could hardly be interpreted otherwise than as tolerance, even as a new confirmation of the University's existence. Any other solution was unthinkable any-way, unless one wanted to break with the traditional Roman cultural policy. Freedom of religion was one of the main pillars on which the Empire rested. Tampering with a re-ligious institution, which was how the School of Jabne should be regarded, would doubtless be considered by all the subject nations as a threat to their cultural centres as well. With the closing of the University of Jabne one would create a danger-ous precedent and much unnecessary disturbance.

Claudius Reginus had with great skill chosen phrases out of the Emperor's own ideology and appealed to Domitian as the guardian of Roman tradition. Now he furtively watched the Emperor's face. The latter was silent, gazed at him for

a moment out of his protruding, near-sighted eyes, in ab-
stracted meditation, then slowly turned his head toward the
other gentlemen. Reginus, meanwhile, an observer for many
years, knew that his words had made an impression on
D.D.D. And so they had. Domitian said to himself that the
arguments of his Reginus were worth listening to. But this
did not suit him at all. For he did not want his freedom
of decision to be disturbed, he wanted to keep his hands
free; the matter should remain undecided. So he sat there,
expressed no opinion, and waited for one of his councillors
to bring up opposing arguments.

He could not admit—for all that Chamberlain Crispinus
pursued the subject, in the lisping, whispering, snobbish
Greek which was the fad at the Universities of Corinth
and Alexandria and was therefore considered distinguished—
he could by no means admit that the Crown had committed
itself by its silence. It had happened before from time to time
that one had let ambassadors, even kings, of barbaric peoples
wait for an audience. They all started a little and looked toward the Emperor, as the Egyptian, giving his hatred full
rein, spoke of the Jews as barbarians. But the Emperor remained motionless.

Chief of Police Norbanus came to Crispinus's aid. "In itself," he said, "the journey of the Jewish High Priest to Rome,
which nobody wanted, is an impertinence and presumption.
If the High Priest has a plea or complaint, then he should be
so good as to address himself to the proper authorities, to the
imperial Governor in Cæsarea. My agents report unanimously
to me that the insolence of the Jews has increased since the
arrival of their High Priest in Rome. The suppression of the
University of Jabne would be a suitable way of squelching
this insolence."

Norbanus tried to keep his face—onto which the fashionable

front curls of his thick, deep black hair fell grotesquely—unconcerned and his tone objective. Yet to the Emperor the coarse-grained phrases of his Chief of Police did not seem fit to invalidate Reginus's case. He sat there, annoyed, was silent, waited. Waited for better arguments which should give him back his freedom of decision. At that moment the very one of his councillors from whom he had least expected it came to his rescue, Annius Bassus. The Lady Dorion again and again had patiently and skilfully repeated arguments to the simple soldier, which were calculated for their effect on Domitian, until Annius thought they were his own. Certainly, he expounded in detail, it corresponded to the old Roman statesmanship and tradition to spare the cultural life of the subject countries, and to leave the conquered peoples their gods and religion. However, the Jews had robbed themselves of the privilege. With tricky intention they had made it impossible for the generous conqueror to separate their religion from their politics, in that they had saturated this religion of theirs to the very core with politics. If one treated them differently from the other subject nations, the latter would understand and draw no false conclusions. For the Jews had always set store on being an exceptional people, and they excluded themselves in a hostile spirit from the peaceful group of culturally autonomous nations of which the Empire was composed. Also their God Jehovah was no god of the type of other nations; He was not a real god, there was no image of Him, one could not, as in the case of the other gods, set up a statue of Him in a Roman temple. He was formless; He was nothing else than the rebellious spirit of Jewish national policy. If they really wanted to subdue the Jews in other respects, they could hardly spare this God Jehovah, and hardly His University of Jabne. For Jehovah was simply a synonym for high treason.

One was not ordinarily accustomed to such clever speeches from the simple soldier Annius Bassus. Marullus and Reginus smiled; they guessed the connexion, they guessed that behind these elaborations stood the Lady Dorion. But the Emperor heard with pleasure the sentences of his Minister of War. Whoever was their source, they seemed to him a serious answer to Reginus's considerations and gave him, the Emperor, his freedom of decision again.

He had heard enough of this Grand Doctor and his University. With a wave of his hand he brushed aside the question and spoke of other things.

THE next evening, however, he dined alone with Jupiter, Juno, and Minerva. A puppet dressed in robes of Jupiter, equipped with an ingenious wax mask which reproduced the face of the god, lay on the dining-couch, and on high golden chairs sat puppets with the wax masks of the two goddesses. With these, then, the God Domitian was dining. The servants, in white sandals, fetched and carried the courses; they were filled with noiseless, fearful assiduity not to disturb the conversation which Domitian was carrying on with his guests the gods.

The Emperor wished to take counsel with his gods about his difficult affair with this foreign God, Jehovah. For divided as the voices of his councillors were the voices in his own heart. He was moved to destroy the School at Jabne, and he was moved to protect it with a strong hand. He could not settle the problem.

With Isis or with Mithras one could deal; one could erect statues to them, and there were many ways to appease them if one had insulted their adherents. But what could one do with this God Jehovah, of whom there was no image and no visage, who was formless as flickering, feverish vapour, which one cannot grasp, which one recognizes only by its evil effects?

Annius Bassus had told him how much in its time the dwelling-place of this Jehovah, the Temple, that white and gold affair, "That Thing," as the soldiers called it, had clouded the souls of the besiegers and brought sickness on them. It had almost driven them out of their minds. Titus had all his life been afraid of the vengeance of this God Jehovah because he had offended Him in destroying His dwelling-place. And the last thing that he had done was to make apologies to the Jew Josephus for that insult.

He, Domitian, knew no fear, but he was the High Priest, he was the earthly representative of Jupiter Capitoline, he honoured all the gods and would be careful not to pick a quarrel with the foreign God and with His High Priest. He would deal carefully with this Grand Doctor. For the Jews were cunning. Just as attacking forces in a siege were protected by their roofed-over tortoise formation, so the Jews hid behind their invisible God.

But perhaps on the other hand it was all a hoax. Perhaps He did not exist at all, the invisible God.

His own gods must help him, must advise him. Therefore he had adorned himself festively and bidden them as guests, therefore he dined with them, therefore pork, lamb, and beef steamed for them on golden platters.

He was making an effort to be worthy of his guests, and now he half raised himself, striving to give his face the expression of his portrait busts. The head with the leonine brow held proudly high, the eyebrows frowning threateningly, the eyes flashing, the nostrils somewhat flared, the mouth half open, he looked deep into the eyes of his divine guests and asked them for inspiration, for advice.

Since Jupiter was silent and Juno had no word for him, he turned to Minerva, his favourite goddess. There she sat. He had freed her from the prettiness, from the cheap idealization of her portraits; he had given her back the owl's eyes which had been hers originally; Kritias, the great specialist, had had to set them in for her. Yes, for him, Domitian, she was the owl-eyed Minerva. He sensed the animal in her, as he sensed the animal in himself, the might of primitive strength. With his own large, protruding, near-sighted eyes he stared into the large, round owl's eyes of the goddess. He felt a deep bond with her. And he spoke to her; out loud, without being embarrassed by the disconcerted servants who tried not to listen and yet had to listen, he spoke to her. He tried to soften his sharp vóice; he gave the goddess pet names, in Greek, in Latin, all that occurred to him. Guardian of the City, he called her, Keeper of the Keys, Defender, darling little Champion, my Untamed One, Conqueror, Despoiler, Inventor of the Trumpet, Helper, Clever One, Keen-Eyed One, Ingenious One.

And, behold, in the end she yielded and spoke to him. This Jehovah, she said to him, is a sly God, an Eastern God, a real fox. He wants to get you into trouble, you the Roman, with His University of Jabne. He wants to tempt you to sacrilege, so that He will have reason to chastise and destroy you; for He is vengeful, and since your brother is already in the lower world He wants to hold fast to you and pull you to pieces. Stay calm, do not let yourself be carried away, have patience.

Domitian smiled his deep, sombre smile. No, the God Jehovah should not get the God Domitian into trouble. He wasn't even thinking of suppressing that silly School in Jabne. But he would not let the Grand Doctor into the secret. If the God Jehovah demanded patience of him, Domitian, then he, the Emperor Domitian, demanded patience of this High Priest. He would let him stew in his own fear. The fellow should melt away and disintegrate with sheer waiting.

Cheerful, in a thankful mood, Domitian took leave of his gods.

AND the Grand Doctor waited.

Soon now the good time of the year would be at an end; soon winter would make the sea-voyage impossible. If the Grand Doctor wanted to get back to his Judæa, he would have to prepare for the journey.

He did not prepare. He paid no attention to the fact that his long stay made an odd, even an offensive, impression. He betrayed by no word how much the behaviour of the Emperor vexed him, the insolent disrespect which the man was showing to Jewry in his person. In princely and gracious fashion he held court as before.

Custom demanded that Joseph should pay a visit to the Grand Doctor. John of Gishala tried to persuade him to it; but Joseph remained absent. He had been forced to experience in Judæa to what a degree of cruelty his office forced this High Priest of Jewry from time to time, and although his reason sanctioned this harshness, his heart repudiated it.

Gamaliel, disregarding the insult, invited him to come to him.

The Grand Doctor had aged greatly in the six years that Joseph had not seen him. Grey hairs were appearing in his short, reddish-brown beard, which was cut in a sharply defined square; and when the stately, powerful gentleman thought no one was watching him, his body would slump from time to time, the arched, brown eyes lose their radiance, and the strong chin its firmness.

Gamaliel took up the conversation where it had ended six years ago as if nothing had happened in the meantime. "What a pity," he began, "that you rejected my offer that time of being the representative of our foreign policy in Cæsarea and Rome. We have many heads of uncommon intelligence among us, but few who could be of help to a man who is condemned to control the politics of the Jews. I am very much alone, my Joseph." "I think," answered Joseph, "I did right on that occasion. The mission with which you wanted to entrust me demanded at once hardness and flexibility. I have neither the one nor the other."

This time, too, Gamaliel was treating him as an intimate. By no syllable did he let Joseph notice that meanwhile his prestige had declined. Rather he spoke to him as an equally entitled leader of the Jews. He made an effort to win him; he behaved exactly as if he had to justify himself to him for his policy.

He tried to prove that the cruel stroke with which in those days he had cut off the Minæans from the Jews had been justified by subsequent developments. "What we needed," he declared, "was clarity. Today we have it. Today there is only one criterion—outside of the belief in Jehovah, of course— which determines whether or not a man belongs to us, whether or not he is a Jew. This criterion is the belief that the Messiah will come only in the future. Whoever thinks that the Messiah has already appeared, whoever thus gives up hope of the rebirth of Israel, whoever renounces the rebuilding of Jerusalem and the Temple, with such a man we have nothing in common. I confess to you frankly, Joseph, I hold that the sufferings with which God afflicted us have been to our advantage. The ordeal helps us to differentiate between those who are strong enough to keep on hoping and those weaklings who let themselves be submerged in the sacrifice which their crucified Messiah is supposed to have brought for them. Let the Minæans with their sweet and tempting gospel win new adherents. I don't mourn for anyone who goes over to them; he never was a Jew. The Minæans' Jehovah, this so-called Jehovah of the whole world, can't be saved now; we have to renounce Him. We have no use for a God who evaporates as soon as one wants to touch Him, as soon as one wants to hold on to Him. Through our customs and laws we shall at least rescue the Jehovah of Israel."

Oh, Joseph knew this tune. He had seen a hundred times that a man who wants to play politics has to alloy his truth with many lies. Just so, then, he heard the Grand Doctor say: "The man who doesn't only preach the idea, who acts for it, has to bargain some of it away. The man who writes needs only a head and fingers; the man who is placed in the world of action needs a fist." No, he, Joseph, had done right to withdraw into the realm of contemplation.

"We have to save our Jabne," the Grand Doctor abruptly, vehemently, came to the point. "One can think what one wants about my politics; but Jabne we must save. It would be all over with the Jews, Jehovah would vanish from this world, if the Seventy-One of Jabne didn't exist any more. Is that blasphemy?" he asked himself, startled that he had so candidly laid bare his inmost feelings before Joseph. "But I think every Jew thinks the same at heart," he reassured himself.

Joseph looked at the man's frank, swarthy, energetic face. He had been justified by success. His fierce will to action had managed to preserve Jehovah by means of a ridiculous little University in Judæa. The Grand Doctor had replaced Jerusalem by his Jabne, the Temple by his School, the Sanhedrin by his Council. Now there was a new place of refuge, and only he who destroyed Jabne destroyed Jewry.

Gamaliel now spoke quite casually, in a tone of light conversation. "In front of you, Joseph," he said, "I can safely call things by their right names. Of course the School and the Council of Jabne are as much a political as a religious institution. We make a special point of saturating the Law with politics. In our position as commentators on the Law we haven't taken cognizance of the fact that the Temple is destroyed and the State no longer exists. We carry on debates on details of the performance of the temple-service with the same assiduity as on details of our daily life, and we give them the same amount of space. We dispute with the same fervour questions concerning those spheres of legal administration of which we have been deprived as questions concerning the ritual which we are permitted to establish. Those questions even take up more space in our curriculum than the others. Let the Romans try to establish where theory ends and practice of law begins, where theology ends and politics begin. What we're doing is nothing but theology. If someone prefers to appeal to the School in Jabne instead of to the imperial courts, isn't that his private affair? Isn't it our duty to give him information when he asks us how his case looks from the point of view of the Law? And if he submits to our decision, should we hinder him? We can neither force him to it nor forbid him. Perhaps, probably, he will do it to pacify his conscience. We don't know; his motives are unknown to us. They're none of our business. In no case have our decisions anything to do with the administration of justice by the Senate and the people of Rome. We limit ourselves to our field, to theology, to the Law, to the ritual." His full lips, his large, widely spaced teeth, smiled slyly from out of his four-cornered beard.

But then that smile disappeared, he jumped to his feet, his eyes began to glow, and, "Admit it yourself, Doctor Joseph," he cried, and his voice grew animated, "admit it yourself, isn't it magnificent, isn't it a miracle, that a people, a whole people, should exercise such tremendous self-discipline? That beside a court of law set up by a foreign power, to which they must submit, they create a voluntary one, to which they submit out of the prompting of their hearts? That beside the high taxes which the Emperor extracts from them they pay voluntary taxes to preserve their God as their Emperor? Isn't such self-discipline something grand, splendid, unique? I find our Jewish people, I find this fierce urge to go on existing, not to let themselves be crushed, the most sublime, the most wonderful thing that exists on this unhappy and darkened earth!"

Joseph saw the man's enthusiasm; he felt carried away by it. But it did not destroy his mental reservations. It was a mighty achievement which had been accomplished here; with admirable acuteness and the utmost energy a vessel had been created to hold the dissolving Spirit. But now that the Spirit was imprisoned in a vessel, it meant contraction, renunciation, surrender; and what had been surrendered was very dear to Joseph.

"And so the Romans of course," Gamaliel went on, light and gay again, "sense the dangerous, rebellious element that is hidden behind our University of Jabne. However," and now again his whole face was one expanse of genial slyness, "they can't find out in just what this dangerous element consists. The Romans can only understand the world insofar as they can squeeze it into legal formulas; they don't know any other kind of spiritual concept; at bottom they're barbarians. But what we've done evades every possibility of being forced into legal formulas. We submit to everything, we are ready to be of service, we don't lay ourselves open to anything, we even opposed the uprising. In short, unless they want to break Roman tradition, unless they want to warp

Roman justice, they can't touch our University. And doesn't this very Emperor Domitian think of himself as ordained by the gods to be the guardian of Roman rights and Roman tradition?

"Now, however, there are our enemies, many and powerful enemies. There are the Princes Sabinus and Clemens and their whole following, there is the Minister of War Annius Bassus, and your former wife Dorion, there is the whole rabble of Minæans. All these enemies of ours are urging the Emperor to suppress us, and he would like nothing better than to give in to these pleas. The only thing, therefore, that stands between us and extermination is the Emperor's reverence for tradition, for Roman principles. So he wavers between his, shall we say, sense of justice, and his antipathies toward us which are fanned by our enemies; wavers, waits, simply won't give us a hearing, won't give us an audience. Looked at from his point of view, it's the best thing he can do. In that way he escapes the odium of having destroyed the University of Jabne, but at the same time he weakens our prestige by keeping me waiting here, he makes Jehovah and Jewry ridiculous, he undermines our Jabne."

Joseph had to admit that one could not state the situation more clearly than this Grand Doctor. The latter continued. "And at that, I'd know," he said thoughtfully, "how to handle this Emperor. I should try to get a hold on him through his traditionalism, through his religion. For, strange as it sounds, that man certainly has religion in him; much of what he does and doesn't do can't be explained in any other way. It may be a queer, a very heathen religion, he certainly believes in many Baals, but it is religion, and with this religion of his one would have to start. One would have to make use of cunning; one would have to make Jehovah into a Baal for him, into a gross, dangerous god, a type of god which he understands and fears. Is that blasphemy again? Do such words sound wicked when spoken by Jehovah's High Priest? But today more than ever the High Priest has to be a politician. Every means is justified if only it helps Jehovah's people to survive this, their third wilderness, not to perish in it. They must stay alive. For the idea, for Jehovah cannot live without His people."

This time Joseph was inwardly alarmed. That last sentence was truly blasphemous and wicked, particularly from the lips of the Grand Doctor. To such perilous heights did politics lead a man who sought nothing but God and God's service.

"Yes, I'd know how to handle this Emperor," Gamaliel resumed. "Only he doesn't let me get to him. I confess to you," he burst out angrily, "sometimes I'm all on fire with waiting and impatience. It isn't for my sake; I'm not vain; I can swallow insults. But it isn't a question of myself; it's a question of Israel. I must have that meeting. But our friends, skilful and well-intentioned as they are, are failing us this time. Reginus isn't managing it, Marullus isn't managing it, John of Gishala isn't managing it. There is only one man who might yet perhaps manage it; you, my Joseph. Help us."

Joseph, thus appealed to, was torn two ways. It was difficult to escape the Grand Doctor's persuasion. The unscrupulous politics of the man who had abandoned the God of the whole world in order to serve the God of Israel revolted Joseph as much as it attracted him. What Gamaliel was demanding from him was action, exertion, practical activity, exactly what Joseph had avoided with full intention through all these years. The man who wants to act must make compromises; the man who wants to act must command his conscience to be silent. The Grand Doctor was ordained to do deeds; that was his task; he had the head and hands for it. But, he Joseph, was strong only in contemplation; it was his office to set down the history of his people and to give it meaning; while as soon as he himself took part in it as an actor, he was a blunderer and a bungler.

What he, Joseph, thought, spoke, wrote, would perhaps in later years reveal to one or another the events of today as he, Joseph, wanted them to be revealed; it would perhaps determine the actions of a much later generation. On the other hand what this Gamaliel said and thought was transformed at once into history; it was translated today and tomorrow into human fates. The thought tore at Joseph: it drew him. The walls in which he had so ingeniously shut himself up to preserve his peace collapsed. He promised the Grand Doctor what he demanded.

WHEN Joseph asked for an audience with Lucia she allotted the very next day to him.

She scrutinized him with unconcealed interest. "It must be two years," she said, "that we haven't seen each other; but when I look at you now it seems to me to have been five. Have I changed so during my banishment or have you? I'm disappointed, my Josephus," she said frankly. "You have aged. And you don't look wicked any more, either." A smile passed over Joseph's furrowed face; so she still remembered the exclamation which had once escaped her on looking at his portrait bust while it was being modelled: "Why, you're a wicked creature!" "What are you doing?" Lucia went on. "We haven't heard anything about you for a long time. You seem to me to be depressed," and she regarded him with sympathy. "What they're doing to your Jews is no doubt really vile. These disgusting, petty tortures. When my cousin Faustina has slept badly she pricks the maid who does her hair in the arm or the back with a pin. Faustina can do that, but the Roman Empire can't treat a whole nation that way. Anyway, I'm sorry that you're depressed. I too have experienced much evil in these last years. I don't repent it, and I wouldn't have missed it. Life would be grey without the change of good and bad."

Joseph was a little hurt that Lucia had found him so changed. He called to mind that first interview he had had with a great Roman lady, the interview with Poppæa, the wife of Nero. How assured his whole being had been then, eager for victory, confident of victory. Something of that young Joseph awakened in him; he braced himself more keenly. "That I can believe, Mistress Lucia," he said with animation, "that you say yes to the bad as to the good," and he looked her in the face with unashamed attention, with the same admiring impudence as once with Poppæa.

Lucia gave her full, vigorous laugh. "Tell me, please," she challenged him, "just why you wanted to see me. For of course you didn't come just to pay me a call. Though the way you just looked at me was pretty brazen; there was a little of the wickedness of the Joseph of that bust in your look, and one might almost have thought you were here out of mere curiosity, to see how my banishment became me. By the way, I looked at your bust in the Temple of Peace again the other day; it's magnificent; still it doesn't give a true picture, because the eyes are lacking. You shouldn't have protested that time when Kritias wanted to put them in for you. But now tell me quickly, how do you like my new coiffure? It will create a big stir." She had arranged her hair in several rows of curls one behind the other, abandoning the towerlike edifice which fashion prescribed.

The briskness, the vitality which the woman breathed forth

refreshed Joseph. Yes, she stood above fate, neither good nor bad could touch her, she was bursting with life, her exile had only made her livelier.

"You are right, Mistress Lucia," he said. "It really is the misfortune of my Jews which weighs upon me, and I have come to entreat your favour for them. We've had to stand a lot in the last ten years. We're accustomed to standing a lot; we regard it as a distinction that our God tries us so severely. We have a great, profound book about a man called Job, whom God chastens because He wishes to set him apart, because He wishes to bring him to see that there is a secret sin in him, a sin which otherwise the man could not recognize and which, moreover, only few call a sin." "What kind of sin is that?" asked Lucia. "Arrogance of spirit," answered Joseph.

"Sin, h'm," said Lucia reflectively. "I too, to a certain degree, have been through an ordeal, but I never investigated my sins because of it. I don't know whether I'm full of spiritual arrogance. I don't really think so. True, I shouldn't want to change places with anyone; I'm content the way I am. All in all, it seems to me that you're considerably more arrogant than I am, my Josephus."

"The writer Flavius Josephus," answered Joseph, "is, I hope, not too arrogant. But the Jew Joseph Ben Matthias is. But the spiritual arrogance of an individual is one thing, the spiritual pride of a people another. It's no sin if we Jews are proud of our Jehovah and our kind of mentality. I believe that the world cannot do without us. We are necessary to the world. We are the salt of the earth."

The quiet conviction with which he spoke amused Lucia. "What people," she said, "did not think itself chosen? The Greeks think so, the Egyptians, you Jews. Only we Romans don't fool ourselves. We calmly let others be the salt of the earth; we are content to make use of that salt for ourselves and to control the others."

But Joseph did not smile as she had expected; he grew serious. "If it were so," he said eagerly; "if you did content yourselves with that; but it isn't so. You want to do more than control. Only the madmen among us resist your rule. Punish them as hard as you like; we shan't complain. But you want to attack our soul. That's why I'm here, Mistress Lucia. Ask the Emperor to stop it. Leave us our soul. Leave us our God. Leave us our Book, our Law. Up to now Rome has left every people their God. Why does it want to deprive us of ours?"

Lucia raised her eyebrows above her widely spaced eyes. "Who wants to deprive you of your God and your Law?" she asked in return, in a tone of refusal. "A great many people want to," answered Joseph, "your cousin, Princess Julia, at their head. They want to close the University of Jabne which Vespasian sanctioned. It's a small theological school, a cultural centre, nothing else. Help us, Lucia," he said urgently, familiarly, without giving her her title. "We really want nothing for ourselves but freedom of spirit, a freedom which costs Rome nothing, which is not directed against the rule of Rome. But that's just what people don't want to leave us. Out of hate. They prevent us from getting in touch with the Emperor because they're afraid we might convince the Emperor. For months they've been keeping the Emperor from seeing our High Priest." "Oh, that High Priest," said Lucia a little scornfully, "about whom they talk so much." Joseph said: "We should all be glad if they talked less about him." "And so you care a great deal," asked Lucia, "that the Emperor should receive him?" "If you accomplish that," replied Joseph, "you would gain great credit among

my people, who more than any other remember favours
done them with passionate gratitude." "You've expressed that
elegantly and politely, my Josephus," Lucia laughed. "But
such arguments are lost on me. I trouble myself little about
what people will think of me after my death. I don't really
believe in a life down below in Hades or anywhere else. Once
I've been cremated I'm afraid I won't be able to feel much
of your gratitude."

She reflected. "Moreover, I don't know," she said, "whether
I'll be able to help you even if I wanted to. The Emperor is
difficult just now," she confided to him, "and not very
favourably inclined toward me. I often have quarrels with
him. I cost him a lot of money." And with friendly, talkative
frankness she told him: "Do you know that I'm always getting more avaricious? I find life magnificent, but just for
that reason I get more and more demanding as I grow older.
I have to have pictures, statues, more and more; I have to
build, I have to have jewellery, plays, many servants, feasts
on which no expense is spared. I've been using up a devilish
amount of money lately. By the way, you Jews are experts
in the question of money; one must grant you that. There's
Reginus, he only half belongs to you, it's true, and then
there's that man with the furniture, Caius Barzaarone, then
another with whom I sometimes have dealings, a certain John
of Gishala, an amusing, crafty, saucy fellow: they all make
money, a lot and effortlessly. The last one even succeeded in
forcing down my prices. You see I know how to appreciate
your virtues. In many respects I'm fond of you." She became
serious. "So Julia, you say, wants to close your University?"
"Yes, Julia," Joseph confirmed; he had chosen the name with
full intention. "She's very much in favour with Vellykins in
the last weeks," Lucia reflected, "and I've as good as vanished
from his field of vision. What kind of man is your High

Priest?" she inquired. "Is he a saint or a gentleman?" "Both," answered Joseph. "H'm, then he would be a great man," said Lucia. "But how am I going to bring around Vellykins?"

"Perhaps by expressing a wish to see the High Priest," Joseph urged her. "Then the Emperor would have to receive him first. It would not do for the Grand Doctor to pay a visit to you, Mistress Lucia, before he has expressed his reverence to the God Domitian." "You really belong at court," Lucia smiled. "And you seriously think that it's important for you that I bring about the visit of your Grand Doctor to the Palatine?" "I knew that you would help us, Lucia," answered Joseph.

DOMITIAN had told himself again and again, in these days that he had not seen Lucia, what there was against her. She lowered his dignity; she made fun of him. Also, it was certainly not out of the question that she was again sleeping with someone else. He had toyed with the idea of having her condemned a second time in accordance with the law on adultery, which he had made stricter, or of sending her without trial into exile and death. But then he saw her bold, imperious face before him, with the pure, childlike forehead and the long, powerful nose; he heard her laugh. Alas, he could not frighten her with his Senate. And if he had her put to death, he would be punishing himself more than her; for she would not suffer thereafter, but he most certainly would.

He was glad that Julia at least, after preliminary resistance, was now after all letting him come closer to her again. He had obviously wronged her; she loved him, and the fruit she had borne had been his child. He was annoyed that the evidence which Norbanus and Messalinus had collected against

Julia's husband, Sabinus, still was not enough in the opinion of those two to do away with Sabinus, unless one wanted to start talk which might be harmful to him. But perhaps he would take that harmful talk into the bargain. Julia was worth it. Without doubt he had underestimated her. She was not at all stupid; for example, not long ago she had made a neat, ironical comment on a long and noble poem of Court Poet Statius's which he himself could not have bettered. Outwardly, too, she pleased him more and more since she was less plump. Basil must model her a third time. She was a beautiful woman, a Flavian, a Roman, a lovable woman. She could replace Lucia for him.

Never could she replace Lucia for him. He knew it the moment that Lucia walked into his room. His whole resentment against Lucia was swept away. He marvelled at how tall and stately she looked in spite of her simple, low coiffure. Julia suddenly appeared ridiculous to him. How could he have thought of doing away with Sabinus for her sake and of giving second place to his duty as a ruler and to his popularity? How could he have stood Julia so long anyway, her everlasting childish sulking, her touchiness about every smallest, imaginary insult, her whole lukewarm, plaintive personality? His Lucia here, with her boldness, her pride, her taking things for granted, she was a Roman, she was the woman who belonged to him.

Lucia, in her unconcerned manner, declared first of all that his bald spot had increased little and his belly not at all. Then she went straight for her object. "I've come," she said, "to give you a piece of advice. For some time the High Priest of the Jews, Grand Doctor Gamaliel, has been staying here, sanctioned in his position by you. You're not behaving toward him the way you should. If you want to suppress his School, then it seems to me that you, the Imperator Domitianus

Germanicus, should have the courage to tell the man so to his face. But neither to see nor send away the man, not to give the man a yes or no, those are methods which remind one of the time when you were still called the Pet or Sproutling. I had thought those times were over. I had thought you'd become more of a man since Titus died and you were Emperor. I regret your relapse."

Domitian grinned. "Did you sleep badly, Lucia?" he asked. "Or did you make a bad business deal? Did you make a miscalculation on an order from your brick-works?" "Are you going to see the Grand Doctor?" Lucia persisted. "You take a strong interest in the man," said Domitian, and his grin grew darkly malignant.

"I shall see him," Lucia decided, and laid a slight emphasis on the "I." "It will create a sensation if I receive him. The Grand Doctor himself will probably find it unsuitable to appear before me before being received by you." "That's Chamberlain Crispinus's affair," returned Domitian.

"I warn you, Vellykins," said Lucia. "Don't make any excuses. Don't try to get rid of this unwelcome business the way you got rid of certain others. Don't send this man away before you have given him a hearing. Don't put him out of the way. That you exiled me didn't become me so badly. If you go on handling this situation regarding the Grand Doctor improperly, then it might happen that I shall banish myself."

THE Emperor, after she had gone, told himself that with her rude talk she had only been forcing an open door. For even if he had wanted to humble this rebellious pack of Jews a little by fear and suspense, he, the ordained protector of the gods of all peoples subject to him, had never seriously thought of depriving the Grand Doctor and his followers of their cultural centre. Yet even now, after Lucia's visit, he could not bring himself to liberate the Jews from their fear, but continued his silence, let them wait, undertook nothing.

The only person who felt the effects of Lucia's intervention for the time being was Chamberlain Crispinus. When he appeared at the Palatine the morning after Lucia's visit, decked out and perfumed as always, the Emperor asked him: "Tell me, my good man, just what do you mean by 'barbarians'?" "Barbarians?" the astounded Crispinus asked in return, and hesitantly he offered a definition: "They're people to whom Roman and Greek culture is foreign." "H'm," said Domitian; "and do the Jews in my city of Rome speak Greek or not? And do the Jews in Alexandria speak Greek or not? So in what way," he broke out suddenly, flushing darkly, "are the Jews more barbarians than, say, the Egyptians? Why should this Grand Doctor wait longer for an audience than your Priest of Isis, Manetho? Do you think, you scoundrel, that because you spend five talents a year for your perfumes you're more civilized than my historian Josephus?" Crispinus had shrunk back; his slender body was shivering beneath the formal, white robe; his pretty, impudent, depraved face had become greenish-pale beneath the brown make-up. "Then I should set a time," he stammered, "for the Grand Doctor to have an audience?" "You should do nothing!" Domitian screamed at him in a breaking voice. "You should get out. You should think things over." The crestfallen Chamberlain hastily removed himself, not knowing how to take the Emperor's rage, not knowing what he was expected to do.

And the Grand Doctor went on waiting, and the Emperor went on hesitating; nothing happened.

Then, on the eighth day after Lucia had called the Emperor to account, a courier arrived at the Palatine bearing the ominous feather; he brought dispatches from the Dacian theatre of war.

Locked in his study, Domitian studied the reports. His Commander Fuscus had suffered a crushing defeat. He had let himself be drawn far into the interior of Dacia by King Diurpan, and there had met his downfall with a large part of his army. The Twenty-First Legion, the "Rapax," was as good as exterminated.

Mechanically Domitian picked up the cylinder which had protected the dispatches of misfortune, lifted it, put it back again. The papers which it had held were partly strewn about the table, partly they had fallen to the floor. With an absent expression Domitian gathered up some of the papers, crumpled them, smoothed them out again, laid them down neatly. Only he himself, Domitian, was responsible for this Fuscus who now had let himself be conquered. He had entrusted him with the chief command in spite of contrary advice from Frontinus and Annius Bassus, who had warned him against his foolhardiness, against his quick impetuosity. But he, Domitian, had insisted. Fuscus's courage was to have balanced Frontinus's and Annius Bassus's prudence. The defeat in Dacia was his, Domitian's, fault.

And yet his calculations were right. One did not reach one's goal by continual waiting. The legions were well tried, well armed; the gamble might just as well have turned out favourably. It was a vile trick of fate to let this war end so badly.

Was it chance? Or was it an injury meant for him personally? Domitian's face suddenly became rigid, almost idiotic. What had happened down there in the East was no chance, it was a deed of vengeance, it was the vengeance of a god, of this God Jehovah. He should not have let the High Priest of this Jehovah wait so long. He was mighty in the East, the God

Jehovah, and He had, to injure the Roman Empire, inspired Diurpan with his vile, cunning stratagem.

Here there was only one course: retreat, speedy retreat. He, Domitian, was not so stupid as to continue the struggle with the God Jehovah. He would end the quarrel with this God, in which he had involuntarily become involved, most rapidly, unmistakably, and once and for all. He would receive this Grand Doctor. He would wish him well with his ridiculous University of Jabne.

When Crispinus appeared the next morning, the Emperor asked him with dangerous friendliness: "Have you now summoned the Grand Doctor and his group for me?" "I didn't know," Crispinus answered, disconcerted, "I didn't want to—your decision—" "What does that mean, you didn't know, you didn't want?" the Emperor interrupted him vehemently. "I wish it, isn't that enough? By Hercules, what a blockhead I've picked for my Minister!" "Then I'll invite the Grand Doctor for tomorrow," Crispinus suggested cautiously. "For tomorrow?" the Emperor raged. "How am I supposed to find a solution by tomorrow to make up for the insult which you've inflicted on this High Priest and his God by your stupidity? Summon the Grand Doctor for the fifth day," he ordered the Chamberlain brusquely. "And to Albanum."

"To Albanum?" Crispinus asked wonderingly. Official receptions of foreign ambassadors customarily took place simply at the Palatine; that the Emperor summoned the Jewish gentlemen to Albanum was contrary to every custom. So, "To Albanum?" Crispinus asked again; he thought he had not heard rightly. But, "Yes, to Albanum," the Emperor confirmed. "Where else?"

HE HIMSELF drove out to Albanum on the next day. It was humiliating that now he had after all to receive this Grand Doctor and his Jews, and assuredly those fellows would look upon it as an admission of defeat. He would have to find something to dampen their arrogance and to sour their pleasure in the rescue of their University. But he must go about it carefully; as he had learned, this mysterious, invisible God Jehovah was devilishly vengeful.

Unfortunately he could not take counsel with his Ministers about it. For the simple soldier Annius Bassus, for the elegant empty-head Crispinus, for the brutal Norbanus, the matter was too subtle and too high. Marullus and Reginus would be more likely to understand what the issue was, but they were partisan. No, he could take counsel on this issue only with himself.

He stalked about in the gardens of Albanum. For a long time he stood in front of the cage of a panther; the beautiful animal blinked at him out of yellow, sleepy, dangerous eyes. But the Emperor's imagination remained unproductive. His misanthropy, which in similar cases had sometimes inspired him with capital ideas, left him in the lurch. He found nothing with which he could injure the Jews without exposing himself to the justified revenge of their God.

He summoned Messalinus to Albanum. He took a walk with him through the wide, ingenious variety of the park. He pretended to be much concerned to spare the blind man every stumble, but not without pleasure he watched how the man tripped from time to time and how fearfully he concealed it. Behind, the dwarf Silenus imitated Messalinus's dignified, intendedly natural movements.

Domitian led his guest into a cellarlike room situated beneath the ground. The extensive palace, on which they had now been working for ten years, was still not finished, and the Emperor did not know for what his architects had intended this unfinished, neglected space. A few rough steps led down into it, the bare earth of the floor was uneven, in a corner a heap of sand was piled, the room was full of a damp twilight which contrasted disagreeably with the brisk clarity of late autumn outside.

Domitian chased his dwarf away, led Messalinus to a kind of step, and asked him to sit down there. He himself crouched on the ground. There, in the dark, mouldy hole, squatted the two of them, the Emperor and his blind councillor, and the Emperor asked him for help in his difficult struggle with Jehovah. Yes, in front of this blind man who was even gloomier and more misanthropic than he, he could talk. And he talked his consuming anger off his chest. He had to leave the Jews their School; he had to receive the Grand Doctor; unfortunately he could not get out of that. But what could he do to spoil the Grand Doctor's pleasure in his School, without bringing the vengeance of his God upon himself?

Messalinus sat on the steps, his ear inclined toward the speaker, as was his habit. In the surrounding twilight, which revealed only outlines, his stately form seemed doubly tall. The Emperor had finished, yet Messalinus remained motionless and did not open his lips. Domitian arose. With soft steps, so as not to disturb his councillor's meditation by any noise, he went up and down the uneven earthy floor of the room. All kinds of animal life were there, woodlice, a mole.

Messalinus, after a while, began to put his thoughts into words. "It is not very easy for us," he reflected, in a voice which issued in a remarkably clear, amiable, and caressing tone from the huge, dark man, "to understand the superstitious imaginings of these Jews and their quarrels. As far as I am informed, the most violent opponents of this School in

Jabne are found not among us Romans, but among the Jews themselves. And they are, indeed, the adherents of a Jewish sect, those people who see their god in a crucified slave, a certain Jesus, and who are called Minæans or also Christians, people of whom you have surely heard, my God and Lord. The difference between the superstition of these Christians and the superstition of the other Jews consists, as far as I have gathered from their confused talk, in the following. One group, the Christians, suppose that their redeemer—Messiah is the word in their language—has already appeared and, indeed, in the person of that very crucified slave whom they worship as a god. The others suppose that the redeemer is coming in the future. In themselves these quarrels can be indifferent to us, but unquestionably they are the reason why the Christians are hostile to the School of Jabne. From this we may no doubt gather that the hope of the Messiah who is to come is the most important doctrine of this University of Jabne. It is said that this Jabne has political influence. If that is so, then those politics are probably connected with the doctrine of that redeemer who is supposed to be coming."

Domitian had stood still soon after the blind man began to speak; he listened tensely, now he squatted down again. "If I understand you rightly," he said reflectively, "then this redeemer, the Messiah, would be a person who wants to dispute my possession of the Province of Judæa?"

"That's exactly what I mean, my Lord and God Domitian," came the clear, polite voice of the blind man. "And no god could hold it against you if you resisted and defended your province against this Messiah."

"Interesting, that is interesting," the Emperor acknowledged. "If one could strike at this Messiah," he reflected, "then one would also strike the Grand Doctor, and remain unpunished. It seems to me you're on the right track there, my resourceful

Messalinus." And since Messalinus had nothing further to say, Domitian continued: "The redeemer, the Messiah. Perhaps the Jew Josephus could give us some information about that, he who once hailed my father as the Messiah, although I don't know how far that was all a plot. In any case it won't be easy to get anything out of this Jew about their secret doctrines; they are stubborn. Nevertheless, I seem to sense that your advice is very valuable, my Messalinus. Will you go on helping me in this direction?"

"If this Messiah is supposed to have something invisible about him," replied Messalinus, "like the God Jehovah Himself, then, I'm afraid, I won't be able to help you, Emperor Domitian. Then the whole track would be wrong; for then he would not be any earthly pretender, and Jehovah would have the right to protect him and fight against you. But if the Messiah should be of flesh and blood, tangible, then we have rights against him, then we shall seek him out, then we shall disable this School in Jabne and the man who stands behind it."

"Quiet, quiet," answered Domitian in a suppressed voice; "don't say that so loud, Messalinus. Think it, but don't say it so loud, just because you might be right. At any rate I thank you," he went on, cheered. "And please put your mind to the problem of whether and how we can track down this Messiah. Think of something quickly, my Messalinus. Don't forget that this affair vexes me and that I'll sleep badly as long as it isn't settled."

Messalinus returned to Rome, but on the third day he was back again. "Did you find out anything?" asked Domitian. "I shouldn't dare," answered Messalinus, "to appear in the presence of the Lord and God Domitian with empty head and empty tongue. I have found out the following. The Messiah who is supposed to raise up their Temple and their State for the Jews again, and to take the Province of Judæa away from the Roman Emperor, is no kind of spirit. Rather he is of flesh and blood and can be seized by the police. In addition he is marked by a plain sign. For according to the belief of the Jews, the Messiah who may make a claim on their throne must have sprung from the line of an ancient Jewish king, a certain David. Only such a man, according to the opinion of the School of Jabne and all Jews, may become their King and Messiah. The crucified Jewish slave whom the Minæans worship as their god is also supposed to have been an offspring of this ancient Jewish king. Descendants of this family, I was told, exist now as before. They couldn't give me exact figures. There are supposed to be several of them, but very few, people of various classes, however: one of them is said to be a fisherman, one a carpenter, but one also a priest and a great aristocrat. At any rate, they can be hunted out, they can be seized, and with them the driving political force of the School of Jabne."

"That is valuable, my Messalinus," Domitian acknowledged, "that is an important pointer. You think, then, one would have only to get the descendants of that Jewish king in one's grasp, crush them, and the University of Jabne would be done for, and perhaps also," he added timidly and avidly, "the Invisible One behind it?" "I should think it advisable," answered the clear, caressing voice of the blind man, "to disarm those people. Then surely the political tension in the Province of Judæa would let up."

"And you think, Messalinus," Domitian inquired further, "it would not be difficult to search out the people who, according to the beforementioned unwritten law, have a claim on the throne of the Jews?" "Very easy it will not be," Messalinus reflected. "It is a secret teaching, they haven't written down anything about it. There are no lists," he smiled. "Moreover, they don't make much fuss about these descendants of David, and they themselves don't exactly conceal their election, but they don't seek to display it either. And no doubt they do have something ridiculous about them, these people. For they are, it is true, elect, but in the end it's only one who's chosen, and even he probably only as father or ancestor of some descendant who will come possibly much later."

"I thank you, my Messalinus," answered the Emperor. "I shall commission Norbanus and Governor Pompeius Longinus to make investigations. But since, as you say, the task is not easy, it would be a good thing, Messalinus, if you yourself took it upon you and tried to find out who falls in the category of these Messiahs." "I am at the service of my Emperor," said the blind man.

IN TWO carriages the gentlemen of the Jewish deputation drove to Albanum; with them was Joseph, whom the Emperor had invited to come to Albanum with the Grand Doctor and his retinue.

Gamaliel and Joseph sat together in the first carriage with Doctors Ben Ismael and Chilkias, representatives of the mild, moderate faction in Jabne. Gamaliel was wearing Roman formal dress. But while at other times he looked very Roman in spite of his beard, today his Roman exterior gave the impression of a disguise. He was not the worldly politician, as Rome and Judæa knew him, but rather one of those fanatical, inward-looking Jews who go through the world around them without a glance, occupied only with Jehovah, the God within their breasts. The Grand Doctor was in truth seeking the God within him during this drive; he called upon Him, within him there was nothing but the ardent prayer: "Lord, give me the right words in the presence of this Roman. Lord, let me guide aright the cause of Your people. Lord, not for my sake, not for our sakes, but for the sake of future generations give strength to me and my words."

If they were silent in the first carriage, all the more talkative were they in the second. Here the leaders in the conversation were the representatives of the severe faction in Jabne, Doctors Helbo and Simon, called the Weaver. With bitter words they expressed their pangs of conscience about the fact that, against their objections, they were driving to the Emperor's just on this day before the Sabbath. It might very easily happen that on their return they would find themselves riding in the late evening, at the beginning of the Sabbath, and to drive across the country on the Sabbath was forbidden by the ritual Law. The whole undertaking was thus endangered from the beginning, since they were exposing themselves to the risk of having to transgress the Law of Moses. If they had had their way, one would have informed the Emperor that the deputation could only visit him two days later. But Gamaliel had overridden them, he had misused his authority and forced them to mount the carriage, he had even forced them by a second peremptory decision to exchange the customary Jewish costume for the prescribed formal dress. They carried on an eager theological debate as to how many of the three hundred and fifty prohibitions they were disregarding by this drive, and how many of the two hundred and forty-eight laws they were being forced to neglect by it. In addition the Grand Doctor had taken along to the Emperor's the heretic Joseph Ben Matthias, that man who had betrayed Israel to Edom. It was doubly necessary under these conditions that they, the Doctors of the severe faction, should make themselves unyielding and not permit Gamaliel, during the audience, to give in to his dangerous tendency toward compromises or to dilute the principles of Jabne.

The Grand Doctor, already amazed at the fact that he had been summoned not to the Palatine but to Albanum, was doubly astounded at the reception which he and his gentlemen found there. He had been told much about the circumstantial, splendid ceremonial of the imperial audiences. But here in Albanum he and his gentlemen were not escorted into an antechamber or a reception room, but were led on circuitous paths through the extensive park, through zoos, across arched bridges and miniature ones, past ponds, by clumps of quaintly trimmed trees, by flower beds.

It was a changeable day in late autumn; the sky was dark blue, flecked with fat white clouds. The Doctors' legs had become stiff from sitting so long in the carriage. Now they tramped awkwardly along the many paths; up and down across terraces they went, over long, winding flights of steps.

Finally the Emperor came in sight. A few gentlemen were grouped around him. Joseph recognized Chief of Police Norbanus, the Minister of War Annius Bassus, and the Emperor's friend Senator Messalinus. Domitian was wearing a light, grey cloak, his face was reddened even more than usual by the sharp air, he seemed in good spirits. "Ah, here are the Doctors of Jabne," he said vivaciously, in his high voice. "I didn't want to postpone making your acquaintance any longer, my reverend Master," he said, addressing himself to Gamaliel. "Not two more hours would I wait, not till the end of the inspection of my new buildings. Now, though, you must permit me to go on with my business here while I speak to you. These gentlemen here," he made the introductions, "are my architects Grovius and Larinas, whose names will be familiar to you. And now, while we chat, I'll continue the inspection. First of all we want to inspect the little summer theatre which I'm in the process of setting up for the Empress."

They began moving again. The Jews, astonished by their

strange reception, stumbled awkwardly on. They and this environment by no means went together, and they felt it. The Emperor, as they walked on, stalked along, tramped heavily, spoke to the Grand Doctor over his shoulder. "Just now," he said, "there is much talk about your University of Jabne. People complain that it is a hotbed of revolt. I should be obliged to you, reverend Master, if you instructed me about this." The Grand Doctor was a flexible man who could adapt himself to every situation. Keeping carefully half a step behind the Emperor, he answered: "I don't understand how our quiet, scholarly activities in Jabne could give rise to such gossip. Our only business is to interpret the old teachings of our God, to adapt them to the requirements of our new, unpolitical, purely religious community, to establish the rules of a life which renders unto Cæsar the things which are Cæsar's, and to our God Jehovah the things that are His. Our first guiding principle is: the laws of the government are also religious laws. By means of this basic rule we have dispensed once and for all with every question of jurisdiction and every conflict of conscience."

In the meantime they had arrived at the building site. The foundations of the little theatre had been laid. The Emperor stood looking at them; it was doubtful whether he had heard the words of the Grand Doctor and had taken them in. For the moment, anyway, he did not answer, but turned to his architect. "The view," he said, "over the stage of this little theatre toward the lake is even more beautiful than I expected. But perhaps after all we should have made the stage somewhat wider, the way I first suggested, by about two metres." And without transition, abruptly, he turned to the Grand Doctor. "But aren't your pretty speeches perhaps mere theory? Isn't your Law by its very nature hostile to the government? Isn't your God also your King, so that His laws cancel out the

laws of the Senate and the people of Rome from the very beginning? Didn't the leaders of that miserable revolt appeal to
you and your Law?"

The architect Larinas explained: "If we had made the stage
wider, the building would have lost the character of a little
jewel box, the way the Lord and God Domitian ordered this
theatre for the Empress." The Grand Doctor said: "We have
outlawed those who joined in the movement of revolt." The
Emperor declared: "I want to look at the building from the
side. I still don't think you're right, my Larinas."

While they were going around to the other side of the little
theatre, Annius Bassus teased the Jewish gentlemen in his jovial, noisy way: "Yes, my reverend Doctors, you outlawed the
rebels, true; but only after the uprising had failed and the
rebels were dead." The Emperor looked over the building.
"You are right, my Larinus," he decided, "and I was mistaken.
The theatre would lose its point if one made the stage any
larger." Doctor Chilkias politely contradicted Annius Bassus:
"It was not possible for the ban to be pronounced before the
rebels were dead. The formalities and the pronouncement,
however much one speeds them up, take at least six weeks."

"So," said the Emperor, "and now show me the pavilion."
Once more they ceremoniously resumed their walk, until they
stood before a small building open on all sides. "Can you imagine, reverend Master," said the Emperor, turning genially
to the Grand Doctor and pointing to the delicate, upward-
springing columns, "how that will look when it's really all finished? Isn't it like something woven of lace, so light and elegant? Just imagine how it will stand out against a hot, blue
summer sky. By Hercules, my Grovius, you've done an excellent job here! . . . Now, what is this about your Messiah?"
he again pounced suddenly on Gamaliel. "I have been told
that you spread an ambiguous doctrine about a Messiah who's

supposed to be coming, to be your King and re-establish your State. If words mean anything, this can only mean that this Messiah is destined to take my Province of Judæa from me."

The Doctors gave a start as the Emperor suddenly began mentioning the Messiah. Domitian was speaking Greek, which was a polite gesture toward the Eastern gentlemen, but some of them were able to follow only with difficulty. These last sentences, however, and their malicious intention, they had all understood. They stood there, bearded, helpless, at a loss, quite uncomfortable in their unaccustomed surroundings; delicately in front of their heavy figures rose the summer pavilion.

The Grand Doctor, however, remained self-possessed. The coming of the Messiah, he explained, was a general prophecy which had nothing to do with politics. The Messiah was a manifestation of God outside of all realistic conceptions; he belonged in the world of the purely spiritual. The Emperor could best imagine him as something like one of Plato's Ideas. Certainly there were people who associated realistic conceptions with the doctrine of the Messiah. These people called themselves Minæans or Christians; the latter designation came from the Greek term for the very word, Messiah. They drew practical consequences from that prophecy. They worshipped a personal, incarnated Messiah. "But we," he declared with dignity and decisiveness, "we, the School and Council of Jabne, we have thrust out these people from our midst as heretics. We have no dealings with that kind of believer in the Messiah."

"Too bad," said Domitian, "that I shan't be able to use the pavilion very often. Just in the summer, regard for the stupid requirements of my position forces me to give large dinners almost daily. But the pavilion is a marvel of its kind." Then, very softly, he said to the Grand Doctor: "But this time you cheated a little, reverend Master. I am better informed than you suppose. The believers in the Messiah of whom you speak, your Christians, they declare after all that the Messiah has already died; their crucified god will therefore hardly deprive me of the Province of Judæa, and the people are quite harmless in that respect. Your Messiah, on the other hand, since you're still expecting him, remains suspicious."

There was visible confusion among the doctors. The prophecy of the Messiah, Gamaliel attempted to explain, referred to a distant future. Concerning the kingdom which he was to found, it said that swords would be beaten into ploughshares, and that there the lion, wolf, and bear would lie down with the lamb. "You see, Your Majesty," he concluded, "it's a matter of a religious Utopia which has nothing to do with real politics." Doctor Chilkias came to his aid. "Only one thing is certain," he said, "namely, that a Messiah will come. But when he will come, and what his function will be, is left up to the individual to picture for himself."

While Gamaliel was speaking some of the Doctors had already begun to whisper together. They obviously thought it blasphemous, unbearable, that from ordained lips such an important part of their faith should be so ambiguously explained, yes, actually denied. Scarcely had Doctor Chilkias finished before Doctor Helbo was correcting him and above all the Grand Doctor. In his deep, cracked voice, awkwardly, in bad Greek, he said: "It may be far, it may be near, it may be this way, it may be that; but the day will come. The day will come," he repeated bluntly, threateningly, and turned his old, angered eyes toward the Grand Doctor and back to the Emperor.

There was an uncomfortable silence. "Interesting," said Domitian, "that is interesting." He sat down on the steps of the pavilion, sloppily crossed his legs, and rocked his foot to and fro; it was pleasant not to be wearing formal, high-soled shoes but comfortable, sandal-like ones. "I'd like to hear more about that," he went on. And still very gently, he turned to the Grand Doctor, shaking a finger at him. "And then you say your Messiah is a Utopian concept, a Platonic Idea." And then again to blunt, old Helbo: "The day will come. What day, please? 'It will come, the day on which sacred Ilium falleth,'" he quoted Homer. "Which Ilium are you thinking of, my Doctor and Master? Of Rome?" he asked point-blank.

The Doctors were now standing somewhat apart. The Romans looked at them, waited for an answer. The Emperor meanwhile, not taking advantage of their embarrassment, interrupted the painful silence and went on, with unwonted joviality: "There must be a number of you who have not imagined this Messiah as something purely spiritual, but as a being of flesh and blood. My Flavius Josephus here pointed out my father, the God Vespasian, as the Messiah. And you, my Flavius Josephus"—he looked him full in the face, softly, mockingly, dangerously—"you surely didn't suspect my father of any intention of taming wolves or lions so that they would lie down with lambs. But well and good"—he turned again to the Doctors—"this Knight Flavius Josephus is by vocation soldier, writer, statesman, and only by avocation theologian and prophet; so let us leave his interpretation to him. But you, however, my Masters and Doctors, you are the ordained exponents of the Jewish Law, the attorneys of Jehovah. I ask you for a clear, unmistakable explanation: who or what is your Messiah? I ask you for as unambiguous an explanation as I expect to find in the reports of my officials."

"It is written," began Doctor Helbo, "in the book of our prophet Isaiah: 'For out of Zion shall go forth the Law, and the word of the Lord from Jerusalem. And he shall judge among the nations, and shall rebuke many people.'" Angrily and dangerously the words issued from his large mouth. But,

"Not so, not so, my brother and Master," Doctor Chilkias interrupted him eagerly; "that is a half-truth which only acquires its correct meaning from later sentences. For the same prophet Isaiah has said: 'It is a light thing that thou shouldest be my servant to raise up the tribes of Jacob. . . . I will also give thee for a light to the Gentiles, that thou mayest be my salvation unto the end of the earth.' " However, "Don't distort things, my brother and Master"—Doctor Helbo grew stubbornly excited—"don't put the emphasis on side-issues! Is it not also written in the book of the prophet Micah: 'He shall judge among many people, and rebuke strong nations afar off'?" But Doctor Chilkias insisted also: "It is you who distort, and for the second time. Because you omit how it goes on in Micah: 'But they shall sit every man under his vine and under his fig tree; and none shall make them afraid.' " But now Doctor Helbo's theoretical ally came to his aid, Doctor Simon, called the Weaver. "And what," he asked pugnaciously, "about Gog and Magog, whom the Messiah will first overthrow?" Now they all began to debate. They were no longer in the gardens of Albanum and in the presence of the Emperor; they were in Jabne, in their schoolroom, they fell from Greek into Aramaic, their voices intermingled heatedly, angrily. The Emperor and his gentlemen listened quietly and barely showed how much they were amused.

"I must confess I haven't become much wiser," the Emperor said at last. Messalinus, in his soft voice, intervened. "May I make an attempt," he said, "to make clear to the gentlemen what our Lord and God really wants of them? His Majesty is interested, my Masters and Doctors, in finding out the following from you as the authorized source. Are there men of flesh and blood, men with exact names, habitation, and year of birth, who have the possible expectancy of being the Messiah awaited by you? I've been told on occasion that one criterion is recognized by all of you as the foundation of such suitability and expectancy: namely, that your awaited Messiah will be a scion of the house of your King David. Have I been rightly instructed on this point or not?"

"Yes," said the Emperor vivaciously, "that's interesting. Is the circle of those from whose midst your awaited Messiah is to come sharply defined? Is he to be sought exclusively among the descendants of your King David? I ask you for a plain answer," he challenged the Grand Doctor.

Gamaliel replied: "It is so and it is not so. Our Holy Book often employs a poetic manner of expression. If among our prophets one or the other declares that a Messiah will come to us from the line of David, then it is expressed vaguely on purpose, and to be understood figuratively. The whole imaginative sphere of the Messiah is poetical. It has," he concluded, smiling, as man of the world, "little to do with a reality which could be pinned down in documents and lists."

Doctor Ben Ismael turned his noble, ivory-colored, wrinkled face toward the Emperor, directed his tired, sunken old eyes straight at him, and declared: "Yes, it is a question of a higher reality. Whoever gives individual details about the Messiah is at best expressing a half-truth and thus something false. For the doctrine of the Messiah is a manifold truth, it cannot be grasped with the understanding alone, it can only be surmised, envisioned. Only the prophet beholds it. One thing only is certain: the Messiah who is to come will be the link between God and the world. His mission concerns not only Israel, but the whole world and all its peoples."

But, "It is not so," the fierce zealot Doctor Helbo declared, "and you, Doctor Ben Ismael, know that it is not so. There are individual details revealed about the Messiah"—he turned to Messalinus—"signs so unambiguous that they cannot be wiped out and that even you Romans can understand them.

The Messiah will be a scion of David. That is the truth, and you have been correctly informed, sir."

"Thank you," said Messalinus.

"What you proclaimed to my father, however, Flavius Josephus," said the Emperor amiably, "doesn't agree with this. For as far as I'm informed about our descent, it goes back to Hercules, not to this David." A ripple of laughter went around; it sounded harmless; the Grand Doctor breathed a sigh of relief. Joseph himself, in spite of the humiliation, was relieved, glad that the danger seemed to be passing by the University of Jabne, passing by the Law. "From the differences among the reverend Doctors and Masters," he defended himself, "the Lord and God Domitian may perceive that the prophecies about the Messiah are obscure and to a large degree left to feeling. What I sensed at the time when I paid homage to the Lord and God Vespasian was sincere; events have justified it, and I am proud of my prophecy."

A deep, angry growl came from Doctor Helbo's throat. If it was already blasphemy that Joseph Ben Matthias, after all a Jew, should address the Emperor of the heathens as Lord and God, then it was twofold blasphemy that he again, in the presence of the Doctors of Jabne, called the dead Emperor Vespasian, Jehovah's enemy, the Messiah. So Doctor Helbo prepared to say something passionate, crushing, an avowal of faith. But neither Annius Bassus nor Norbanus nor even Messalinus was pleased that the conversation had turned back to those old, long-past events. They were eager to pin down the Doctors to definitions which could be used for certain practical measures. "So much at any rate we can regard as certain," Annius Bassus summed up, "that the common man everywhere among the Jewish people regards a man who is a descendant of King David as belonging to the circle from which the genuine Messiah will come." "Yes, that is so," grim

Doctor Helbo admitted. "Well, now," Chief of Police Norbanus declared with satisfaction, "there anyway we have something solid, comprehensible, tangible." And, "Are there such descendants of David?" Messalinus at once pressed on in his soft voice. "Does one know them? Are there many? And where does one find them?"

Except for Joseph and Gamaliel probably none of the Jews knew about this Senator Messalinus's sinister function. Nevertheless, a shiver ran over the Doctors. They noticed the evil intention behind the mild question; they recognized that this was the most dangerous moment of this fateful conversation, the most dangerous moment of this hazardous trip to Rome. What should they answer? Should they surrender the names of the scions of David and their heads to these evil-intentioned heathens and their Emperor? Not that they were highly revered, those whom today the people designated, and not even with certainty, as the scions of David; through the many generations there had been many elect. Yet they were sacred, for among them was the chosen one or the ancestor of the chosen one. And the hope of the chosen one was the brightest part of the Law. Yes, a great light would be extinguished for ever if they wantonly abandoned the line of David and with it the possibility that the Messiah would ever appear. Around the hope of the Messiah was a web of secrecy, an ancient holiness of great fascination; if this holy, secret element disappeared from the world with the line of David, the Law would be deprived of its deepest magic.

What should they do? If they evaded the blind man's soft, tricky question, if they refused to give the names, surely the anger of the Emperor would descend on the School of Jabne. Should they deliver up the scions of David?

The wind had grown stronger; it came in gusts and billowed out the formal robes. Dark green shone the box and yew, silver glittered the olive trees; from below, lightly ruffled, gleamed the lake. But no one noticed. The Emperor sat on the steps of the pavilion; the others stood about. They looked at the Grand Doctor; now it was up to him to answer, and what would he answer? Even the architects Grovius and Larinas forgot their annoyance that the exhibition of their achievements had been interfered with by the presence of the barbarian deputation. What would the High Priest of the Jews say now?

However, before he could answer, Doctor Helbo's cracked, rough voice rang out. Had not this Joseph Ben Matthias just now again committed the sin of blasphemy and thus destined himself for extermination? So, "Those of the line of David are elect," Doctor Helbo said, "but only few are chosen. For example, there is this Joseph Ben Matthias, former priest of the first rank, but now outlawed and a heretic. How could such a man be chosen? And yet he is of the line of David, if only from his grandmother's side. His father, at any rate, has boasted of this in my hearing."

"Interesting," said the Emperor, "interesting."

All eyes turned to Joseph. A small open space had formed around him; it was like the time when the ban had been pronounced against him and all had kept seven paces' distance. With a strange detachment he stood there, as if they were speaking of a third person; the formal robe with the narrow purple stripe clung to his lean limbs in the wind; with an absent stare he looked at the ring on his finger, the golden band of the second rank. Within him was panic. "Of the line of David," he thought. "It's probably true. Of royal lineage from my father's and from my mother's side, of the line of David and the line of the Hasmoneans. That this comes upon me now is my punishment for once having hailed the Roman as the Messiah."

Meanwhile, however, the Grand Doctor had found his answer. In his superior, worldly manner he declared: "If the people designate one man or another as a descendant of David, then it's vulgar superstition, based on not the faintest trace of evidence. Sometimes they're very common men to whom this superstition attaches itself, a fisherman, a carpenter. How should a scion of David fall so low?" This time he was put right by the man of whom no one would have expected it. "But sometimes there is a great radiance upon those lowly men," said the mild voice of old Doctor Ben Ismael.

"Let us look at you, my Josephus," smiled Domitian, "see whether the radiance is around you." He stood up, came close to the Jew. "In any case this affair of your Messiah remains obscure and suspicious," he decided; it sounded conclusive.

But now the Grand Doctor thought of what he had deduced about this Emperor's piety and fear of God, and he felt it was time for him to take the offensive. "I entreat Your Majesty," he requested, "not to regard the situation as critical. The doctrine of the Messiah is obscure, but do not the gods of many peoples wrap themselves in obscurity?" He now stood face to face with the Emperor; his voice sounded clear, strong, courageous, threatening. "It is not a good thing," he warned, "when man attempts to pry too deeply into the secrets of the divine. Perhaps it happened for such reasons that our God chastised us so severely." A little quiver passed over the face of the Emperor, scarcely noticeable, but Gamaliel noticed it. He had not hoped to accomplish more; to go on threatening the Emperor would only have spoiled the effect. So Gamaliel let matters rest with his veiled statement; he even acted as though he had not brought forward any warning, but only an excuse, and continued more softly: "He is not a light, cheerful God, our God Jehovah; it is difficult to serve Him; He is easily offended."

The Grand Doctor's threat caused the Emperor uneasiness by its very ambiguity, Gamaliel's ringing voice reminded him painfully of his brother Titus's voice, and that last hint, that Jehovah was easily offended, upset him profoundly. "What does he want," he thought, "the Jewish priest? After all, I'm not even thinking of closing his University. It would just suit this Jehovah for me to undertake something against Him and give Him an excuse to hear me. I'll do nothing of the kind."

"I have heard," he said with a rush, decidedly, "that you were afraid that we might close your School. How did you get such an absurd notion? How can you give credence to such senseless gossip?" He drew himself up; flashing, imperial, he stood in the strong wind. "Rome protects the gods of the peoples who have entrusted themselves to her care," he announced, and, "Have no fear," he continued genially. "I shall give you a written statement to my Governor Pompeius Longinus, which will relieve you of any further anxiety." With a light, graceful gesture he laid his hand on the Grand Doctor's shoulder. "One should not become at once disheartened," he said with amiable irony, "and despair, under the rule of Domitian whom the Senate and people of Rome call their Lord and God. And perhaps also one should have somewhat more faith in one's own gods." And turning to Joseph, in closing, with an easy and yet princely gesture, he said: "Are you satisfied with me, my Flavius Josephus, historian of my line?"

THE next week, in spite of the bad time of the year, the Grand Doctor and his gentlemen embarked for Judæa. Joseph and Claudius Reginus accompanied Gamaliel to the boat.

Now again Gamaliel found cordial and highly respectful

words with which to thank Joseph for having procured him the audience with the Emperor. "Again," he said, "you have gained great merit in the cause of Israel. I only hope that in the end you won't have to pay the price for our privileges. Since Domitian hasn't as yet taken any steps as a result of our Doctor Helbo's thoughtless utterances, I hope he will continue to abstain."

Joseph was silent. But Claudius Reginus shook his head anxiously, and said: "Domitian is a slow god."

Then the Doctors embarked, happy in the possession of the Emperor's graciously phrased, autographed letter. All hearts were filled with gratitude to Joseph. Only Doctors Helbo and Simon the Weaver continued to bear him a grudge.

A SHORT time afterward Senator Messalinus invited Joseph to visit him. The Emperor was doing the Senator the honour of dining with him, and wished Joseph to read aloud the chapter on the Jewish King David from the manuscript of his *History*.

Then Joseph knew that Claudius Reginus had been right, and that the slow god, Domitian, had postponed measures against him, but not abandoned them. He felt terror in his heart. But at the same time he decided that if God really had destined him to be a sacrifice in place of Jabne, he would not protest, but take this sacrifice upon himself full of humble pride.

While Domitian lay lazily on the couch, Messalinus explained to Joseph that the Emperor was interested in certain Jewish questions, and since the Doctors of Jabne were no longer in Rome, he wished to gather information from Josephus as the best expert in the field. "Yes"—the Emperor nodded indolently and benevolently—"it would be kind of you, my Josephus, if you would instruct us."

Joseph, addressing himself only to Messalinus, asked: "Am I to regard this interview as a hearing?" "What harsh words, my Josephus," the Emperor reproached him from his couch, and, "It's mainly a matter of a discussion on historical subjects," the blind man again emphasized amiably. "The Lord and God Domitian is interested, for example, in what you, a man of the East, think of the fate of Cæsarion, that son of Julius Cæsar and Cleopatra." "Yes," the Emperor agreed, "that interests me. Cæsar obviously loved him, that son of his," he explained, "and planned that he should play the part of the mediating ruler between East and West. It appears also that Cæsarion developed into a young man of many gifts." "And on what," said Joseph, stunned, "do you wish my opinion?" Messalinus leaned forward, fixed his blind eyes on Joseph's face as if he could see, and asked slowly and very distinctly: "Do you think that Augustus was right in doing away with this Cæsarion?"

Now the issue was clear to Joseph. Domitian, before he dispatched the scions of David, wanted in addition to have one of his victims affirm that he was right in doing away with him. Cautiously he said: "Julius Cæsar would certainly have been able to advance sound and convincing arguments before the tribunal of history to condemn Augustus's deed. Augustus for his part would doubtless have had arguments no less sound to justify his deed." Domitian laughed a little laugh. Across the blind man's face also a smile flitted, and he said in acknowledgment: "Well answered. However, what interests us here is not Cæsar's opinion, nor Augustus's opinion, but only your opinion, my Flavius Josephus." And, "Do you think," he repeated slowly, underlining every word, "that Augustus was right in doing away with the pretender Cæsarion?" He inclined his ear in Joseph's direction, greedily.

Joseph bit his lips. Shamelessly and directly the man was stating the issue: the removal of undesirable pretenders, his, Joseph's, removal. He was a skilful speaker, he could have evaded them further and withdrawn from their cheap trap; but his pride rose up against it. "Augustus did right," he judged boldly and without evasion, "in doing away with Cæsarion. Success has justified him." "Thank you," said Messalinus, as he had a habit of doing in court when his opponent had been forced to admit that he was in the right.

"And now tell us about your King David," he continued cheerfully, "whose descendants are destined to be your future rulers." "Yes," Domitian agreed, "read aloud to us what you have written about your ancestor. Our Messalinus asked you here for that purpose."

At heart Joseph loved dark, tortured Saul more than that David for whom so much was easily and happily fulfilled, and he knew that the chapters about David were not the best in his work. But today, as he read, his subject carried him away, and he read well. It gave him satisfaction to tell this Roman Emperor about the great Jewish King, who had been such a mighty ruler and conqueror of peoples. Joseph read well, and Domitian was a good listener. He had some feeling for history, he had some feeling for literature, Josephus interested him, King David interested him; his face mirrored his sympathy.

Once he interrupted Joseph. "It is no doubt quite a long time ago that he reigned, this David?" he asked. "It was about the time of the Trojan War," Joseph informed him, and proudly he added: "Our history reaches very far back." "Our Roman history," the Emperor admitted peaceably, "only begins with the flight of Æneas from burning Troy. At that time, then, you already had this great king on your country's throne. But go on reading, my Josephus."

Joseph read, and as he read aloud there to the Roman Emperor, he seemed to himself a little like that David, playing the harp before distraught King Saul. He read for a long time, and when he wanted to stop, the Emperor ordered him to read on.

Then, when Joseph had finished, Domitian made some thoroughly understanding comments. "He seems to have had the knack of ruling, your David," he suggested, "although I don't approve of his various fits of generosity. He obviously acted foolishly when he spared Saul after he had been delivered into his hands, and that even a second time. Later on he acquired more knowledge and behaved more intelligently. One deed above all seems good and kingly to me: namely, that he punished the assassination of the King, even though that murder was committed against his opponent and was therefore to his benefit."

Yes, that action of David's, ordering the man who had murdered Saul to be executed, seemed to stimulate the Emperor's imagination, and with a slight shudder Joseph had to note with what ingenious skill Domitian was able to abstract something for his own use even from seemingly the most remote event. "Emperor Nero"—he turned with an example to Messalinus—"was of course my family's enemy, and it was a good thing that he perished. Yet I can't understand how the Senate could allow this murderer, Epaphroditus, to go on living. Whoever raises a hand against an Emperor must not continue to exist in the world. And is he still living, that Epaphroditus? Isn't he living here in Rome? Doesn't he walk around like a two-legged incitement to regicide? I don't see how the Senate could stand for it so long." Messalinus, in his most amicable tone, excused his colleagues. "Much," he said, "of what the

Conscript Fathers do and omit to do is incomprehensible to me, my Lord and God. In the case of Epaphroditus, though, I hope to refer my colleagues with success to the example of the ancient Jewish king." Joseph felt a dark stab of grief. He valued Epaphroditus; he was a good man, he loved and fostered art and science; Joseph had spent many a pleasant hour in his company. And now, without intending to, he had brought about this man's downfall.

A little later, under some pretext, Messalinus left the Emperor alone with Joseph. Domitian raised himself half-way on his couch, and smiling, with inviting intimacy, he said: "And now, my Josephus, speak openly. Was that crude fellow among those of Jabne right when he declared that you were a scion of the house of David? It is, as your Doctors indeed explain, more a matter of feeling, of intuition, than of documentary evidence; I can follow you in that train of thought. If, for example, I myself think that I am a descendant of Hercules, then I am. Surely you have already understood, my Flavius Josephus, what I'm aiming at. It is this: I put it in your hands whether you want to be regarded as a descendant of David or not. For we are making up lists. We are taking note of those who are to be counted as descendants of the great king whose virtues you described so excellently. Administrative considerations make the setting up of such a list seem desirable to my government. Now how is it in your case, my Josephus? You are an enthusiastic Jew. You are proud of your people, of its great cultural achievements. You are a believer. I trust the believer, Josephus. Whatever you tell me, I shall believe you: it will count. Tell me: I am a scion of the house of David, and you are one. Tell me: I am not, and your name will not appear on that list." He rose, he came quite close to Joseph. With a smiling, almost grinning, horrible familiarity, he asked him:

"How is it, my Jew? All princes are related. Are you a relation of mine? Are you a scion of David?"

Joseph's thoughts and feelings raged chaotically within him. If the people declared that one man or another was of the line of David, it was pure talk and not subject to further proof. And he himself had never made much of it. So it would be senseless now to flaunt the courage of confession and to declare: "Yes, I am of the line of David." No one would be benefited by it; the only thing it would accomplish would be his own destruction. Then why was he driven so strongly to say yes? Because this Emperor of the heathens was strangely right. He, Josephus, knew from his feelings, and thus from a deep knowledge, that he actually belonged to the elect, to those of David's line. The Emperor of the heathens wanted to humiliate him and tempt him to deny the best in his nature. And if he let himself be led to do so, if he denied his great ancestor David, then this Emperor would scorn not only him, but his whole people, and rightly. What was being enacted here between Domitian and himself was one of the many battles in the war which his people were waging against Rome for their Jehovah. But where was the right course? What did the Godhead expect of him? It was cowardice if he denied his "election." But was it not spiritual arrogance if he, against his reason, confessed to his feeling?

He stood there, quiet, haggard. No trace of his desperation showed on his fleshless face; he kept his burning eyes beneath the broad, high, furrowed forehead fixed on the Emperor, thoughtfully, seeing and unseeing, and only with difficulty Domitian stood his gaze. "I can see already," he said, "that you don't want to say yes to me, or no either. I understand that. But if that's the case, then, my good fellow, I know a third choice for you. You hailed my father, the God Vespasian, as the Messiah. If you acted rightly in that case, something of that Messianic nature must be in me as well. So I ask you: am I the son and heir of the Messiah? Think well before you answer. If I am the heir of the Messiah, then what the people gossip about the scions of David is empty drivel, nothing more, then the scions of David present no threat, and it isn't worth while for my officials to draw up lists. So do not evade me, my Jew. Save your scions of David and yourself. Say it, say the word. Say to me: 'You are the Messiah,' and fall down and worship me, as you worshipped my father."

Joseph paled deeply. This he had already experienced. But when? When and how? He had experienced it in spirit. Thus it was described in the tales of the pure and the fallen angel; and thus also, in the writings of the Minæans, the Tempter, the Slanderer, the Diabolus, tempted the Messiah to deny his own being and to worship him, and promised him in return all the riches of the world. Strange, how in his own life the tales and legends of his people were mirrored. He was so saturated with the past of his people that he himself was metamorphosed into the figures of that past. And if he now obeyed this Roman Emperor, the Tempter, and worshipped him in the way he demanded, then he would betray himself, his work, his people, his God.

He was still looking immovably at the Emperor; his gaze had not changed; his burning eyes retained that profound thoughtfulness, that seeing unseeingness. But the Emperor's face had changed. Domitian smiled, he grinned, with hideous, revolting cordiality. His face was heavily flushed, his near-sighted eyes winked at Joseph with false, simulated, inviting familiarity, his hand waved grotesquely in the air, it was as if he beckoned to him. There was no doubt, the Emperor, the Lord and Devil Domitian, *Dominus ac Diabolus Domitianus,* wanted to enter into an understanding with him, the kind of understanding which he suspected between him and his late father, Vespasian.

Joseph's thoughts, calm as his face remained, became clouded. He could no longer even say with certainty whether Domitian had really spoken those last words, that he should fall down before him and worship him, or whether it was only the recollection of the fallen angel of ancient legend and the Diabolus of the Minæans. In any case his temptation by Domitian had lasted but a very short moment. Already the Emperor was again only the Emperor; arms angularly pressed back, he stood there, with a commanding air, and said formally: "I thank you for your interesting reading, my Knight Flavius Josephus. Concerning the question which I put to you, whether you are a scion of the King David you have described, you may think over the answer in peace. I expect you in the course of the next few days at my morning reception. Then I shall ask you again. But where is our amiable host keeping himself?"

He clapped his hands, and, "Where is our Messalinus?" he said to the hurriedly approaching servants. "Call my Messalinus. We desire his company, I and my Jew Flavius Josephus."

DURING those days Joseph wrote the "Psalm of Courage":

Much do I praise him, the man who yields not in battle.
Stallions rush at him, arrows whistle, iron clangs,
Arms with axe and sword crash down before his eyes.
He flinches not.
He sees death, he defies it, and faces it squarely.

He must have courage. But courage no greater
Than that of all men who would rightly be called so.

Valour in battle is never so hard;
Courage there springs from one man to another,
No man believing that death will descend on him.
Never do you believe more firmly
In a multitude of days still before you
Than in time of battle.

Higher yet ranks the courage of him
Who ventures forth into barbarian deserts, there to explore,
Or of him who pilots his ship ever farther into waste oceans,
There to seek whether new lands and new riches may be
    discovered.

But as the moon pales when the sun rises
So fades the glory of the adventurer
When faced with the glory of him who fights for the invisible.
They wish to force him
To speak a word, insubstantial, intangible,
Which no sooner spoken, has vanished utterly;
None hear it then, and it is there no longer.
But he speaks not the word.

Or else his heart bids him to speak
Only one word, one certain word,
And he knows that the word brings him death.
No price is set upon the word except destruction,
And he knows it and yet speaks the word.

If a man offers life to gain gold, to gain might,
The price of the gamble is known;
It hovers before his eyes, it is solid, and he can weigh it.

But what is a word?

Therefore I say:
Hail to the man who takes death upon him,

That he may speak because his heart bids him.
Therefore I say:
Hail to the man who says what is so.
Therefore I say:
Hail to the man who cannot be forced
To say what is not.

For he takes it upon him, the hardest of all.
Clear-eyed in the sober light of noon,
Beckons to death and says to it: Come.
For a bodiless word he faces his death;
That if a falsehood, he may deny it,
That if a truth, he may confess.

Hail to the man
Who for that faces ruin,
For his is the courage God most approves.

O N ONE of the following mornings Joseph had himself carried along the Sacred Way up to the reception at the
Palatine, in obedience to a summons from the Emperor.

At the entrance to the palace he was searched for weapons
along with all the other visitors, and only then admitted to the
first antechamber. There were several hundred people there;
the attendants called out their names, Chamberlain Crispinus's
officials wrote them down, turned them away, admitted them.
The guests were crowded in the second antechamber. The
ceremonial officials hurried from one to another and arranged
the lists according to Crispinus's directions.

Joseph's presence attracted attention. He saw that his visit
disturbed Crispinus and noticed, not without a little smile,
that Crispinus, after some hesitation, did not put him among

the most privileged on the lists of "Friends of the First Admittance," but only on the list of all the others of the second rank. On the way Joseph had taken courage and had told himself that the sooner the agonizing hour was over, the better; now he was glad that, since he was only on the second list, he might perhaps leave again unnoticed and without accomplishing his mission.

At last the cry rang out: "The Lord and God Domitian has awakened!" and the doors which led to the Emperor's bedchamber were opened. They saw Domitian half sitting up on his broad couch; officers of the guard in full uniform stood on his right and on his left.

The criers called out the names of the first list and, one after another, the bearers of those names entered the inner chamber. Those standing outside peered in avidly to see how the Emperor greeted each one. To most he merely stretched out his hand to be kissed; only few were honoured with the embrace prescribed by custom. It was understandable that he did not want day after day to kiss a number of people who were repugnant to him, quite aside from the danger of infection. Still, no Emperor before him had shown so openly what a disagreeable task he felt this greeting to be, and it aroused bad blood that Domitian above all, the guardian of tradition, should withdraw more and more from this noble custom, and many were offended.

After a little while the Emperor made a pause. He yawned without regard for the crowd of his guests, stretched himself, cast dull, peevish glances over the assembly, beckoned to Crispinus, looked over the lists. Then, suddenly, he came alive. Clapped for his dwarf Silenus, whispered with him. The dwarf waddled into the antechamber; all glances followed him; his path led to Joseph. Into the absolute silence, bowing deeply,

the dwarf said: "The Lord and God Domitian summons you
to his bed, Knight Flavius Josephus."

Joseph, before the eyes of the whole assembly, went into the
inner chamber. The Emperor asked him to sit down on his
bed; it was a high distinction with which no one else had been
honoured that day. He embraced and kissed him, not reluctantly, but slowly and solemnly, as the custom prescribed.

But while his cheek was pressed to Joseph's he whispered:
"Are you a scion of David, my Josephus?" And Joseph answered: "It is even so, Emperor Domitian."

The Emperor freed himself from the embrace. "You are a
courageous man, Flavius Josephus," he said. Then the dwarf
Silenus, who had heard everything, escorted Joseph back into
the antechamber. This time he bowed even more deeply and
said: "Farewell, Flavius Josephus, scion of David." The Emperor, however, ordered the doors of his bedchamber to be
closed; the reception was over.

A FEW days later the following announcement was made in
the official news bulletin: The Emperor had examined
the historical work on which the writer Flavius Josephus was
now engaged. It had become apparent that this book did not
promote the well-being of the Roman Empire. Thus the said
Flavius Josephus had not fulfilled the hopes which had been
attached to his first work, the book on the Jewish War. The
Lord and God Domitian had therefore ordered the bust of this
writer Flavius Josephus to be removed from the Hall of Honour in the Temple of Peace.

And so that bust of Joseph's head, turned slantingly over one
shoulder, lean, bold, was removed from the Temple of Peace.

It was handed over to the sculptor Basil, so that the precious metal in it—Corinthian bronze, a unique alloy formed during the burning of Corinth by the mingling of melted metals from various statues—might be used for a bust of Senator Messalinus, which the Emperor had commissioned him to model.

"WAS that a slip of the tongue or didn't I hear right?" Reginus asked Marullus, turning his fleshy head around so suddenly that, for all his skill, his private barber almost cut him. "Neither one nor the other," replied Marullus. "The accusation against the Vestal Virgin Cornelia will be advanced; that's certain. The courier from Pola yesterday brought the order. D.D.D. must care a lot about the affair. Otherwise he wouldn't have given the command while travelling, but would have waited until he was back." Reginus muttered something, the heavy, sleepy eyes under the bulging forehead had an even more thoughtful expression than usual, and before the barber was really finished with his work, he waved to him impatiently to be off.

But then, alone with his friend, he said nothing. He contented himself with slowly shaking his head and shrugging his shoulders. And he really did not need to say anything; Marullus understood him without words; for him the occurrence was quite as unbelievable. Didn't D.D.D. have enough with the storm raised when he had brought those other two of the six Vestal Virgins to court, the sisters Oculatæ? And wasn't the popular temper cool enough without that, just now, after the not exactly brilliant Sarmatian expedition? What, by Hercules, did D.D.D. think he would accomplish by dragging out the old-fashioned, brutal laws and having the Vestal Virgin Cornelia charged with unchastity?

Junius Marullus, sucking at his aching tooth, calmly scrutinized his vexedly snorting friend with his sharp, blue-grey eyes. He guessed his thoughts to the very word. "Yes," he replied, "the popular temper is cool; you're right there. To the man in the street the conclusion of the Sarmatian expedition doesn't

look brilliant, although it's quite a substantial success. But perhaps that's just why. Our good Senators will certainly falsify
the outcome of the war into a defeat. The Vestal Virgin Cornelia is related and cousin to half the aristocracy. Perhaps
Vellykins thinks the gentlemen will be more careful if he
doesn't shrink even from an accusation against Cornelia."

"Poor Cornelia," Reginus said, instead of any answer. Both
of them now saw Cornelia before them: the face of the twenty-
eight-year-old girl, delicate yet fresh and gay, beneath her
brownish-black hair; they saw her as she smiled at them from
her honorary box at the Circus, or, as she, with the five other
Vestal Virgins, went up the steps of the Temple of Jupiter at
the head of the procession: tall, slender, untouched, gracious,
and quietly self-assured, priestess, girl, great lady.

"One must admit," said Marullus finally, "since the uprising
of Saturninus he has an inner justification to use every means
against his enemies, if only they accomplish his ends." "In the
first place this means doesn't accomplish the end," returned
Reginus, "and in the second I don't believe that this proceeding
is directed against the Senators. D.D.D. knows as well as we
that there would be less dangerous measures for that. No, my
dear fellow, his reasons are simpler and deeper. He's just dissatisfied with the conclusion of the expedition and wants to
prove his divine mission in some other way. I can already hear
him rolling out big words. 'Through such examples of strict
morality and piety, the century of Domitian will cast a radiance
far into the most distant times.' I'm afraid," he ended, sighing,
"he sometimes believes his own speeches."

For a while the two sat silent. Then Reginus asked: "And
does one know who's actually supposed to be the unfortunate
Cornelia's partner?" "One doesn't," answered Marullus, "but
Norbanus does. I guess it's Crispinus who's mixed up in the
affair." "Our Crispinus?" asked Reginus incredulously. "It's

just a guess," replied Marullus quickly. "Norbanus of course hasn't said a word to anybody; it was on looks and half-gestures that I based my conclusion." "Your guesses," Reginus admitted, running his tongue reflectively from one corner of his mouth to the other, "have the peculiarity of being right, and Norbanus is very resourceful when he hates someone. It would be a pity if, just because Norbanus is jealous of the Egyptian, that delightful creature Cornelia should really be thrown to the wolves."

Marullus, partly because he did not want to harbour any sentimentality, partly from old habit, assumed a frivolous manner. "Too bad," he said, "that one didn't hit on the idea oneself: that Cornelia isn't just a Vestal Virgin, but a woman. But, by Hercules, when she went up to the Capitoline in her heavy, old-fashioned white dress and her old-fashioned coiffure, even a tough old materialist like myself didn't give a thought to what might be hidden under that dress. And yet, something sacred, something forbidden like that, is just my meat. Once, in my wildest period, I slept with the Pythia at Delphi. She wasn't particularly pretty, a trifle on in years too; the pleasure was in no proportion to the danger; what appealed to me was only the sacred element. One shouldn't have overlooked a girl like this Cornelia. One shouldn't have left her to a Crispinus."

Claudius Reginus, usually no prude, did not enter into that spirit today. As he bent down, groaning, to tighten his shoe-laces, which had once again become loosened, he said: "D.D.D. makes it hard for one to stay his friend." "Have patience with him," Marullus urged him. "He has many enemies. He's now forty-two," he reflected, and sought the other's sleepy eyes with his own sharp ones. "But I'm afraid we have a prospect of surviving him."

Reginus was startled. What Marullus had said there was so true and so foolhardy that it should not have crossed anyone's lips even among close friends. But now that Marullus had gone so far, Reginus did not want to restrain himself either. "Such abundance of power," he said, trying to lower his high, oily voice, "is a disease in itself, a disease which speedily devours the life of even a healthy man. "Yes," said Marullus, now also almost whispering, "a man's spirit must have devilishly firm walls if he isn't to burst with such an abundance of power. D.D.D. has stood fast amazingly long. Just since Saturninus's *coup d'état* he's become so"— he groped for the word—"peculiar." "And yet," replied Reginus, "just in that affair he had such superhuman luck." "Cæsar and his luck," Marullus returned sententiously. "But that much luck is just what no man can stand." "Cæsar," reflected Reginus, "got to be fifty-six before his luck deserted him." "Too bad about him," said Marullus rather obscurely. And, "Too bad about Cornelia," said Reginus.

"HE WILL not dare it!" burst suddenly from Senator Helvidius. They had been speaking about the garrison reinforcements in the north-east which must result from the conclusion of the peace and what hot-tempered Helvidius had suddenly interjected had not the faintest connexion with the subject. Yet all knew what he meant. For even when they talked about other things, the thoughts of all turned constantly to the disgrace which the Emperor was about to bring upon the Vestal Cornelia, and in her person upon the whole ancient aristocracy.

Domitian had committed many atrocities against them, the four men and the two women who had gathered here in Helvidius's house. There were Gratilla, the sister, and Fannia, the wife, of Cæpio whom he had had executed. And all here had been friends of Prince Sabinus and of Ælius and of the nine other Senators who had had to die with Cæpio, because they had been involved in Saturninus's unsuccessful *coup d'état*. Still, though the Emperor had killed these men, even if he took measures against the very persons who were assembled here, such atrocities had meaning from his point of view. But Cornelia's persecution was nothing but a filthy, utterly meaningless whim. It was inconceivably shameless if this Emperor, if this lascivious brute of a Domitian, laid hands on Cornelia, our pure, sweet Cornelia. Wherever she appeared one had the feeling: "The world is not lost after all, since she is in it, Cornelia." And she, of all people she, had to be picked out by that inhuman creature.

It was, without their having to say much about it, the symbolical nature of the event which so deeply outraged the four men and the two women at Helvidius's house. If Domitian, that two-legged embodiment of depravity, ordered the truly noble girl Cornelia to be convicted of unchastity by false witnesses, and disgracefully executed, then the event would graphically reveal the whole leering rottenness of this Rome. There was nothing in the world from which the Emperor would shrink. Under his rule the noble was distorted into the base.

"He will not dare it." With that they had comforted themselves from the first day on which they had heard about the rumour. But in how many cases they had comforted themselves with similar words. As often as there was talk of some new, shameless intention of the Emperor's they had muttered between clenched teeth: He won't dare that; the Senate and the people won't stand for that. But, especially since the unfortunate uprising of Saturninus, he had dared everything, and the Senate and the people had stood for everything. Darkly the recollection of these many defeats lay within them, but they would not let them rise up. "He will not dare it." They pinned their hopes to the words which Senator Helvidius had blurted out so furiously and confidently.

But then the youngest among them opened his lips, Senator Publius Cornelius. "He will dare it," he said, "and we shall be silent. Shall accept it and be silent. And we shall be right in doing so; for it is the only thing left for us to do in these times."

But, "I won't be silent, and one should not be silent," said Fannia. She sat there, with her aged, earth-coloured, bold, and gloomy face, and fixed her angry gaze on Publius Cornelius. He was a close relative of the endangered Vestal Virgin, her fate was more his affair than that of the others, and indeed he already almost regretted what he had said. He might have spoken thus before those of the same opinion, but not in the presence of this old Fannia. She was the daughter of Pætus, whose republican courage of confession under Nero had brought about his death; she was the widow of Cæpio, whom Domitian had had executed after the suppression of Saturninus. Whenever Fannia spoke, doubts overcame Cornelius whether perhaps after all he was not wrong in calling heroic that silence which he recommended with so many reasonable arguments. Perhaps, in the last analysis, the demonstrative martyrdom of a Fannia was the better virtue.

Slowly he turned his face, severely ravaged and sad in spite of his youth, from one to another. Only moderate Decian gave him half a glance of understanding. So without much hope Cornelius tried to explain why he considered any kind of demonstration, particularly in the case of the Vestal Cornelia, as harmful. The people loved and honoured Cornelia. Legal proceedings against her, or even her execution, would not, as Domitian probably wished, appear to the people as an act of stern service to the gods, but simply as something inhuman, blasphemous. But if we of the Senatorial party make a demonstration, then with that we simply force the affair out of the sphere of general humanity down into the political.

Decian agreed. "I'm afraid," he said, "our Cornelius is right. We are powerless; we can do nothing but keep silent." Yet he did not utter these words with his customary soberness and restraint, but with such agony and such a lack of hope that the others glanced up in consternation.

This was the trouble: Decian had received a message from Cornelia. A freedwoman of Cornelia's had brought it, a certain Melitta. In agitated words this girl had told him that at the Feast of the Good Goddess in the house of Volusia, the Consul's wife, something extremely distressing had occurred. In what this distressing event had consisted, Decian had not been able to gather from Melitta's confused words; certain it was that Melitta was mixed up in it and Cornelia seriously endangered. Now the quiet, no longer youthful Senator Decian loved the Vestal Cornelia, and thought he had observed that she too smiled more deeply and cordially when she saw him. It was a silent, unobtrusive love, as good as hopeless. To approach Cornelia was difficult, almost impossible, and when she would be allowed to leave the House of Vesta he would be an old man. That she had appealed to him for help had moved him deeply. Melitta, in the name of her mistress and friend, had implored him to get her out of Rome, to make it impossible to find her. He had done everything to help Melitta; he had had her taken by his confidential agents, with great secrecy, to his estate in Sicily, where she now lived safely hidden, and probably in her person the main witness whom Cornelia's enemies might have summoned had disappeared. However, if Domitian seriously intended to destroy Cornelia, matters did not depend on one witness more or less; no doubt justice hardly controlled the decision, but actually hatred and caprice. This feeling of being bound and helpless had doubly attacked Decian now while Cornelius was speaking, and his anguish had sounded through his words.

Fannia meanwhile paid no attention either to Decian's anguish or to Publius Cornelius's reasonableness. She sat there, her earth-coloured face hardened from suffering and severity. "We must not be silent," she insisted, and her voice came sonorously from her aged lips. "It would be a crime and a disgrace." "That creature lives according to the pattern of a school reader," thought Publius Cornelius discontentedly, "and wants to carry on the heroic tradition of the family at any cost. And for all that, at most she'll be no more than a good figure for a little episode in my historical work—she won't make history." Yet in spite of his dispassionate criticism he could not help admiring the woman who stood out so heroically and foolishly among her contemporaries, could not help regretting his own rationality.

Gratilla, the dead Cæpio's sister, a self-possessed, distinguished, rather stout, elderly lady, agreed with her sister-in-law Fannia. "Reasonableness," she said scornfully, "caution, politics—all very well. But how can anyone with a heart inside him swallow this Domitian's horrors for ever without resisting? I'm a simple woman, I don't understand anything about politics, I have no ambitions. But my gall rises when I think of what later generations are expected to think of us one day, our sons and grandsons, if we stand for this rule of falsehood and violence without protest."

"When will your biography of Pætus be finished, Priscus?" Fannia spoke up again. "When will it appear? It's a profound satisfaction to me that at least one man isn't silent, that at least one man speaks and doesn't lock up his anger."

Priscus, thus appealed to, looked up, turned his completely bald head from one to another, and saw that all were looking at him, waiting in suspense for his answer. Priscus was re-

garded as the greatest lawyer of the Empire; he was famous
for weighing carefully every pro and con. So he did not overlook Domitian's merits in managing the Empire, but he also
saw very exactly the capriciousness and lack of responsibility in
this personal regime, the many plain violations of justice. But
of this understanding he could speak only in the circle of his
intimates; before all others, unless he wanted to bring a suit
for *lèse-majesté* upon himself, he had to bury it deep within
him. He had now found a personal solution for himself. He
was silent, and yet he was not silent. He vented his resentment
in a historical work, in a representation of the life of the great
Pætus Thrasea, Fannia's father. It fascinated him to set down
the life of this republican (whom Nero had had executed for
his liberal views) with the greatest objectivity, stripped of all
legendary traits, and to present him so, that this Pætus Thrasea,
even without the mythical accessories, appeared as a great man
and worthy of the highest veneration. Fannia could give him
much material for this work of his, a great quantity of unknown and exact detail.

This work, however, now almost finished, was intended only
for the author and his closest intimates, especially for Fannia.
To publish such a book under Domitian's regime meant risk-
ing position and income, even life, and he had never thought
of doing that. So when Fannia now declared that he, Priscus,
was not silent, that he was not locking up his anger, it was, to
put it mildly, an exaggeration and a misunderstanding. For
actually he had in a certain sense intended to do just that. To
lock up his anger, to lock his book away safely, that was exactly what he had intended, and his only purpose had been to
lighten his heart. He promised himself little from publication.
Such an act would have been nothing but a demonstrative gesture, and Publius Cornelius here was right, three times right:
nothing was accomplished by such ostentatious gestures; they

could not actually change matters; how should literature resist power?

Such were Priscus's opinions. But now he saw the expectant glances of everyone fixed upon him, he saw Fannia's severe, challenging face, he knew that all would take him for a coward if he now withdrew, and he could not get up the courage to appear cowardly. While his brain was saying: "What are you doing there, you fool?" his lips said sharply and bitterly: "No, I shall not lock up my anger," and before he had finished the sentence he already regretted it.

"To what purpose does he want to imitate Pætus?" Decian thought sorrowfully, and, "Another fool and hero," thought Publius Cornelius, and out loud he said grimly: "It's a man's business to control himself; it's a man's business to go through these times in silence, so that he may survive them."

Fannia's old, earth-coloured, furrowed face was a mask of scorn and refusal. "Poor Cornelia," she said, and challengingly she asked Publius Cornelius: "Are you at least going to get up the courage to join us when we visit your uncle Lentulus?" Cornelia's old father had long since retired from public life and lived quietly on his Sabine estate; such a group visit meant a demonstration against the Emperor. "I'm afraid," said Publius Cornelius, unmoved by Fannia's scolding, "we shan't be very welcome to my uncle. He has his sorrows, and takes little pleasure in people." "So you aren't coming?" asked Fannia. "I shall come," answered Publius Cornelius with impersonal politeness.

"Poor Priscus has to publish his biography," he thought, "and I have to make this stupid visit, because this hero-woman demands it. It's all so hopeless. We have dignity; Domitian has the army and the masses. What dismal impotence."

IT STILL was winter when Domitian returned. He contented himself with offering the laurel to Jupiter Capitoline, and forwent a big, public ceremony in his own honour. In the Senate they made malicious jokes about it. Marullus and Reginus felt the situation was not easy for Domitian. If he celebrated a triumph, they would make fun of the fact that he falsified his defeats; if he forwent the triumph, they would jeer that his defeats were so great that he himself had to admit them.

Domitian, as a wise expert in popular psychology, instead of having personal honours bestowed on him, decreed a great distribution of gifts, whose costs were to be covered by his share in the Sarmatian booty. Every resident citizen of Rome had a claim on a share of the donation. The Emperor was exceedingly magnanimous when it was a question of this kind; it did not matter to him if such donation consumed many millions. In this particular case it would make it possible for him in addition to prove how huge the Sarmatian booty must have been.

So there he sat on his throne in the pillared Hall of Minucius, behind his head his favourite goddess Minerva, roundabout him his court officials, scribes, officers. In huge swarms the people crowded in; each man, in the order in which he came, received his token of clay, lead, bronze, and, if his list number chanced to be lucky, of silver or gold. There were certificates for very considerable presents among them. The rejoicing when someone received such a token! With what honest enthusiasm he praised the Lord and God Domitian, who brought joy to Rome and his people! And not only the receiver of the gift praised the Emperor, but his friends and relatives did the same; yes, everyone was happy, for everyone had a claim, and if he did not receive a gold token today, perhaps it would shine for him the next time. Thus Domitian's distribution of gifts turned into a more brilliant triumph than the most lavish parade could have been.

But he himself, the Emperor, was enthroned above them in front of his wise, shrewd counsellor, Minerva. He had become very much stouter in the last seven years; his face was red and bloated. Motionless he sat there, like a god, and enjoyed the jubilation of his people. Those to whose lot the golden gift tokens had fallen had the right to kiss his hand. He stretched it out without looking at them, but none regarded this as unseemly pride; they were made blissful just the same. The enraged Senators had to admit it: the people—or, as they called them, the rabble—loved their Lord and God Domitian.

The next day the festival of gifts came to its conclusion with an exhibition in the Flavian arena, the Colosseum, that largest circus of the world, which Domitian's brother had had erected. Coins were scattered about; by means of an ingenious piece of machinery airy, merry spirits flew over the arena and showered gift tokens on the crowd; at the end even the goddess of bounty herself appeared, Liberalitas, and poured gifts out of her cornucopia, certificates signed by the Emperor for estates, privileges, remunerative offices. The rejoicing was boundless, and it did not injure his prestige that in the crowd women and children were crushed or trampled to death.

Domitian gave a banquet on the evening of that day for the Senate and his friends. He honoured many by graciously addressing them, but his misanthropic wit made a number of his cordial phrases rather sinister. To Chief Judge Aper, for example, a cousin of the overthrown, rebellious General Saturninus, he spoke in his high, sharp voice about the joy which the masses had manifested at the great donation. This influx of the masses had been a scene worth seeing, even more so than the scene on that occasion when he had ordered the head of the vanquished mutineer Saturninus to be exhibited in the Forum. Then again he spoke about his good luck, which had begun to be proverbial since Saturninus's defeat. For at that time the carefully prepared *coup d'état* had failed solely because of an accident of weather: the sudden commencement of a thaw had prevented the barbarian troops, won over by Saturninus, from crossing the frozen river and bringing the rebel general the aid agreed upon. Yes, Domitian declared, one could really compare his luck with that of the great Julius Cæsar. True, that fortunate Cæsar had indeed finally fallen beneath the daggers of his enemies. "We princes," he said lightly, in the midst of a group who sat there as if turned to stone, "don't have an easy time of it. If we seize our opponent in time, before he has carried out his planned *coup,* then people reproach us and say that we just invented the criminal plots of our enemies as an excuse for doing away with them. They only believe in the conspiracies against us when we've been successfully assassinated. What do you think, my Priscus, and you, my Helvidius?"

For the time being he let no word drop about his intentions in the case of the Vestal Cornelia. For one could hardly draw any conclusions from the fact that one of the first acts which he undertook after his return consisted in the punishment of another religious violation, committed by an insignificant man.

A freedman, a certain Lydus, had in fact, while drunk, made water into one of those little troughlike ditches which it was the custom to dig in order to bury lightning in them. For every shaft of lightning which had struck in a public place and died out there had to be decently buried, like a dead man, if it was not to have evil consequences. So, at the spot where it had struck, the earth was thrown up, the priest sacrificed onions, human hair, live fishes—living objects from the three realms of life—and then a kind of coffin was buried in its depths; above it, however, a square ditch as large as the coffin was filled up to ground level and adorned with the inscription: "Here lightning is buried." Such an old lightning grave, then, still from the time of the Emperor Tiberius, was situated near the Latin Gate, and in this sacred spot the unhappy Lydus had made water. The Emperor, in his character of High Priest, had ordered him to be brought to court. He was condemned to be flogged out of the city, to lose his property, and the fire and water of Italy were forbidden to him.

THEN, a few days later, Domitian called a meeting of the highest priests, the Council of Fifteen, to his palace at Albanum. The invitation, as always, had come in great secrecy. Nevertheless, everyone knew about it, and when the Fifteen set out for Albanum, the whole of Rome lined the street.

For rarely were they to be seen, those highest priests, and curiosity and awe surrounded them. The Sacrificial Priest of Jupiter in particular was, for the inhabitants of the city of Rome, probably the strangest to look at, the most ancient. On the rare occasions when he left his dwelling, a lictor walked ahead of him, calling out that every man must lay aside his work, for the Priest of Jupiter was approaching; there must be feast day where he appeared, and religious awe; he must see no man working. Also, no man bearing weapons and no man in chains. His whole life was arduous and holy. As soon as he awakened he had to put on the full official costume and could take it off only when he went to sleep again. But this costume consisted of a thick woollen toga, which had to be woven by the priest's own wife, and with it belonged a white, peaked felt cap, ending in a tassel and wound around with an olive twig and a woollen thread. Never, even in his house, was he permitted to put off this sign of rank. Nothing tied or knotted might be found on his body; his robe had to be fastened with brooches; even his signet ring had to be a broken circle. He always had to carry a little staff with him to keep people at a distance, for he was elevated above every human touch.

So to see him and the other members of the Council of Fifteen the people thronged the street. There was excitement and a great spreading of rumours. All knew what the issue was: the fate of Cornelia, the Vestal Virgin, the favourite of Rome.

The sinister element about the meetings of the Council of Fifteen was that, in all cases of crime against religion, they could pronounce the verdict of guilty or not guilty according to their own free will. They had to grant the accused neither a hearing nor witnesses; they were responsible only to the gods. The accused was handed over to them without recourse. True, they had only to decide whether a person was guilty or not; to pronounce the sentence was the privilege of the Senate. But since the latter could not reverse the "guilty" of the Sacerdotal Court, and since the law prescribed the punishments without allowing for varied interpretations, they had the thankless task of merely carrying out the verdict brought in by the Sacerdotal Court.

That evening, filled with terror and yet slightly titillated, one man whispered to another the decision of the Council of Fifteen. The Vestal Virgin Cornelia had been found guilty of unchastity.

For this crime, the unchastity of a Vestal, the barbaric custom of old had established a barbaric punishment. The guilty woman was to be dragged on a willow mat in front of the Hill Gate and there flogged, then she was to be buried alive in an underground cell, and there, with a little food and a lamp, left to a slow death.

Before Domitian no Vestal had been accused of unchastity for a hundred and thirty years. Domitian had been the first to institute such proceedings again, against the Oculatæ sisters. Yet he too had not had the sentence fully carried out; he had softened it by giving the sisters free choice in the manner of their death.

What would he do now? What would happen to beloved and honoured Cornelia? Would he dare it?

ON THAT evening, after the members of the Sacerdotal Court had made their departure, only the Emperor and Chamberlain Crispinus were left in the extensive palace of Albanum.

Crispinus crouched in his study, inactive, consumed with burning suspense. D.D.D. had not admitted him to his presence the whole day; now he waited fearfully to see when he would be called. The habitually elegant gentleman seemed to have disintegrated. Where was his aristocratic, superior composure, where that bored manner which had made his fine, thin, long face seem so imperious? Now that face was nervous and distraught, and on it there was written only fear.

Again and again he thought over what had happened, could not understand it, could not understand himself. What evil spirit had given him the insane idea of attending the Mysteries of the Good Goddess in disguise? Any little child could have told him that D.D.D., for all his friendship, would not let him get away with that. Every other vice he would overlook in him, but not a religious crime. And at that he had not been thinking of offending the gods at all; he had only stolen into the Feast of the Good Goddess because there simply was not any other way of getting close to Cornelia. That was what Clodius, the famous gallant of Julius Cæsar's time, had done in his day, to get access to Cæsar's unapproachable wife. For Clodius the affair had ended well on that occasion. But those were liberal times. Our D.D.D., on the other hand, unfortunately would not understand a joke when religious principles were at stake.

But did they really have proof against him? Nobody had seen him when he had crept in woman's clothes to the Feast of the Good Goddess, which no man might attend. Only that Melitta could bear witness against him, the freedwoman with whom he had had the agreement. But she had vanished, and Cornelia herself had all good reason to keep silent. No, there was no witness against him. Or was there? Norbanus had a hundred eyes, and when it was a question of him, Crispinus, those eyes were sharpened by hate.

He had hoped that the return of the Emperor would bring a clarification of his position. But nothing had been clarified: D.D.D. had treated him as calmly and cordially as always. Yet he knew his D.D.D., he knew that meant nothing, and the dreadful burden had not been lifted from him. All that time he had felt as if any moment the earth would open and swallow him. His pretty face had become hollow. He had had to pull himself together not to fall silent suddenly in the midst of conversation and lose himself in thought. The most exquisite dish, the most fashionable woman, the handsomest boy, all had lost their attraction for him. He paid no attention to the clothes which his valet laid out for him; his barber could confuse his perfumes without his noticing it. His pleasures were no longer pleasures, and when at night he lay sleepless, many times a terrible vision came to him, always the same one. He saw himself being dragged to the cattle market, being chained to a block before ten thousand spectators, and flogged to death in accordance with the wording of the law. Strangely enough, the ten thousand spectators all had his own face; even the official who conducted the execution, and the executioner, had his face; also they all spoke with his voice. And he heard himself—and this terrified him the most—in his whispering, elegant Greek, making cutting little jokes about the unbearable, mortal agonies of his torture and his horrible dying.

Today, at Albanum, throughout the whole day while the Council of Fifteen were in meeting, the feeling of impending destruction was even more oppressive, that feeling as if a mountain were coming toward him and slowly sinking down to bury him; it was so physical that at moments it took away his breath. He wandered around in the endless hallways of the palace, through the large park, through the zoos, the hothouses, between the animals' cages, unseeing; if someone had asked him where he was he could not have said.

Then night had come, and, from hiding, he watched the members of the Sacerdotal Court make their departure. Something in him, a remainder of the old Crispinus, noticed with impish derision how much pains the gentlemen had to take not to let their ridiculous peaked, white felt caps fall off their heads while getting into the carriage. At the same time, though, the new Crispinus within him, whose life was in danger, thought: "What have they decided?"

And now he crouched in his study, full of helpless rage that it had been entirely in the hands of these absurdly dressed fellows to condemn him to a disgraceful, martyred death, him, the great Crispinus, the Emperor's all-powerful Minister. Had they done it? Had they dared it? His hands were like a dead man's, his brain kept turning over the one question:

"Did he condemn me, did he dare? Did he condemn me, did he dare?"

At last he was summoned to appear before Domitian. He gave abrupt, impatient directions to the valet who helped him to put on the formal robes and the high shoes, but his voice would not obey him properly, and when he buttoned and tied something himself his hands shook, and when he walked through the long corridors, the servant with lights before him, his knees shook. He tried to concentrate on his shadow, which accompanied him grotesquely, so as to distract himself from his fear and appear composed before the Emperor. In his thoughts too he no longer called Domitian D.D.D., but only the Emperor.

The Emperor lay on a wide couch, in his dressing-gown; he looked tired, slack, fleshy. He stretched out his hand to him, and Crispinus, careful not to leave any trace of lipstick, kissed the hand. "That was a strenuous day, today," said Domitian, yawning. "Yes," he told him, "we had to condemn her. That was a blow for me. I took over city and Empire in a bad condition. It's a neglected garden; one must weed and weed, only to see new weeds always growing up again in spite of one's efforts. Why are you so silent, my Crispinus? Say something comforting to me. The Lord and God Domitian thirsts for the comforting words of his friends today."

Crispinus did not know what to make of these words. If Cornelia was condemned, then it could only be on account of what had happened at the Feast of the Good Goddess, and then he, Crispinus, was surely a fellow-culprit. So what did the Emperor want? Was he making one of his gruesome jokes? "I see," Domitian went on talking, "it has robbed you of speech. I understand that. Since the times of Cicero no Vestal Virgin has been condemned. And in my reign, only the Oculatæ sisters, and now this girl. The gods don't make it easy for me."

Crispinus, his own voice sounding oddly unfamiliar to him, asked painfully: "Were there proofs?" The Emperor smiled. It was a long, deep smile, and by that smile Crispinus recognized that he was lost. "Proofs?" said Domitian, shrugging his shoulders and spreading out his arms a little, the palms of his hands toward Crispinus. "What do you want, Crispinus? Our Norbanus collected a number of facts, circumstantial evidence one says in legal phraseology, I believe, conclusive circumstantial evidence. But what are proofs? If one had given Cornelia a hearing, and the man and woman whom Norbanus indicated as fellow-culprits, the three defendants would surely have advanced just as many and just as conclusive contrary proofs. What are proofs?" He drew himself up, leaned toward Crispinus, sitting there stiff and cold, and said to him, familiarly, right to his face: "There is one solitary proof. That weighs more than all that Norbanus brought forward against Cornelia, and all that Cornelia and her fellow-culprits could have brought forward in their favour. To the Masters and Priests of my Council also, this proof seemed fully conclusive. Namely, I am not satisfied—I can say it to you, after all, my Crispinus—with the conclusion of the Sarmatian expedition. The gods did not bless my weapons. And why? For this reason"—he jumped to his feet—"for this reason: because the city of Rome is full of sin and immorality. When Norbanus informed me of what had happened at the Feast of the Good Goddess, my eyes were opened. Then I saw why this Sarmatian expedition did not bring in the harvest that I had expected. What do you think, my Crispinus? Tell me honestly, express yourself: isn't that conclusive proof?"

"Yes," stammered Crispinus. He too had sprung to his

feet when the Emperor rose; with knocking knees he stood
there, the pretty tan of his narrow face showing as a greenish
hue through his make-up. "Yes, yes," he stammered, and, as
he could not restrain himself any longer: "But who, if I may
know, were the fellow-culprits?" he asked. "That's another
point," said the Emperor, slyly, yet still in the same tone of
cordial frankness. "Of course it's a question of the occurrences
at the Feast of the Good Goddess. But no doubt you know
that yourself," he said in passing, as a matter of course, and
a fresh shudder ran over Crispinus as the Emperor let fall
that "But no doubt you know that yourself." "What he did,
the fellow who defiled the feast," Domitian went on, "was
fundamentally nothing but an unspeakably stupid imitation
of that Clodius of Julius Cæsar's time. And just for that
reason I still can't believe what our Norbanus reports, sound
as are his foundations. I simply can't believe that in our
Rome, in my Rome, anybody could think of such an unspeakably idiotic idea. I don't understand it. The men of
those days might forgive a Clodius; but my Sacerdotal Court,
my Senate—after all, anybody with even the brain of a chicken
could have told himself that—I and my judges, we do not
forgive such crimes."

But at that Crispinus's strength gave way, his limbs melted,
he crumpled before the Emperor. "I am innocent, my Lord
and God Domitian," he whimpered on his knees, and again
and again, wailing, whining, "I am innocent."

"Well, well, well," said the Emperor. "So then Norbanus
is mistaken. Or a liar. Well, well, well. Interesting. That is
interesting." And suddenly, with a purple face, seeing that
Crispinus while kissing his dressing-gown had soiled it with
rouge from his cheeks and lips, he burst out: "And on top
of everything you besmirch my robe with your miserable
lips, you leper, you son of a drunken teamster and a bitch!"

He drew breath, he stepped back from Crispinus, who remained prostrate, he strode up and down and spoke angrily out loud to himself: "Thus do they betray one, whom one has raised from the dirt. My Cornelia! They befoul the best thing one has. They lie with one's daughters. Probably you didn't know, you to whom the gods gave an empty egg for a head, that the Vestal Virgins are my, the Arch-Priest's, daughters. Probably you don't even grasp, you scum of an Egyptian, what you have done. You have torn my bond with the gods, you piece of carrion, you thrice-abandoned scoundrel. And at that it isn't the first time you have thrown me out of favour with the gods." And now he let it pour out, what he, slow avenger that he was, had stored up inside him for seven years. "It was you too, you pestilential wretch, you piece of offal, you miserable fool, who involved me in my struggle with the God Jehovah, seven years ago. Who else was responsible for my letting the Grand Doctor wait so long that time? It should have been your business to draw my attention to the fact that I had to receive him. And now on top of it all you lie with my Vestal Virgin, you faithless wretch, you jackal, you Egyptian."

Crispinus had crawled into a corner. The Emperor, groaning a little, walked toward him like a fleshy colossus. Crispinus squeezed himself against the wall; the Emperor kicked him. His bare foot in the sandal had no force; the kick did not hurt. Yet Crispinus cried out, and his terror was sincere. The Emperor's protruding upper lip curled even more scornfully. "Not a spark of courage in the jackal," he said, and let him alone.

Yet, unexpectedly, he approached him again, bent down to the whimpering man, and softly, whispering, very close to his ear, he asked: "And how was it? Did you at least get something out of it? How was she, the Virgin Cornelia?

Was it a great pleasure? Did she please your appetite? Was she different from the others, this holy maiden? Say it, say it." But since Crispinus stammered: "But I don't know anything, I'm really—" the Emperor straightened up again, and, "Very well, of course," he said, distantly, haughtily. "Norbanus slandered you, you're a poor innocent, you don't know anything about it. You've told me so already, anyway. Very well." And suddenly, turned away, over his shoulder, he threw at him: "You can go; you are to stay in your room. And I advise you to take a bath. You've filthied yourself completely, you coward."

"Grant me my life, my Lord and God Domitian," the Egyptian began to wail again. "Grant me my life, and I'll thank you as none of the others has ever thanked you." "What a pile of dirt," Domitian said out loud to himself, with revulsion, indescribably haughty. And: "Don't dare to commit suicide—you hear? But you wouldn't do it, anyway."

Crispinus was already at the door. Domitian, again completely the Emperor, said: "As for your life, the decision doesn't rest with me. It rests, after the Council of Fifteen has spoken, with the Senate."

But while, from his judicial heights, the Emperor was speaking those profoundly ironical words, the dwarf Silenus, who up to that moment had probably been hiding in some corner, suddenly appeared. Now he stood behind the Emperor, imitating his posture. And when Crispinus, during the few days that still remained to him, pictured the Emperor to himself, in his thoughts the dwarf Silenus was never separated from the Emperor. For this was the last time that the Minister Crispinus beheld Domitian, and the scornfully solemn words were the last which he heard from his lips.

CORNELIA's cell was the second on the left from the entrance. Like all six cells it was simply furnished; only a curtain separated it from the great hall, which the dining-room adjoined farther in the rear.

Weeks ago the Priest of Jupiter, as the Emperor's representative, had already informed her that she had been relieved of her duties, and that she might no longer leave her cell. Behind her drawn curtain she heard the others continuing to live their lives. The service of Vesta was regulated down to the smallest details: the fetching of the sacrificial water in the pitchers which were pointed at the bottom so that they might never touch the ground, the pouring out of that sacred water, the guarding of the sacred, virgin fire; every step in the simple, ancient, holy shrine was prescribed. So Cornelia knew every detail of the daily routine, she knew which of her religious sisters now had the watch, now had to make this sacrifice, now bake that bread. She knew that through her banishment the three sisters who had entered the holy shrine after her were now each promoted a step. Soon, as soon as the Emperor returned, twenty girls, all under ten years and descendants of the oldest families, would be presented as candidates and one would be chosen to replace her, the banished Cornelia, as the sixth. To enter the holy shrine of Vesta was one of the highest honours which the gods and the Empire had to bestow. Daughters of all the old families competed for it; they fought one another jealously to be called and chosen. Would Cornelia ever learn who was to replace her?

Whoever this new girl might be, Cornelia envied her, as a matter of course, that she could now lead the life which until then had been hers, Cornelia's. Exactly twenty years it was now that she had spent in the holy shrine, monotonous, strictly regulated years, with rules for the day, the hour, the minute. And yet how beautifully stirring were the days of that life, how quietly, evenly, and yet with ever-constant change, they glided past her. One felt as if one floated on a stream, so guided, channelled, regulated. Everything obeyed a divine law.

The quiet, pious joyfulness which the people had observed on Cornelia's face when at the great festivals the Vestal Virgins walked along in the processions, that quiet, pious joyfulness which made her more than the five others the favourite of the whole city, was no disguise. From the first day on, when she had been brought to the House of Vesta as an eight-year-old, she had felt at home there. The sense of oppression which the others were supposed to have felt sometimes, as little girls, in the twilight of the sacred dwelling, she, Cornelia, had never known. She had felt no fear when her father Lentulus in the great, solemn ceremony handed her over to the Emperor as Arch-Priest—it was Vespasian at that time—and when she, with childish zeal, repeated the formula after the slyly and genially smiling old man, swearing to the goddess and to the Empire to keep her soul pure and her body undefiled. Then, for ten years, she had been instructed with friendly seriousness by the High Priestess Junia. The individual functions which had to be discharged were not difficult, but there were very many of them, and if the state was not to suffer from the wrath of the goddess, no slightest omission must occur. But ten years were a long time; one could learn everything so that it came as naturally to one as breathing in and out. Cornelia, moreover, learned with enthusiasm; she liked to fetch the water in the pointed pitchers, to watch the fire and keep it going according to strict rules. They learned to weave wreaths to decorate the pale grey donkeys which the millers brought them on the feast days of Vesta. They learned to prepare the sanctified dough which was to protect women from illness and misfortune. The many tasks were all light, but they had to be carried out with dignity and grace, for any number of these services took place before the eyes of the whole people. When the Maidens of Vesta went up to the Capitoline, when they occupied their honorary seats in the theatre or the circus, always, next to the Emperor, they were the ones to whom the tens of thousands gave most attention.

Cornelia loved the customs, and she liked herself well when she appeared in public. Better than any of the others she knew how to perform her services with a pious, joyful expression, and as if she did not know that a hundred thousand eyes were fixed upon her. Inwardly she felt with great joy that those eyes were upon her and that she, Cornelia, did not disappoint those eyes. To be the central figure of a beautiful, holy, and joyful drama filled her completely, and to know that it promoted the well-being of the State, when she attended to her responsibilities with orderliness and composure, warmed her heart.

In them, in the six Maidens of Vesta, were embodied the simple gravity and the chaste dignity of the old Roman home. They were the guardians of the hearth; entrusted to their care were the palladium and the most important documents of the Empire. Chastity and vigilance had become a matter of course for Cornelia.

The Vestals had many honorary titles. To her, Cornelia, the title "Amata—Beloved" was the dearest, and she was conscious that she bore this title rightfully. She felt that she was loved, not by one person, but by the gods and the Senate and the people of Rome. Of course there were little jealousies among the six girls who lived together constantly, but even in the circle of the sisters she was the most beloved.

At most Tertullia would feel a very slight satisfaction about her, Cornelia's, misfortune. Tertullia had never liked her. What ugly looks she had cast, for example, when at the Capitoline games she, Cornelia, had it fall to her lot to ascend the steps to Jupiter hand in hand with the Emperor. And yet it was precisely from that ceremony that she had not had much pleasure. True, Domitian was very grand to look at, and she had felt that her serious and joyful grace made twice its usual impression next to the Emperor. Yet she was not glad, and that day was one of the not very many when she had felt actual uneasiness, confusion, "troubling," as she had called it to herself. The hand of the man with whom she had walked up the steps, that hand of the Emperor, of the Arch-Priest, of her "Father," had been a cold, damp hand, and as she laid her own in it she had felt fear and repugnance as at the Feast of the Good Goddess.

Yes, it had been a premonition, a warning, and not a matter of chance, that she had felt the same "troubling" from the very beginning and with everything connected with the Feast of the Good Goddess. For the others the Feast of the Good Goddess was the high point of the year, but she had always, when that festival approached, feared it more than looked forward to it.

The feast took place every year, in the winter. The hostess was the wife of the highest official of the Empire, the Consul. He had to leave the house to his wife for this purpose for two days; he himself was not permitted to enter it, for to him, as to every man, access to the festival was forbidden on pain of death. At that feast ancient incantations were spoken, strange sacrifices brought, dark, exciting rites performed, all under the guidance of the Vestals. Toward the end of her apprenticeship, shortly before she became eighteen, Cornelia had had the significance and meaning of these rites and customs explained to her by her teacher Junia. Now the Good Goddess was a close relative of Bacchus, she was the goddess of domestic fertility, and as wine was the attribute of Bacchus, so hers was the vine. But her drink, although it was wine, was not called that but given the name of the "milk of the Good Goddess." This milk of the Good Goddess was the symbol of domestic fertility, of chaste, yet for that no less voluptuous, sensual pleasure. All this was explained to the novice, and in the same way also the dark, exciting rites were explained to her which were practised at the Mysteries of the Good Goddess. Festively decked out with grapevines was the house of the first lady of the Empire, which received the guests of the goddess; grapes in abundance were there, now in the middle of winter, grown in hothouses; in their pointed, antique pitchers the Vestals fetched the milk of the Good Goddess—wine—and all the women were adorned with vine leaves. They embraced and kissed each other, at first in a stiff, severe ceremony; they performed sacred dances, every gesture prescribed. Then gradually, in the second hour, the dances became wilder, the embraces of the women more passionate, they kissed and clasped each other more excitedly, the milk of the Good Goddess flowed in greater abundance. As the night wore on the feast became more dissolute. But it was a long winter night, and when at last, shortly before daybreak, the Vestals left the house, it was full of women who lay around in the corners, in groups of two and three, and no longer recognized anyone who spoke to them.

Often now, in the loneliness of her cell, Cornelia tried to recall in exact sequence the events which had occurred at the last Feast of the Goddess and upset her whole life.

Melitta, the freedwoman, had announced to her that a woman was waiting for her in their hostess Volusia's dressing-room. What kind of woman? she, Cornelia, had asked. A peculiar woman, Melitta had answered, who had something peculiar to discuss with her and was asking her for peculiar help—and with those words Melitta had smiled in a strangely provocative way. It really had been that smile which had brought it about that now, alone, despised, and banished from the service of her goddess, she sat in her cell. So she had gone into Volusia's dressing-room, with not quite her usual carefree feeling and yet lighter than usual, since she had enjoyed the milk of the Good Goddess. Her white dress had been torn in dancing, the tear revealed her legs, and she remembered that as she walked she had tried to hold the stubborn tear together.

Strangely enough, while she was going to Volusia's dressing-room, she had thought of Senator Decian, that quiet, friendly gentleman who always greeted her with such especial respect and with more than respect. Yet it was senseless to associate this man in particular with the Feast and Mysteries of the Good Goddess.

The woman who awaited her in Volusia's dressing-room had appealed to her. She was tall, slender, with a brownish complexion that had a tinge of olive, with knowing eyes and knowing lips; that she had noticed when the woman had greeted her with the kiss of the Good Goddess, and at once the "troubling" had become stronger, that peculiar and alarming feeling which for her was associated with the Feast of the Good Goddess. "I am very bold," the woman had said to her, "but I can't help it: I have to ask you, just you, Mistress and beloved Cornelia, to initiate me deeper into the Mysteries of the Good Goddess; for I shan't be able to sleep if I don't learn more about these Mysteries." "Do I know you, my Lady?" she, Cornelia, had asked in return. And, "Yes and no," the unknown woman had answered, had seized her hand and embraced her as was the custom at the Feast of

the Good Goddess. During the embrace, however, the aware-
ness suddenly came over her that the unknown woman had
no breasts.

Naïve as she was, and filled with imaginings from an-
tiquity when gods and mythical beings peopled the world,
she had thought at first that the other was an Amazon born
after her time. Late, too late, comprehension of the whole,
horrible reality had dawned on her. She had of course heard
about that Clodius who once, at the time of the great Julius
Cæsar, had stolen into the Feast of the Good Goddess, dis-
guised as a harpist. But that had happened in times long past
which were as unreal as the times of the gods and half-gods.
That such a thing could still happen today, in the tangible
reality of present-day Rome, was simply inconceivable.

The thought that it actually was happening had paralysed
her. It still paralysed her. Even at this moment she did not
know exactly what had happened; it was at once real and
unreal, she did not grasp it, but she continued to feel it, to
this moment, daily, hourly. They were not happenings and
visual images which had become dammed up inside her as
a result of that occurrence; rather they were feelings, tremors
of excitement, an obscure, painful, frightening confusion, revulsion and disgust, and a minute trace of curiosity—an ugly
mixture.

It had been violation, that was certain. Perhaps she should
have screamed. But if she had screamed, all would have known
that the Feast of the Good Goddess had been defiled, and
from such a bad omen the worst evil would have sprung
for the expedition and the Empire. It was better that she had
fought silently, grimly, panting. She had fought, she had
resisted with all her force, and she was strong. But she had
been as if dazed by the enormous and unthinkable outrage.
And she had been hampered by her heavy, old-fashioned

dress. What had terrified her most, immediately after, was that that sacred dress had been besmirched with the traces of the crime, literally besmirched, as was her skin also.

The whole thing had lasted an eternity and yet probably only a very short time. Of the external consequences of that night she had not thought at all. Whether her absence and her agitation had attracted attention—with that she had not occupied herself. Only on the next day, when Melitta came to her and urged her to save her in her own interest, had the danger dawned on her. She had given Melitta that letter to Decian. What had resulted from it she did not know. She had only her obscure recollection of the short and everlasting embrace of that "woman" and of a few confused sentences from Melitta. No one else had spoken to her about the events of that night and their consequences. Nor had the Sacrificial Priest of Jupiter given her the reason why he had banished her behind the curtain.

What was likely to happen to her? Never had she, never had anyone, thought otherwise than that one day, when she was dead, her statue would be erected with the inscription: "To the most chaste, most modest, most pure, most vigilant maiden, Pulchra Cornelia Cossa." Instead, now she would have to descend into the vault outside the Hill Gate; for when she had laid her hand in that of the Lord and God Domitian during the procession, she had felt that he did not love her, and he would not permit her to determine the manner of her death as he had once done with the sweet and beloved Oculatæ sisters. Instead she would be entombed with a pitcher of water and a little food, a willow mat would be spread over the vault in which she was perishing miserably, and those who passed the place would fearfully make a circle of horror and disgust around her grave.

Yet she had not really violated her oath. She had not wished for what had happened, she had been dragged into it, she had not done it. Perhaps too it had not actually happened; she did not know; perhaps she had merely imagined it all in her "troubling." Perhaps, if she offered to undergo the test before the Sacerdotal Court she would succeed, as in her time the Vestal Tuccia had succeeded; perhaps she would manage to dip water from the River Tiber with a sieve and carry it before the priests.

She was dreaming. It had happened, and they would not let her undergo the test; fate had decided against her, fate had wished it so; no one inquired into the motive. She would be entombed in the vault.

The curtain was lifted from below. A hand shoved under a bowl of food and a pitcher of milk. Cornelia recognized the hand which attended to this; it was Postula's hand. The food had been prepared with love, it was her favourite dish, and covers had been carefully laid over it, so that it would keep warm. The others loved her; the others were sorry for her. "Amata—Beloved": she bore that title with right.

She would not be buried with sacerdotal honours along the Attic Way, she would have no commemorative column, her name would be erased from every stone and every page. Nevertheless, the others would think of her, often, lovingly; not even Tertullia's hatred would be able to prevail against that. When they prepared the sacred dough, they would think of her, and when they renewed the fire of the goddess on the first of March—how she would have liked still to experience that first of March! And they would whisper about her, full of awe, secrecy, and tenderness, when they fetched and dedicated the holy water, and when one watch relieved the other at the fire of Vesta.

This thought reassured Cornelia a little, and she ate the good food with relish. Then she slept, and in her face was

that serious and joyful repose which had won for her the
loving reverence of the people.

D URING this period, immediately after his return from the
Sarmatian expedition, the Emperor was seldom in
Rome; he stayed almost all the time at Albanum. While
before he had liked best to linger in front of the animal
cages, now he preferred to wander about in the remote sections of the park, from which his head gardener, Toparius
Felix, had banished every original trace of nature, transform-
ing its area into a kind of enormous carpet. The flower beds,
hedges, walks were geometrically laid out. Dainty and stiff
stood the clumps of box and yew, the individual trees trimmed
into spheres and pyramids; thin and rigid rose the cypresses;
all kinds of flowers and plants formed initials, figures, even
little paintings. The walks were carefully gravelled; the parts
of the big zoo which were not planted were paved. Fountains
and waterworks spouted on every hand; there were all kinds
of resting-places: circular benches, artificial grottoes, arbours,
tree-stumps made of stone, artificial ruins, and a labyrinth.
There were ponds with swans and herons; on gleaming white
outdoor staircases peacocks preened themselves. Arcades dec-
orated with frescoes divided off certain parts of the garden.
Here and there terraces and outdoor staircases connected the
various sections of the giant park, since it was laid out over
hilly country. Wood and stone bridges spanned the brooks;
the whole area sloped to the shores of the lake. Everything
was delicate, dainty, stiff, solemn, artificial, showy.

When Domitian walked in this artificial garden, the thought
elated him that one could alter living things in this way,
subject them to discipline, make them conform to established

norms. Since Toparius Felix was successful in bringing about miracles and metamorphoses in living, blossoming growth, how could he, the Emperor, help but succeed in fashioning human beings according to his will, in shaping them, like a second Prometheus, according to his desires and knowledge?

Absorbed in such reflections, the Emperor wandered through his gardens at Albanum. With him was the dwarf, at some distance followed the head gardener, somewhat farther behind again were the litter-bearers with the litter, in case the Emperor should grow tired. With satisfaction he gazed at the arbours, the grottoes, the whole fussily broken up, overartful distortion of nature. From time to time also he fingered the climbing vines, the ivy, the morning glories, the ramblers, which had to grow in the directions man prescribed for them. Then again he would call the head gardener to him, have him explain one thing or another, and warm his heart with a description of how one could force even tall, strong trees to take the form which the organizing mind dictated to them.

Most of all he liked to stay in the hothouses. Everything there appealed to him: the artificial ripeness, the artificial warmth, the cunning glass with which one caught the sun. With thoughtful satisfaction he saw that one could thus force trees and bushes to bear in winter the fruit which they were meant to bear in summer. That was a simile which he relished.

I T WAS in a hothouse too, on a couch which he had had set up for him, that he lay dozing, brooding, when Lucia came to him.

The Emperor's relations with her had again become more dangerous. Yes, they had lately been so full of abysses that Lucia would not have been surprised if Vellykins had suddenly raised his hand against her in a second, fatal blow.

This change had begun when he had ordered Prince Sabinus to be executed. Domitian had spared Sabinus a long time, since he had a guilty conscience toward Julia, although Norbanus had collected enough evidence in the course of years to justify his condemnation by the Senate. Only after Sabinus's participation in the unsuccessful *coup* of Saturninus had been proved without a doubt—a letter from the imprudent, arrogant Prince, in which he accepted the general's offer to make him Emperor in Domitian's place, had fallen into the hands of Norbanus's agents—had Domitian let the blow fall. And at that time Lucia had made a grave mistake. Since she had not credited Sabinus with so much stupidity and had assumed that it was a case of Domitian's acting arbitrarily, she had reproached him with having had his cousin executed solely out of jealousy of Julia. But with that she had obviously wronged him, and for a long time he had had the advantage over her.

Her relations with Domitian had, however, become seriously dangerous only since Julia's unhappy death. It had happened this way. Julia had become pregnant after Sabinus's death, at a time which excluded any doubt of Domitian's fatherhood. Domitian intended to adopt the child, and therefore wished that it should not come into the world as a bastard. He suggested a new marriage to Julia. Julia, who had had enough to suffer from Domitian's jealousy during her first marriage, refused. Domitian wanted to force upon her the man he had selected. She resisted. The Emperor had an attack of rage. Contradictions he had suffered from one person only up to then, from Lucia. He was not willing to resign himself now to Julia's also becoming arrogant, a second Lucia, as a result of her pregnancy. Rather he would do without a son. In the course of two ugly discussions, he forced Julia to consent to an abortion. From this operation Julia had died.

Domitian suffered from Julia's death, of which he was guilty. But he did not want anyone to notice this, least of all Lucia, and he had asked her in his jeering fashion: "Well, my Lucia, are you satisfied that you are rid of Julia?" The Empress had never liked Julia; she had treated her with cool, faintly mocking arrogance. Her death, however, made her indignant; the woman in her grew indignant at Domitian's masculine despotism, and his silly question completely incensed her. She made no attempt to conceal her feelings, her large, bright face twisted with aversion and disgust, and she said: "Your love, Vellykins, doesn't seem to agree with those affected by it."

Although Domitian had forgiven her accusation in the case of Sabinus because it was unjust and absurd, this remark about Julia wounded him the more deeply because it was true. The element of antagonism which had been in his relation with Lucia from the beginning grew sharper, and from then on there was just as much resentment as desire in his embraces. Such a relationship was perfectly agreeable to Lucia. It vexed him, however, that he could not free himself from her; he was small in his own eyes when he was with her. He controlled himself, his embraces became increasingly rare, and finally his meetings with her were limited to those occasions when they had to show themselves together in public. Their encounters became formal, watchful; they were on guard against each other. For several weeks, for more than a month, Lucia had not seen the Emperor at all.

So it had been a risk to gain access to him now, unannounced; it had not been quite easy to get past the many guards and valets; and in rather uncomfortable suspense Lucia waited to see how he would behave.

"You here, Lucia?" he greeted her, and already from his voice she noticed that he was pleasantly rather than unpleasantly surprised. This was indeed the case. If Domitian had avoided interviews with her during the last months, it was because he was afraid that she would tell him truths which he was not inclined to hear. This time, however, he guessed that she came because of Cornelia—she was related to her and liked her, as everyone in Rome liked her—and in the Cornelia affair he felt himself secure; he actually looked forward to arguing this case with her.

Surely enough, after a few sentences, she began to speak about Cornelia. She talked to him, without regard for Silenus squatting in the corner, but not without flattery, for she wanted very much to save Cornelia. "I presume," she said, "that you want to frighten the Senate. You want to show that there's nobody in the Empire, however venerated and beloved, to whom you would give way. Besides, you probably intend to show the Senate that you're a stricter guardian of Roman tradition than anyone else before you. But you're too clever not to know yourself that in this case the reward isn't in the right proportion to the cost. What you can gain at best doesn't balance what in any case you must lose. Spare Cornelia." Domitian grinned. "Interesting, your point of view," he said, "interesting. But you've overheated yourself, my Lucia; I'm afraid that staying in this glass house doesn't agree with you. May I suggest a walk through the garden?"

They went along an avenue of plane trees. They were now alone, as the Emperor had driven away everyone around them with a vehement gesture. "I know that such talk about my intentions is going around Rome," he said in passing, "but you, Lucia, shouldn't repeat such cheap gossip. The case is extremely simple. It's a matter of religion, of morality, of nothing else. I take my office of Arch-Priest seriously. The sacred shrine of Vesta, her hearth, is entrusted to my protection. I can forgive when it's a question of my own hearth"—he smiled at Lucia with malicious politeness—"but it's impossible for me to forgive when it's a question of the purity of that hearth which symbolizes the spotlessness of the whole."

He wanted to turn into a side path, but she preferred to go back along the avenue of plane trees, and he followed obediently. "Don't you notice," she asked, "that you're acting, shall we say, inconsistently? A man who lives a life like yours—they say that lately you have played around with a number of women in blind Messalinus's presence, mocking him and urging him to guess which one, what, and how—a man who lives that kind of life makes an odd impression when he plays judge to the Vestal Cornelia."

"Once again," said Domitian gently, "I have to advise you, dear Lucia, not to borrow my Senators' cheap drivel. No one knows better than you that there's a difference between Domitian, the private individual, who fills one of his rare idle hours with pleasure, and the Lord and God Domitian, the Censor, appointed by the gods as judge of the morality, actions, and traditions of the Empire. It isn't I who persecute Cornelia; I neither love her nor do I hate her; she's completely indifferent to me. The state religion is the persecutor, the *imperium,* Rome, whose pure flame she's supposed to guard. You must understand that, Lucia, and I know you do understand it. There simply are certain differences established by fate and the gods. Everything that has a smooth face and a lap isn't alike. A woman who possesses Roman citizenship, a *mater familias,* and especially a Vestal, is something different from the other women of the world. Those other women can do, and not do, what they want, they can whore around like flies in the sun, can let themselves be laid when and by whom they like. They just exist from the waist down. A

Roman citizen, and especially a Vestal, only exists from the waist up. One shouldn't blur the differences, one shouldn't confound the substance, one shouldn't falsify the values. The private individual Domitian can be measured by the same standards as a Cappadocian porter, for all I care; but I protest, I forbid it, if anyone confounds the amusements of my idle hours with the activities of the God Domitian."

Now, after all, they had turned off into the side path. "I thank you," replied Lucia, "for your illuminating instruction. Only one thing puzzles me: namely, that you don't grant the Roman citizens what you grant yourself. Why can't a Roman citizen also differentiate between the amusements of her idle hours and the activities she carries on as a Roman citizen? Why can't she too divide herself in half, the way you do, and at one time be only the Roman citizen, existing only from the waist up, and at another be like any other girl?"

Domitian would not agree to this. "Come now, understand me, my Lucia," he begged. "It really is the Prince's, the Arch-Priest's, consciousness of duty that condemns Cornelia, and nothing else. I want to restore to this society, to this aristocracy, which has degenerated under a line of bad rulers, their feeling for the severity, the simplicity, the sense of duty of the ancients. I want to lead this people back to religion, to the family, to the virtues which insure the present and guarantee the future. People shall say of the age of Domitian, with more truth than of the age of that Augustus: 'No more does unchastity shame the pure home. Virtue and justice have driven out lewdness and vice. Honour be to the women, for the child looks like the father. And punishment runs not behind guilt, but keeps step beside it.'" Somewhat theatrically, in his sharp, high voice he declaimed Horace's noble lines.

But at that Lucia could not restrain herself any longer. She burst into her rich, deep laugh. "Excuse me," she answered. "I do believe that you mean it sincerely. But the verses sound too funny in the mouth of the man who was Julia's lover and Lucia's husband." And, as Domitian flushed deeply, she went on: "I don't want to hurt your feelings. I didn't come here, by Hercules, to hurt your feelings. But do you actually believe that forcible measures will serve to increase the amount of virtue in Rome? This Rome, as for better or worse it is, this period of ours, as for better or worse it has developed, the real age of Domitian, do you think that you can turn it back and make it into the age you want? To do that you'd have to tear down all of Rome and forbid three-quarters of her institutions. Do you want to abolish the prostitutes? Do you want to suppress the theatres, the comedies about cuckold husbands? Do you want to have the amatory exploits of the gods scratched off the frescoes in the houses? Do you think you're really accomplishing anything by burying Cornelia? I don't know what you're able to prove against her; but this I do know; my cousin Cornelia, whatever she may have done, has more chastity in her little finger than you and I together. When Cornelia walks by, the people feel what chastity is. When the people see you, however strict the laws you decree, I'm afraid they don't feel it."

"I don't think you're right," he replied and tried to suppress his anger and keep his voice steady. "But be it as it may, I want to teach your Senators that their aristocracy doesn't merely give them privileges, but also imposes duties. All right, I afford myself this pleasure or that; but someone who's as close to me as you are must also see, after all, that the Emperor Domitian denies himself a thousand delights which fire his blood, and instead takes upon himself a thousand burdens. Do you think, perhaps, it was a pleasure to go on the Sarmatian expedition? You shiver just being here, under the sun of Rome; you should have been there with the Sarmatians to know what cold is. And you should have seen those barbarians with whom we had to deal. When one saw the corpses of those fellows on the battlefield, when one looked over the prisoners who had been brought in, one shuddered at the thought of the dangers escaped. One had to have a stout heart to face the onslaught of those uncouth half-humans, tens of thousands of them, with their accursed arrows. My dear, do you think I wouldn't have preferred lying in bed with you to jogging over icy battlefields on a slipping, stumbling horse? And if I demand that of myself, then I demand a few things of my Senators too." He stood still; he stood tall beneath the daintily trimmed trees, and made a speech. "The gentlemen take it easy. Their service to the State consists in drawing lots among themselves for the provinces and taking turns in exploiting them. But they won't have such an easy time of it much longer with me. Whoever belongs to the first rank should not waste his strength in erotic adventures or in womanish dreams and beliefs about the Minæans' superstitions or anything of that kind; he should save his strength for the State. Only a god such as I can combine both things. A society which indulges itself and plays around, like the aristocracy of Rome, ends up with having no more officials and no more soldiers, but only debauchees. The Empire will perish if its aristocracy continues to degenerate like that."

Lucia's bold, bright face wore that mocking expression before which he was helpless. "So that's why you're having Cornelia put to death?" she asked. "For that reason too," he said, but it did not sound quarrelsome. With gentle force he led her away from the light part of the garden to a grotto, drew her within, into the shade, away from the bright, early spring day. "I want to tell you something, Lucia," he confided to her, almost whispering. "Those Eastern gods, that Jehovah and the God of the Minæans, they hate me. They are dangerous, and if I don't guard against it in time, they'll get the better of me. If I want to prevail against them I need the whole support of our gods. I can't make Vesta my enemy. I can't leave any crime against her unpunished. If I want to hold the centennial games this year they must take place in a pure Rome. And I shall continue to tread the path I have entered. The gentlemen of the Senate, whose opinions you're so fond of repeating, said during my first years that I was a severe Emperor. Since I revenged the conspiracy of Saturninus they have said that I was cruel. They will have to search a long time for a word to express what they think of me after they've experienced my later years. But that won't deflect me from my path. It is calculated, step for step. I pull up the weeds. I hold critical inspections of the Senate. I crush the Eastern disorders underfoot. I shall make certain people lose their taste for flirting with those Eastern superstitions. Jupiter has a good servant in me."

He said all this softly, yet such an air of determination shone from him, such a sombrely vehement faith in his ordination, that Lucia found him by no means ridiculous. She wanted to leave the grotto and get out into the light, and he had to follow her whether he would or not. "All right, Vellykins, all right," she said, running her large hand lightly over his hair which was getting more and more sparse, and, in a tone between respect and irony, she admitted: "In many respects perhaps you're even right. But you're certainly not right in your intentions against Cornelia. Cornelia is the most beloved woman in the Empire. The people, who love you, will love you very much less if you really intend to carry

out the sentence against her. Don't do it. You'll have to suffer
for it." Unconsciously she tried to loosen the hard winter
earth with her shoe; she could not do it. A slight shudder
ran over her. To have to go down under the earth as a living
body, a straw mat overhead!

He smiled his imperious, sinister smile. "Have no fear,
my Lucia," he said. "My people will go on loving me. Shall
we make a bet? May I remind you of it when it has been
proved that I am right?"

THE Senators went most unwillingly to the session at which
they were to pronounce sentence against the Vestal Cornelia and her fellow-culprit Crispinus, both of whom the
Council of Fifteen had found guilty. It was repugnant to
them to confirm the doubtful verdict and to lend their authority to the barbaric measures which the Emperor obviously
wanted to have taken. Domitian, however, had had the news
spread that he would attend the session, and this plain warning moved the Senators to be present almost without exception.

The people too seemed to be very discontented. A great
crowd surrounded the Curia where the session was to take
place, and even the Emperor was not greeted with acclama-
tion and homage as usual; instead there was nothing around
him but excited whispering or hostile silence.

From the very opening of the session the Senate was un-
ruly. Helvidius was the first to claim the right to speak. He
had to make an announcement to the Conscript Fathers, he
explained, which changed the whole aspect of the affair which
they had assembled to discuss. It was their business to pronounce sentence against Chamberlain Crispinus, the Em-

peror's Minister. A definite report had arrived that the man had escaped the judgment of the Senate: he had slit his veins; he was dead.

The presiding Consul could not manage to keep the session in order any longer. The Senators had jumped up, they spoke and shouted in confusion. A better excuse to escape the unwelcome task could not have been found. The only witness who could have been brought against the Vestal Cornelia had disappeared; the condemnation of the Sacerdotal Court was shaken; how could one pronounce sentence in a case like that? Only with the greatest difficulty was the Consul able to restore quiet.

Messalinus tried to calm them. With practised rhetoric he elaborated the point that no stronger confession could be imagined than this suicide, and since one of the guilty had escaped vengeance they were particularly obliged, in order to appease the wrath of the gods, to punish the other all the more severely, before the eyes of the city and the world. But his speech had no effect. The uproar had only increased. From outside—the doors had to remain open, according to the law, so that the people could follow the discussions—they could hear the debates and angry cries of the crowd, and within and without the Senate they were pressing the point that, if anyone had sinned against the goddess, certainly it was only this Crispinus, who had now died in such a comparatively mild fashion, a fashion pleasing to the Emperor.

Inside the Curia, meanwhile, Senator Helvidius was answering Messalinus. It was incomprehensible, he declared, that the Council of Fifteen had not prevented Crispinus's suicide by a stricter arrest and guard. Frightened by such a bold speech, the Senators looked at the Emperor. He sat there, his face dark red, violently sucking at his upper lip; he was

furious at these insolent Senators and at himself. He had
wanted to spare Crispinus and make suicide possible for him,
but, as sometimes happens in such cases, he had given ambiguous
orders in order to shield himself from his own conscience.
Helvidius came to his conclusion. It was, he found, after this
strange death of Crispinus's, the duty of the Senate to refer
the case of the Vestal Cornelia to the Council of Fifteen
again, so that they might once more review the proofs.

Next Priscus took the floor, and after Helvidius's bitter and
indignant speech the great lawyer's objectivity made a doubly
convincing impression. There were, he explained in his high,
cuttingly clear voice, no precedents. To the Senate the case had
been presented as a proceeding against Chamberlain Crispinus and his fellow-culprits. It was not possible now suddenly to separate the Vestal Cornelia's case from the main
case. For that a new trial and a new recommendation from
the Sacerdotal Court would be required. Moreover, he had to
confess that, with all due respect to the Sacerdotal Court, he
had attended this session only with the gravest qualms. From
the very beginning, as he was a man who observed the actions
of the gods with the greatest reverence and who saw meaning
and connexion in all events, a grave doubt had tormented
him. If one of the Vestals had really committed such a sin
and thus called down the wrath of the gods upon the Senate
and people and on the head of the Emperor, how then, he
elaborated with cunning logic, could the Lord and God Domitian have achieved the glorious victories of the Sarmatian
expedition?

This argument, clothed in irreproachable objectivity, was
the most coldly malicious insult to the Emperor that could
be imagined; everyone in Rome understood it and took pleasure in it, and Priscus himself was filled with deep satisfaction as, in his sharp, ringing voice, he hurled those sentences

into the assembly and into the world. Domitian caught on, Domitian understood him fully, Domitian's heart stood still for a moment; but Priscus himself was to pay bitterly for his sweet revenge, for from that moment on the Emperor was certain that very soon he would send this Priscus after Sabinus and Ælius and the others who had dared to deride him.

Messalinus took the floor and set himself to contradict Priscus, and order the indignant Senate back within bounds. Did he have to remind the honourable assembly, who defended their rights with such jealousy, that they were about to create a dangerous precedent in wanting to interfere with the functions of an equally honourable autonomous body? The wording of the law did not give the Senators the right to examine the reasons which might have moved the Masters and Priests to make their pronouncement. These reasons were not the business of the Senate. Cavilling and formally legalistic scruples such as the honourable Senator Priscus had just advanced might carry weight before secular judges, but they were insubstantial and vapid before the Council of Fifteen, who made their pronouncements as representatives of the gods and under their guidance. Once the Council of Fifteen had reached their verdict, their pronouncement stood fast for eternity; there was no appeal from it; and it was up to them, the Senators, merely to pass the sentence on the basis of this verdict.

With extreme reluctance the Senate set itself to its hated task. A great number of motions were made, all aiming at relieving the Senate of the responsibility. The wording of the sentence which was finally accepted skilfully thrust the responsibility back onto the Emperor. The sentence declared that the Vestal Cornelia should be punished in the same way as the Oculatæ sisters in their time. However, although the latter had been condemned to suffer the death prescribed by law—that is, death by entombment in the vault—they had also been recommended to the mercy of the Emperor, and as a matter of fact Domitian had then given them free choice in the manner of their death. Thus the Senate, by its ambiguous pronouncement, had avoided being the one to condemn Cornelia to the cruel punishment; it had transferred the responsibility for the manner of her death to the Emperor again.

Fearful because of their own boldness, the Senators looked at Domitian. As the law ordained, the presiding Consul asked the Emperor whether, in his character of highest judge and Arch-Priest, he approved the sentence and would command its carrying out. All looked in suspense at the Emperor's large, darkly flushed head. Norbanus, sitting behind him, a little lower, turned his face up to him that he might better receive his answer; but there was no need for him to announce it to the Senate. All saw that the heavy, dark-red head nodded yes, even before Norbanus had put the question.

Thus, then, the Consul announced the sentence, the Crown approved it, the scribes wrote it down, and the executioner made his preparations.

UNTIL that time the Emperor had been loved by the masses. Even the bloody severity with which he had punished Saturninus's *coup d'état* had found a sympathetic reception. Cornelia's execution met no sympathy. The Romans grumbled. Norbanus tried to intervene. The Romans would not let their mouths be stopped; they scolded and grumbled more and more loudly.

They told one another touching details about Cornelia's

execution. As she was about to walk down the steps into her grave, her dress had caught. One member of the execution committee had wanted to help her free it; but she had repulsed his hand with such abhorrence that anyone would have had to recognize how her pure nature recoiled from the touch of man. So deeply did this account impress itself on everyone's heart, that two weeks later, when at a performance of Euripides' *Hecuba* the line, "Ever she strove to die with dignity," was recited, the public burst into long, demonstrative applause. Besides, it was said that friends—Lucia herself was mentioned—had surreptitiously given Cornelia a little bottle of poison, and her quiet, pure dignity had so impressed her guards that they had not dared to take it from her. On top of all this came the fact that Crispinus had addressed letters to various friends before his death, stating that he was dying innocently. Copies of these letters circulated all over the Empire. Nobody believed in Cornelia's guilt any more; the Emperor was regarded as a senselessly raging tyrant.

From day to day it was increasingly apparent that Lucia had been right and that the Emperor would have to pay for the sentence against Cornelia with his popularity. Until then the masses had been cold to the Senators of the opposition, had been on an almost hostile footing with them. Now the people greeted the ladies Fannia and Gratilla with sympathy wherever they appeared. A play was performed, entitled *Paris and Œnone*, which was full of allusions to the Emperor's relations with Lucia and Julia, and it had an enormous success. On the street complete strangers spoke to Senator Priscus—would he not publish the speech which he had made in the Senate for Cornelia?

So far, however, Priscus did not venture. Yet he did now set himself to fulfil the promise which he had once made to old Fannia, to lock up his anger no longer, to put his *Life*

of Pætus before the public. He handed the completed work
to Fannia, for whom he had written it, and allowed her to
hand on the little book. Soon copies were circulating throughout the Empire.

In this book, moreover, the life of the republican Pætus
was set down with beautiful clarity. How this man, brought
up with the old Roman severity, had, as the tyranny of Nero
became increasingly unbearable, refrained from participation
in the sessions of the Senate in order to demonstrate his
opinion. How he had, it was true, maintained complete silence,
silence, silence, but on the other hand his whole behaviour
had shown his deep resentment at the course of public affairs.
How finally Nero had ordered him to be accused and condemned. How calmly, even gladly, since he no longer had
to live in that degenerate Rome, he had slit his veins and died
with a Stoic's courage. That was now twenty-seven years ago.
Priscus did not say the slightest word against Emperor Domitian in his biography; rather he limited himself with exemplary objectivity to an exact representation of his hero,
using the dates which he had been given by Pætus's daughter
Fannia. Nevertheless, and just because of its objectivity, the
book became one single, enormous accusation against Domitian, and as such it was read and understood.

Such attacks were the daring deeds of individuals; shortly
afterward the Senate in its entirety took up an open battle
against the Emperor. This occurred in connexion with the
case of Governor Ligarius.

On this Ligarius, one of his favourites, Domitian had conferred the office of Governor of the Province of Spain, and
the man had used his position to plunder the entire country
without mercy. Now representatives of the province had come
to Rome, to bring an accusation against their dishonest governor before the Senate. Formerly, before Domitian's prestige

had been shaken by Cornelia's execution, the Senate would barely have permitted such proceedings against a favourite of the Emperor. Now, when it felt its power growing day by day, it not only forced the Emperor to agree to these proceedings but also drew everyone's attention to them.

The Senate appointed Senator Helvidius as attorney for the Province of Spain. He let loose his whole wild eloquence; the Senate followed his lead and accepted almost every one of his presentations of proof. In the most minute detail they investigated the extortions which Ligarius, friend and favourite of the Emperor, had perpetrated against the unhappy Province of Spain. Full of secret triumph the Senate listened to Ligarius being convicted and loaded with the foulest abuse. When the hearing of the witnesses was concluded, it was as good as certain that the Senate in its next session, which was to take place two weeks later, would not only condemn the Emperor's favourite to the restoration of the stolen gold and goods, but beyond that would confiscate his income and sentence him to banishment.

This was the kind of blow to Domitian which no one would have thought possible a few months before. Now it was true that there were certain tablets of law stored up in the state archives which allotted more functions to him than any one man had ever held at once since the founding the City, but Domitian knew that he must not dare to exercise those functions. On the contrary, for two generations the Senate had not dared to offer the ruler so much defiance as this Senate was doing now.

He lay in the hothouse at Albanum, stretched out on the couch which he had had set up there. He was thinking over what had happened, and how it could have happened. Had he presumed too far? Had Lucia been right? She had not. He had only to find the strength to control himself, not to let the blow fall too soon, not to let it fall at the wrong moment; he had to find the strength to wait. And that he could find. He had practised waiting. It had been a long road from his bitter, miserable youth to the present.

Much could be accomplished by patience. Many plants could be forced to grow in the direction one dictated to them. What did not adapt itself, one pruned away, one uprooted. At the moment he had to prune his own power, but the day would come when he would be able to do the uprooting. He knew that he was in agreement with the gods. Lucia would not be right for ever.

Why was it that the people of Rome would not understand that he could not have done anything else than condemn Cornelia? He was conscious of the fact that the guilt of many a man whom he had condemned had not been established beyond doubt. But Cornelia actually had been guilty; why was her guilt alone not accepted by the people? It must be possible to make Cornelia's proven guilt plain even to the stupid eyes of his incredulous subjects.

He summoned Norbanus. Had he not mentioned a certain Melitta, the Vestal's freedwoman, who knew about the occurrences at the Feast of the Good Goddess? Where was she, that Melitta? What an incompetent his Chief of Police was to have let that Melitta get away, not to have kept her at his disposal. The Emperor railed at Norbanus in ugly, mean words; then again he flattered him and entreated him to produce the vanished Melitta so that one could torture her and extract a confession.

Norbanus remained as unmoved by the Emperor's entreaties as by his curses. Squarely he stood there, his powerful head rested on his broad shoulders, grotesquely the black curl fell into his low forehead, and his eyes, the brownish eyes of a faithful but perhaps not completely tamed dog, gazed at the

Emperor, scrutinizing, ready to be of service, and a little bit superior. "The Lord and God Domitian knows," he said, "that he can depend on his Norbanus. The sinner Cornelia lies beneath the willow mat, condemned to oblivion because of her well-proven guilt. I shall give you the means, my Lord and God, by which to convince even the stupid rabble of her guilt."

SHORTLY after this, Decian, who was living in almost complete retirement on his estate at Baia, was told that he had an unexpected guest, Senator Messalinus. Decian asked himself uneasily what that sinister being could want of him, yet in his inmost heart he knew as soon as the servant spoke the name of Messalinus. The man wanted Melitta.

And very soon the blind man brought the conversation around to the Vestal Cornelia. "What a pity," lamented Decian, "that that woman had to perish." It was incautious of him to speak in that vein, but he had to do it; he was strongly moved to express his grief for Cornelia.

"Would it not be a still greater pity," asked Messalinus, "if she had died in vain?" There they were, at the subject for whose sake the man had obviously come. Decian decided that he would under no circumstances betray the dead Cornelia; yet even while he swore that oath he felt an inner certainty that he would not keep it.

It had, Messalinus was elaborating meanwhile, cost D.D.D. a great deal of self-control to have the harsh sentence carried out. Now, however, certain obstinate republicans were trying to rob the Emperor of the success of his painfully achieved harshness and Cornelia of the significance of her death. They were spreading the rumour that Cornelia had died innocently, and thus they were endangering the aim and purpose of the sentence's exemplary severity and the advancement of morality and religion. It was with grief that every true friend of the Empire must witness this activity, as insane as it was godless.

Decian knew that his own life was at stake. Yet he forgot his fear for a moment and eyed the blind man with curiosity and revulsion. So it was with such soft, cajoling, fiendish logic that these people knew how to turn their crimes into the opposite. Perhaps they even deceived themselves; at least that man in whose name this Messalinus had come believed that the arguments advanced here were the pure truth. "It's simply a fact," he answered bravely, "that Cornelia possessed a certain radiance with which the gods bless very few; and so," he concluded with polite ambiguity, "it will be difficult to make her death seem reasonable."

"There is a man," replied Messalinus, "who could be of help to the Lord and God Domitian in this undertaking. You are that man, Decian." With a light wave of his hand, as if he could see the simulated indignation and amazement on the other's face, he cut off his superfluous reply and went on: "We know where the freedwoman Melitta is. We want to avoid seizing her by force, only because we don't wish to increase the scandal around Cornelia's downfall. It would be reasonable, Decian, for you to hand over this Melitta to me. You would spare yourself great grief, Melitta much that would be very painful, and us the scandal. It seems to me that would really be in the spirit of our dead Cornelia."

Decian had become very pale, and it was some satisfaction to him that at least the blind man could not observe his pallor. "I don't understand what you want," he replied steadily.

Messalinus made a polite little gesture of negation. "You are no wooden-headed fool like certain of your friends," he remonstrated. "D.D.D. values you as a man of the world and of intelligence. We understand that you wanted to shield Cornelia.

But what do you expect to gain by continuing to put up re-sistance? Do you think you can force a declaration of dead Cornelia's innocence out of D.D.D.? Show us your well-known intelligence. Hand over Melitta, talk her into being reasonable, and you will have gained quite a lot. I won't try to fool you. Even if you do hand over Melitta to us, an accusation against you for having helped conceal Cornelia's crime will have to follow. But whatever the verdict of the Senate, I can assure you that you'll get off with a light sentence of exile. Don't give me any answer now, Decian. Think over carefully what I've told you. I'm convinced that you'll come to the con-clusion that there's no other sensible solution. Make it your business to save Melitta from torture and yourself from death, and begin at once, today, to send everything you own in the way of movable possessions out of the country, for the two or three years which you'll have to spend outside of Italy. I can promise you that Norbanus won't find out much about it. Be-lieve me, the advice I'm giving you is the advice of a friend."

Decian, after Messalinus had left, said to himself that the Emperor and his councillors probably cared nothing about the dead Cornelia, and that they only wished to win back Domi-tian's lost popularity. As soon as the Senate could no longer count on finding support among the general masses, it would have to surrender again the positions which it had lately won in its fight against the Emperor. Decian knew this well. Should he, in order to save his own life, help the Emperor weaken the Senate once again?

He should not. But what would be accomplished if he sacri-ficed himself? He could let Melitta disappear permanently. Then what would Messalinus and Norbanus do? They would arrest him, they would extract a confession from him, how and why he had made Melitta disappear. Nothing would have been gained. The Emperor's triumph over the Senate, which must, after all, be the final result, would be postponed for a few weeks by his sacrifice, but it would not be prevented.

Decian informed Messalinus where Melitta might be found.

Decian was commanded to preserve silence, he was not allowed to leave his estate at Baia, he was watched. The freed-woman Melitta was apprehended with all possible speed and secrecy.

Domitian smiled deeply and with satisfaction. "I have good friends," he said to Messalinus; "I have good friends," he said to Norbanus, and in the presence of his most intimate council, which now consisted only of Reginus, Marullus, Annius Bassus, and Norbanus, he declared: "This affair is to remain among us for the moment. We won't bring any accusation against Decian yet, we will let the gentlemen of the Senate calmly continue their activities, we will see what they still have to bring up against Ligarius and against us." He smiled more broadly. "Let the enemies of the Empire plunge even deeper into their ruin; we can wait."

So the gentlemen of the Senatorial opposition had no inkling of what had happened, nor were they aware that the Emperor was now in a position to silence all the talk about the guilt of the executed Vestal whenever he liked. Instead they thought, Helvidius and Priscus and the other gentlemen of the Senatorial opposition, that they had already re-established the republic, that the Emperor had really been pushed back into the place assigned to him by the constitution, that he was no longer the first among equals, but that they were in truth his peers. Old Helvidius went around beaming; his battered face had grown young again with pride at the victory achieved. He was the great republican, the advocate of the good cause, he had revenged the oppressed Spaniards against Ligarius and against the Emperor; he sunned himself in his success, he plumed himself, and with him the other leaders of the Senatorial cause,

Priscus and his followers and the relatives of the executed Pætus, Fannia, Gratilla. On the day after tomorrow the Senate was to pronounce sentence against Ligarius, the exploiter of the Province of Spain. A few of the Senators wished that it might be satisfied with condemning Ligarius to confiscation of property and to banishment, but they, the leaders of the opposition, were not going to be so modest and moderate. They would demand that the Emperor's friend, the criminal, be condemned to death, and they would carry the motion.

Ministers Reginus and Marullus of course knew about this talk. They were elderly gentlemen, they had innumerable experiences behind them, they had seen many friends and acquaintances die an unexpected death, and they had not always been able to avoid giving their assistance in bringing about that speedy death. They had become weary, they were by nature good-hearted rather than malicious, they were conciliatory, and now they felt a mild regret when old Helvidius began to rush so blindly and wildly to his death. The man could not be permanently saved, but why should he not have a few years still, or at least months? They were human; they wanted to prevent him from hastening his own downfall.

It was not unusual for the two gentlemen, whose generosity was known even to their opponents—they called it flabbiness— to carry on more or less frank discussions with those opponents, which, it is true, remained theoretical in character. Now again Marullus and Reginus looked for an opportunity for one of those confidential talks. On the day before the Senate was to pronounce sentence against Ligarius, it happened that they were able to talk it over with Helvidius, Priscus, and Cornelius, as they had wished.

"You've helped your Spain to achieve victory, Helvidius," said Marullus, "and you've overthrown Ligarius. That's a lot; one can congratulate you on that. But what else do you actually want? If a man like our Cornelius here behaved so stormily and youthfully it would be understandable. But a gentleman of our age—that's unnatural." And Reginus, in his easy-going way, added: "Why, really, are you acting so blood-thirstily? After all you know just as well as we do that D.D.D. at best might confirm a sentence of confiscation of property and banishment, but never a death sentence. So such a proposal would be a pure piece of theatre. Is that necessary? You'll only compromise your victory."

"I want to show the Senate and the people of Rome," said Helvidius sombrely, "that this regime doesn't hesitate to entrust the most important positions to criminals." "My dear Helvidius," asked Reginus, "isn't that a doubtful generalization? Even in times when the Senate reigned without restriction a governor is reported to have been condemned for embezzlement now and then. We learned something about that in school. I remember a few speeches about such subjects, speeches without whose example even your excellent summation against Ligarius couldn't have been made." And, "If you want to be honest," Marullus seconded him, "you must admit that it's just under this our Lord and God Domitian that the government of the provinces has improved. Granted, Spain got a bad man; but after all, the Empire has thirty-nine provinces, and in the memory of man there have never been so few complaints coming in from the provinces as now, under D.D.D. No, Helvidius, what you're trying to do there, your proposal of a death sentence, hasn't anything to do with objective politics, it no longer aims merely at the abolition of abuses; it's simply a demonstration against the regime as such." And Reginus again: "Try to persuade your friend, my good Priscus, and you, Cornelius. He isn't benefiting anyone by making such a proposal—not us, not you, and not himself. Only evil can come of it." He spoke in an especially quiet, actually comfortable tone. Yet Priscus and Cornelius heard the warning behind it.

But nothing was noticed by Helvidius, who, still intoxicated with his success, thought only in big words. "Of course," he said brusquely, "I'm not fighting against the individual Ligarius as such; it's indifferent to me whether he's banished or executed. What I'm fighting against—and you know that perfectly well—is that Rome should be embodied in one single man. I'm fighting for the sovereignty of Senatorial jurisdiction. I'm fighting for Rome's freedom." Those were dangerous words, even now, and prudent Cornelius tried to change the subject. "You're making a speech, Helvidius," he said, "you're not sticking to the subject." But Reginus reassured the worried young man with a little wave of his hand. "No danger," he said, smiling. He did not want to be deprived of the opportunity of saying a few words himself, for once, on this subject of freedom about which the Senators were so fond of indulging in absurd phrases. So, "Freedom," he repeated Helvidius's last word, and in his high, oily voice he gave his definition: "Freedom is a Senatorial prejudice. You want Rome to be embodied not by one single man, but by the two hundred families of the Senate, and that's what you call freedom. Just imagine that you'd achieved your aims a hundred per cent. You'd have gained more power for the Senate than for the Emperor. What, by Hercules, would then have been attained? What kind of freedom? In what would it consist, your freedom? In an ugly confusion, in an unplanned hither and yon between the two hundred quarrelling families who would be scuffling, swindling, and bargaining with one another for the provinces, the privileges, and the monopolies more than they do now. If you follow your reason and not your feelings, you'll have to admit that such freedom for all would turn out worse than the planned rule of an individual, which you want to dispose of with the convenient catchword despotism."

Helvidius wanted to answer, but Priscus held him back; he had too much to answer himself. "You say disparagingly: feelings," he replied, and his cuttingly clear voice contrasted oddly with Reginus's high, oily tones. "You forget, you don't want to realize, how the feeling of being abandoned to the whim of an individual oppresses one. The consciousness that one's actions are subject to the judgment and the conscience of a carefully chosen group is like fresh air; the feeling of being at the mercy of one individual is like suffocation." And even Cornelius could not restrain himself any longer, but added in his deep, grave, threatening voice: "Freedom is no prejudice, Reginus. Freedom is something very definite, tangible. If I have to stop and consider whether I may say what I have to say, my life becomes narrower, I become poorer; finally I can't think unrestrictedly any more; I force myself against my will to think only what is 'permitted'; I degenerate; I imprison myself in a thousand miserable considerations and doubts, instead of taking a broad view of broad issues without hindrance; my brain becomes atrophied. In slavery one breathes; one can live only in freedom."

But now Helvidius would not wait any longer. "The Emperor," he stormed, "makes violent efforts to restore discipline and virtue in Rome. In his ragings he makes use of punishments which have been unknown for a century and a half. What has he accomplished? When the Senate ruled—that you yourself won't deny—there was more morality in Rome, more virtue, more discipline." And Priscus added: "More justice." But Cornelius concluded by adding: "More happiness." "Words, gentlemen," said Reginus comfortably, "nothing but big words. Happiness. You demand that a government make people happy? By that you simply prove that you're not fitted to rule. You demand morality of a government, virtue, justice? I admit to you, we're much more modest in our demands. We,

Marullus and I, consider a government good when it abolishes as many causes as possible from which unhappiness can arise: famines, plagues, wars, too uneven a distribution of property. If I have to choose between one regime and another, if I have to weigh which is the better, I don't quarrel about the name, it's utterly indifferent to me if one calls it liberal or despotic; I ask only one thing: which regime guarantees better planning, better organization, better management, better administration. To demand more of a government, to demand justice or happiness, that's asking for milk from a hen. Give a population a generous supply of bread and circuses, give it some meat and wine, give it judges and tax collectors who aren't too corruptible, and prevent the privileged groups from making themselves too fat; then the rest—justice and discipline and happiness—will come of its own accord. In your inmost hearts you know as well as I that under Domitian the population has had more bread, more sleep, and more pleasure per capita than would be possible under a Senatorial rule. Do you think that the hundred million inhabitants of the Empire would give up that additional bread and sleep and pleasure for your 'freedom'? Not even half a million of that hundred million want a different form of government."

They all wanted to reply. But Marullus was tired of the fruitless debate and said, bringing it to a close: "At any rate, my good Helvidius, I advise you to enjoy your triumph over Ligarius; don't challenge the gods, and be satisfied with that." And, "I think that's good advice," Claudius Reginus said dryly, comfortably, and yet very emphatically.

The three Senators were honestly indignant at the cynicism of the two Ministers, but they knew them well enough to understand that the warning was meant sincerely. Priscus and Cornelius, accordingly, urged the hot-headed old man to moderate his intentions and content himself with Ligarius's banishment. This was very much more than they would have dared to hope only half a year ago. Popular moods were changeable; one must not irritate the Emperor too much; after all, the army stood behind him; very rapid and bold and successful advances had been made; it was wise to pause for breath. Yet Helvidius was obsessed by his plan. He had told so many people that he would not content himself with Ligarius's banishment, that he would propose his death; he could not humble his pride by retreating now. He decided to carry through his intention.

And so he did. The warning from Domitian's friends made him only more bitter, and he spoke more wildly, passionately, and eloquently than ever. Even Cornelius and Priscus forgot their doubts when he spoke. It was a great moment. The old republicans held their breath, their eyes shone, they were giddy with joy, when Helvidius, magnificently working up to a climax, demanded for the criminal Ligarius the severest punishment provided by law—death, death, and again death.

For many long years, since Domitian had assumed power, the opposition in the Senate had been as good as silenced. Now, in these last months, it had suddenly reappeared; it had won one victory after another; now one of its members even dared to demand the death penalty against a friend and favourite of the Emperor's. Had the days of freedom come again? Helvidius's speech, this proposal of his, was the opposition's greatest victory.

It was also its last.

This became apparent at once when the defendant answered the prosecutor. Up to that moment Ligarius had behaved quietly and modestly, as befitted a man who with good reason has been accused of such a serious crime. So it had been expected that after this speech and the proposal he would be utterly crushed, that he would humbly implore the mercy of the Senate. Instead, Helvidius's proposal did not seem to de-

press him at all; on the contrary, he smiled when Helvidius
made the motion, his face actually lighted up; yes, it was as if
he had longed for such an excessively severe statement. And
from his very first words it was clear that he was quite sure
that he would never have to suffer the penalty demanded by
Helvidius, whether the Senate passed it or not. From the first
word, his speech was not a defence but an accusation.

Of what he had been guilty, he declared, the state and the
world knew well; he had confessed it, he had shown himself
ready to repent and pay the penalty which the Senate assigned
to him. But with all his might he would protest and defend
himself against such proposals as Senator Helvidius's. He,
Ligarius, was still a Senator and a man of consular rank. As
such he was defending the dignity of the Senate, which was
being threatened by proposals as extravagant and utterly unreasonable as Helvidius's. Such a suggestion no longer expressed justified indignation against a guilty individual, but
entirely and solely personal hatred—brutal, senseless, vicious
enmity. Now, however, no sort of enmity existed between Helvidius and himself. Against whom, then, against whom alone
was this outrage directed? Doubtless it could only be against
that personality who should be furthest removed from such
miserable enmity, against the Lord and God Domitian. It was
he, and he alone, whom Helvidius was trying to attack in his,
Ligarius's, person. The proposal was a brazen provocation, the
proposal was really a case of *lèse-majesté,* and since it was no
longer possible for him, Ligarius, after today's session and sentence, to make the accusation of *lèse-majesté,* he called on the
Conscript Fathers, still his colleagues, not to let the shame of
Helvidius's outrage rest upon them, but to defend the dignity
of the Senate and the prestige of the Empire by bringing an
accusation of *lèse-majesté* against Helvidius.

It was plain that Ligarius would not have dared to make

such a speech if he had not been certain that he would be protected by the councillors of the Emperor. It was plain that Domitian must have found the means to defend himself with new force against the Senate. At any rate the Emperor had decided not to tolerate any further defiance on the part of the Senate; probably he had also found the means by which to transform the popular temper. As always, it was not advisable to venture any further; one would do better to see to it that Helvidius's proposal was rejected by a practically unanimous vote. Not even the proposals for confiscation of property and for banishment were accepted. Ligarius, the friend and favourite of the Emperor, was sentenced merely to replace the sums which he had illegally extorted from the Province of Spain.

And soon it became apparent that the Senators had rightly interpreted Ligarius's speech, and that the Emperor was in possession of witnesses who would be able to restore his popularity among the masses and force the Senate back into its old state of impotence.

Only a few days after the sentencing of Ligarius the Senate was confronted with an accusation against Decian. Decian was accused of having attempted to conceal the crime of the condemned Vestal Virgin Cornelia.

The Emperor himself attended the proceeding in the Senate. Decian had not appeared. In his place, after the statement of the accusation, his attorney declared: "Senator Decian declines a defence. I am here more as messenger than as attorney. Senator Decian informs the Conscript Fathers through me that he confesses to the crime of which he is accused."

One single proposal was advanced: death for the guilty man and disgrace to his memory. No voice was raised in opposition. Then Domitian himself intervened. He begged the Conscript Fathers to let mercy temper their decision against the confessed and repentant sinner. So they sentenced him only to banishment, and confiscated those of his possessions which were to be found in Italy.

As he withdrew, the Emperor, with a genial smile, shook his finger at a group of Senators who had gathered around Helvidius and Priscus: "See, gentlemen, now even your friend Decian has acquitted me of certain accusations."

The masses were taken aback when they heard that a man as respected for his integrity as Decian had borne witness for the Emperor and against the Vestal. Melitta too, Cornelia's friend and freedwomen, had borne witness against her. Consequently one had been doing Domitian an injustice. Quickly the indignation against him shifted back into the old enthusiasm. People reproached themselves for their credulity, and were heard to curse the Vestal Cornelia who by her lewdness had almost robbed the Empire and the great, good Emperor of the assistance of the gods. Domitian was praised for having taken things so energetically in hand, without regard for the individual, to avenge the goddess. What an effort it must have cost the good Emperor to bring someone like Cornelia to court and to take the odium of such a condemnation upon himself! What a great Emperor they had! Finally enthusiasm reached such a pitch that Cornelia's condemnation saved Domitian a public donation.

A FTER having restrained himself for so long, Domitian now enjoyed his revenge to the full. In rapid succession a number of proceedings were instituted which finally did away with those leaders of the old aristocratic faction whom his father and his brother and he himself had hitherto not dared to touch.

The first against whom he had accusation brought were

Senators Helvidius and Priscus, and the Ladies Fannia and
Gratilla. The accusation was one of *lèse-majesté*. It was shamelessly pieced together. The whole lives of the defendants had
been searched and everything they had done, and everything
they had not done, was interpreted as an insult to the Emperor. Every harmless little witticism they had permitted
themselves was twisted and distorted until it became a highly
treasonable speech. Cautious Priscus, who, so as not to endanger himself, had lived for many years in retirement in the
country, found that this very precaution was interpreted as a
crime; it was an insult to the Emperor that just under his rule
a man of Priscus's gifts and abilities should withdraw from
service to the State. Naturally his biography of Pætus was
presented as a seditious hymn to a rebel, a veiled insult to the
Emperor. Without reprisal the prosecutors showered the defendants with mean and cold-blooded abuse. The Senate did
not dare to protest. The Curia, where they sat, was surrounded
by the Emperor's personal guard. It was the first time since
the founding of the city that the reigning body had to make
its decisions under armed threat.

Two episodes in these proceedings lingered especially in the
memory of the Romans. One was Fannia's trial. The prosecutor declared that Priscus was said to have written his seditious
biography on her, Fannia's, instigation, that she more than
anyone was supposed to have distributed the book, and he
asked her if this was true. All knew that a "yes" would cost
her her possessions. "Yes," she replied. Had she, the prosecutor
went on, given Priscus material for his book? All knew that if
she said "yes" a second time she would at best be banished
from Rome, that she might be executed. "Yes," she replied.
Had her sister-in-law Gratilla known about this? they asked
her further. "No," she answered. Those three simple, unafraid,
and scornful words, that double "yes" and that "no," consti-

tuted all of Fannia's testimony, which impressed itself more deeply on the Senate and the people of Rome than the prosecutor's excellent oration.

The second event was this: Helvidius, who knew he was lost, used this last opportunity of once more addressing the Romans to make a sombre, powerful, threatening speech against the Emperor, who would not escape the vengeance of Rome and the gods. They listened in silence. But blind Messalinus arose, and with a sure step, as if he could see, walked through the benches toward Helvidius to lay his own hands on the slanderer. But then—it was the first time that this had happened to the blind man—the others jerked him back, they shouted at him: "This man is a hundred times worthier than you!" They cursed him, they pulled him down.

But these outbursts of rage did not hinder the Conscript Fathers from condemning Helvidius and Priscus to death, the Ladies Fannia and Gratilla to banishment, and Priscus's book to be burned.

Two days later they prepared the bonfire for the book in which Priscus, who was about to be executed, had described the life of Pætus, who had been executed. The burning took place late in the evening. The flames were pale when they were lighted, for it was still daylight, but they gleamed more and more fiercely as nightfall approached, and the cries of the onlooking rabble became louder and louder. Priscus had been sentenced to watch the burning. He did so. He held rigid his round, completely bald head; with his small, deep-set eyes he stared into the flames that consumed his book. The copies which had been chosen for the burning were written on parchment—for old Fannia the most precious material had not been costly enough for that book—and the parchment burned slowly and toughly, it resisted destruction. Priscus was a cool, objective person, he had often smiled at his friend Helvidius's metaphors and similes, yet now his own imagination associated many touching thoughts and images with that pyre. Fire gave light, fire purified, fire was eternal, fire linked man to the gods and in a certain sense made man mightier than the deity. Perhaps, probably, just because of this fire, his *Life of Pætus* would last longer than the rule of Domitian and of the despots who might succeed him; but probably none would succeed him any more.

That was the last fire that Priscus saw, his last evening and his last night. In that night also, battered, passionate Helvidius paid for the satisfaction he had felt when in his proposal against Ligarius he had hurled his whole hate and his whole scorn into the Emperor's face, and followed his father to Hades, like him sent there by violence. Domitian, however, could say to himself that now old Vespasian would be satisfied.

Then a week later the condemned women went into exile. It was a wild, barbarous region to which they were being sent. Plump Gratilla with her ladylike indolence, accustomed to having three maids about her for personal attentions alone, would not have an easy time of it now, living alone with gloomy old Fannia in the rough little house on the cold, inhospitable shores of the north-eastern lake. True, Fannia took Priscus's eulogy of her dead husband, which had caused her exile, into that exile with her. True, when the women approached the Latin Gate on their way out of the city, many people lined their path. But their dead husbands were not brought to life by that, nor did it make the Pontus the Tiber.

Along their path Senator Cornelius, the writer, stood among the others. He had not wanted to have any hand in the death of his friends and had remained absent from the session in which their case was tried. That had been bold. Not too bold, however, for of course he had taken the precaution of calling three doctors to his bedside as witnesses to an attack of pneumonia. Even now the prudent man had debated with himself at length whether he should mingle with the crowd, to salute the women passing there for the last time. He had conquered his caution, he had taken the risk; there he stood, blaming himself for his excessive boldness, waited, and, when the women came by, raised his right arm to bid them farewell once more, for a long time, perhaps for ever. But in his heart he thought: "How senseless and useless it all is. Poor, foolish friends. Why didn't you wait for the right moment to overthrow the Emperor? Then, after his death, you would have been able to say much more clearly and forcefully what there was against him than you were able to say now. Poor, foolish, dead friends, who didn't understand that this age makes one single demand of us: to survive it. Poor, foolish, heroic women. Your only hope is that I, who am less foolish, may perhaps be able to erect a memorial to you some day."

AFTER Domitian had purged the city of the people who were his and the deity's enemies, he began his centennial celebration. Since the founding of the city eight hundred and forty-nine years had passed, and it needed a bold manipulation of chronology to calculate that a new century had now been concluded. However, Domitian was a bold man; he managed it.

The people were called together by heralds. The Council of Fifteen ordered the instruments to be handed out with which each man was to purify himself: torches, pitch, and brimstone. The people for their part brought the Priests' Council the first fruits of their crops and the first-born of their cattle as a tribute to the gods. The Emperor himself sacrificed to Jupiter and Minerva on the Campus Martius, in his presence women of the nobility prayed to Juno, a live trout was sacrificed to the earth, choruses of youths and maidens sang hymns, and the Emperor dedicated a piece of land to Vulcan, that he might henceforth protect the city against fire.

On that night the Emperor slept with Lucia. "Do you remember," he asked, "what you prophesied to me at the time of the Vestal's execution? Well, now, my Lucia, who was right?"

His victory over the Senate filled Domitian completely; it confirmed his belief that he had rightly conceived his priesthood and his office, as the gods wished. The thought supported him, elated him; he was happy.

He had always liked to work; now he took his work and his duties even more seriously. Formerly the passionate, restless man had loved to traverse his huge Empire from one end to another, in spite of the many hardships of travel, and one year had found him in Britain, the next on the lower Danube. Now he spent the greatest part of his time in council with his Ministers or at his desk.

He had chosen a small room as his study; he had to have narrow, closed-in walls around him in order to concentrate. In the solitude of this locked room he was able to delve deep into his inmost consciousness. Sometimes, in such moments of concentration, he could actually feel in his physical being that he was the heart and brains of that thoroughly alive and powerful organism, vaguely and abstractly called the Roman Empire. For him alone, in him alone, this Roman Empire actually lived. The rivers of this Empire—Ebro, Po, Rhine, Danube, Nile, Euphrates, Tigris—were his, the Emperor's, veins; the mountains—Alps, Pyrenees, Atlas, Hæmus—were his bones;

it was his blood that warmed and gave life to those huge territories; the millions of inhabitants were the pores through which his own life breathed. This life multiplied by millions made him in truth a god, elevated him above all human measure.

But so as not to let this mighty vitality dissolve and escape, he had to construct its frame with even greater strictness and precision. Rigidly he followed his programme. That he had conquered his rebellious Senate had been the first lap of a course which he had mapped out for himself exactly. Now, since he had assured himself of the aid of the gods, he could begin the difficult part of his course. Now he could set about the task of putting an end to the subterranean upheavals with which that foreign, sinister, and uncanny God Jehovah was threatening him.

It was by no means the case that he had wanted to attack Jehovah for His own sake. Not at all; that would not be suitable for him, the defender of religion. Jehovah's doctrines should continue in force; but only among Jehovah's people. If these doctrines, however, overstepped their boundaries, if they began to poison his, Domitian's, Romans, then it was his duty to defend himself against them, to burn these doctrines out of the hearts of the Romans for ever.

He took counsel with his Ministers. With Reginus, Marullus, Annius Bassus, and Norbanus he worked at a plan for driving the East out of Rome, for pushing it back within its boundaries.

First it was a question of doing away with Jacob of Sekanya, the miracle-worker. Jacob was regarded as the leader of the Christians in Rome. The whole city was interested in him. He went in and out of Prince Clemens's house. Many of the Senators evinced interest in him and his ideas in order to demonstrate their opposition to the Emperor in this temporarily safe manner. The people looked up to the miracle-worker with timid reverence. Seventeen people had seen with their own eyes how the lame Paulina, a freedwoman, had risen up and walked after he had laid his hand on her head and murmured a few Aramaic phrases. It was true that this Paulina had died on the same day; but the event was none the less a miracle, and the man who had accomplished the miracle was none the less worthy of awed reverence. At any rate the Emperor and his Chief of Police were of the opinion that it would be better if Jacob of Sekanya performed no further miracles in this their city of Rome.

But how did one prevent a man from working miracles?

There were, Norbanus suggested unambiguously, very thorough means.

In silence they all thought over those thorough means. Then Reginus said it was perhaps after all not wise to resort to the thorough means in the case of the miracle-worker. If they resorted to them, it would look as if the followers of the State religion were afraid of the miracle-worker's God. This would presumably not crush his followers, but only reinforce them in their superstition.

Perhaps, suggested Marullus, one could invite the miracle-worker to perform a miracle at the Emperor's court. Then one could investigate and expose him. "Who told you," Bassus objected, "that the miracle won't come off?" The Emperor, however, declared conclusively: "I don't want to throw any doubts on the abilities of the God Jehovah. I merely want to prevent the miracle-worker from making converts."

Marullus, not at all offended by this reprimand, said that they should first make it clear to themselves how far the dissemination of the Jewish doctrine was permitted, and where it began to be proselyting and therewith a crime. "If the Lord and God would give us his opinion," he said, "he would be granting us all a favour." The Emperor loved such formal, legalistic distinctions, and Marullus counted on the fact that Domitian would welcome a chance to define his views on the question.

And Domitian seized the opportunity. "The Jewish religion," he explained, "is and remains permissible. I am not unconscious of the fact that this religion denies the basic principle which unites all the other nations of the Empire, namely, the principle that the Godhead is manifested in the Emperor. While all others, the followers of Isis and Mithras no less than of the barbarian divinities of the Germans and the Britons, are agreed that sacred reverence is due the image of the Roman Emperor and his insignia, the Jews alone will not grant this plain acknowledgment. Now, tolerant Rome doesn't by any means think of violently forcing a poor, stiff-necked people, whose miserable character has been confirmed by their enormous defeats, to recognize the truth." After this preamble he could not resist declaiming his favourite theory as if he were in the Senate. "Rome does not forbid religious opinions. Rome permits to every man his belief, even if that belief is a false one. Every man can have his god, however strange that god may seem. Let every people have its rites, but let them not offend our laws," he declaimed, and Reginus as well as Marullus noticed with an inner smile that he was soaring off into verse. "But here," Domitian continued, "exactly at this point, is the boundary. One thing Rome does not permit, that the god of another people should interfere in the sphere of her, Rome's, State religion. Rome's Arch-Priest cannot allow these Eastern people to dare to spread their superstition further through persuasion and propaganda. You asked, my Marullus, how far the dissemination of the Jewish doctrine is permitted. I answer: to confess to that faith and to practise its rites is permitted without restriction to all those who, to their misfortune, are born of that people and of that faith. It is not permitted that this superstition be spread by teaching or even by deed. Whoever wishes to make a convert to the Jewish religion, by word or by the knife of circumcision, is committing a crime against the majesty of Rome and of the Emperor."

"That's clearly formulated," said Marullus. But Claudius Reginus objected cautiously: "If we state that basic principle publicly, won't people accuse us again of being afraid of this Jehovah and the convincing force of His doctrine?" "Caution is not fear," replied Norbanus brusquely. "If I lock the doors of my house, it's justified caution, not fear." But the simple soldier Bassus declared bravely: "I'm afraid of this doctrine. It's becoming contagious. I was in Judæa. I experienced what an atmosphere of awe this God Jehovah and His Law diffuse around them. The Temple, 'That Thing,' terrified my soldiers, paralysed them. It isn't good for the army to let the preachers of this doctrine loose on them."

They were embarrassed by the frank confession. "I don't like to hear such words, Annius," said Domitian. "But however that may be, I do not wish the dissemination of the doctrine; I want to shield my Romans from the doctrine; it is not to be preached. I have spoken."

"So what are we going to do with our miracle-worker?" Norbanus said, coming back to the point of departure with brief practicality. Marullus, with a little smile, said: "If I have correctly understood the Lord and God Domitian, this miracle-worker may go right on performing his miracles, but among his Jews, not here in Rome." "I thank you, my Marullus," answered the Emperor. "I think that's the right course." But candid Annius grumbled: "The Province of Judæa is near, many people have business there, many ships go there. I'd rather know the man to be farther off. Why not banish him beyond the boundaries of the Empire? He can work his mira-

cles for the Scythians or the Parthians, but for no Roman subject." They were all pleased by the straightforward soldier.

Domitian, however, did not content himself with limiting
the discussion to the case of Jacob of Sekanya. He wanted his
gentlemen to understand that the action taken against the
miracle-worker was only the first step on the road to much
more important things. He explained: "So that there won't be
any misunderstanding, I shall sum up once more. There are
three kinds of Jews. In the first place the kind who, born Jews,
limit themselves to practising their faith. That they are free to
do; they will not be persecuted. In the second place there is the
kind who spread propaganda and proselytize. Their presence
is not permitted either in Italy or in any other province of the
Empire, their habitation is restricted to the Province of Judæa,
and even there they are subject to the surveillance of the police. Then, however," he spoke more slowly, enjoying every
word, "there is still a third kind of Jew, and that, it seems to
me, is the worst." He interrupted himself, savoured to the full
his Ministers' suspense, and finally explained: "I mean those
who, born to the State religion, deny it in order to go over to
the God of the Jews and cast doubt on the divinity of the
Emperor."

"Which would fully clarify the question," said Marullus
dryly. But practical Norbanus at once drew the immediate in-
ferences. "So I suppose," he said, "we shall banish Jacob the
miracle-worker as a first step, and as a second bring an accusation against Senator Glabrio." The others glanced up. Senator
Glabrio was a peaceful man, whom one could not accuse of
hostility against the regime; that he occupied himself a great
deal with exotic philosophy, especially with the doctrine of the
Christians, was regarded by most people as a lovable eccen-
tricity. Bassus made an attempt to soften the proposal. "Perhaps," he suggested, "we should first institute proceedings

against a few little people who, among the masses, follow the
false faith of the Jews; that would be a kind of warning." "I
wouldn't persecute the little people," Reginus objected; "it only
injures the Emperor's prestige among the masses." Domitian,
with his malicious smile, decided: "Glabrio is small enough."
"So I am to gather the evidence against Senator Glabrio because of offence against the State religion?" replied Norbanus.
"Yes," agreed Domitian, almost feigning boredom, "first
gather together the evidence against Glabrio."

It was clear to all what that "first" meant. It was aimed
very high; it was aimed at the Emperor's cousin, Prince
Clemens.

WHILE Sabinus had not been able to resist the temptation
of becoming involved in Saturninus's conspiracy, Prince
Clemens was without a trace of political ambition. He spent
most of his time far from Rome on his Etruscan farm, near
the little town of Cosa, in that old farmhouse which was the
oldest possession of the Flavians. Even Norbanus, certainly no
friend of Clemens's, could only report to the Emperor that
the Prince's days were filled with the study of Eastern philosophy. But the doctrine of the Jews and Minæans was aimed
at the mentality of little people; it preached against resistance,
talked foolish drivel about a kingdom which was not of this
world; so that one had nothing to fear in the way of dangerous political activity from Clemens.

Domitian considered this view most fitting for his Chief of
Police; but he himself, the Censor Domitian, evaluated this
Clemens's personality and activities quite differently. Even if
a nobody, a man of second rank or an unimportant Senator,
approached the Christian way of thought, it was reprehensible;

for the Christians preached withdrawal from the things of this world, and inactivity ill befitted a man of old Roman family. But if Prince Clemens, the Emperor's cousin and next to him the first man in the Empire, adhered to this superstition and thus evaded his duties as citizen of the State, instead of pursuing significant political or military activities, this criminal indolence set a highly pernicious example. How was he, the ruler, to educate his Senators to be good servants of their country when his own cousin evaded the responsibility of that service?

It was not only national and religious considerations of such a general nature which enraged the Emperor against Clemens. Rather it offended him personally that this lazy, slack fellow Clemens would not recognize his, Domitian's, divinity, his genius. Not that Clemens would have directly denied the Emperor's divinity; he was even willing to sacrifice to the Emperor's image as the law demanded; yet Domitian felt, behind the unapproachable, indolent politeness of the Prince, how little the latter respected him. It was indifferent to Domitian, if, for example, that miserable Domitilla, Clemens's wife, glared at him with her wild, dry eyes; it amused him more than it annoyed him. But Clemens's scorn offended him. In particular, no doubt, because it was precisely this Clemens who was the father of the Princes Constans and Petronius, "the little lions." The twins were now eleven years old: Domitian liked them more and more the older they grew; since Julia's death he had become increasingly determined to adopt them. The one disturbing thing about them was this Clemens. Everything about the phlegmatic man irritated him; he could never reproach him enough for his lazy, spineless personality, he was always finding new words of blame for him, calling him self-indulgent, leaden, dawdling, stupid, lifeless, negligent, lazy, cold-blooded, impotent, dull, slothful, dilatory, flabby, sluggish, indolent. But against that very indolence all the Emperor's scoldings glanced off. Clemens came when the Emperor summoned him, listened politely to the Emperor's reproaches, promised improvement, went back to his estate, and remained the same. Domitian would have forgiven the father of his little lions a conspiracy against his life; this passive resistance he could not abide.

Clemens himself was much less occupied with the Emperor than the latter was with him. The Prince was no deep thinker. For all his forty-four years he still made a very youthful impression; the delicate skin, the pale blue eyes beneath the light, ash-blond hair emphasized the appearance of boyishness, of immaturity. Yet while the Prince was slow of understanding, he was not shallow. Once he had grasped something, he revolved it within him and considered it until it had sunk deep into him and fused with his very being.

What made the strongest impression on him, in the teachings of the Christians, were the dark prophecies of the Sibyls. The gods who were now worshipped as gods were nothing but the dead ghosts of ancient kings and heroes. But the rule of those beings long dead was drawing to a close. Rome too worshipped such dead beings, and therefore Rome too would fall. Its rule would be succeeded by the rule of the Messiah. Rome's arm was still strong, strong was every muscle and every bone, but the heart of this strong body was dying, was turning to stone, and could no longer breathe life into the limbs. However mighty this creature appeared, a profound sadness went out from it. Its exhalations paralysed the whole world; there was no peace and no joy any more in that world; satisfied desire no longer satisfied; and a deep longing for something else filled all living beings.

Thoughts and feelings of this kind occupied the Prince's simple soul. He was by nature friendly, even gay. Yet he saw what was happening on the Palatine and in the Senate as interpreted by the Sibylline oracles; it all seemed senseless and dead to him, and this sense of death weighed on the whole world and crushed life and happiness. That he was forced to be part of this universal death made him melancholy. He became always more deeply involved in the world of Jacob the miracle-worker and the Sibyls; it became more and more difficult for him to fulfil his duties as representative of the imperial family at the court and in the city; he longed more and more to be allowed to withdraw permanently from the Palatine and to live quietly on his farm with Domitilla and the children and the books and teachings of the Eastern faith.

This was Prince Clemens's position at the time when Domitian, strengthened by his victory over the Senate, decided not to let the God Jehovah intrude further into his domain.

As a first step, Clemens's friend and teacher, Jacob of Sekanya, was torn from him. Prince Clemens had seen many friends and relatives go into exile, but he had never seen a man accept his sentence of exile with such quiet confidence as Jacob. His life in the little town in Judæa, which henceforth he would not be allowed to leave, would not be easy. He would have to live there as the only Christian among heathens and Jews, hated by both, in the most extreme poverty, deprived of his income and forbidden to receive the visits or gifts of friends. But he bore this without rebellion; he went into misery and exile as if he were going toward a joyous future.

Then came the trial and execution of Senator Glabrio, and although Clemens and Domitilla paid little attention to Roman affairs, they had to recognize that the danger was now threatening their own persons. Domitilla spoke to Clemens about it, with the dry clarity that was characteristic of her. She had thought herself strong in her faith, but now that she lacked Jacob's presence and advice, she was not willing to suffer without resistance, but determined to defend herself with all her strength against their threatened fate. She was all the more amazed when at this juncture she came up against Clemens's decided opposition. Jacob's banishment and Glabrio's execution had created a mood of bitter martyrdom in him. Not that he had become arrogant. He did not feel himself ordained to seize the martyr's crown with his own hands and to draw the Emperor's vengeance down on his head by a demonstration of faith. Rather he wanted to go on living as before, not to resist the Emperor, to submit to him willingly; but he was just as firmly determined to undertake none of the plans for escape which Domitilla suggested. Whatever might happen, he would not evade the fate for which the Deity had destined him.

And so he waited. He knew that D.D.D. let his decisions ripen very slowly, and that therefore he too might perhaps have to wait a long time. But then it happened that by a conversation with the writer Quintilian he brought upon himself that martyrdom which he had wanted the Deity to impose on him.

It happened in this way: Domitian had wished that his future, adopted sons should be brought up in the Roman tradition, and had for this purpose given them as their teacher Quintilian, the great orator, the first literary stylist of the period. Quintilian was instructed to keep from the boys everything which was not suitable for the future rulers of the Roman Empire, but on the other hand to avoid conflicts with their parents. Contradictory as these instructions sounded, Quintilian, a stately, polite, very dignified, flexible, yet very definite gentleman, had managed to follow them. In a polite and very subtle form a silent struggle was being carried on between the boys' parents and their teacher; and Quintilian, without actually placing himself between the parents and the children, yet managed to estrange the boys from them in a cautious way that was hard to pin down.

Several times Clemens made an attempt to have a frank discussion with the teacher and his children. But he was in no way a match for the skilful orator and stylist, and it was during one of those conversations that he finally, against his will, let himself be carried away to use such incautious words that the Emperor was at last given a handle against him.

Quintilian had declared it was his aim to instruct the children more in what was useful than in what was true. A good teacher, he thought, might as a matter of course feed his pupils with lies, if this was done for a noble, that is, a Latin or Roman, end. "I have never," he said, "as a speaker in court, had any qualms about making doubtful statements, if I saw no other way of bringing the judges over to the good cause." "Do you always know so exactly," Prince Clemens could not help asking at that point, "what the good cause is?" "In our case," answered Quintilian, "I know it exactly. In front of Princes Constans and Petronius every statement is right and justified which contributes to their being brought up as Flavian rulers. The good cause which I have to serve is the sovereignty and duration of the Flavian dynasty." "I envy you your certainty," Clemens returned. "The good cause," he went on thoughtfully, "so many people mean so many different things by that. I, for example, know surely that the reign of the Flavians will collapse, and just as surely I know of another kingdom which will endure."

To this highly un-Roman statement, expressed, moreover, in sloppy Latin, Quintilian made no further answer. But Clemens asked himself at once, why had he really made that statement? It was a superfluous confession, one of those useless demonstrations which Jacob the miracle-worker and Domi-

tilla severely condemned. For to speak of the Godhead and
the truth had a point only in front of people who were receptive to that truth.

Repentantly he told Domitilla what had occurred. She was
deeply alarmed. Jacob had impressed on them so forcefully,
before he went into exile, that they must not thrust themselves forward as martyrs, that they should be as wise as ser-
pents and try to survive the rule of That One, of the Anti-
christ. But she said nothing of this, nor did she complain; all
the more deeply was Clemens moved by the few, resigned
words which issued from the narrow lips of his dearly loved
wife.

He honestly repented his thoughtless utterance. But if, as
was probable, his fate was to be hastened by it, then at bottom
he was glad. He had become more and more weary of the
ugly, ruthless life around him, and it cost him no effort to depart from this empty, burdensome world. He was by nature
modest, he did not think that he was one of the elect, yet if
the Deity had destined him to bear witness for Him, his "lazy,
indolent life" would have gained more significance and would
cast a brighter radiance into the future than D.D.D.'s restless,
active career. The thought made him smile. His expectation of
what Domitian would do took more and more the form of
confident joyousness, and while Domitilla was fearful, Clemens waited with exalted serenity.

About two weeks after that conversation with Quintilian, a
courier delivered a letter to the farm at Cosa, in which Domitian, in particularly cordial language, urged Clemens to come
soon to the Palatine, as the Emperor longed for an intimate
talk. Domitilla paled deeply; her light-coloured eyes gazed before her in a lost stare; her narrow mouth was not firmly
closed as usual, the lips had gone dry, she held them slightly
parted. Clemens knew exactly what she was thinking. Such

intimate talks with the Emperor rarely came to a good end; with Sabinus, too, D.D.D. had had a long and especially amiable conversation before he had had him killed.

Clemens deeply regretted that Domitilla felt nothing at all of the joyful calm which filled him. The light, delicate face of the forty-four-year-old Prince seemed even younger than usual when he said good-bye to her; it revealed an almost gay composure. He kissed the twins on their pure foreheads, he stroked their soft hair. "My little lions," he thought—he too had learned something from Domitian.

D OMITIAN received his cousin in his dressing-gown. He had awaited him with impatience; he hoped for a lot from this interview. He loved such conversations. For matters stood as Clemens and Domitilla had guessed: after his cousin's treasonable utterance Domitian felt justified before himself, before the gods, and before Rome in purifying the atmosphere around the boys who were his future successors, and so he had decided to let Clemens die and to send Domitilla into exile. But beforehand he wanted to have a discussion with his cousin. And because the hours in which he had discussions with the men he had doomed to death were his pleasantest, he had relaxed, that he might fully enjoy the interview, and he received Clemens with great warmth.

First he questioned him about conditions on his farm: how had they adjusted themselves to the changes which had resulted from his decree restricting wine cultivation? Then he came back to his old complaint about Clemens's spending so much of his time in the country and thus evading the duties of a Roman Prince. Once again he reproached him for his "indolence" and pointed to all that he, Domitian, undertook.

Just five days ago he had been able to attend the opening of a new road, a great highway between Sinuessa and Puteoli. It had cost much effort and sweat, that Via Domitiana, but now after all it was there, and would make life easier for many millions of people, today and for the whole future.

"I congratulate you," answered Clemens. "But," he went on thoughtfully, without sarcasm, "don't you think it would be more important to build the masses a quicker and easier road to God rather than to Puteoli?"

Flushing, with an angry glance, Domitian eyed his cousin. He was about to shout him down, to let loose the lightning of his wrath upon his head; but then he remembered that he was in his dressing-gown just because he had made up his mind to be not like Jupiter but very human. And Clemens had doubtless had no intention of making fun of him; rather it was merely his usual dullness and idiocy which had caused him to make that stupid remark. So Domitian restrained himself. In reality he was not eager to crush Clemens; what he wanted was for Clemens to admit that he was in the right. For although the Emperor had formerly been proud of the fact that he alone had perception, and although he had felt this isolation as a distinction with which the Deity had blessed him, he was now depressed by the lack of understanding which he found all around him. Was it really impossible to have others share in the light? Was it really impossible, for example, to convince this Clemens? So Domitian restrained himself, only answered his cousin's bold question with: "Stop that silly joking, Clemens," and went on to another subject.

Half reclining, half sitting, comfortable on his couch, he began: "I have been told that those Eastern philosophers with whom you occupy yourself so much lately, those Jewish, or rather more exactly those Christian, wise men, address themselves in particular to the rabble; they try to help the lowly and oppressed; their teachings are for the masses, the spiritually impoverished, the millions. Is that so?" "In a certain sense it is," answered Clemens. "Perhaps it's just for that reason that this doctrine appeals to me." The Emperor suppressed his annoyance at this unseemly comment, remained lying down, and went on: "Now I have done away with a few of my Senators; people like to enumerate their names. But there aren't many of them, there are about thirty; you can't make it more than thirty, however many I'm accused of having overthrown. It isn't the number of the names, it's more their old aristocratic lineage that makes the list of my 'victims' seem so important. On the other hand, nobody can deny that I've used by far the greatest part of the confiscated property of those 'victims' in such a way that hundreds of thousands, yes, millions, are very much better off. With that gold I have prevented famines and plagues, or at least lessened them, and likewise general misery and poverty." He looked attentively at his hands, and concluded slowly: "If it hadn't been for my regime, hundreds of thousands, perhaps millions, would no longer be alive; other hundreds of thousands might never have been born at all without my measures, which were possible only because of the execution of those thirty men."

"And so?" asked Clemens. "Now then, listen carefully, my Clemens," answered the Emperor. "You, who set as your goal the happiness of the lowly, the happiness of the masses, you should have understanding for me, you should love and honour me. Do you do that?" "Perhaps," replied Clemens, amiably, almost humbly, "perhaps we mean something else by happiness and life than you do, Domitian. We mean a life directed toward the Godhead, a confident preparation for the other world."

But now Domitian's composure was at an end. "The other world," he jeered, "Hades.

'Rather on earth would I dwell, naught but a portionless
    hireling,
Than in the depths of Hades rule over lifeless shades,' "

he quoted Homer's Achilles. "Hades. The other world," he
went on excitedly. "That's the very thing I blame you for. You
don't dare to look life in the face, to come to grips with it;
you talk a lot of drivel about the other world, you try to get
out of everything, you run away. You don't believe in yourselves or anyone else, or in the duration of what man has created. What cowardice, what a pitiable sight, when a Flavian
doubts the duration of the Flavian dynasty! It will not perish,
I tell you." Now he stood there in his imperial pose, in spite of
the dressing-gown, and with his arms angularly pressed back,
in his high, sharp voice, he crowed the verses into the other's
face:

" 'Never shall I vanish. Much of me endures,
    Challenging destruction.'

If a poet may say that, and not without justification, how
much more so may a Flavian Emperor? But what doesn't resist destruction, what will perish, is the kingdom of your invisible Messiah. You dwell in dream palaces, you're shades
already in your lifetime. Rome is life, but your Christianity is
death."

Surprisingly, but with the gentle, humorous friendliness
which he had shown throughout the whole conversation,
Clemens suddenly declared at this point: "So you want to send
me to Christianity?"

That quiet, cheerful, and, as it seemed to him, mocking
statement completely robbed Domitian of his composure. He
stood there darkly flushed, violently sucking at his upper lip.
But one last time he restrained himself, and, speaking to the

other with almost amiable persuasiveness, he said: "I want you to acknowledge that I'm justified in sending you to your death." "If your gods exist," answered Clemens, always with the same unshakable, unapproachable, humorous calm, "then you are justified in sending me to my death." And after a very brief pause, and this time with quiet, emphatic composure, he added: "Moreover, you're doing me a favour."

Domitian, even after Clemens was long dead, often pondered those words, wondering whether the man had really believed them or whether they had been a pose.

JOSEPH

I

THEY drove in three carriages. In the first sat Mara, fifteen-year-old Jalta, thirteen-year-old Daniel, and one of the serving women; in the second was fourteen-year-old Matthias with the two men servants and a large part of the baggage; and in the third the rest of the baggage and Mara's freedwoman Jarmatja. Joseph rode along beside Mara's carriage; his groom brought up the rear. Sometimes Matthias took the groom's horse and gave the man his seat in the carriage.

It was a beautiful late autumn day, very brisk; a light wind blew from the sea; the intense bright blue of the sky was flecked with a few very white clouds. Joseph's mood was happy and excited. When he had bought the Be'er Simlai estate four years ago he had promised Mara to return to Judæa when he had completed his work. Now he had arrived at that point; the *Universal History* was finished. But it was a good thing that he had found a "temporary solution" which made it possible for him to spend the winter still in Rome. Mara, Jalta, and Daniel could now easily go ahead to Judæa; he and Matthias would follow in the spring. He looked forward to the winter with his son Matthias.

He loved Mara, he loved her dearly, but they had now lived together with short interruptions for twenty-five years. She had become more difficult in the course of those years; he was willing to admit that sometimes he too had made things very difficult for her. It had taken a long time for the blind worship with which she devoted herself to him to melt away; and often he had wished that she would learn to think more independently, even about him. But now that it had happened and she accepted his weaknesses with an almost motherly indulgence, but let him notice that she saw through him, he sometimes would have preferred things as they were before. For at times her criticism pricked him sharply, mildly as it was expressed. It was the persistence of that criticism which annoyed him; at heart he knew well that she was right, although in a dispute he could effortlessly put her in the wrong with his practised dialectics.

Above all she had been right when throughout those last years she had urged, quietly but insistently, that they should at last leave the city of Rome. Since the Emperor had ordered his honorary bust to be removed from the Temple of Peace, all his friends had implored him again and again to get out of dangerous Rome, away from the eyes of the Emperor, of Messalinus, of Norbanus. John of Gishala had enumerated a hundred common-sense reasons to him, reasons against which his, Joseph's, arguments had not held good as they had against Mara's; and then when new persecutions broke loose, Justus himself had told him that to stay any longer was more theatrical than courageous. And once he had actually gone back to Judæa; he looked over his new estate, Be'er Simlai, carefully; but he had only found that under the excellent care of his old Theodore Bar Theodore it was prospering at least as well as under his own eyes, and he had gone back to Rome.

But now he was glad that events had shaped themselves so that he had spent those bad years in Rome, apart from things and yet in their midst. Now his work was finished, and the excuse with which he had justified his stay to himself and to Mara—the excuse that his work would turn out better far from Judæa—was untenable; the fulfilment of his promise was due. Yet he had simply not been able to embark now, to bury

himself in Judæa. So finally he had found the "temporary solution," the new argument by which he could justify his stay
in Rome at least for a while longer. If the *Universal History*
was to have an effect, he had pretended to Mara, his presence at the moment of the book's appearance was important,
almost indispensable; he owed that to Claudius Reginus
alone, who had spent so much love, patience, and money on
making that work possible. It was a faulty argument, Mara had
smiled resignedly and a little bitterly, and there had been
some uncomfortable moments when he had suggested to her
that she should journey ahead, that he would follow with
Matthias in the spring. But now those unpleasant moments
were behind him; now they were already in the sixth day of
their journey; tomorrow, at latest the day after tomorrow,
they would have arrived at Brundisium, and the ship would
set out to sea, carrying Mara and the children to Judæa. And
then it would be winter, and before the next spring he would
not have to think about travelling to Be'er Simlai.

The wind reddened and tightened Joseph's face. Today one
would not have guessed from his appearance that he was in
his late fifties. He grew impatient at the slow speed of the carriages; he rode ahead a little distance.

Sharply his horse's hoofs rang on the paved highway. One
had to grant this Emperor Domitian that under him the Appian Way was kept in better condition than at any time under
his predecessors. An endless train moved past on either side.
Joseph overtook carriages and riders, and carriages, riders, and
litters came toward him. As he squeezed his horse between a
wagon and a litter a teamster called out to him: "Hey, there,
not so fast—are you being chased by the police?" and Joseph,
in good humour, called back: "No, but I'm riding to my girl,"
and everyone laughed.

He halted on a little rise, having left the carriage far behind, and waited. His boy Matthias came riding up; he had not been able to stand it inside the carriage again; gaily he spurred toward him, forcing the rather heavy horse into a gallop. Joseph rejoiced when he looked at his son. He came rushing up, a big boy—at fourteen he was almost as tall as Joseph himself. His Matthias had the same lean, bony face, the long, slightly aquiline nose, the thick, glossy black hair. His skin was flushed by the wind; his hair, though not long, fluttered lightly; his intense eyes glowed with pleasure in the rapid movement. How like him he was, and yet unlike him. Matthias had nothing of the excessive sensibility which had caused him so many joys and tortures; instead he had inherited much of his mother's harmlessly friendly personality, of the childlike traits which were hers even today. He had his mother's open nature also, he made contacts easily and amiably, but without being pushing. No, he was not a handsome boy, thought Joseph, as Matthias came riding up in the wind, bareheaded; actually no single feature of his face was handsome, yet how lovable he was, how his frank, boyish heart was reflected in his face, and his naïve, vigorous grace in his gestures. He was a young man and yet still completely a child; no wonder that he attracted everyone's friendship. Joseph envied him that childlike nature, and he loved him for it. He himself had never been a child; at the age of ten he had been precocious and an adult.

Matthias reined in beside him on the rise. "You know," he said, in a voice which already sounded noticeably deep and manly from out of his very red lips, "one just can't stand it— the snail's pace of that carriage. I'm already looking forward to when we ride back, you and I." "I'm curious," answered Joseph, "whether, when you actually see the ship, you won't be sorry after all that you're not going along." "Oh, no!" the boy answered vehemently. "I don't want to serve my appren-

ticeship in Judæa, not in the army or in the offices." Joseph
looked at his son's lively face and was glad that he had decided
to keep him in Rome. Youth, expectation, a thousand hopes
shone from the boy's passionate eyes. "Not to mention an
apprenticeship at court?" Joseph supplemented Matthias's sentence It was a rather thoughtless remark; he noticed that from
the violent effect which his words had on the boy. Now an
apprenticeship in the army, in government offices, or at court
was the customary educational programme in aristocratic families. But an apprenticeship at court was not easy to get, it was
considered a great distinction, and one had to have good relations with the Palatine if one wanted to be accepted there.
"Do you really think," Matthias asked in turn, and his whole
face was one glow of desire, "that would be possible? Would
you let me? Would you get it for me?" "Don't count on anything," Joseph said, quickly trying to take back his overhasty
words. "I haven't yet thought it over enough. I can't tell you
anything at all yet. Be satisfied, my Matthias, that you're staying in Rome for the winter. Or aren't you? Isn't it enough for
you?" "Oh, yes, yes it is," Matthias replied hurriedly, quite
sincerely. "Only," he reflected, and his eyes grew large as he
imagined it, "what a triumph it would be, what would Cecilia
say, if I got admitted to court for my apprenticeship!"

Joseph did not have to question Matthias very long to find
out what this Cecilia had to do with the problem. She was the
sister of a schoolmate of his son's, and once in a quarrel she
had prophesied to him that he would end up on the right bank
of the Tiber, where the poor Jews lived, as a pedlar. Otherwise
Matthias had never suffered from his Jewishness. Joseph had
sent him to a school where he was the only Jew; it had happened that his schoolmates had laughed at him because of his
Jewishness. He, Joseph, would scarcely have been able to get
over that as a boy. He would have brooded about it for months,

years; he would have hated those who made fun of him. His Matthias was obviously more surprised than hurt by the derision of the others; he had not taken it hard, he had fought it out with them, and he had laughed at them, and he had on the whole got along well with the others. Only this little Cecilia's remark had stuck fast in his memory. But at bottom this was quite agreeable to Joseph. At bottom he was glad that his boy had ambition.

The carriage approached. Joseph rode beside Mara for a while. He was full of tenderness for her, and he loved his other children too, Jalta and Daniel. Then why was it that he now felt such a deep bond with his son Matthias, a deeper bond than with the others? Only a year ago he had left the upbringing of the growing boy essentially to Mara. Now he could no longer understand how he could have done so. Now he felt a slight twinge of jealousy that he had left the child in her care so long, and his heart swelled at the thought that he was to spend the winter alone with him. Why was it that one suddenly loved one of one's children so much more than the others? The Lord had blessed him in days past with Simeon, Mara's first son, but he had let that blessing slip through his fingers and foolishly wasted it. Then the Lord had punished him and cursed him with Paulus. Now He had blessed him a second time, with Matthias, and this time he would not waste the blessing. This Matthias would be his fulfilment, his Cæsarion, the perfect fusion of Greek and Jew. With Paulus he had not accomplished it; this time he would succeed.

ON THE day after the next they arrived at Brundisium. The ship *Felix* lay ready; early the following morning they would set out to sea. Once more, for the twentieth time, Joseph

talked over with Mara everything there was to be discussed.
He had already given her letters of recommendation to the
Governor at Cæsarea, as well as a roll of important instructions from John of Gishala, which she was to go over once more
with his steward Theodore. The main point was for her to
come to an understanding with Theodore, so that he would
bring up the boy Daniel to be a good steward. Daniel was a
quiet boy, not stupid and not clever; he was looking forward
to the Be'er Simlai estate; when Joseph himself came to Be'er
Simlai in the spring he would find a good helper there. No
word was spoken on that last day about Joseph's personal relations with Mara. They had experienced so much together,
good and bad. Mara, although she had not Joseph's deep understanding of human nature, and could not follow his philosophy,
knew more about him than anyone else in the world, and he
was aware of that. He was aware that she loved him with a
womanly and motherly love, which knew each of his weaknesses and in a quiet way fought them and accepted them.

The boy Matthias had immediately gone over the ship thoroughly, into every last corner. It was a gallant ship, seaworthy
and spacious, but it would have been much too slow for him.
He explained this enthusiastically to his father and his brother
Daniel; he hoped very much that when he sailed with his
father in the spring they would have a faster ship than the
Felix. To go fast, before the wind, under full sail, on a slender,
narrow, terribly fast ship—that was what he was looking forward to; his eyes shone.

The next day the moment of departure arrived. Joseph and
Matthias stood on the quay; Mara stood at the rail with the
children. The pleasant, invigorating wind was still blowing,
and the busy little white clouds were still in the sky. All around
them, on the ship and on the quay, there was shouting and
bustle. Then slowly the rail swung away from the land, and

with it the faces of Mara and the children. Joseph stood on the quay and looked after them, looked with concentration; his gaze absorbed the three figures deep into his being, and he thought of all the good which he had experienced in his many years of companionship with Mara. Her voice came from the ship: "Come on the first boat in spring," she called; she was speaking Aramaic, but in the wind and the shouting around them her words could not carry far. And then the ship was already distant from the docks, and despite Matthias's scornful opinion it sped fast before the favourable wind.

Joseph looked after it until he could no longer distinguish any faces, only the gliding outlines of the ship, and in those moments his thoughts were concentrated with their full warmth on Mara. But then, barely had he turned away when it was as if she herself had vanished with the sight of the ship, and he thought only of the lovely winter in Rome which lay before him, of the winter with his son Matthias.

It was a joyous return journey. Joseph and his son rode fast, leaving the groom on his poor borrowed hack far behind. Joseph's spirits were light and gay; he did not feel his years. He chatted with the boy, and fast and merrily his thoughts came and went.

How he loved him, this Matthias, now in truth his eldest. For Simeon was dead and Paulus even more unreachable than if he had been dead. With a little shudder he thought of how Mara was sailing to the country where Paulus lived, an enemy now, the worst enemy imaginable.

But he had his Matthias now. All winter long he would have his Matthias. How different was this Matthias's frankness from his own, however sincere he tried to be. Matthias's nature drew out other people, it won him their hearts; while he, Joseph, had never known how to moderate himself, and when he poured out his feelings to another person, it was sometimes to find that the other, uncomfortably before such lack of restraint, would shrink from him.

How had it happened that his whole love had suddenly concentrated itself on this son of his, Matthias? All those years the boy had lived alongside him, and he, Joseph, had not really seen him at all. Now that he saw him he knew that Matthias was by no means so gifted as Paulus, or even as Simeon. Why, when his plan of bringing up Paulus to be his continuation and fulfilment had failed so badly, did he believe that it must succeed with this Matthias? Why was he putting all his hope in him, giving him all his love?

Why? That was what Matthias was always asking, and very often about questions which no mortal could answer. In such cases Joseph had to put off the boy with a vague answer, or he had to admit directly: I do not know. It was the same for Matthias as it had been so often for him, in his days at school in Jerusalem. When a problem came up about which the Doctors had been quarrelling for decades, perhaps for centuries, how often then—and just at the point where things became most exciting and involved—he had had to content himself with the answer: *Kashya.* But that meant: "A problem, an undecided problem, not settled, not to be answered for the time being."

Quicker than they expected they arrived in Rome. When Joseph had bathed it was afternoon, two hours before sunset, still much too early for dinner. Short as his absence had been, Joseph felt like a man returned from a long journey, and he decided to use the hours until mealtime to take a walk through the city.

Happily he strolled along the lively streets of the bright city, shimmering in the brilliant autumn sunlight. After the long ride it did Joseph good to stretch his legs again. He felt light and free as he had not felt in years. His work was finished, no duties awaited him, no wife with silent, unexpressed admonitions. He was a different man; his years no longer weighed on him; it was as though he had a new skin and a new heart. His thoughts followed different directions from those of the past years. With different eyes he looked at Rome, familiar as it was to him.

He had been in Rome all those years; daily, hourly he had lived in the midst of those streets, temples, and houses, and he had not noticed at all how tremendously it had all changed since the first time he saw it. When he had first entered the city it had been under Nero, shortly after the fire. The city had not been so well planned then, nor so clean; it had been more disorderly, but on the other hand more liberal, more varied, gayer. Today it was more Roman; the Flavians, especially this Domitian, had made it so. The city had more discipline now. The booths of the tradesmen no longer took up half the street, the litter-bearers and pedlars bothered one less, and one no longer ran the risk of stumbling over garbage pails or of being doused with offal from an upper story. The spirit of Norbanus, the spirit of the Chief of Police, ruled the city. Huge and powerful it rose around him; the houses paraded their magnificence insolently, on a gigantic scale; the ancient and the modern were often fitted together by main force; power and wealth were on display. The city showed that it ruled the world. But it no longer showed off with the amiable boasting of the disorderly, liberal Rome of Nero's day; it displayed itself coldly, threateningly. Rome meant order and power, but it was order just for order's sake, power just for power's sake, power without a soul, meaningless power.

Joseph remembered exactly the thoughts and feelings with which he had looked on the city of Rome for the first time. He had wanted to conquer it, to vanquish it by cunning. And in a certain sense he had succeeded; though it had then become

apparent that his victory was a veiled defeat. Now the outlines
of the struggle were clearer. This Rome of Domitian's was
harder, nakeder than the Rome of Vespasian and Titus; there
was nothing in it of the jovial spirit of that Rome which the
young Joseph had conquered. It was harder to conquer; he
who would do so needed more strength; but since it so openly
displayed its whole power one was less likely to make any mistake about the size of the undertaking.

All at once Joseph recognized that, just as in the days of his
youth, he was suddenly filled with a tremendous ambition,
with a burning desire, to conquer the city. Perhaps that was
why he had so violently opposed the idea of leaving Rome.
Perhaps, probably, it was the tempting desire for that fight
which held him here in Rome. For only here could the fight be
carried on. It was a fight with the ruler of Rome, with Domitian.

No, the battle was very far from having been fought to the
finish. Though the Emperor had remained silent so long, it
was not by any means because he had forgotten him; he had
merely postponed the great encounter. But now it was approaching, and if not the Emperor, then Joseph himself would bring
it about. He felt that this was the favourable moment for him.
He had completed his work, he had finished the *Universal
History*—it was the pebble with which the little Joseph would
bring down the giant Domitian. And he felt new strength in
him; it flowed into him from his son; he drew fresh youth
from the youth of his Matthias.

He was so absorbed in his thoughts that he no longer saw or
heard anything around him. But then laughter and cheerful
chatter coming from a small marble building awakened him,
and at once he was no more the heated, ambitious fighter. He
was only a man who had completed the work of many years
and was strolling gaily and relieved of his burden, through the
city which he loved, which in spite of everything had become

his home. Smiling to himself, he listened to the laughter and cheerful chatter issuing from the small marble building. Rome had four hundred such public toilets. Every seat had a sumptuous back of wood or marble, and there the Romans would sit together, comfortably chatting with each other while they relieved themselves. They were experts in comfort—one had to grant them that. They made life easy for themselves. Joseph's amused and bitter smile deepened as he listened to the merry chatter coming out of the handsome white building where the men were relieving themselves. They had comfort, they had abundance, they had power. They had all the externals, everything that did not matter.

Yes, Rome was order, meaningless power; Judæa was God, was the realization of God, was the giving of meaning to power. One could not exist without the other; one complemented the other. But in him, Joseph, the two elements flowed into each other; Rome and Judæa, power and spirit. He had been chosen to reconcile them.

But now enough of those thoughts. For the moment he did not want to have anything to do with all that. He had a long, difficult piece of work behind him; now he wanted to rest.

The walk through the city had made him tired. How huge it was. If he went home on foot it would take him almost an hour. He hired a litter, let down the curtains, shut himself off from the colourful brilliance of the street which had forced itself so violently upon him. He lolled in the twilight of the litter, pleasantly tired, only a tired, hungry man who had a great and successfully completed piece of work behind him and who happily and with an enormous appetite was about to have dinner with his beloved son.

"I CONGRATULATE you, Doctor Joseph," said Claudius Reginus and pressed his hand; it happened rarely that he pressed anyone's hand; usually he contented himself with carelessly touching the other's hand with his fat fingers. "This really is a universal history," he went on. "I learned a lot from it, although your history wasn't entirely unfamiliar to me. You've written an excellent book, and we'll do everything to make the world find that out." It was an unusually warm and decided speech for Reginus, who was habitually sceptical and reserved.

With animation he explained what they could do effectively to publicize the book. The technical side—manufacture and sale—was mainly a question of money, and Claudius Reginus was no skinflint. But where the technical side ended, everything began at once to be a problem. For example, what should the portrait of the author be like, which according to custom they would put in the front of the book? "I don't want to pay you compliments, my dear Joseph," said Claudius Reginus, "but at the moment you look exactly the way I do, that is like an old Jew. Of course I like you the way you are now, but I'm afraid the public will be of a different opinion. How would it be if we stylized the portrait a bit? If we simply painted the elegant, beardless Joseph of the old days, naturally a little aged? My portrait painter Dakon does that kind of thing excellently. By the way, it wouldn't be a bad idea if in your own person you'd let people see a little more of the worldly Josephus just now, instead of the cloistered, withdrawn scholar. For example, it wouldn't do any harm if you had your beard scraped off again."

Joseph took the man's blunt talk in good part, since he felt the sincere respect behind it, and Reginus was an expert. Lately everything was turning out well for Joseph. Reginus's interest almost guaranteed the external success of the book, and Joseph longed for such a success. The period was over in which he had not cared that they had removed his honorary bust from the Temple of Peace. In this new spirit Joseph took advantage of Reginus's good mood to bring up the other matter which now occupied him, Matthias's apprenticeship. It had been very rash of him to have given the boy hope of an apprenticeship at court. Only Claudius Reginus could really help him in this affair.

So Joseph explained the situation to him. It was now more than a year since Matthias had celebrated his *bar mitzvah,* his entrance into the Jewish community, and it was time for him at last to put on the toga and thereby be declared a Roman man and citizen. On that occasion it was customary to announce on what career the young man intended to embark. Joseph wished for himself and for his son that the boy should have a chance to serve his apprenticeship not only in the army and in the government offices but also at court. He was strongly moved to tell Reginus, whom he knew to be his friend, about the problem. "I feel," he explained, "a deeper bond with my Matthias than with my other children. Matthias is to be my fulfilment, my Cæsarion, the perfect fusion of Greek and Jew. I didn't succeed with Paulus." It was the first time that he admitted it so frankly to another person. "He has too much of his Greek heritage in him, the Greek Paulus; he refused to follow my plan. Matthias is entirely my son; he is a Jew and willing."

Reginus lowered his untidily shaven, fleshy head, so that the heavy, sleepy eyes under the bulging forehead were invisible. But he had listened carefully. "Your fulfilment?" he said, catching up the word, and with friendly irony he went on to ask: "Which Joseph is supposed, and which Joseph is going, to fulfil himself in this Matthias, the cloistered scholar or the poli-

tician and soldier? Is he ambitious, your Matthias?" And without waiting for an answer, he concluded: "Bring the boy here
to me in the next few days. I want to have a look at him. And
then I'll see whether I can advise you."

When Joseph accordingly arrived with Matthias a few days
later at the gate of Reginus's villa, where they had been invited, the secretary received them. Reginus had been unexpectedly summoned by the Emperor, but hoped not to have to
make Joseph wait too long. "By the way, here is something
which might interest you," said the secretary with assiduous
politeness, and showed Joseph the portrait which the painter
Dakon had just delivered for the *Universal History*.

A little fearful and yet fascinated, with shining eyes, Joseph
stared at the portrait. But the boy looked at it with even greater
curiosity. The long, brown head, the passionate eyes, the
marked eyebrows, the high, deeply furrowed forehead, the
long, slightly aquiline nose, the thick, glossy black hair, the
thin, curved lips—was this clean-shaven, proud, noble face his
father's? "If I hadn't known," he said, and his deep voice came
from his very red lips with a manly richness, and with such
feeling that the secretary glanced up, "if I hadn't known, I'd
have doubted whether that was you, my father. So that's what
you can be like if you want to." "We all probably have to show
ourselves to the world a little different from what we are," replied Joseph, attempting to joke, a little uncomfortably. He
had almost felt afraid of the ambition with which the boy tried
to idealize his father. But incidentally he decided that he would
now actually follow Reginus's advice and have his beard
shaved off.

The secretary suggested that they take a walk in the park
until Reginus came. It was an extensive garden, the beautiful,
clear autumn weather still held, and it was a pleasant walk.
The air was invigorating; his son's presence made Joseph

young and cheerful; he could talk to Matthias as to an adult and yet as to a child. What eyes the boy had! How eager for life they looked out from under his honest, well-formed forehead. Happy, youthful eyes, they had seen nothing of the horrors of which his were full, they had not seen the burning of the Temple. All that Matthias had had to feel of the sufferings of the Jews had been that one small girl teased him a little.

They came to the peacock run. With boyish pleasure Matthias eyed the showy birds. The keeper came up, and when he saw the interest with which the boy looked at his peacocks he explained his animals at length to his master's guests. The first year there had been seven birds: five came from the famous strain of Didymus, two had been brought directly from India. It was not a good time just now—at the moment the birds had lost a good part of their trains. Only at the end of February, when they were pairing, did their full splendour become apparent.

The keeper told them all this, and Matthias could not hear too much of it. He carried on an animated conversation with the keeper, asked him his name. It turned out that he was from Crete and was called Amphion, and the boy got him to tell them more and more. Matthias stroked the gleaming blue breast of one of the peacocks; it suffered him to do so and that made the keeper also become more confiding, and he told them how difficult the creatures were to handle. They were arrogant, domineering, and greedy. Yet he loved his birds with passion. He managed to get several of them to spread their fans simultaneously, and Matthias was filled with enthusiasm at the play of colours. It was like a meadow of flowers, he said, the thousands of eyes reminded him of a starry sky; and he clapped his hands. But at that the peacocks all at once folded up their splendour and magnificence and rushed apart with ugly screams.

Joseph sat idly on a bench, listened with half an ear, and

made malicious observations to himself. The peacock, he thought, was just the right bird for Rome: gorgeous, screaming, domineering, unbearable, vain, stupid, and greedy. Outward form, appearance, was everything for these Romans.

That Matthias took such an interest in the peacocks did not disturb Joseph. It was only that he was completely a boy, full of interest in everything he saw that was new, and little as he wanted to know about general problems, all the greater was his interest in all concrete, living things. With approval the proud father Joseph saw how well his Matthias and the peacock keeper got on together. He smiled at the boy's enthusiasm. When one looked at him he seemed very mature, but that was an illusion; in reality he was still completely a boy.

With a little smile Joseph noticed also with what innocent eagerness Matthias tried to make as unimportant a man as this keeper like him. Matthias was not actually vain, but he sensed the impression he made, and unconsciously he was always trying to confirm that impression to himself.

Then, finally, Claudius Reginus came waddling toward them. His business at the Palatine had not lasted too long, but now, before they went in to dinner, he wanted to walk a few steps after his drive. He was in a good mood, and it soon became plain that the boy appealed to him. He again spoke about Joseph's work, the *Universal History,* and asked Matthias what he had to say about his father's big book. Matthias, in his deep, manly voice, declared with modest frankness that he was not much of a reader; he had read the *Universal History* a long time, but only the events of recent years as described by Joseph had really stirred him. He probably did not have enough knowledge to grasp the ancient events completely. He said this nicely, it sounded like an apology, but he did not conceal the fact that he did not take his lack of understanding very much to heart. Always what the boy said was average, not particularly clever and not particularly stupid, but always it seemed to be something out of the ordinary because of the fresh and charming way he expressed it.

Joseph had come there to procure his boy a place in service at court; he approved of his son's plans, of his ambition. What Joseph's ancestors had been—scholars, priests, writers, intellectuals—and what he himself was, for that the boy was not suited, and Joseph accepted the fact. Since he himself had decided to let only the contemplative side of his nature fulfil itself, since he had forcibly suppressed the desire for action which he so frequently felt, why should he not now give the boy full scope and every possibility for satisfying his thirst for action? That was what he had told himself; thus it was right and reasonable. Yet he felt a twinge of regret, when he heard the boy chattering along so flatly and glibly about the *Universal History,* that he lacked any feeling for his father's work. He was comforted immediately, however, when he noticed how much the boy appealed to Claudius Reginus. And at the same time, with a kind of naïve calculation, he told himself that it was precisely his son's natural, fresh, and unspoiled personality which would make an impression at the Palatine.

They went in to dinner. Reginus had a famous cook from Alexandria. Matthias ate with a good appetite; Reginus himself grumbled that he was forced to be content with a restricted diet. They talked a lot; it was a merry, harmless conversation, and Joseph was pleased to see how quickly the boy won over even a difficult old codger such as Reginus.

After the meal, without much beating around the bush, Reginus said: "It's obvious, Joseph, that your Matthias has to serve his apprenticeship at the Palatine. We'll have to think over to whom we ought to entrust him as page." The boy's warm brown face flushed with joy. But Joseph's joy, although this was what he had wished for, was not unclouded. For if

Matthias was now going to enter the house and circle of a great gentleman as his young friend, then he, Joseph, would at once be separated from him after having had him to himself for such a short time.

Reginus, in his energetic way, was already discussing practical considerations. "The boy could enter my household," he said; "he wouldn't be badly off here and he could learn all sorts of things from me too. There are many and peculiar pieces of business which the Emperor gives me to do, and your Matthias would learn quickly that on the Palatine the crookedest path is often the shortest. But probably I'm already too much of an old fogy. Or what do you think, my boy?" "I don't know," answered Matthias, smiling frankly. "It's all come so suddenly, if I may speak freely. I do think we'd get along together, and your house and park are simply marvellous, especially the peacocks." "Well, yes," answered Claudius Reginus, "there's a lot to be said for that, but it isn't the decisive factor. The second possibility would be Marullus," he went on, considering. "From him he could learn some valuable things which I couldn't teach him, for example, manners. Otherwise Marullus is as much of an old fogy as I am, and just as un-Roman. Our man must be a Friend of the First Admittance," he reflected, "not too old, and not an anti-Semite. Those are three qualifications hard to find in one person."

Matthias listened quietly while they talked over his future; his lively eyes glanced trustingly from one to the other of the two men. "When do you want him to put on the toga?" Reginus asked unexpectedly. "We can wait three months more," Joseph informed him. "He isn't quite fifteen yet." "He looks manly for his age," said Reginus approvingly. "You know I have an idea about this," he went on in explanation, "but one would have to have some time for it, one would have to feel out the lay of the land, make preparations; one mustn't rush this business."

"Of what are you thinking?" asked Joseph in suspense, and Matthias's eyes too, although he was keeping a well-mannered silence, were fixed on Reginus's lips.

"One might possibly persuade the Empress to take him into her household," Reginus said calmly, in his high, oily voice. "Impossible," said Joseph, recoiling fearfully. "Nothing is impossible," Reginus corrected him, and lapsed into a morose silence. But before long he regained his animation. "At Lucia's he could learn all sorts of things," he explained. "Not only manners and courtly behaviour, but knowledge of human nature, politics, and something which only she has these days: Romanness. Not to mention business dealings. I tell you, my Joseph, that woman with her brick-works is more than a match for an old hand like me." "The Empress!" said Matthias ecstatically. "You really think that would be possible, my Lord Claudius Reginus?" "I don't want to rouse your hopes," answered Reginus, "but it isn't impossible."

Joseph saw the glow in Matthias's face. Thus, almost a generation ago, he himself had glowed, no doubt, when he was told that the Empress Poppæa awaited him. Something like fear overcame him. But immediately he shook it off. "That girl Cecilia," he thought, "was wrong in any case. My Matthias won't end up on the right bank of the Tiber."

For the time being the *Universal History* had no real success, in spite of Reginus's efforts. Most of the Jewish readers found the work too cold. They had expected an enthusiastic representation of their great past; instead here was a book which sought to persuade the Greeks and Romans to accept the Jews into the circle of civilized peoples with a great past. Was that necessary? Had not they, the Jews, a much older, prouder history than those pagans? Did they, God's chosen people, have to beg humbly not to be looked upon as barbarians?

But neither did the Greeks and Romans give Joseph's work a warm reception. True, many found the book interesting, but they did not dare to express their opinions. The Emperor had ordered the bust of the writer Josephus to be removed from the Temple of Peace; it was not advisable to be enthusiastic about him.

There was one solitary group of readers who dared to praise the book openly and loudly, and that was made up of people on whose approval Joseph had least counted: the Minæans or Christians. When an author dealt with them they were accustomed to having him mock or attack them. All the more astonished were they that this Josephus not only did not rail against them, but that he even presented with respect the lives and beliefs of certain forerunners of their Messiah. In their opinion the book was a lay supplement to the story of their Saviour.

The man whose judgment Joseph awaited with greatest fear and suspense remained silent. Justus remained silent. Finally Joseph invited him to his house. Justus did not come; whereupon Joseph called on him.

"In the thirty years that we have known each other," said Justus, "you haven't changed and I haven't changed. So why do you bother me? You know anyway in advance what I have to say about your book." But Joseph persisted. He almost longed for the pain which the other would inflict on him, and he pressed Justus until he spoke.

"Your book is lukewarm and undecided, like everything you've done," Justus finally declared, and he uttered that unpleasant nervous titter which so irritated Joseph. "Tell me, what are you really trying to do in your book?" "I wanted the Jews to learn," answered Joseph, "to see their history objectively at last." "Then," Justus rejoined sharply, "you should have written much more coldly. But for that you didn't have the courage. You were afraid of the criticism of the general mass of Jews." "Furthermore," Joseph defended himself sullenly, "I wanted to arouse enthusiasm in the Greeks and Romans for the great history of our people." "Then," Justus declared immediately and mercilessly, "you should have written more warmly, with a great deal more enthusiasm. But you didn't dare to do that; you were afraid of the criticism of the experts. It's the way I said," he concluded. "Your book isn't warm and it isn't cold; it's a lukewarm book; it's a bad book." The sullen opposition on Joseph's face drew him on to express pitilessly everything that he had against the book. "No one knows better than you that the ends which underlie a policy may be moral or immoral, but the means never. The means can only be useful or harmful, in respect to the desired ends. But you arbitrarily confound measure for weight, you measure political occurrences by moral standards, although you know perfectly well that that's nothing but stupid, lazy, cheap convention. You know perfectly well that the individual may be evaluated by moral standards, but never a group, a mass, a people. An army can't be brave; it consists of brave and cowardly men; you experienced that, you know it, but you don't want to admit it. A people can't be stupid or pious; it consists of stupid and clever men, of saints and rascals; you know that, you experienced it, but you don't want to admit it. You always confound the values for the sake of effect, out of cheap caution. You haven't written a historical book, you've written a moral tract for blockheads. You haven't even succeeded in that; for you wanted to write for both sides, and so haven't even had the courage to use the demagogy at which you excel."

Joseph listened and no longer defended himself. Although Justus, his hostile friend, exaggerated immeasurably, there was some truth in his objections. One thing at any rate was true:

the book on which he had spent so many years, so much life, was not a success. He had forced himself to remain cold in face of the history of his people and to look upon it reasonably. By doing so he had driven all life out of those events. Everything was half true and therefore quite false. Now, when he read over his book, he recognized that everything was seen crookedly. His stifled feelings revenged themselves, they rose up again with twice as much vigour; the reader Joseph did not believe a word of the writer Joseph. He had committed a basic error. He had written entirely according to the dictates of his rational judgment and often against his feelings—that was why large parts of his book were lifeless, worthless; for the living word springs into being only when feeling and judgment coincide.

All this was cruelly clear to Joseph; all this he told himself harshly and unsparingly. But then he put away his book, the *Universal History,* once and for all. Whether successful or not, he had given what he had been able to give, he had done his duty, had struggled, worked, denied himself many things; now he had laid down the work, and, free of it, he wished to continue his life for himself. The portrait which Reginus had set in the front of the book had made him see how old he had grown. He had not much more time. He did not want to waste the rest of his strength in brooding. Let Justus philosophize; now he wanted to live.

And a thousand wishes and thoughts arose in him which he had believed long dead. He was glad that they were not dead. He was glad that he still felt thirst, that he thirsted again for deeds, for women, for success.

He was glad that he was in Rome and not in Judæa. He had his beard shaved off, and presented to the world the naked face of the earlier Joseph. It was harder, sharper, but it was a younger face than he had worn during all the past years.

The crooked old house in the suburbs now suddenly became too cramped and mean for him, although Mara and the children were gone. He went to see John of Gishala and asked him to find him an elegant modern house which he might rent. On that occasion he had a long talk with John. The land dealer had read the *Universal History* with attention, and spoke about it with animation and understanding. Joseph, of course, knew that John was not an objective judge. He had a very active life behind him, rather like Joseph's own; at bottom he was frustrated, and so he tended to look upon the history of the Jewish people in the same light as did Joseph himself and to mistrust all enthusiasm. Nevertheless, John's recognition pleased Joseph and comforted him a little for Justus's condemnation.

He became talkative; now that he was living alone with Matthias in Rome he opened up much more easily than in the old days. He told John about his plans for Matthias. John was sceptical. "It's true that the times still permit a Jew to satisfy his ambition," he said. "You've accomplished a lot, Joseph, admit it freely; Caius Barzaarone has accomplished a lot; I've accomplished a few things. But I consider it wiser not to make a display of what we've accomplished, not to show the others too clearly our money, our might, our influence. It only arouses envy, and for that we're not strong enough, for that we're too isolated." Joseph's face had been joyful when he had told John about his hopes and doubts; now the joy was extinguished. John saw that, did not insist, but added. "If you want to accomplish anything for your Matthias, you should abandon your plan of going to Judæa in the spring in any case. I'd be glad," he added courteously, "to see you stay longer in Rome." Joseph said to himself that John was a good friend and was right in both his criticisms. If he found one of the gentlemen at the Palatine to be friend and patron to Matthias, then of course he

would have to stay longer in Rome; also if he moved into a
new house it would only make sense if he made arrangements
for a longer stay. But at heart he was glad to postpone his trip
to Judæa, his return to Judæa, and every excuse was welcome;
for, oddly enough, it seemed to him as if the return to Judæa
would mean the final renunciation of everything which required a little youth, as if by that return he would declare himself once and for all an old man. And as far as John's other
warning was concerned—that it was unwise to strive for external glory and honours—his friend was probably right about
that. But Joseph had seen the glow of joy on his boy's face; he
could not hurt Matthias by abandoning the plan now, he could
not do that to Matthias, or to himself.

The new house was found quickly, and Joseph set about
furnishing it. Matthias helped him enthusiastically; he had a
thousand suggestions. Joseph was now seen frequently about
the city; he sought the society of others. While before he had
spent months alone and shut off from the world, now he appeared almost daily in Marullus's, in Reginus's circle. Benevolently, a little mockingly, and with a slight tinge of anxiety,
his friends observed the change. Matthias loved and admired
him even more.

Joseph spoke to Claudius Reginus about John's misgivings.
In Reginus's opinion John was a clever man, but he could no
longer really understand the new times, or a Jewish younger
generation which had not seen the burning of the Temple and
for whom the State was nothing but a historical memory, a
legend. He, Reginus, was in a certain sense an example of the
fact that even the most conspicuous power did not always bring
misfortune upon a Jew. Joseph did not like that example too
well; under no circumstances had he wanted Matthias to abandon his Judaism as completely as Claudius Reginus had done.
Yet he willingly let him strengthen him in his decision. He

listened avidly when Reginus informed him that he had been doing a little listening around at the Palatine among people who were kindly disposed. Although at first everyone had been actually staggered at the boldness of the idea of making a Jewish boy page to the Empress, in the end most of them had thought that the novelty of the idea did not exclude the possibility of its realization. So he, Reginus, was of the opinion that they could now set to work. He suggested to Joseph that he should publicly celebrate Matthias's investiture with the toga in the Roman manner although that was not customary. To blunt the point of any derisive comments in advance, Joseph should invite to this celebration the Empress, who was now as always kindly disposed toward him. It had been criminal carelessness for Joseph to have made such scant use of the favour which Lucia had shown him from time to time. But now he had a good chance to make up for lost opportunities. He should bring the Empress his new book and on that occasion invite her to Matthias's feast. The worst that could happen would be a refusal, and after all he had swallowed worse defeats.

The idea appealed to Joseph; yes, the proposal tempted him. He was a man in his late fifties; his feelings were no longer what they had been when, tense in every fibre, he had gone to see the Empress Poppæa; but he was more excited than he had been for a long time as he entered Lucia's presence, book in hand.

Claudius Reginus had skilfully prepared the way for him; he had told Lucia about Joseph's transformation. Yet she was surprised as he now appeared before her with his clean-shaven, rejuvenated face. "Well, well, look at this," she said. "Now the bust has disappeared, but to make up for it the man has transformed himself into the bust again. I'm glad to see that, my Josephus." Her bright face, fresh although her first youth was past, openly radiated her pleasure. "I'm glad that the book's here now, and that the old Joseph is back again. I've kept the whole morning free for you. We must have a good, long chat for once."

Joseph was elated by this warm reception. Inwardly, it was true, he mocked at himself a little and thought he was the same fool as an ageing man that he had been as a youth; yet his heart swelled almost as it once did in the presence of the Empress Poppæa. "What I like about you," said Lucia commendingly, "is that, for all your philosophy and art, at bottom you're an adventurer." That was praise which did not overly please Joseph. But she at once interpreted her words in a way that must flatter him. It meant little, she said, if a man became an adventurer who came from nothing, who therefore gave up little. However, if a man who from the beginning had possessed great estates and security chose to be an adventurer, it was proof of a lively, restless soul. Such adventurers of the soul and not of external circumstance had been Alexander and Cæsar. She herself felt something of such an adventuress in her, and between such aristocratic adventurers of all periods there existed a secret kinship.

Later she asked Joseph to read aloud to her from his book, and he did so without standing on ceremony. He read to her the stories of Jael, Jezebel, and Athalia. And he also read her the stories about the wild, proud, ambitious women at Herod's court, from one of whom he was descended.

Lucia's comments surprised Joseph. For him the people whom he described were not of the real world; they performed on a stage which he himself had built; they were stylized, they were creatures of air. That Lucia looked upon these characters of his as if they were people of flesh and blood who were walking around on earth—that was something new to him, and it disturbed him. At the same time it delighted him that he had thus, as a little god, created a living world. He and Lucia got along excellently together.

It did not need much courage for him to broach the subject of his visit. He told her about his son Matthias, that in the next weeks he would put on the toga. "I've heard," said Lucia, "that he's a nice boy." "He's a wonderful boy," declared Joseph enthusiastically. "What a proud father you are," said Lucia, smiling.

He invited her to attend the feast which he intended to give on the occasion of Matthias's investiture. A slight shadow passed over Lucia's face which mirrored every feeling. "I'm certainly no enemy of the Jews," she said, "but won't it seem a little odd if you of all people celebrate that festival so demonstratively? I'm not so well versed in the origins of our customs as Vellykins. But isn't the ceremony of the investiture with the toga above all a religious act? I don't believe that Roman culture and the service of the gods always coincide, but I'm pretty certain that in the case of this ceremony of investiture our gods have something to do with it also. I'm the last person to interfere with your relations with your fellow-countrymen, but I fear that your Jews won't be very happy either if you make so much of that ceremony. I'm not refusing your invitation," she added hastily, when she saw that Joseph grew gloomy as she stated her misgivings, "but as your friend I ask you to consider it all carefully before you arrive at your final decision."

Joseph was much struck by the fact that Lucia's objections were very much like John's. But in the meantime his decision had only become firmer. He had brought his son into the Jewish community through the *bar mitzvah;* why should he not in a similar fashion take him into the Roman, to which after all he belonged? It seemed to him symbolical to celebrate both ceremonies magnificently, and if that gave rise to misinterpretations—it had been his experience that everything he did and did not do was misinterpreted. Also, he had already promised Matthias this feast, he looked forward to it with such childlike joy, and Joseph could not bring himself to inflict an enormous disappointment on his beloved son.

He gave Lucia a half-answer, thanked her for her advice, promised to think over everything once again; but in his inmost heart he was firmly determined. At home, half jokingly, half seriously, he asked Matthias: "If someone asks you whether you're a Roman or a Jew, what do you answer?" Matthias, in his deep voice, said laughing: "I'd answer: don't ask such a stupid question. I'm Flavius Matthias, son of Flavius Josephus." Joseph was pleased by the reply. The misgivings of the others seemed to him more and more to fade away. Should he, Joseph, show less courage than old Claudius Reginus, who saw no danger in sending the boy to the Palatine?

They began the celebration. Matthias went about walking on air. He invited the girl Cecilia. She gave him one of her snappish answers. He informed her that the Empress would attend his feast. Cecilia grew quite pale.

Since Joseph had to avoid everything which might be interpreted as worship of a Roman divinity, as idol worship, he was forced to resort to a number of evasions in the ceremonial of the feast. There was no altar to the domestic gods in Joseph's house, nor did Matthias wear the golden amulet of the Roman boy which he could have hung up on that altar. So the actual ceremony in the house was limited to Matthias's exchanging the bordered toga of the boy for the pure white one of the man. The simple new costume became him magnificently; his young yet already manly face, at once happy and serious, was set off by the plain, pure robe.

Then Joseph and a huge company of friends, at their head the Empress, brought the young man into the Forum on the southern side of the Capitoline, to the archives, that there he might have his name solemnly inscribed on the lists of those granted the rights of citizenship. And from that moment on the boy was called Flavius Matthias Josephus. The Empress set on his finger the gold ring which marked his admittance to the second rank.

Then, while the non-Jewish guests betook themselves to Joseph's house, where the banquet was to be held, Joseph himself, Matthias, and the Jewish guests attended to a piece of business which was to be the talk of the city, even of the Empire, for weeks afterward. Custom prescribed that the young citizen go to the Temple of the Goddess of Youth, there to offer a coin and perform a sacrifice. Since the Jew Matthias could not do this, he went instead, accompanied by his father and his friends, to the proper office of the treasury, had himself entered on the lists of Jews, and paid the double drachma which, since the destruction of the Temple, the Jews had to deliver to the Capitoline Jupiter instead of to Jehovah. That Joseph made a festive act out of the payment of the tax which had been intended as a disgrace caused many of the Jews to forgive him for having had his boy declared a Roman in such demonstrative fashion.

Joseph's courage appealed to the Empress. Joseph's son also appealed to her. She had noticed with what princely poise he had behaved in that proud hour when she had set the ring of the second rank upon his finger; now during the banquet she was told that he had undergone the ignominy of being registered in the list of Jews with the same simple grace. The boy sat beside her. His eyes were fixed upon her with boyish worship yet he did not become self-conscious. She talked to him. He obviously knew how well the white toga became him, and he knew that the eyes of everyone were fixed upon him, yet his fresh and natural behaviour did not suffer from it.

Claudius Reginus had already prepared Lucia for Joseph's

asking her to take his son into her service. Everyone could see that the boy appealed to her, so Joseph could be sure that he would not ask in vain. Still he did not present his request with the sureness which was his at other times, and Lucia too gave her consent in a strangely veiled voice, and within her and on her face there was an unaccustomed confusion.

Joseph's heart was aflame with joy. He had raised his beloved son to the position of which he had dreamed for him. But he had a sensitive ear, and in all his rejoicing he did not forget the voices of the friends who had warned him.

So henceforth Matthias was in the Empress's retinue and lived for the most part at the Palatine. It happened as Joseph had foreseen: Matthias, Lucia's young Jewish adjutant, with his air of young manhood, charming and cheerfully serious as he was, gave the impression of something out of the ordinary especially at the Palatine. People spoke much about him, many sought his friendship, and women encouraged him. He remained unself-conscious, it seemed natural to him that things happened as they did, and probably it did not mean so very much to him; yet he would have missed being the centre of attention, being sought after.

That Matthias was in the Empress's retinue brought Joseph also into much closer contact with her. Lucia had already crossed his path several times, but never had he seen her with such receptive eyes as now. Her robustness, her merrily bold frankness, the Roman brightness and vitality which emanated from her, her mature, womanly beauty—all that made a much deeper impression on him now than ever before. He was an ageing man, but with amazement he observed that since the days when he had burned with passion for Dorion the company of a woman had not so disturbed him as did his present meetings with Lucia. He did not disguise his emotion, and she was pleased by it. Much that he said, and much that she said, was now ambiguous; half-phrases passed between them, and their looks and gestures become equivocal. He read all kinds of symbolical meanings into their relationship. If she attracted him so much, if she too was not unresponsive toward him, was that not a symbol? Was it not an image of the mysterious relation between victor and vanquished? Once he could not resist hinting something of this nature to Lucia. But she simply laughed outright and said: "You just want to sleep with me, my dear fellow; and that you look for such deep meanings behind it is proof that you yourself are aware how impudent you actually are."

In that period Joseph lived a serene, happy life. He enjoyed what had been vouchsafed him; it seemed to him very much. He was now seeing Lucia daily; they understood each other better and better, forgave each other's weaknesses, and enjoyed each other's virtues. And for Joseph's beloved, radiant son everything was turning out as he had wished. Bright and pure he walked through the Palatine which was filled with so many disorders and vices; the whole world loved him; no envy and no enmity touched him. Yes, the Deity loved Joseph. It showed that by bestowing so many pleasures on him, now before he finally crossed the threshold of old age, while he still possessed the strength to enjoy them.

There was much talk about Joseph and his son in the city of Rome; too much, thought the Jews. And there came to Joseph a delegation from the Jews consisting of Masters Caius Barzaarone and John of Gishala. Anxiously they asked him to consider that his good fortune and glory would arouse even more envy and more enmity against the Jews if he displayed them so openly. Hatred and oppression were increasing throughout the Empire as it was. "If a Jew is happy," warned John of Gishala as he had once before, "he should keep his happiness within his four walls and not display it in the streets."

Yet Joseph remained unreceptive, obstinate. His son Matthias simply was a radiant person, and it was the characteristic of light to be visible. Should he hide his beloved son? He would not think of it. He was infatuated with his beautiful, lovable son and his good fortune.

And he tossed the words of the men to the winds, and continued to enjoy his lot. He reaped successes where he willed and as many as he willed. There was only one thing which offended him. His book, his *Universal History,* was now as before without visible effect.

And on top of everything a book appeared called *The Jewish War,* by Justus of Tiberias—published, moreover, like his own works, by Claudius Reginus. It was a history at which Justus had been working for decades.

Joseph's own book about the Jewish War had had the greatest success of all the prose works of the period. The whole reading public of the Empire had read that *Jewish War,* not only for its subject matter, but above all for its attractive presentation; Vespasian and Titus had supported the book and highly honoured its author; the work had already acquired, a brief generation after its appearance, the stature of a classic. So it was an enormous piece of audacity for Justus to publish a book on the same subject at this time.

Joseph had read a part of the book many years before, and he himself and his own achievement were paltry and miserable when confronted with Justus and his book. With actual fear he now read his hostile friend's completed work. Justus painstakingly avoided all big words and every obvious effect. His presentation was one of hard, crystalline objectivity. Nor did it ever occur to him to inveigh against Joseph's book. But he

mentioned Joseph's activity during the war, his actions at the time when he had been commissioner in Galilee, the activity, in short, of Joseph the statesman and soldier. He presented only the facts; he refrained from any evaluation. But just through that naked presentation, just because of it, Joseph appeared as a pure opportunist, a miserable, vain fellow, a man who harmed the cause which he had undertaken to represent.

Joseph read on. He had in his day constructed a glittering legend about his activity in Galilee, he had skilfully set forth that legend in his book, and he had finally believed it himself, and with his book the legend of his personality had gradually been recognized as historical truth. Now, in Justus's book, the ageing man saw the war as it had really been; he saw himself as he had really been; he also saw the book which he had wanted so much to write—only it was Justus who had written it, not he.

He saw all that. But he did not want to see it; he could not see it if he wanted to go on living.

Full of suspense he waited to see what would happen to Justus's work, what people would say about it. Not much was made of Justus's book. There were, it was true, a few who recognized the importance of the history; they were people whose judgment Joseph valued highly, but they were very few. Still Joseph was forced to recognize that in the eyes of those few Justus's work eclipsed his own writing. He was forced to recognize that Justus had discredited his, Joseph's, activity, that Justus was regarded by those few as the final, true, incorruptible judge.

Joseph made an effort to forget the bitter taste of that recognition. He told himself that as a writer he had been spoiled as almost no other man among his contemporaries, and that the opinion of the few had no weight against his fame, which in spite of everything was well founded. But that helped not at all; the bitter taste remained. Yes, the bitter taste grew more bitter. Joseph was the friend and favourite of the Empress, he had procured for his beloved son a position which the boy and he himself had desired. He had, as soon as he had so wished, again become one of the men who were well in the forefront and focus of public attention. But the bitter taste spoiled his satisfaction in all those pleasures.

He told himself that he had become peevish, and old, and that he could no longer perceive anything but the disagreeable and never the pleasant. Then again he told himself that he had let his faith in himself and in his work be destroyed by Justus's immoderate, envious criticism. He brought out his *Universal History*. He read a few chapters of it, the best, and told himself stubbornly that what Justus had advanced against him was nonsense.

But in the end it remained a fact that the *Universal History,* on which he had lavished so many pains, was not a real success, in spite of all Reginus's efforts. He was accustomed to all the accidents of success and failure, but at this particular moment he needed reassurance from outside, at this particular moment he needed literary success. All his other achievements were of no use to him. The only thing which could help him would be reverberations of the *Universal History,* reverberations so loud that they would drown out the voice of Justus. He had to have reassurance now, if only for his beloved son's sake, to further his career.

Sullenly, accusingly, he asked Reginus what was responsible for the fact that the success of the *Universal History* was not developing at all. Reginus rather reluctantly explained to him that the main obstacle was the Emperor's attitude. Those whose judgment was of importance did not dare to express their opinion of the work so long as they did not know what the Emperor would say. Even if D.D.D. spoke against his work it would be an advantage, for then at least one would have the opposition on one's side. But D.D.D., crafty as he was, kept silent, and expressed not even an unfavourable opinion; he expressed no opinion at all. He, Reginus, had tried to break that hostile silence. He had asked Vellykins whether Joseph might present him with a copy of the book. But Vellykins had avoided hearing the question, as only Vellykins knew how, and had said neither yes nor no.

Gloomily and with great annoyance Joseph listened to him. The thoughts with which he had returned to Rome after he had sent Mara to Judæa rose up in him again. At that time he had looked forward to the fight with Domitian, to the fight with Rome. He had felt a fresh youth in himself, and he had thought that he had a weapon in his completed book. But now the Emperor evaded the encounter. He simply would not take a stand.

What Reginus went on to say only confirmed this belief of Joseph's. D.D.D., Reginus told him, had not uttered the name Joseph for ever so long. That was odd. He must certainly have heard about Joseph's new friendship with Lucia, about the defiant way in which Joseph had had his son registered in the list of Jews, and about Lucia's new Jewish page. If, moreover, the Emperor was not thinking of making use of his power and simply destroying Joseph, then from D.D.D.'s viewpoint, these tactics were the wisest. For his silence, D.D.D.'s silence, diffused silence all around the book, a silence which would finally smother it.

Joseph thought over what he might do to break that crafty silence, to draw the Emperor, his enemy, out of ambush, to force him to take a stand. It was the custom, upon the appearance of a book, for the author to give a reading from it before a large audience. Joseph had not wanted to do this when his work was published; at that time there was in him still too much of the mood in which the *Universal History* had been created. The Joseph who had written the *Universal History* had scorned the public. To that Joseph it would have been absolutely indifferent what Domitian thought or said about the book. But the Joseph who now sat before Claudius Reginus was a different man. "How would it be," he suggested, "if we held a recitation, if I read aloud from the *Universal History?*"

Reginus glanced up in amazement. If Joseph, after he had preserved silence so long, again appeared before the public eye it would be a sensation. Such a public reading was perhaps the only means, if there were any, to draw the Emperor out of his reserve. The plan tempted Reginus, yet he did not conceal from Joseph that the undertaking would be very dangerous. It was daring to challenge the Emperor to an expression of opinion. Joseph, however, since Reginus had not refused point-blank, was already all afire with his plan. Like an actor who hungers for a new part he advanced all the arguments in favour of the undertaking to Reginus and to himself. He did not read badly; the slight Eastern accent in his Greek appealed to people more than it offended them; after he had not let himself be heard from for such a long time all Rome would be curious about his appearance in public. And then, overcoming a slight feeling of embarrassment, he confessed to Reginus, to his friend, the secret wish which had arisen in him with the first thought of such a recitation. "And what a pleasure," he said, "it would be to shine before the boy, before Matthias."

That evidence of the naïve vanity of a doting father won over Reginus completely, and he said: "It still is a devilishly risky business; but if you want to risk it, you old youngster, I'll go along with you."

Joseph took the greatest pains with the preparations for his reading. For a long time he talked over with his friends where the lecture should take place. Reginus, Marullus, above all

Lucia, discussed the question as if it were a matter of State policy. Should the reading take place at Joseph's house, before a small, select circle? Or before a larger audience at Marullus's house or at Reginus's? Or perhaps even at the Palatine itself in the great hall of Lucia's house?

Lucia had an idea. How would it be if Joseph held his reading in the Temple of Peace?

In the Temple of Peace? In the building from which the Emperor had ordered his bust to be removed? Was that not a tremendous challenge? Would not the great hall lie empty then, because no one would dare to take part in such dangerous proceedings? Was there not a possibility that the Emperor would have Joseph arrested immediately before his reading?

Lucia said: "We're not getting anywhere this way. We always come up against the same stumbling-block: D.D.D. I'm not going to stand for it any longer. He wants to undermine us by his tactics. He wants to murder our Josephus with his silence. But he won't succeed there. I want to know where we stand. I'm going to see him."

WHEN Lucia was announced, Domitian guessed at once that it would be about the Jew or his son.

During the last months he had encountered Lucia only rarely. He was out of temper most of the time; he was getting fatter and slacker in body; he had used a great number of women without their having given him any real pleasure. He received exact reports about everything which happened in Lucia's circle. Suspiciously, maliciously, he considered the fact that now she had taken the young Jew into her court, the son of that dangerous Josephus. Since Josephus was getting old, he was probably having his son take his place.

The Emperor received Lucia politely, with distant, ironical amiability. They talked for some time about indifferent subjects. Lucia looked at the fat, bald, ageing gentleman; he was not many years older than she, yet he was old and she was young. She had the feeling that he was more a stranger to her than he had been for years, she had little power over him any more, and she asked herself whether perhaps she would not do better to abandon her plan and not even speak about Joseph. But then her natural audacity overcame her caution.

She had lately, she began, advancing toward her intended subject, heard a lot about the persecution of the Jews in the provinces, and about petty annoyances to which the Jews in the city itself were subjected. She had, as he knew, Jewish friends, so she was interested in this problem. She felt that he too, the Emperor, should occupy himself with these matters. "You once explained to me, my dear Domitian," she reminded him, "that there was a war between you and the Eastern God. If I were you I'd think over every step in that war ten times before I took it. I myself, as you know," she smiled, "am a little lukewarm in the performance of religious duties, but I am a good Roman and believe in the gods. Even if I don't do much to show my reverence, I do avoid everything which might offend them. But now with the greatness of the Empire the number of its gods has also increased. I think, Domitian, we are agreed on the point that you as censor are ordained to protect all the gods of the Empire. I don't know whether you are thoroughly informed about this difficult God Jehovah whom you consider your enemy. He is a difficult God, and perhaps it would be wise if you would inform yourself as exactly as possible about His character and being."

"Are you thinking about our Jew Josephus, my Lucia?" asked Domitian, smiling very politely, and he looked into her large, bright face with his near-sighted, somewhat protruding eyes. "Yes," she answered without evasion, "Josephus has published a book on which he's been working for many years, and in my opinion it's a book which we Romans should read with the greatest attention. When you have read this book, Domitian, you'll be much better informed about the character of your enemy, the God Jehovah."

"Do you remember, Lucia," answered the Emperor, still very politely, "that after I had read parts of that book I ordered the bust of this Josephus of ours to be removed from the Temple of Peace?" "I remember very well," replied Lucia. "I already asked myself at the time whether that grave insult to a great writer, a man to whom Rome was indebted, was not rather hasty. After having read his book I'm convinced that it was. I advise you strongly, my Lord and God Domitian, to read the book. Then I'll leave all further steps up to your good judgment."

"Go right ahead and finish what you have to say, my Lucia," said the Emperor, and now his smile had turned into a grin, but he spoke especially softly and especially politely. "What do you want me to do?" Lucia felt that today she had little power over him. Again, for a very short moment, she thought of giving up her intention. But after all she made one more attempt, in a different way, in her old way. She went up quite close to him and stroked his ever-thinning hair. "You must have lost at least twenty-seven hairs," she said, "since I last counted them. There would be a very simple means," she went on without transition, "by which you could rectify the injustice which you did this writer and perhaps his God, and at the same time receive instruction from ordained lips about the God Jehovah. For example, you'd only have to attend a reading which our Josephus is planning to hold with your permission."

"Interesting," answered Domitian, "very interesting. So my Josephus, our Josephus, your Josephus wants to read aloud from his new book. And you like it very much, this new book? You really think it's very good?" "If it weren't for your silence," she answered with conviction, "the whole world would be saying it was by a second Livy. Even when his first book appeared, under Vespasian and Titus, they called him that. Only now, since you had the bust melted down, people have become more cautious."

The Emperor made a little grimace. "True," he said, "my father liked to converse with him, and Titus valued and loved him. Perhaps you did your part in making Titus value and love him. And so now you want to convert me also to show honour to your favourite's new book. Let me tell you, in case you don't know it, that I already am acquainted with certain parts of the book. They are neither boring nor interesting. And about the other parts, people tell me, people who certainly aren't hostile to your Josephus, that they're a little long-winded and neither hot nor cold." "It would be a good thing," Lucia insisted, "if you would hear them yourself and form your own opinion. I'm honestly convinced that it wouldn't harm you to find out more about Jehovah."

A very slight feeling of uneasiness overcame Domitian at her warning. He eyed Lucia's bold, open face, which made no effort to conceal her anger and sympathy. "You really take great interest in your favourite, my Lucia," he said. "He couldn't find a more zealous champion." Distrust, jealousy sounded in his spiteful words. Lucia noticed it. So Vellykins thought she was sleeping with Josephus. She pictured it to herself. She smiled. Then she looked at Domitian and simply laughed outright.

But he was relieved by that laugh. For all his distrust, he had never seriously thought of a love affair between Lucia and that Jew. She was very Roman, although in somewhat devious fashion, and that God Jehovah and His people must seem strange and somewhat ridiculous to her. "Do you want to stay and have dinner with me, my Lucia?" he asked. "And then we'll think over further what we should do about your Joseph."

Public readings were popular in the city of Rome. People were convinced that the spoken word made a deeper and more lasting impression than the written, and that it expressed more of the author's personality. In the last years, however, there had been an excess of readings, people had had a little too much of them, and at the present moment authors who gave readings no longer found it easy to fill their halls; people sought all kinds of excuses to evade attendance at such affairs. Joseph's reading, however, was an event to which the whole city thronged. The official bulletin had announced that the Emperor would attend the performance. People came from far off to hear Joseph. It was not only the sensation which drew them, but now, since the Emperor had indicated by his promise to be present that there was no longer any objection to the author, there were many—Romans, Greeks, and Jews —who were glad to declare publicly that they supported the writer and his work.

Joseph prepared himself for the reading more carefully than he had ever prepared for any event. Ten times he looked up the chapters which he intended to read, chose, rejected, chose, and rejected again; there were political and literary considerations to be weighed; boldness and timidity swayed him in turn. He took counsel with his friends, read the chosen passages aloud to them to try them out, like a beginnner.

He devoted attention to preparing his outward appearance as well. Like an actor or a young coxcomb he thought over his costume and haircut, debated whether the hand which was to hold the manuscript would be better adorned or bare. And he took potions and drugs to make his voice strong and flexible. He did not know before whom he wished to shine the most: before the Emperor, before Lucia, before the Romans and Greeks, before the literary circles, his friends and rivals, before the Jews, before Justus, or before Matthias.

When the hour arrived he felt in good form and sure of himself. His barber and Lucia's facial specialist had worked on his head at length, he looked masculine and impressive, and his eyes gazed out over his audience with fire and yet with composure. Everyone who was of any importance in Rome was there: the Emperor's friends, because of course they were not allowed to be absent when their master was present, the Emperor's enemies, because they considered it a confession of defeat that the Emperor appeared at the reading of a writer in a place whence he had banished that writer's bust. So Joseph saw them all, saw and recognized them: Lucia, to whom he felt deeply indebted, the Emperor, his mighty enemy, young and radiant Matthias whom he loved, the writers, waiting for every weakness he might expose. He saw that whole sea of light and dark faces; he felt confident; he looked forward to making them all bow to him, to his work, to his faith.

First he read some chapters from the early history of his people, the warmest and proudest he had been able to find. He read well, and what he read was suited to hold the interest of an unprejudiced public. His listeners were scarcely prejudiced, but they did not dare to express their opinion. They all felt that every utterance, approval as well as disapproval, might become dangerous; they knew that Norbanus's and Messalinus's agents were keeping their eyes and ears open and sharply watching the listeners' hands and lips. Even Reginus's claque had been instructed not to put itself forward so long as the Emperor himself gave no sign.

But Domitian gave no sign. He sat there, upright, imperially clad although not in full gala dress, his·arms angularly pressed back, exuding gravity and discomfort. With his protruding, rather near-sighted eyes he stared now at Joseph, now straight in front of him; at one moment he closed his eyes, then again he coughed; he listened politely, yet it was very possible that he was bored.

For the Empress, Domitian's behaviour was profoundly annoying. She looked upon the occasion as her own affair, and D.D.D. knew it. She waited in suspense to see whether he would persist in his attitude through the whole reading. For in the latter half Josephus wanted to read a few chapters from the sixteenth book of his history, a section which related the story of Herod's family in a grand and deeply stirring vein. Too bad that he would be able to read only the beginning and early complications of the plot—the intricate and strange relations of the Jewish king to his sons, how those sons were slandered and how he had them arrested and brought to trial. But unfortunately he would not be able to read the conclusion of the story, namely, how Herod cruelly put those sons to death. For if Josephus read that passage, the listeners would be painfully reminded of D.D.D.'s execution of Princes Sabinus and Clemens. Lucia was sorry that her Josephus was therefore forced to omit the best part, the end of the story and his especially well-put evaluation of King Herod.

Still, the events which preceded the execution were told with great power, Joseph read excellently, one could see that

what he read excited him anew, and Lucia noticed to her satisfaction with what interest people were listening. But the Emperor's face and attitude did not change. Then Lucia could
not stand it any more; she would not maintain a subservient
and well-mannered silence any longer. When Joseph had finished a passage that was written with particular vigour and
yet with great calm, she clapped, and called out her approval
in her loud, ringing voice. A few joined her; even the claque
made an effort. But most of the audience looked at the Emperor, and as he remained silent, they too remained silent and
did not stir.

Joseph heard the applause; he saw Lucia's face and the loving, admiring, happy face of his son Matthias. But he also saw
the rigid, cool, negative face of the Emperor, of his enemy. He
knew that it was a question of one thing and one thing only:
he must force that expression to change. He saw that the man,
his enemy, was determined to continue his tactics of silence,
not to let his face be moved, and thus to bury his, Joseph's
work for ever. At that an immeasurable fury seized him, and
he swore to himself: "Yet will I force that face to move."

And he did not stop reading at the intended point, but read
on beyond. At first with dismay, then with a growing excitement made up of alarm at such madness, admiration for so
much courage and wild suspense as to what would now
happen, Lucia, Marullus, and Reginus—those who knew Joseph's book—heard him continue his story. With beautiful expression, in well-turned phrases, with bitter and indignant
calm, he told how the Jewish King Herod brought his sons
to court and had them put to death.

While he read he knew perfectly well that it was foolhardy
in the extreme to read such a story right into the Emperor's
face, before thousands of listeners. For much less daring allusions the philosopher Dio had been brought to trial, and

Senator Priscus had been killed. Yet while Joseph was telling himself this, he remained completely in control of what he was doing and read effectively and with self-possession. With profound satisfaction he noticed that now the rigid face was stirring. Yes, it was happening: the Emperor's face reddened, he violently sucked his upper lip, his eyes began to flash darkly. Joseph was elated, a dizzy exhilaration uplifted him, all the more glorious because he knew that in the next moment he might suddenly and horribly meet his downfall. And he read on and on, he read the magnificent psychological evaluation of Herod, the moral which he had attached to his narrative. Perhaps he would have to pay with his life for reading it. But it was worth a life to hurl those sentences, to hurl his faith, into the face of the Roman Emperor, his enemy.

As he read he noticed more and more plainly that the parallels between his Herod and the Domitian who sat there before him were unmistakable. Surely among those several thousand breathless listeners there was not one who at this moment was not thinking of Princes Sabinus and Clemens. But just for that reason Joseph read on: "If he felt endangered by them, it would doubtless have been a sufficient precaution to keep them in captivity or to have banished them from the Empire, so that he would not have had to expect a sudden attack or open violence. But to murder them out of hate and passion— was that anything else than a tyrant's cruelty? That the King delayed in carrying out his plan, in ordering the execution itself, for a long time, condemns him more than it excuses him. For to let oneself be carried away in the first heat of passion to perform cruel acts is indeed horrible, but understandable. If, however, a man commits such a vicious deed only after careful deliberation and frequent vacillations, his action cannot be interpreted as anything other than a sign of a brutal, blood-thirsty character."

Joseph had finished; he was silent; his own boldness robbed him of breath. It was so quiet in the great hall that one could hear the rustle of the manuscript as he mechanically rolled it up. Then, into that absolute silence, a high laugh rang out. It was not even a malicious laugh, yet all started in alarm as if death had entered their midst. Yes, Domitian laughed, he laughed shrilly, not very loudly nor very long, and in his high voice, again not very loud, he said into the wide, deep silence: "Interesting, very interesting."

But that laugh exasperated Joseph beyond measure. Since everything was lost now in any case, and since surely he would never be able to hold another reading in his life, why should he not show Rome, gathered together in this place, how a man met his downfall in the grand and Jewish manner?

"And in conclusion," he cried into the deathly silence of the hall, "I shall read to you, my Lord and God Domitian, and to you, my most honourable guests, an ode which conveys the meaning of my *Universal History,* the state of mind in which the work was written, and the philosophical attitude which dominates the history of the Jewish people. They are not perfect verses, they are stammered in a language which is not the author's native tongue, but I think the clarity of their content has not suffered by that." And he spoke the verses of the "Psalm of Courage," he proclaimed:

> "Therefore I say:
> Hail to the man who takes death upon him,
> That he may speak because his heart bids him.
> Therefore I say:
> Hail to the man who says what is so.
> Therefore I say:
> Hail to the man who cannot be forced
> To say what is not."

Frozen with horror, the thousands listened to the Jew who dared to declare to the face of Rome and its Emperor that he denied them. Frozenly they gazed at their Emperor, who listened unmoving. Unmoving they all sat when Joseph had finished; for half a minute the whole gathering remained motionless; Joseph, very pale, sat motionless on his platform, the Emperor motionless on his raised seat.

Then, into the enormous silence, Domitian's voice rang out: "What do you think of it, Silenus, my fool? This is an ode of which you seem to me a competent judge." And Silenus, in his usual way imitating the Emperor, arms angularly pressed back, answered: "Interesting, what that man up there's been saying—a very interesting conception."

Then, still in the midst of absolute silence, Domitian turned to the Empress. "You held out to me," he said, "the possibility that, if I attended the recitation of our Jew Josephus, I should receive all manner of instruction. I have received it." And, "Are you coming along, Lucia?" he asked. But Lucia, her voice a little strained, replied: "No, my Lord and God Domitian. I'll stay for a while yet." The Emperor, however, bade her a ceremonious farewell; and, followed by his retinue, through the ranks of listeners bowing silently to the ground, he went out of the hall.

Quickly the hall emptied itself. Around Joseph there remained only his intimates. Soon these too left; first Caius Barzaarone, then Marullus, then John of Gishala. Finally Joseph was alone with Lucia, Claudius Reginus, and Matthias.

The abundance and the tension of will-power which Joseph had had to summon to stand the past hour was not yet exhausted. He had the strength to say to his friends, compos-

edly, even with a little smile: "And yet it was a good thing
that we held the reading." Reginus looked at the empty niche
where Joseph's bust had once stood. "It doesn't look as if you
were going to get a new bust there," he said, "but the book
will doubtless be read now." "It was a grand moment," said
Matthias naïvely. "And it doesn't matter that they didn't really
understand you. At readings of this sort," he said precociously
and sententiously, "it's probably always just the sensational,
the cheap stuff, that's successful." "Well, there was plenty of
sensation," said Claudius Reginus. But Lucia said: "I can appreciate courage. But what in the world actually came over
you, my Josephus, that you suddenly undertook to launch an
attack against the whole Roman Empire single-handed?"

"I don't know myself what possessed me," said Joseph. His
artificial tension disappeared, he sank down wearily on one of
the benches; he was suddenly old despite the arts of the facial
expert. "I was insane," he said, trying to explain to the others
what had happened. "When I saw that the man had made up
his mind to keep on preserving silence, when I saw how they
were all cowards and that none of them dared follow your
lead, my dear Lucia, but all just stared at him, and when I
saw the derision and hostility on his face, madness seized me.
From the very beginning I was rash and presumptuous, even
at that moment when the idea of this reading came to me,
even when I asked you to invite him, Lucia. You could not
know, my friends, how rash it was, but I should have known.
I had had certain encounters with him, and I should have
known that it could only end this way. I shouldn't have been
allowed to undertake this reading. My helpless rage at having
nevertheless undertaken it drove me insane."

"I don't know what you all want," said Matthias dissatis-
fiedly, in his deep, young, innocent voice. "I think it's a tremendous, eternally memorable victory that the Emperor of the

Romans came to Flavius Josephus. You said, my Father, that he was your opponent. That makes the victory all the greater. The Emperor, with his hundred million Romans behind him, looks upon the single man Joseph Ben Matthias as an enemy whom he must make a personal effort to overthrow. But Joseph Ben Matthias is not afraid and tells him the truth. I think that's a mighty victory."

The three adults smiled inwardly, almost touched at the boy's awkward attempts to comfort his father. Claudius Reginus and Lucia discussed, this time not without anxiety, what Domitian was likely to do next. But one could foresee nothing; one could only wait. And there were no measures of precaution which one could take. It would have been senseless and would only have increased the danger if, for example, Joseph had tried to leave the city.

Joseph, when he was alone, saw perfectly that his action had sprung from the same madness which ten years ago had driven the Zealots to their senseless revolt. But what was permissible for them, for those boys, those twenty-year-olds, was not permissible for him at the age of fifty-eight. And yet it was an honourable defeat, a defeat which filled the heart of the vanquished with a proud, exalted pain, a defeat a hundred times better than those shallow triumphs of reason which had made his heart so arid and cold during the last years. He was by no means crushed, he was proud of his defeat, and even the expectation of what was going to happen made him happy.

For the time being his act of madness brought him only joy. Matthias looked up to him with such admiring love as he could not help but feel after such a great success. Lucia scolded him, to be sure, but her scolding was mingled with an almost tender understanding of his fifty-eight-year-old heart which still caught fire so youthfully. And the Jews, this time the Jews of the whole Empire, wildly acclaimed Joseph. The misgivings of a few cautious individuals were drowned in an enormous wave of popularity. Joseph, who had hurled the truth of Jehovah at the head of the anti-Semitic Emperor in the midst of a gathering of thousands, became the greatest rebel of his period. Claudius Reginus had been right: soon the *Universal History* was read by even more people than in its time *The Jewish War*.

FOR the moment it was not Joseph himself to whom ill fortune accrued as a result of that memorable reading, but Matthias. For with the exception of Joseph's very few intimate friends the aristocracy of the city of Rome now closed their doors to Joseph, and Matthias was made to feel this more than his father.

How quickly Matthias's glory had paled, especially in the homes of society, he was forced to notice the next time he met the girl Cecilia. Cecilia had looked upon him in the last months with increasing respect; there had been no more mention of the right bank of the Tiber or of a prospective pedlar's career for Matthias. All the more violent now was the reaction. Her teacher of literature had told her in her Homer class about the great Egypto-Jewish interpreter of Homer, Apion. On that occasion there had also been talk of the most famous of Apion's books against the Jews, and some of the most contemptible and spiteful of this Apion's arguments Cecilia had adopted. Flushing, zealously, she used these arguments against Matthias; she jeered at him as one of the members of a barbarous, dirty, brutishly superstitious race.

When Matthias told Joseph of this dispute, the silly affair wounded him more deeply than was to be expected. He was

not only annoyed that he was forced to see evidence of the injury which he had done his son's career by his rash piece of
folly, but he was even more excited by the fact that he had
once again come up against Apion. With anger he recalled
that hour with Phineas, his Paulus's teacher, when he had
senselessly bellowed at him because of Apion's arguments.
Now, when Matthias told him about the girl Cecilia's words,
his hatred suddenly brought that dead Apion back to life for
him. It was many, many years since he had seen him; he had
been very young at that time, and Apion had been the rector
of the University of Alexandria. Joseph remembered plainly,
as if it had been only that morning, how the man had stood
there, vain, puffed up, important, in the white shoes which
were the insignia of the anti-Semites of Alexandria. Again and
again during his varied life Joseph had come up against A-
pion; all the enemies of the Jews drew their arguments from
Apion's poisoned well. The image of his foppish, mean, conceited, and highly successful opponent, who had filled the
whole world with clamour as foolish as it was malicious, became for Joseph the symbol of anti-Semitism everywhere, even
the symbol of all the victorious stupidity in the world, and for
him as for Socrates stupidity was synonymous with evil.

In the study of his handsome, bright new house he strode
up and down and argued with Apion, his opponent, whose
mouth was so full and whose head so empty. How different
was this Joseph who now, filled with his God, prepared his
new work from that other one who had written the *Universal
History*. Perhaps the goal which he had set himself with the
Universal History had been a higher one, but that goal had
been attainable only through the faith in reason of a Justus.
He, Joseph, had been presumptuous in striving toward it. He
was not suited to that, and he had done everything wrong.
Now he had come to know himself, now he was wise, now he

cared not a straw for that lofty goal. He turned back to the
path he had left. He had wasted many years, but it was still
not too late. He had become young again with his Matthias.

With relief he felt the heavy burden of critical responsibility
fall from his shoulders, the cramping duty of filtering all feelings through the sieve of reason. He thought of Justus and,
behold, there was in him no longer anything of the gnawing
feeling of inferiority, of the loving hatred of the bigger man.
He would no longer keep an eye on his judge, on posterity.
He would let himself go. He would write as his heart bade
him, not objectively, but with heat and anger, with the whole
fury which his opponents deserved, their arrogance, their su-
perficiality, their stupidity. He would give them what they deserved, this dead Apion and those before and after him who
had poured their cheap mockery upon the high and holy
things, upon what was unattainable for them, upon Jehovah
and His people.

And he sat down and wrote his book, *Of Apion, or Of the
Ancient Culture of the Jews*. What a good feeling it was to
sing the praises of his own people from an unburdened heart,
without the constricting bands of the scientific attitude! Never
in his life had Joseph experienced greater pleasure than in the
two weeks when, without interruption, he wrote down the
five thousand lines of that book. He saw them before him: the
White Shoes, the anti-Semites, those Hellenized Egyptians,
those Manethos and Apions. Big and puffed up they stood
there, and he knocked them together, them and their arguments, he knocked them to pieces, to dust, until there was
nothing left of them any more. Words came to him in floods
until he could barely cope with their abundance, and while he
wrote his brilliant chapters he thought of the Egyptian Greek
woman Dorion and his son Paulus, and it was the Manethos
and Apions who had estranged them from him. With bitter

wit he made fun of those Greeklings, the dwarfs, who had command of nothing but pretty, light, easy, elegant, dainty words. And he contrasted them with the true Greeks, the great Greeks, a Plato or a Pythagoras, who knew the Jews and valued them; otherwise they would not have taken parts of their doctrine into their own philosophies.

After Joseph had thus annihilated his opponents, he crowned all those noes with one great, passionate, glowing yes. There was nothing left now of his cosmopolitanism. All that he had painfully suppressed during his work on the *Universal History,* his whole immeasurably proud love of his people, he now allowed to pour into his book. In glowing words he praised the nobility of his people. They had wisdom, literature, law, history, long before the Greeks existed. They had had a great law-giver a thousand years before Homer and the Trojan War. No people had a purer worship of God, no people's love of morality was deeper, no people's literature richer. We have assembled our canon out of the tens of thousands of our books; we have chosen only twenty-two out of those myriads; and those twenty-two books we have combined into one Book. But what a Book it is! The Book of Books. And we are the people of that Book. We love it, we read it, we interpret it. The Book is the content of our lives; it is our soul and our State. Our God does not manifest Himself in physical shape; he manifests Himself in the spirit, in this Book.

In barely two weeks he had completed his *Apion.* But now, after the elation of writing, after the tremendous intoxication of work, he came down to earth. Fear overcame him—had he been able to give his enthusiasm enough form so that it would convey its meaning to others and sweep them off their feet? The thought of Justus was already back again, and the chilling feeling—how would his *Apion* appear when compared with Justus's *Jewish War?*

Timidly and filled with suspense he brought the book to
Claudius Reginus. The publisher was obviously sceptical because of the rapid completion of the work. He lay lazily on
his couch and asked Joseph to read aloud to him. With half-
closed eyes he lay there, not very much inclined to believe
what he heard, and soon he interrupted the reader and said
teasingly: "This will hardly appeal to our Justus." Joseph had
been thinking much the same thing while he read, and it cost
him some self-control to go on reading. But gradually the intoxication seized him again, and soon Reginus also opened his
eyes, and soon he sat up, and finally, after Joseph had been
reading perhaps half an hour, he tore the manuscript from his
hand and, "You read too slowly for me. Let me read it myself,"
he said, and while Joseph sat there silently, Reginus went on
reading to himself, avidly, and, "My scribes must get to work
on it at once tomorrow," he said, and, with an unusually animated expression: "If the Jews had Olympic Games, then you
would have to read this book to them, as Herodotus in his day
read his history to the Greeks in Olympia." And that was a
more enthusiastic utterance than Claudius Reginus had made
for many a year.

And as it happened to Reginus, it happened to all the others. Lucia, stirred by the warmth and passion of the book, declared: "I don't know whether everything you advance here is
true, my Josephus, but it has the ring of truth." Matthias was
carried away. Now he had the material he needed so badly to
hold his own against Cecilia and her Apion. Now he knew
why he was so proud of his people, of his family, of his father.
Everybody, friend and foe, was gripped by the book; it became
a greater success than Joseph had ever had. Now Flavius Josephus was incontestably the foremost writer of his period.

There were hours when that success seemed shallow to Joseph. He avoided seeing Justus, but sometimes when he was

alone, above all at night, he had debates with Justus. He heard Justus's derision, and he tried to justify himself, and he pointed to the enthusiasm of the others. But what use was that to him? He had betrayed his mission. He knew that Justus was right, and that those who acclaimed him were wrong. And he felt tired, tired of successes and defeats.

However, he had not many such hours. He had thirsted for success so long, and now he enjoyed his success. He tasted to the full his triumph that the Jews, who had misunderstood and railed against him so long, now had to see him as he was, their most effective champion. He tasted to the full the triumph that his Roman and Greek enemies had to feel the force of his book. And the glory which he had lacked so long was a new, a very welcome proof of his abilities before Lucia, and above all before Matthias.

MARA too had read *Apion*. In her simple, naïve words she wrote him about it, full of enthusiasm. This was a book which she could completely understand, this was a book after her own heart. Then, without transition, she reported on the Be'er Simlai estate. The steward, Theodore Bar Theodore, was a man of sound understanding and loyal heart, and he was instructing Daniel with fine success. Daniel took to farming; they all felt well, although here in Samaria and near Cæsarea they were living in the midst of heathens, and the Jews didn't make it easy either; they looked askance at everything which belonged to Joseph, especially because of the privileges which the heathens granted him. But perhaps that would be better now, after *Apion*. A suitor had presented himself for their daughter Jalta who pleased her, Mara, very well. He had his doctorate from Jabne, was nevertheless not proud,

but followed the trade of a silversmith simply and industri-
ously. True, he worked mostly for the heathens, and she was
not sure whether that was not an objection. But now the
spring was here, and Joseph would no doubt soon be on his
way to them, and then everything would arrange itself. And
it would be good for Daniel if he came under his father's eye
again, and surely for Matthias too it would be good not to
stay too long in Rome. Incidentally, on the *Felix* they had been
given a lot to eat, but the food had not agreed with them.
Joseph would please take care that he did not spoil his diges-
tion.

Joseph read, and he saw Mara before him, and he was filled
with a warm, tender feeling. But he did not even consider the
possibility of going to Judæa. Now more than ever he belonged
here in Rome. Now, especially after he had written *Apion*.
He felt happy, and his happiness had come just in time, at a
time when he could still enjoy it, while he still had the
strength to enjoy it. And Rome was the right setting, the only
setting, for that happiness. He now felt ordained to write only
as his heart bade him; he was chosen as the great panegyrist
and defender of his people. But that could be only in the heart
of the hostile capital.

And should he by any chance leave Matthias alone? He
could not take him away from Rome, tear him away from his
service to Lucia; that would shatter all the boy's glorious
dreams, that would shatter the boy himself. No, he did not
even think of it. And to separate himself from the boy, of that
he would not think either. It was the best thing he had, this
radiance which went out from Matthias, the love and admiration of his son. How he loved the boy! Just as the patriarch
Jacob had loved his son Joseph, idolatrously, criminally, so did
he love him. And if Jacob gave his son a gorgeous coat of
many colours, which brought envy and misfortune upon him,

he, Joseph, could understand that. He would have done exactly the same to adorn his Matthias with all that was lovely in the world. And if there were those who had misgivings, he had none the less done right in placing his Matthias in the midst of the glitter of the palace. Whose heart did not open at the sight of the boy? The Palatine was too paltry for him. The coat of many colours was still not gorgeous enough. Moreover, since the appearance of *Apion,* even John of Gishala had fallen silent and had no more misgivings.

Yet the danger was by no means over, the danger which he himself had created by his boldness before Domitian. But he took that danger lightly. Even if Domitian should revenge himself on the author of *The Jewish War,* of the *Universal History,* of *Apion,* even if he sought his life, what then? Through such a death Joseph would only bear witness anew for Jehovah and his people; he would thereby set the seal of martyrdom upon his book and assure himself and his work of immortality.

Joseph went about Rome happy, radiant, like his Matthias's elder brother. Daily he was at the Palatine, at Lucia's. The woman was becoming daily more indispensable to him. He felt a friendship for her which was mingled with a physical desire that sometimes confused his words, and made him, the skilful speaker, fall silent. They did not speak about their relation; frank, open Lucia was as reluctant to put into words what lay between them as Joseph, the skilful speaker. That very silence, laden with many and confused feelings, was the best and most charming part of their friendship.

Long-forgotten feelings and thoughts awoke in him when he was in her company, thoughts and feelings such as he had felt when, as a very young man, he had withdrawn into the desert to live only for God and wisdom. He felt as if God would consider it to his merit if he kept himself from Lucia;

he felt as if he gained strength if he kept himself from Lucia.

Once, as they sat thus together, Lucia said, with a strange smile about her curved lips: "My Josephus—if he knew!" "He would rage," answered Joseph, "he would rage and fall silent and have me die a martyr's death. But it would be no martyrdom, since it would be happening for your sake." "Oh," laughed Lucia, "you're thinking of Vellykins. I wasn't thinking of him. I was thinking of Matthias." And suddenly very serious, and looking at him thoughtfully out of her widely spaced eyes, she said: "Do you know, Josephus, that we should be betraying him, your son Matthias?"

It had happened that the boy Matthias, like countless others, had fallen in love with Lucia. Her frankness, her gaiety, the abundance with which her vitality poured forth, the insatiability with which she gave and took life, fascinated him. To be like her was the highest state a mortal could reach. She often joked with him, in a harmless, familiar way, and that bound him even closer to her. Yet she also took him seriously; she listened to his advice. He esteemed it highly that on his recommendation she had instituted peacock runs at her villa along the Appian Way and at her country house at Baia, and appointed as keepers the people whom he had had named to him by his friend Amphion, Reginus's peacock-keeper. He did not know what to call the delicate, groping feeling which bound him to Lucia. It would have seemed blasphemous to him to call it love, even in his thoughts, and he was shocked when he felt something rise up in him which could hardly be called anything else than desire. To desire her was as madly presumptuous as if a Roman boy had desired the Goddess Venus.

That did not prevent him sometimes from almost envying his father for the way that Lucia looked at him and he was allowed to look at her. For it was a fact that the two did not actually make an open display of their friendship, but on the other hand made no serious effort to conceal it. Matthias forbade himself any disrespectful thoughts toward his father or toward the Empress, his mistress, but such bold doubts were far from being dead for all that. He tried to master them by heightening even further his admiration for his father. Where in the world was there another man who simply by his word moved people of all realms, all classes, and all kinds, who moved the simple peasant Jews of Galilee as much as the refined, depraved Greeks, and that great, lofty woman, the Empress?

But he was twice as eager to serve her, Lucia, just because of his rare and immediately banished suspicions about her and his father.

So NOW he was gone, and she did not even regret it very much. She felt an emptiness within her, that was true, but when she probed her feelings carefully she recognized that she was not sorry now that he was gone.

The hopes which she had pinned on her Paulus had not been fulfilled. He had become flat and ordinary. Phineas's education and her own had borne no fruit. He was arrogant, her Paulus, but it was not the æsthetic arrogance of her father, the great painter Fabullus, and neither was it the wild, nervous arrogance of Josephus, nor the sharp, domineering arrogance which had been her own. No, her son Paulus's pride was nothing but the stupid, empty, brutal national pride of the Romans, the pride of belonging to those who had overthrown the world with blood and iron.

Gently and evenly the litter swung on the shoulders of the trained Cappadocian bearers. Dorion was coming back from the second milestone on the Appian Way; she had accompanied her son up to that point. Yes, the litter moved almost without rocking; she had privileges; the forerunner held high the russet shield with the golden wreath, and the russet curtains of the litter also bore the golden wreath, the sign that one must make way for the litter because it belonged to the household of an imperial Minister. But the easy swing of the litter did not make the Lady Dorion's thoughts more pleasant.

So now Paulus was on his way back to Judæa. He had got somewhere, he had proved himself as a soldier, he was adjutant to Governor Falco, he had a voice in those affairs; to his step-father Annius, Paulus had appealed quite especially this time. He would have a career. He would distinguish himself in the next expedition, and some time, since he wished it so

passionately and had the energy, he would become Governor of
Judæa and show the Jews what a Roman was. And it was not
at all impossible that his highest dreams would be fulfilled,
and that he would some day be in charge of the armies of the
Empire as Annius was now. He was very Roman, and the period was very Roman, and the Emperor was very Roman, and
Annius loved the excellent officer Paulus; why, after all, should
he not become Annius's successor?

And what would happen when he had achieved all that?
He would think himself on the heights of life. And he would
believe that she, Dorion, was also utterly satisfied by what he
had accomplished. Alas, how little he knew about her, her son
Paulus.

Grimly she thought of the vulgar outbreaks of Jewish hatred
to which he had given way at table, her once so princely
Paulus. His ugly and foolish talk had been doubly unpleasant
to her because shortly before she had read *Apion*. She had hesitated whether she should do so, but since everyone was talking about the book, she had done it. And she had had the same
experience as everyone else, for she had heard the voice of Joseph while she read, she had not been able to get that voice
out of her ears, and often it seemed to her as if he spoke to her
alone through the book. She was full of glowing rage while
she read, and she was full of glowing shame, and—why should
she not admit it to herself?—some of those old, passionate
feelings had stirred in her for the man who spoke to her out
of that book with such heat and such violence.

Several times she had thought of giving the book to Paulus.
She would reproach herself again and again for not having
done so. But she was glad that she had not done it. For it was
altogether possible that even about *Apion* he would have been
able to utter nothing but flat, spiteful nonsense, and she would
have found that hard to bear.

Life was full of strange chances. Perhaps now that she had had to suffer such a disappointment in Paulus, she would have all the more pleasure in Junius, her second son, For the time being, however, it did not look like it. For the time being it looked as if he would turn out like his father, like Annius, as if he would become an honest, noisy, self-confident, very Roman young gentleman, and adapt himself well to his period. It often happened that she was unwilling to admit that; often she imagined all kinds of qualities in her Junius. But now, in the litter, coming back from the second milestone on the Appian Way, everything in that respect also seemed dreary and hopeless to her.

From outside, through the drawn curtains of the litter, the noise of the city of Rome pressed in upon her. The citizens of the great city were making way for her litter; they gave her respect and the right of way. No doubt they envied her. Had she not indeed attained great heights, the daughter of the painter who had been consumed with never-satisfied ambition? He would have enjoyed what she had achieved. She had her reliable husband who loved her: the Minister of War Annius Bassus, firmly established in the Emperor's favour for so many years. She had her two—what was the phrase?—her two blooming sons, both turning out well. She belonged to the first rank of the Empire, and her sons would, according to all mortal calculation, occupy the first offices of the Empire. So what did she want?

She wanted very much, and while in the daytime she managed to drive away her evil thoughts, her nights were full of bitterness. Where was she, the slender Dorion of long ago with the light, pure profile and the delicate, imperious face? When she looked in the mirror today, a brittle, sour, joyless, ageing woman gazed out at her, and it was little comfort that her honest Annius would not see that and was as attached to her as ever. She was in her forties, middle age had arrived, and what had she had of life? But how much she could have had! She had bungled her life, she had frivolously ruined it. She had ill-intentionedly separated herself from the only man to whom she belonged. And if her son's life had become empty and mean and base, she bore the responsibility because of that very separation. For if she had stayed with her husband, Paulus would have remained as he had been in his boy-hood.

Lately she had heard a lot, whether she would or not, about her former husband. Wherever she went his name greeted her. She had heard about the departure of Mara and Joseph's children, and she had shrugged her shoulders. She had heard about the *Universal History,* and she had read it, and she had shrugged her shoulders and laid the book aside, and she had heard that others had done the same. That had been a satisfaction to her. The man was a good writer as long as he was filled with passion, as long as he was together with her and desired her, and since she had separated herself from him he had written himself out. Then she had heard that he had got his son into the Palatine and into Lucia's service, and she had shrugged her shoulders. He had always been a climber, this Joseph, and since he was no longer getting anywhere with his literature, he was trying to do it by social climbing. Let him. She was glad that she could cover up his image with a film of scorn and indifference. And she had heard more about him. She had heard that he intended to hold a reading, and strangely enough, in the Temple of Peace, and that the Emperor would attend this reading. She came within an ace of going. But she reflected that it would mean a great deal of whispering and that it would not be pleasant for Annius, and she really did not care so much about Joseph that she was will-ing to take that upon herself, merely to be present when he showed off in his vanity. And she had shrugged her shoulders and had not gone to the Temple of Peace.

But then she had heard something else, and she had intensely regretted that she had not attended the reading. For he had not behaved like a climber at that reading, one could really not say that; yes, it must have been actually magnificent when he hurled his truth and his accusations into the Emperor's face, in front of three thousand listeners. No, cowardly he was not, cowardly he most certainly was not. True, her Annius was not cowardly either, nor her Paulus. Neither of them would flinch in battle. But the courage of Joseph was quite a different kind of courage, a much more fascinating kind. A little self-advertising, perhaps, but none the less magnificent. If he had not had that strange, self-advertising, shameless, and magnificent courage, he would doubtless not have taken the whipping upon himself that time for her sake. A very slight flush tinged her brownish face as she thought of that.

She would not think about it any longer, she would not be alone any longer, she would distract herself, she would see people. She ordered the litter to halt and had the curtains flung up. Now the colourful life of the city thrust itself upon her, the multitude of faces; many greeted her, and from time to time she stopped the litter and spoke now to one, now to another. She managed to drive away her evil thoughts.

Yet when she had arrived at home she found a guest there who forced her to occupy herself even more urgently than before with her past and with Joseph. Phineas was waiting for her, the Greek Phineas, her Paulus's teacher, Joseph's enemy.

When Dorion entered he stood there completely calm, his large, extraordinarily pale head gazed out unmoving above his thin body, and he held his thin, long hands completely still. But Dorion knew how much self-control that appearance of

calm cost him. Phineas was devoted to Paulus. Although he
had given many of the best years of his life in a vain attempt
to make his beloved, princely Paulus into a real Greek, although the boy had eluded his grasp and become what the
Greek Phineas abhorred so deeply—a true Roman—Phineas
continued to be deeply attached to the boy. When Paulus had
been in Rome two years ago, Phineas had made ardent efforts
to win him back, to re-create a personal relationship between
his beloved pupil and himself. But Paulus resisted, he had
been stiff and obdurate and full of uninterested amiability, and
it had moved Dorion's heart to see how dignifiedly and without cheap irony, how like a Greek in the great sense, Phineas
had taken it. With what anxious suspense Phineas must have
looked forward to his arrival when Paulus had come to Rome
this time; how he must have waited to see whether Paulus
would come to him or summon him! But Paulus had had
enough of his uncomfortable friend, he had come and gone
without letting his teacher see him.

So there stood Phineas and waited with burning suspense
for what she would have to report to him about Paulus. But he
showed none of his impatience, he made conversation, he
spoke politely about indifferent subjects.

Dorion was sorry for him. For all the reserve of their external contacts they were on very intimate terms; he knew
about her confused relations with Joseph; their disappointment that their Paulus had strayed far from them, that he
had become strange and coarsened, bound them together; and
Phineas was probably the only person who fully understood
how little Dorion was satisfied by her own brilliant life and
her brilliant son.

Soon she herself began to tell him about Paulus without
waiting for his question. She described her conversations with
him, objectively and without judging them; she did not com-

plain, she reproached no one. But when she had finished she said: "And it is all Joseph's fault," and while her manner and voice remained calm, an ungovernable rage flared up in her sea-coloured eyes.

"That may be," answered Phineas, "and it may not be. I don't understand Flavius Josephus, I don't understand what he is, or what he does; he's strange to me, uncomprehended and incomprehensible as an animal. And while I once thought I understood his motives, later it appeared repeatedly that things were interrelated in quite a different way. For example, not long ago we marvelled at the courage with which he confessed his insolent and seditious beliefs to the Emperor's very face. What he did and said, and the way he did it, seemed ridiculous and unreasonable to us, of course, but we recognized the courage which expressed itself in his absurd behaviour. But now it appears that our Josephus didn't need the courage for his heroic act with which we credited him."

Dorion looked him attentively in the face with her sea-coloured eyes. "Please go on, Phineas," she urged him. "He didn't need much courage," Phineas explained in his deep, sonorous voice, "because he was sure of very powerful protection from the rear, from the lady whose intercession is the most powerful in the Palatine." "You disappoint me, my Phineas," answered Dorion. "First you behave as if you had something new to tell me, and then you inform me impressively that Lucia has a soft spot for the Jews and especially for Josephus. To whom is that new? And how does that minimize Joseph's courage? A friendly word from our Empress isn't a strong shield against certain dangers."

"A friendly word perhaps not," said Phineas, "but certainly the knowledge that the first lady of the Empire, the woman the Emperor can't live without, would stake her whole being to protect him, the hero, from any danger——"

But now Dorion had paled. "You're not one of those gossips, Phineas," she said, "who pass on the rumours of the Palatine without investigation. You must surely be in possession of reasons and proofs if you're going around with such dangerous information." "I'm not going around with it," Phineas corrected her gently. "I'm telling you about it, Mistress Dorion. And reasons and proofs?" He smiled; he began on a longer speech. "You know, Mistress Dorion, that I do not agree with very much that our Lord and God Domitian pleases to say and do. Rather I am—I've always talked to you bluntly—an enemy of the State in Norbanus's sense: I demand a much more extensive autonomy for Greece; I endanger the existence of the Empire. You and Annius Bassus should really not tolerate me in your house, and some day I'll surely come to a bad end. It's a miracle that the Emperor hasn't yet had me executed or at least banished beyond the border, like my great friend Dio of Prusa." "You're talkative," said Dorion impatiently, "and you're not sticking to the subject." "I am talkative," answered Phineas, without taking offence, "all we Greeks are talkative—we take pleasure in the well-turned phrase. But I am sticking to the subject. Since some of the discontented Senators are familiar with my opinions, and know that I'm an enemy of the regime, they are frank in my presence and don't exclude me when they talk disparagingly about the Palatine. So I know that Senator Proculus related the following in the circle of his intimates. He has now had three opportunities to observe the Jew Josephus in conversation with the Empress when Mistress Lucia and the Jew thought themselves unobserved. He says that on those occasions he noticed certain glances, half-phrases, little gestures—nothing more—yet he now knows, with a certainty more irrefutable than if he had been witness to their sleeping together, that it is more than an attraction to a talented writer which binds Mistress Lucia to this man. Now there are a number of things to which one can object in Senator Proculus—he's a cranky republican and rigidly Roman—but one quality one must grant him: he has the gift for practical psychology which is characteristic of many Romans. That is all, Mistress Dorion; and now say again that I haven't been sticking to the subject."

Dorion had paled more and more deeply. She had never been jealous of the many women with whom Joseph had slept. But that there should be a relationship between Lucia and Joseph such as this Senator Proculus was supposed to have observed agitated the depths of her being. Her vitality had always been rather artificial, she had had to scrape it together from every corner of her being. Now she had used up her allotted share of vitality and was an old woman, but since Annius still saw the earlier Dorion in her she had been able until then to make herself believe that Joseph also, when he thought of her, would still be thinking of the earlier Dorion. But Lucia was what Dorion would have liked to be—wild, exuberant life. Lucia was, although so different in nature, a Dorion fulfilled, a younger, better Dorion. And Lucia was more beautiful, Lucia was more alive, Lucia was the Empress. If it was true, what Senator Proculus was supposed to have observed, then Lucia would drive the last shadow of Dorion out of Joseph's heart. Then nothing of Dorion would be left in Joseph.

But it was not really the truth. The whole thing was nothing but the gossip of a discontented Senator, a rigid republican whose hatred made him make a mountain out of every molehill, and Phineas's hatred had added its bit.

Even if it were true, what then? Did she still love Joseph?

Of course she loved him. And she had always loved him. And she was a fool to have separated herself from him. And now she had Annius instead of Joseph. And Joseph, the clever man, the son of good fortune, had exchanged her for Lucia. He was not even clever, he had not even intended it to happen, he had wanted only her, Dorion; but she had forced him to look for a substitute, she had driven him into Lucia's arms.

No. She would not tolerate that. It must not be so. She would not think of standing aside and looking on. She would put a spoke in his wheel.

"And Domitian?" she asked unexpectedly.

Phineas looked Dorion full in the face; his glance burned with an evil, cunning, hateful, intimate flicker. He had wanted her to ask that. He had very definitely been sticking to the subject, with great skill; he had wanted to lead her to that point; the plan was to come into being in her. Just as before, in the case of the University of Jabne, he had now again found the spot where he could wound his enemy; true, many roundabout methods were necessary, but the spot was weak, it was vulnerable, and the prospects were good that this time he would at last strike a deadly blow at Josephus, his hated opponent. "Yes, Domitian," he answered accordingly, "that's just the question: how is Domitian taking it?" Dorion, just as slowly as he, said in her thin, drawling voice: "He's very suspicious. He often guesses more than there is. How can he not have discovered what actually exists?" But Phineas said: "Who can look into the Emperor's heart? He is even harder to penetrate than the Jew Josephus." "It's strange," Dorion went on broodingly, "that he left Joseph unharmed after that reading. Perhaps there's some connexion. Perhaps D.D.D. knows something and doesn't want to admit it."

And Phineas proposed: "Perhaps one could force the Emperor to admit that his wife is on offensively intimate terms with the Jew Josephus."

But Dorion, and this time there was the same light, evil flicker in her sea-coloured eyes as in his, answered: "In any case I thank you, my Phineas. Your talkative report wasn't as far off the subject as I originally thought."

Fʀᴏᴍ that time on the whispering which went around Rome about the Empress's relations with the Jew became louder and louder; soon it could be heard on every street.

Norbanus, remembering the Emperor's rage when he had reported to him Ælius's joke about Lucia, discussed with Messalinus whether one should tell D.D.D. about the gossip. "Lucia is in Baia," reflected Messalinus. "The Jew Josephus spent several weeks in Baia. I can't see any reason to keep that from D.D.D." "D.D.D. will wonder why we should report that to him. It really isn't strange and doesn't mean anything that the Jew Josephus wants to be near his son, in Baia. D.D.D. will think it grotesque that anyone should get offensive ideas from that." "It is grotesque," the blind man admitted in his soft voice. "Yet perhaps it would be proper to inform D.D.D. that the Empress takes an interest in the Jew and his son which is causing offence." "That would be proper," replied Norbanus, "but it's a ticklish business. Would you undertake it, Messalinus? You would earn the gratitude of the Roman Empire." "D.D.D. has to hit upon it by himself," urged Messalinus. "It seems to me to be your business, my Norbanus, to get D.D.D. to hit upon it himself." "And even if he did get such an idea," Norbanus reflected, "Lucia would have only to laugh and those thoughts would disappear, and what would be left would at most be some dangerous feelings against the man who put such an idea into his head." "It is not good," said Messalinus sententiously, "that the Lord and God Domitian is so closely and deeply attached to his wife. Perhaps you should dare to put him onto the aforesaid idea after all, my Norbanus. It simply belongs in your field, and you would earn the gratitude of the State."

Norbanus thought over that conversation for a long time. He was a good friend of the Emperor's, he was loyal to him, he considered him a great Roman, and he hated Lucia for many reasons. He sensed thoroughly that her kind was nobler than his, and the amiably detached way in which she sometimes made fun of him embittered him profoundly. He would much rather that she had hated him and tried to turn D.D.D. against him. Also it offended him that she, whom the Lord and God Domitian honoured by his love, obviously did not fully value that love. He honestly believed that her influence harmed the Emperor and the Empire. That she occupied herself with the Jew at all made D.D.D. seem small, it was harmful to his prestige, and, moreover, one could fully expect Lucia to sleep with the Jew.

But what could he, Norbanus, do about it? Messalinus could well say: "Put the Emperor onto it." How could that be managed? What could Norbanus do to get the Emperor to the point where he would take steps against the Jew and against his wife?

One day, while he was torturing himself with such thoughts, he came across a confidential letter which had just arrived from Falco, the Governor of Judæa, on conditions in the province. In that letter the Governor related among other things that he had found in his archives a list of the so-called descendants of King David. At one time Rome had urged his predecessors to keep a special watch on those people, but in recent years the affair seemed to have been forgotten. Now he had instituted new investigations and found that, insofar as they existed in Judæa, there were only two of those descendants of the old king left alive, a certain Jacob and a certain Michael. Lately there had been more talk and agitation about these two,

who incidentally called themselves not Jews but Christians or
Minæans. So he himself had had the two arrested, and since
he thought it would be wise if at least for a while they were
outside the country, he had had them put on a ship bound for
Italy, so that the Palatine might look them over more carefully
and decide their fates. The so-called scions of David, Jacob and
Michael, were now, therefore, on their way to Rome.

As Norbanus read this letter from Governor Falco, he saw
plainly before him the graceful summer pavilion in the park at
Albanum, and in front of it the heavy figures of the Doctors of
Jabne, and suddenly he thought of the fact that the Jew Josephus was also a so-called scion of David. Therefore he and
his son Matthias, according to the faith of the Jews, had the
expectancy of the rule of the world. All at once the "Psalm of
Courage," which Josephus had recited with the greatest insolence right into the Emperor's face, appeared to him in a completely different, much more dangerous, light; and the friendship
of Josephus and his son with Lucia suddenly acquired a very
different, much more ominous significance. It was a declaration
of war on the Emperor and the Empire. Norbanus's broad,
square face wrinkled in a smile that bared his large, strong
yellow teeth. He saw how he, without endangering himself,
might draw his master's attention to the danger which sprang
from Josephus's relations to Lucia. Once reminded of the Jewish superstition about the scions of David and the Messiah, the
Emperor would certainly let his thoughts take the same direction as his own. At the mention or at the sight of the two scions
of David, Jacob and Michael, D.D.D. would necessarily remember that Josephus and his son had the same characteristic,
and then cautious, suspicious D.D.D. would be forced to reflect
thoroughly about the Jew Josephus, his son, and the relation of
the two to Lucia.

He sent a courier to Albanum to ask whether the Lord and

God Domitian would do him the honour of admitting him to his presence in the next few days.

The Lord and God Domitian was again spending the greatest part of his time at Albanum and alone. It was a beautiful early summer, but he took no pleasure in it. He lolled in his hothouses, he stood in front of the cages of his wild animals, but he was as little conscious of the artificially ripened fruits as of the panther which blinked at him sleepily from a corner of its cage. He forced himself to work, but his thoughts wandered. He summoned his counsellors; he listened to their expositions with half an ear and then not at all. He summoned women, and let them go as they had come.

He had not forgotten the insolence of the Jew Josephus, and of course he did not think of letting his offence go unpunished. But the punishment had to be considered. For the monstrous deed—that the Jew had declared war on him and his world and his gods in the hearing of all—had been done not only at the prompting of his own heart, but as the messenger of his God. And that Lucia also had talked him into attending that recitation of the "Psalm of Courage" had not happened from sheer ill-will, but because behind her too, probably unknown to her, stood his evil enemy the God Jehovah. It was strange and it interested the Emperor, even apart from his personal interest in Lucia, that Jehovah had succeeded in getting this woman on His side and drawing her away from Jupiter, to whom after all she belonged by birth. He was an exceedingly cunning God, this Jehovah, and Domitian must consider each step with the greatest caution.

He rejected from the outset every suspicion that the relation between Lucia and the Jew was a question of their sleeping together. If it were a question of physical desire, the two would conceal their relation. Instead the Jew, obviously dazzled by his

God, had challenged him to combat before all of Rome while the Empress applauded.

The simplest thing, of course, would be to annihilate them all: the Jew Josephus and his offspring the boy Matthias, and Lucia along with them. But unfortunately Domitian knew well that those simple remedies had by no means the radical effect which one might expect. Too many had been infected by the poison of the Jewish madness, and the death of the few thus infected would not terrify the others but make them only greedier for the poison. When people died for an illusion it did not become more bitter, but sweet.

How could he exterminate this Eastern insanity? Every means was welcome to him: cunning, love, threats. But where could he find the means? He found none.

He pulled himself together, he went into his private shrine, he turned for advice to his goddess, the goddess of clarity, Minerva. He flattered her, he threatened her, flattered her again, immersed himself in her. He stared out of his large, protruding, near-sighted eyes into the large, round owl's eyes of the goddess. But she would not let herself be forced, she would not answer him; silent and dark she gazed back at him. But he pleaded with her again, summoned all his strength, implored her. And at last succeeded, he tore speech out of her; she opened her lips, she spoke. "Oh, my Domitian," she said, "my brother, my best beloved, my favourite, why do you force me to speak to you? For my heart pains me that I must tell you what I do not wish to tell you. But Jupiter and the Fates have commanded me to do so. Listen, then, and be brave. I must leave you; I may no longer advise you; my image here in your private shrine will become an empty and lifeless shell. Oh, how it grieves me, Domitian, my dearly beloved, but I must henceforth be far from you; I may no longer protect you."

Domitian's knees went weak, his breath stopped, his whole body was bathed in cold sweat, he had to lean against the wall. He told himself that it had not been the voice of his Minerva; his enemy, the God Jehovah, had spoken out of her image, treacherously, to strike terror into him. It had been a day-dream, one of those false visions which were so frequent in the land of Jehovah and of which his soldier Annius Bassus had told him. But these comforts were of no avail; the pale, cold fear remained.

His hostility toward humanity and his suspiciousness grew. He gave orders to his Chamberlain and his Captain of the Guard to make access to him more difficult by every means, and to have everyone who entered the palace searched more carefully for weapons. And he instructed his architects to line the living-rooms and reception rooms with a reflecting metal, so that wherever he stood, walked, or lay he could see everyone who approached him.

Thus had the Emperor been spending his days at Albanum when the Chief of Police came to him. He was glad to see Norbanus. He looked forward to rising up out of the world of his dreams into the world of facts. With curiosity and good-will, even with a certain tenderness, he looked into his Norbanus's faithful, brutal, and crafty face, and as always he took pleasure in the way the fashionable curls of his deep black, thick hair fell untidily and rather grotesquely over the forehead of his square face.

"Well, now," he invited him, settling himself comfortably, "let me hear in detail what's new in Rome." And Norbanus complied; he gave a detailed report on the latest events in the city and the Empire, and his vigorous, firm voice really was suited to drive away the Emperor's ugly dreams and lead him back into the world of sober reality.

"And what do we hear from Baia?" the Emperor asked after

a while. Norbanus had determined to speak as little as possible about Lucia, Joseph, and Matthias; the Emperor should hit upon the connexion by himself. "From Baia?" he repeated cautiously. "The Empress feels at home there, as far as I'm informed. She takes part in a lot of sports, she goes swimming although it's so early in the year, she arranges rowing races in the bay, she has a lot of people about her, people of all kinds, and she occupies herself with books." He made a very slight pause, but then he could not resist adding after all: "For example, she had the Jew Josephus read aloud to her from his new book, which my agents report to be a glowing defence of the Jewish superstitions without overstepping the permissible bounds." "Yes," replied the Emperor, "it's a violent and very patriotic book. When my Jew Josephus shows himself so openly I like him much better than when he preaches his Roman-Greek-Jewish hotch-potch wisdom. Moreover," he went on reflectively, exactly as Norbanus had done earlier, "it's not particularly odd to me if my Jew Josephus stays in Baia, since the Empress has taken his son into her court." And since Norbanus remained silent, he added: "She's very well pleased with this young son of Joseph's, I hear." Norbanus would have liked to say all kinds of things about Josephus and his young son, but he had determined not to do so, and he remained true to his decision. He was silent.

"And what else?" asked Domitian. "Nothing else, really," answered Norbanus. "Or at most one point more—that I could suggest to the Lord and God Domitian an amusing little way of passing the time. Perhaps Your Majesty remembers that we once found out, in the course of an entertaining interview with some Jewish Doctors, that the Jews see in the descendants of a certain King David the candidates for the throne of the world. We drew up a list of those pretenders at the time." "I remember." The Emperor nodded. "Now Governor Falco reports to me," Norbanus went on, "that in his Province of Judæa there are two of those scions of David left. Lately there's been talk and agitation about those two. So Falco has sent them to Rome for us to pass judgment on them. Now I wanted to ask the Lord and God Domitian whether perhaps he would like to amuse himself by looking over these two candidates for world domination. They're a certain Jacob and a certain Michael."

Exactly as Norbanus had intended and foreseen, this suggestion awakened in Domitian's soul countless thoughts, conclusions, wishes, and fears which had been waiting to be awakened. Domitian had really forgotten that the feared and despised Jew Josephus and his son were regarded by a number of people as the descendants of a king and his equals. But now, since Norbanus had refreshed the memory of that remarkable conversation with the Doctors and its consequences, the idea that this Josephus and his son were pretenders, rivals, sprang up in him again with tremendous life. Ridiculous as were the claims of those people, they were none the less existent, and none the less dangerous. It was clear that these scions of David thought that now the time had come for them to announce their claims anew. And it was obviously through this claim, he grew aware in the course of Norbanus's report, through this supposed descent from the old Eastern kings, that Josephus had captured Lucia's imagination; through this assertion he had managed to get her to take his young, ridiculous son into her service. And so also, insisting on his right as the scion of kings, he had dared to hurl his poem about "courage" into his face. He, Domitian, had therefore been right in suspecting his great enemy, the God Jehovah, behind it all.

Yet these reflections did not last five seconds. True, the Emperor's face had flushed as always when he was excited and upset, but his behaviour showed nothing of that excitement.

"That's a good suggestion," he declared cheerfully, and, "Good," he said, "bring the fellows to me, my Norbanus, and soon."

S o the very next week the scions of David, Jacob and Michael, were brought to Albanum.

A sergeant of the bodyguard led them into a small, gorgeous room. There they stood, broad, uncouth, and awkward in the midst of the costly frame. They were men of peasant appearance: they had the long, coarsely woven garments of Galilee wrapped around their bodies, and wore large beards on their quiet faces; Michael looked about forty-eight, Jacob forty-five. They spoke little. Their strange surroundings seemed to make them uncomfortable, but not afraid.

The Emperor entered with his stiff gait, followed by Norbanus and some gentlemen, including an interpreter, for the two men spoke only Aramaic. As the Emperor entered they said something in their jargon. Domitian asked what they said; the interpreter explained that it was a greeting. Had it been a respectful greeting? asked Domitian; the interpreter, somewhat hesitantly, replied that it had been a greeting customary between equals. "H'm, h'm," said the Emperor. He walked around the men. They were ordinary men, peasants, coarse of limb and face like peasants; they also smelt like peasants although they had surely been washed before being admitted to his presence.

Domitian, in his high, shrill voice, asked: "So you're of the line of your King David?" "Yes," Michael answered simply, and Jacob explained: "We are related to the Messiah; we're great-grandnephews." Domitian, after the interpreter had translated this, looked at them uncomprehendingly out of his protruding, near-sighted eyes. "Now what do they mean, these men?" he said, turning to Norbanus. "If they're descendants of the Messiah, then obviously they presume that the Messiah was here a long time ago. Ask them," he ordered the interpreter.

"What does that mean, that you're great-grandnephews of the Messiah?" asked the interpreter. Michael explained patiently: "The Messiah was called Joshua Ben Joseph and died on the cross for the salvation of mankind. He was the Son of Man. He had a brother named Judah. We are descendants of that brother." "Can you follow, gentlemen?" Domitian asked, turning to his retinue. "It seems somewhat confused to me. Ask them," he commanded, "whether the Kingdom of the Messiah is already here, then." "It is here and it is not here," explained Jacob. "Joshua Ben Joseph of Nazareth died upon the cross and arose again—that was when it began. But he will arise once more, and only then will he reveal himself in all his glory, judge the living and the dead, and treat each man according to his deserts." "Interesting," said the Emperor, "very interesting. And when will that be?" "That will be at the end of time, on Judgment Day," Michael explained. "That isn't a very exact date," commented the Emperor, "but I suppose the fellow means it will be a long while. And who will rule in the Kingdom of the Messiah?" he went on asking. "The Messiah, of course," answered Jacob. "Which Messiah," asked the Emperor, "the dead one?" "The resurrected one, certainly," replied Michael. "And will he appoint governors," asked Domitian, "substitutes? And whom will he appoint in that case? His relatives no doubt in the first place. Tell me, what kind of rule will his be?" "We know nothing of governors," said Jacob negatively, and Michael insisted: "It will be no earthly, but a heavenly, Kingdom." "These are clumsy dreamers," said the Emperor. "You can't talk with them. And so you're of the line of David?" he made sure again. "We are that," replied Jacob.

"What taxes do you have to pay?" inquired the Emperor. "We have a little farm covering thirty-nine plethra," Michael informed him. "We live on our income from that land. We farm it with two hired men and a servant woman. The tax collector assessed our property at nine thousand denarii." Domitian reflected: "That's not high revenue for the descendants of a great king and claimants to kingdoms and provinces. Show me your hands," he ordered unexpectedly. They showed them to him; Domitian looked them over carefully—they were hard, callused peasant's hands. "Give them something to eat," the Emperor decided, "and send them back, but on one of the less luxurious boats, and don't spoil them."

But to Norbanus, after they had gone, he said: "What a ridiculous people the Jews are, to see pretenders to the throne in such people! Weren't the two of them amusing in their simple-minded pride?"

"Those two were amusing," answered Norbanus, and he laid stress on "those." At that Domitian grew very red, and then again pale, and then again red. For Norbanus was right; those men were amusing, but other scions of David, Josephus and his son, were not at all amusing; and the fear of Josephus and his God Jehovah arose again in Domitian.

Thus far the interview with the scions of David had had exactly the effect which Norbanus had promised himself. Then, however, it took a turn which was certainly not desirable in the eyes of the Chief of Police. For the Emperor, suspicious as he was, told himself suddenly that it was very possible, nay probable, that Norbanus had intentionally caused those thoughts to arise in him. Probably that was why Norbanus had laid so much weight on those two scions of David, although he too must have recognized from their appearance how harmless they were.

So Norbanus too had recognized from the very beginning

how dangerous Josephus was, and when he drew his, the Emperor's, attention to it he was only doing his duty as a faithful friend, was doing it, incidentally, with a tact with which he, Domitian, would never have credited him. Nevertheless, it was hard to bear that this Norbanus could guess his thoughts so exactly; it bordered on sedition if a subject dared to direct the thoughts of the Lord and God Domitian. He had let Norbanus approach him too closely. Now there was someone in the world who knew him too well. Such were the feelings which moved the Emperor; they were not thoughts—he did not even let his confusion take that much form—but he could not keep his gaze, which rested on his Chief of Police's head, from showing distrust, something like fear. True, it lasted only a fraction of a second; for the face he saw was strong, dependable, brutal, the face of a faithful dog, exactly the face of the Chief of Police that he wanted.

Norbanus had supplied him with welcome entertainment by bringing in the scions of David; he had given him some welcome insights. He was grateful to his loyal Chief of Police for that, and he told him so, but he dismissed him quickly, almost abruptly.

Alone, he reflected. What made this struggle with Jehovah peculiarly difficult was that he could really not confide completely in any person about this particular problem. Norbanus was faithful, but his soul was not quite subtle enough to grasp completely anything so complicated, so profound, as the enmity of this invisible, intangible Jehovah, and, moreover, the Emperor did not want to let him look any more deeply into his heart just now. Marullus and Reginus would understand perhaps what the struggle was about. But even if he were able with great effort to explain himself to them, what would he have accomplished? Both of them were old men, indolent, tolerant, liberal, not the kind of fighters which this fight de-

manded, where blow followed blow. Annius Bassus would be
a good fighter, but he was certainly too simple-minded for such
a cunning and slippery enemy. There remained Messalinus.
He had the head to understand who the enemy was and where
he stood, he had courage and strength enough, and he was
loyal. But Domitian remembered his uneasiness when he had
been forced to acknowledge that Norbanus saw through him.
He would turn to Messalinus, but only when he was no longer
able to find a way out alone.

But he would find a way out. He was sitting at his desk; he
had taken out his writing-tablets. He brooded. He tried to pull
himself together. He could not do it. His thoughts dissolved in
all directions. True, he pressed his stylus into the wax of the
tablet, but he was not forming words, he was mechanically
drawing loops and circles. And with alarm he noticed that it
was the eyes of Minerva he had drawn, the large, round owl's
eyes which now remained empty and without light and without counsel for him.

And all at once the danger which had threatened him so
often, the assassination which his opponents had so often fore-
told for him, was no longer an unreal idea, no longer an abstrac-
tion such as death usually was for a healthy man of his age—
something which would reach him one day, in the distant
future—but something very real, very near. He was not cowardly. But the feeling of boundless security which had filled
him until now, as long as he had known himself to be in the
goddess's protection—that feeling had deserted him. Death,
until then something remote to him, had become something
near which forced itself upon his consideration.

If he should join the gods, if he should vanish from this
earth, he, the flesh and blood of the man Domitian, what would
become of his idea, what would become of his conception of
Rome, which he had realized more profoundly and freshly

than those before him? Who, when he was no longer there, would protect that conception and carry it on?

This conception of Rome as he understood it was closely bound up with the rule of the Flavians. In his innermost heart, very secretly, he had in spite of everything still hoped for heirs from Lucia. But to cling to that nebulous hope any longer, now that he was in danger, would be madness. Down with that hope, away with it! Too bad that he had been afraid of the impudent tongues of his enemies, that he had not let the child which Julia had borne him come into the world. How wonderful it would be if he could appoint as his successor a son conceived by himself.

But that simply was not possible. The Flavian dynasty depended on the two boys, the twins Constans and Petronius. At least the boys were of pure Flavian blood from the father's and from the mother's side. And it was a good thing that he had exterminated the influences which might have spoiled the two, that he had sent Clemens to his death and Domitilla to the Balearic Islands. Now the young lions were growing up under the wise instruction of the very Roman Quintilian, and removed from the influence of the God Jehovah.

He had not, it was true, entirely removed them from the influence of Jehovah. During these hot months Lucia had taken the boys to Baia with her; she did not want the boys, who were severely affected by their parents' fate, to go on living in the dreary house of their dead father and their banished mother, and he had consented. How could he have permitted it? It was of course simply a trick of the God Jehovah to give Lucia the idea of doing something for dead Clemens's sons. Perhaps our Josephus was behind this again, Jehovah's agent. It was incomprehensible that he, Domitian, had not seen through it all immediately. He had, however, felt himself to be the boys' cousin, their relative, and he had not wanted to appear too

severe to them, for he had cared, he still cared, for the twins'
love. But above all—he would be frank with himself—he had
not wanted to seem too harsh in front of Lucia.

Now there would be an end to that. And he knew how. He
would at last realize his old plan of adopting the twins. He
would call them to his court, so that they would automatically
be removed from the atmosphere of Josephus and his Matthias.
Then if, unprotected by Minerva, he should have to depart
from this earth, he would have done his part toward leaving
behind new defenders for his conception of Rome.

His concentrated expression relaxed, he smiled. Something
agreeable had occurred to him. If he adopted the boys, that
was a natural excuse to summon Lucia as well into his presence. And once she was there, many points would be cleared
up. In spite of everything, in spite of having been led astray by
Jehovah, she had always had understanding for his ideas, for
she was a Roman. He, the Roman man, would speak to her,
the Roman woman; he felt in himself the strength to win
Lucia back.

He smiled. Even without the protection of Minerva he did
not feel lost. Even the bad had its good sides. If the danger
which Jehovah threatened had not again arisen so visibly before him, he would have postponed the adoption of the twins
even longer. But this way, through this rapid adoption, he
would accomplish two ends at one stroke. Not only would he
be establishing a new security and a new protection for the
future of his concept of Rome, but he would in all probability
draw Lucia, the new-won convert, away from Jehovah again.
Lucia was Roman through and through; Lucia loved him—
there was no question of that, although it was in her proud,
rebellious way. The God Jehovah had clouded her understanding. But he, the God Domitian, would succeed in dis-
persing those unhealthy mists with which the Eastern God

had darkened her mind, so that she would once more see things as clearly as he himself.

Without delay he set to work and made the necessary preparations for adoption. And on the very same day he wrote a detailed letter to Lucia. He did not dictate it, but wrote it himself and took pains to phrase the sentences personally and very warmly. For the sake of the continuance of the dynasty, he wrote, and since he could hardly expect further heirs from her, he considered it his duty to adopt the descendants of that Flavius Clemens whom he had unfortunately been forced to have executed. The twins were close to his heart, and he had observed with pleasure that they seemed to appeal to her also. So he hoped that she would welcome his decision. Already he had postponed the matter far too long. So now he was hastening it all the more. On that same day he was giving Quintilian instructions to set out with the boys to Albanum. He considered it proper to have the boys don the toga of manhood immediately after the adoption despite their tender age. He intended to observe both ceremonies, the adoption and the investiture with the toga, with solemn festivities. He wanted to hammer into the Romans' heads the idea that he was grafting new shoots onto the dynasty. It would be a great pleasure to him if she decided to heighten the significance of this planned occasion by her presence.

WHEN the twins arrived with their tutor Quintilian at Lucia's house in Baia, they had been deeply upset. The death of their father, the banishment of their mother, had cast an air of reserve over their naturally open faces, and Quintilian had had need of great discretion to get them through that difficult time without grave emotional disturbances. Now, at Lucia's,

they slowly became more relaxed, less shy. Domitilla, before
she had left for her Balearic island, had made Lucia promise to
take an interest in her sons and to work against Quintilian's
Latin influence. Lucia treated the boys completely as adults;
she handled them carefully but without showing her pity too
obviously. And gradually the boys' frozen surface melted, and
they became once again confiding and youthful as they once
had been.

This was above all to Matthias's credit. A healthy boys'
friendship had quickly developed between him and the two
princes. The twins had pleasant natures; they were even more
strongly impressed than the others by the radiance, the aura
of young manhood, which surrounded Matthias; they recognized without envy that he was their superior. When they were
together with him they could be innocent, even happy as before, and forget the intrigues and conflicts all around them, in
spite of the gloomy occurrences which they had been forced to
live through. Then they took part in all kinds of sports with
boyish ambition, wrestled together, and played about.

It did not disturb them that people mocked at their friend
Matthias because of his Jewish descent. They were familiar
with Minæan modes of thought through their parents; they
were proof against anti-Semitic whisperings. That their father
had had to die for his Judaizing tendencies made it a point of
honour with them to take Matthias's part; they attached themselves to him with zealous friendship.

Matthias not only liked his playmates, but it heightened his
self-esteem that the two princes, the closest relatives of the
Emperor, were so devoted to him. Once he heard an Egyptian
slave who had just entered the service informing Cecilia, who
had inquired after him: "The three princes are out fishing."
Then his pride was such that he felt as if he had wings.

Quintilian was annoyed by this friendship. He had had mis-

givings from the very beginning about letting the princes come
here to Baia, into the Empress's cloudy atmosphere. One could
not deny that Lucia was to a high degree Roman, yet most of
what she did, read, and said disturbed him, and he was made
uneasy by the knowledge that his pupils were near her for such
a long time. And now, on top of everything, they had involved
themselves in this friendship with the young Jew. Quintilian,
always striving to judge fairly, granted that there was nothing
about Matthias's behaviour which offended against Roman
character. He refrained, accordingly, from making complaints
to the Emperor about his pupils' relations to Josephus's son,
and limited himself to gentle warnings which, without hurting
Matthias's feelings, could at the same time not be misunderstood by his pupils.

So a persistent struggle was going on for the souls of the
twins between him on the one side and Lucia and Matthias on
the other. This struggle was carried on silently, underground.
Yet once the contrast was revealed openly and before everyone's eyes.

Matthias had infected his friends with his boyish pleasure in
the peacock farm which he had been allowed to set up on
Lucia's estate. Daily the three visited the run; they knew the
individual birds; they loved to bring one or the other of them
to the outside staircase of the main building and delighted in
the spectacle of the birds standing on the beautiful, spreading
stairs of the white-gleaming house, opening and shutting their
fans as if they were fanning coolness to the sunny palace.

Now one day, when Senator Ostorius, a famous gourmet,
was visiting Lucia, a pie of peacock meat was set before him.
In the absence of Lucia and the boys the major-domo and the
cook had forced the unhappy peacock-keeper to hand over to
them six of the costly and beloved birds. The boys raged. Quintilian tried to calm down their excitement to a reasonable level.

A pleasure of the palate, he said, was in no way inferior to a pleasure of the eye, and noisy grief such as Matthias and the boys were showing for the slaughter of the birds was un-Roman, was Eastern sentimentality. The boys fell silent, but they brought up the subject again in Lucia's and Joseph's presence. Joseph said that he found it strange that a Roman felt no repugnance in eating the meat of the peacock, the bird which was holy to the Goddess Juno. Quintilian declared that it showed little feeling for reality if one confused the significance of an object, the idea of an object, with the object itself. That was like considering the paper of a book as something sacred because great things were written upon it. Such an equalization was utterly foreign to a realistic Roman. Quintilian, the great orator and distinguished stylist, got the better of Joseph in the debate, especially since the latter had no possibility of expressing himself in his native tongue but had to defend his arguments in an acquired language.

After this episode Quintilian had been seriously considering whether it was not after all his duty to ask the Emperor to remove his pupils from the harmful influence of the young Jewish gentleman, when, with relief, he received the Emperor's letter ordering him to come to the Palatine with the princes for purposes of adoption.

For Lucia, too, the Emperor's decision to adopt the twins provided more joy than annoyance. True, she was sorry when she thought of how the boys would henceforth have to live in the company of the warped and Romanly severe Domitian. On the other hand she was sincerely glad for the boys that D.D.D. was at last realizing his decision and raising them to such a high position.

Moreover, at the Palatine they could hardly keep the twins altogether separate from her and Matthias, and she would continue to do her best to protect the boys from Quintilian's frozen

Latinity. But quite aside from that she would probably have a good assistant. For if D.D.D. had destined Domitilla's children to be his successors, then probably he would also be found willing to recall the mother from banishment. Lucia did not like Domitilla at all; on the contrary, Domitilla's cold fire, her sourness, were unpleasant to Lucia. But Lucia was free of the formalistic sense of justice of Flavian Rome; she did not approve of thus restricting the individual's liberty of conscience, and she had been indignant at the violence done Domitilla. What crime had Domitilla really committed? She had occupied herself with the philosophy of the Christians, that was all. So in actuality she had been banished because of one of the Emperor's arbitrary, violent whims. D.D.D. must recall her, he simply must; she, Lucia, would get him to do it.

She felt in her the strength to persuade him. She was very honest by nature and had difficulty in disguising her feelings. She could not get anything out of D.D.D. if she felt repelled by him. But if she felt attracted by Vellykins she could show it unconstrainedly and then she could do anything with him. Lately she had shut herself off from him; his long silence had allowed a fear to ripen in her that in his slow and treacherous way he was preparing a blow against Joseph and against Matthias. His letter reassured her. At bottom his personality had always attracted her; his fierce obstinacy, his excessive pride, his exaggerated, twisted, warped, supra-dimensional forcefulness—all that had drawn her to him from the beginning. And she was also conscious that he loved her, in reality only her. So his letter warmed her heart, and she looked forward to seeing him.

She eagerly prepared herself for her trip to Albanum. Filled with a fighter's enjoyment she thought of the coming discussion with Vellykins. Certainly she would manage what she had determined to do. What she wanted to accomplish was to

have the path from the twins to her and Matthias remain
open; what she wanted to accomplish was to have Domitilla
recalled from her Balearic island.

The first three days of her being together with D.D.D. again
in Albanum were filled with the solemn ceremonies of adoption. They were above all religious festivities, and one could
see how profoundly the Emperor was moved by them. His
family was to him a sacred concept; the altar of his family
gods, the hearth with the eternal flame which stood in his
atrium, were for him no empty symbols, but something living,
and he was deeply stirred by the idea that he could bring before his family gods these young beings who would revere
them in the future, for the gods were kept alive only by the
worship of their believers. And he himself, who would some
day be one of these gods of his household, could only ensure
his own continuance by ensuring the worship of his family
shrine. So this celebration was something vitally important to
him; through it he acquired a new, living contact with his
divine fathers. The words of the ancient, holy incantations had
deep significance for him, and it was no empty, legal transac-
tion, but serious reality, when he took the boys under his pa-
ternal protection and gave them their new names, Vespasian
and Domitian. He had thereby transformed the young boys,
made them into new persons. Now he and they had new responsibilities and duties to one another; an unbreakable chain
bound them together.

From the very first moment he felt that Lucia had come to
him in a friendly spirit. But pedantic as he was, he postponed
dealing with her and clarifying their relationship until later.
Now, in these days of the adoption, his thoughts and feelings
were filled with serious, significant symbolical acts which left
him no time for anything else. They were happy, elevating
days; his new sons, the young lions, pleased him; the only

thing which disturbed him about them was that they were bound so closely to the Empress's youngest adjutant, to Flavius Matthias.

After the official ceremonies were over and the countless guests had departed, Domitian gave a family dinner. Besides the twins and their tutor there were present only Lucia and Matthias.

The Emperor naturally thought that the best thing would be to cut the bond between his new sons and the young Jew at once and for ever. Why he did not do so, but instead even included Matthias in this intimate gathering, he could not exactly have said. He told himself that he did it to have a chance for once to feel out Josephus's son thoroughly; for he could not help but recognize after the first glance that a great radiance and a great fascination went out from the boy, so that it would not be very easy to efface his image from the hearts of the twins. If he was to succeed in doing that, he must first study this young person thoroughly. And then—but he did not really admit these further reasons to himself—he also included Matthias because he did not want to put Lucia and the boys out of sorts at the very beginning. Above all, however, he did it out of cunning. He wanted to lull Matthias and the God Jehovah behind him into a sense of security; for so much was plain: it was one of the God Jehovah's tricks that of all people he should set this young man, graced with so many charms, in the path of the pair whom he, the Arch-Priest of Rome, had destined to be the future rulers of the Empire.

During that dinner at Domitian's table Matthias was filled with elation. Within him lay the memory of words which his mother had often said when she praised Joseph: he had been the table companion of three Emperors. Now he, Matthias, was the table companion of three Emperors, he, to whom the girl Cecilia had said that he belonged on the right bank of the Tiber and would end up as a pedlar.

Matthias's happiness made him even more radiant than usual. He made an impression through sheer personality, through his animated face, his gestures; his voice, so young and yet so manly, captivated everyone as soon as he opened his mouth. The Emperor turned to him more than to all the others. But within Domitian, while he spoke to his Lucia's protégé, there were feelings and thoughts of many kinds. He found Matthias's unaffected charm appealing; he enjoyed it as he might the droll awkwardness of the young wild animals in his cages. As he was a good observer, he did not fail to note how much the boy was attached to Lucia, and he felt a consciously ridiculous, but for that no less powerful sense of triumph at the thought that he, Domitian, slept with this Lucia and not the lovable young favourite of the God Jehovah.

Quintilian put all his efforts into showing off his pupils' Latin education to the Emperor. The young princes did valiantly without revealing any particular abilities. Matthias also showed no particular aptitude but he expressed what he had to say in a modest and pleasant manner and proved that he was permeated with Roman education. "The clever son of a clever father," Domitian admitted. The twins, moreover, did not conceal even at table that they looked up to Matthias as to a superior-favoured being, and for the Emperor this was a kind of grim confirmation. So his fear was well founded: the God Jehovah was making use of this Matthias with a deep cunning to worm His way into the boys' souls.

Then at last, after the meal was ended, Lucia was alone with the Emperor. They were in his study, which he had had covered with the reflecting metal. It was the first time she had seen it. "What are these awful mirrors you've got here?" she asked.

"That," he replied, "is to give me eyes even behind my back. I have many enemies." He was silent for a moment, then went on: "But now I have taken precautions. Now if something happens to me, at least the young lions are here. I'm glad that I adopted the boys. It took decision to give up hope of children from you. But I feel relieved since I know that my hearth will not be extinguished." "You're right," said Lucia understandingly. "But," she brought out point-blank, "what bothers me is the thought of Domitilla. I don't like her, the dry, finicky crea-ture, but after all she's the one who bore the children. I don't like knowing that she's on a desolate island in the Balearic Sea while you're intending to bring up her sons as the rulers of Rome."

Domitian's distrust had awakened at once. Aha, she wanted to have an ally in winning the twins to her side. He was tempted to answer sharply, but as he found her very attractive he restrained himself. "I shall try, my Lucia," he began, "to make plain to you the reasons why I have to keep Domitilla at a distance. I have nothing against her. Clemens and Sabinus I hated; I found their slackness, their laziness, their whole be-haviour repugnant. It's different with Domitilla. She's a woman, no one demands of her that she be active in service to the State; also she has something tough, something strong about her which would be more likely to appeal to me. But unfortunately this superstition of the Minæans had simply got a hold on her twisted brain. In itself it's completely unimportant what Flavia Domitilla thinks or does not think, and I could let it go. But it's a question of the boys. These boys are to be instructed by the tutor whom I chose for them, and by no one else. I don't want Domitilla to be near them. I don't want the hard, clear principles which my Quintilian teaches the boys to be softened and blurred by silly, womanish, superstitious talk about that crucified God. Everything about that faith, which unfortunately Domitilla does profess—its unworldliness, its aversion to reality, its indolent attitude toward the State—all that is dangerous for such young people."

Lucia decided to enter into battle, to advance to attack. Turning her bold, bright face toward him with an actually threatening expression, she asked: "And do you consider it dangerous for the boys to be in contact with me?" The Emperor hesitated. He should have said yes; it would have been his duty to Jupiter and Rome to say yes. But the nearness of his beloved's face confused him; he wavered. He tried to avoid her face, he turned his glance away, but in the reflecting metal all around them her face encountered him again and again. Lucia, noticing his hesitation, went on: "To be frank with you, I find Quintilian pretty much of a bore. I think it's very necessary for a fresh breeze to blow about the boys now and then." Domitian had prepared an answer. "Of course," he said gallantly, "I have no objection to my young lions' also enjoying your presence, my Lucia. But I do not wish your young Matthias by any chance to infect them with his beliefs, or the Jew Josephus with his sentimental nonsense about the sinfulness of enjoying peacock pie."

Lucia was annoyed that the proud Roman Quintilian had obviously not had enough dignity to keep his mouth shut, but had had to tattle about Matthias and his father right away as if he were one of Norbanus's spies. But she took D.D.D.'s words as a concession—at least he would not forbid the twins to communicate with her. "It's kind of you," she admitted, "that at least you don't want to prescribe whom I may see and whom not." But she did not labour this delicate point any longer, but came close to him, stroked his sparse hair, and said: "I must pay you a compliment, Vellykins. You haven't lost by my not having seen you for some time; on the contrary, you're more attractive than I remembered you." Domitian had longed for her touch; he had to control himself not to breath harder. She's flattering me, he thought, she's making up to me; I must be firm, I mustn't let her get around me. "Thank you," he said rather stiffly.

Lucia, leaving him alone for a moment, became practical. She thought out loud: "Isn't there any other way of keeping that doctrine away from the boys than by banishing their mother? Don't such drastic measures constantly direct the twins' attention to their mother's guilt, that is, to the very subject which one wants to keep away from them; and apart from all that, won't it seem improper to the city and the Empire that you elevate the twins to such heights but continue to leave their mother on her Balearic island? Doesn't that hurt the young lions' prestige? And doesn't it warp the boys' souls, which you want above all to grow straight?"

"I should never have guessed," said the Emperor maliciously, "that Domitilla had such a warm friend in you." "I am completely indifferent to Domitilla!" Lucia repeated vehemently. But immediately she regained her self-control and changed her voice and behaviour. "It's only for your sake, Vellykins," she said, "that I'm advising you to pardon Domitilla. You let people plead with you a long time before you called me back from exile too," she joked, "and did you repent it? Don't do yourself harm," she begged. "You adopted the boys—that was splendid. But if you don't complete your action by recalling Domitilla, you'll ruin its effect. Nobody knows better than I how often and how badly you are misunderstood. Take care that the service you've rendered the twins isn't misinterpreted because of the thought of the mother. Recall Domitilla."

Domitian avoided answering her. He looked her up and down with his near-sighted eyes and, "You're very beautiful," he said, "when you get excited for a cause." Lucia, however, would not let him go. "Don't you understand," she said softly, in an urgent, affectionate tone, "that I get excited for your sake?" Again she was very close to him, and, with an arm about his shoulders, she begged: "Won't you recall Domitilla?"

"I'll think it over," Domitian evaded her uneasily. "I promise you I'll think the matter over carefully with Quintilian." "With that bore!" Lucia disposed of the great stylist with annoyance. "Think it over with me," she urged him. "But not here. Here, between your awful mirrors, one can't really think. Come to my rooms. Sleep with me and think it over." And she left without giving him time to answer.

He decided to let her wait in vain. No, he would not come. She wanted payment for letting him lie with her. No, my dear, that would never do. He whistled to himself, a couplet which was popular at the time.

> Even a bald-head a pretty girl can hold
> If he is willing to pay his weight in gold.

Norbanus had thought of forbidding the couplet, but Domitian had not allowed that. No, he would not go to Lucia.

Half an hour later he was with her.

Yet even in bed she could get only a qualified promise out of him. If Domitilla made no attempt to interfere with the bringing up of the boys, then, he promised, he would recall her.

Incidentally, while Lucia slept with him she had the feeling that she was betraying Joseph with him, although, or perhaps just because, she had withheld herself from Joseph. It was the first time in her life that she had had such a feeling. Was it Joseph's influence? So this was "sin," about which she had heard so much? She was almost glad that now she had come to know these things also—conscience, sin.

Aᴆᴛᴇʀ Lucia had returned to Baia, the Emperor locked himself in his study, to consider what he had saved and what he had surrendered.

He had them under his protection now, his new sons who were to continue his family and preserve his Roman idea for the future. But he had not yet fully safeguarded them against the poison of Jehovah. He should not have given Lucia that promise to recall Domitilla. At least he had kept his head enough to give himself a respite. He would keep his promise; he, the Arch-Priest, the guardian of oaths, would stand by his word. But first Domitilla must stand the test. First she must prove that she would keep quiet, that she would not interfere with the upbringing of the young lions. That would take some time.

Lucia had demanded payment; he had paid her for her embrace; that was weak and shameless.

> Even a bald-head a pretty girl can hold
> If he is willing to pay his weight in gold,

he whistled angrily to himself. But yet—Lucia loved him, there was no doubt of that. When he thought of the fire with which her embraces had filled him, every other woman seemed a clumsy whore. But Lucia was alive, she was a glowing human being, she was the woman who was right for him, the God, and she loved him.

Yet even though she was Roman through and through, she had not been able to keep herself altogether sane and untouched. Something of the poison of that Jehovah was in her also. Although she probably laughed at most of the things that the Jew Joseph and his son might try to whisper to her, she had not been able to close her ears to them completely. But Jehovah, that sly, treacherous, vindictive God, had most certainly picked agents who could not have been improved upon. That boy Matthias! Domitian called up his image: his burning, darting, yet merry and innocent eyes; he heard his deep, young voice. If he, Domitian, were a boy, he would not be able to escape this Matthias's fascination himself—let alone the twins.

Yet not once since they lived with him had they spoken to him about Matthias. Domitian, however, was suspicious; probably Lucia had impressed upon them that they should not mention Matthias's name for the time being. She was no doubt counting on the fact that she would surely be able to retie the bonds between his young lions and her young Jew once she was near to them again.

Lucia was very much attached to him, to this adjutant Flavius Matthias. Not that there was anything of criminal passion in the attraction. The Emperor had watched closely. It was simply the boy's radiance which drew Lucia; she felt for him the tenderness of a mother, of an older sister.

But what were the relations between her and Joseph? Nonsense. Joseph was a worn-out, faded fellow on the threshold of old age. It was laughable, insane, inconceivable, that Lucia, the Roman Empress, should throw herself from the arms of a Domitian into the arms of this Jew. There was nothing between Lucia and Joseph but the somewhat sentimental and snobbish friendship between a cultivated woman and a famous writer.

It was a case of self-control, self-control on her part and on his. But he, Domitian, had not been able to resist; he had become weak before Lucia through greed, through lust. Before his wife, the Empress, the Roman, the whore, he had let himself be tricked into the promise to call back Domitilla. He had sinned against his new sons; he had neglected his duty toward Jupiter and the gods of his household.

He must make up for it. He must get the enemy and his

brood out of the way: Joseph, who had dared to mock at him, to hurl the poem about courage into his face, and that Matthias, the scion of David, the candidate for world domination, the favourite of the Eastern God.

True, since he had had the boy at his table the task seemed even harder. He must do away with the boy, but how should he go about it without calling down the justified wrath of the Eastern God upon his head?

About this time the Emperor was visited by Messalinus, the only person left him, the only person to whose ears and heart he could confide his troubles.

It was the first very hot day. The wind was from the south and the atmosphere sultry; the sultriness could not be shut out entirely even from the darkened, artificially cooled room in which Domitian received Messalinus. The odours of the garden penetrated it heavily; a fountain splashed; its noise accompanied the men's conversation evenly and soothingly.

The Emperor recalled his encounter with the scions of David, speaking about the details of that meeting with ironical benevolence. "The Jews," he concluded, "can't gain much prestige with their pretenders. Can you imagine, for example, that a faded old writer like our Josephus would cut a very good figure as the Messiah? A man who can't even speak decent Greek?"

The soft voice of the blind man sounded through the quiet splashing of the fountain: "Still, this Josephus is said to have a son, handsome to look upon and well formed in mind also."

The Emperor was startled that, as soon as the subject came up in conversation, the same disquieting thoughts arose in the other as in himself. "He's a handsome youth, the boy Matthias," he admitted hesitantly. With a twinge of fear he waited for Messalinus's answer. For a brief moment—but it seemed long to him—there was no sound in the room but the regular splash of the falling water. Then at last, in his carefully measured,

courteous way, Messalinus said: "Heaven deprived my eyes of
sight. But the Lord and God Domitian has good eyes, and he
can judge whether this boy Matthias has enough charm to endanger the peace and safety of the Province of Judæa because
he is a scion of David."

"You speak of a subject," replied the Emperor, and he lowered his shrill voice so that it was almost drowned out by the
fountain, "which it is no light thing to touch upon." He began
to speak, he swallowed, then made up his mind and told the
other his secret. "I have concluded a kind of truce with the
God Jehovah," he whispered. "I do not want to interfere with
His decisions. I do not want to anger Him," and in louder
tone, almost grandly: "No man shall be endangered because
he happens to be pleasing to the God Jehovah and chosen by
Him." Now it was out; his heart beat so loudly that he was
afraid that the other would hear it despite the fountain. Had
Messalinus understood him? He feared it; he longed for it. In
suspense he waited for the blind man's answer.

Then it came. "The thoughts of the Lord and God Domitian," he said respectfully and very calmly," are so lofty that a
mortal can never fully grasp them, that he can at most surmise
them. We see only Flavius Josephus and Flavius Matthias,
people of flesh and blood. The God Domitian sees what is behind them."

It had annoyed Domitian that Norbanus saw through him;
that Messalinus understood him gave him satisfaction. The
blind man was after all almost an equal spirit. How subtly he
had put into words what he, Domitian, felt. Yes, the blind
man's intuition came close to his own lofty reality which was
hidden from others. "You are very wise, my Messalinus," he
said, and now his voice sounded loud and relieved, "and you
are my friend. Fundamentally you are my only friend. Perhaps
that is why you are so wise. Matters stand exactly as you have

said. Unfortunately it is not the human beings whom I have to fight, it is the God. If the God didn't stand behind them I would blow them away with one breath from my lips. Since you have understood me so well, my Messalinus, you will surely understand this also. Think about it, think it over well and give me your advice."

Again for a long time there was nothing in the room but the sound of the fountain. Domitian waited in excitement, full of confidence. He was sure that his good, his faithful friend would be able to advise him. And, surely enough, Messalinus began to speak. Very cautiously he amplified Domitian's statement: "He is a scion of David and therefore your opponent. But you spare him and don't antagonize him because as a scion of David he is under the God Jehovah's protection and you don't want to have anything to do with this God Jehovah. Have I rightly understood the wisdom of my Lord and God?" "You have done so," replied Domitian. "But," continued Messalinus, "what if the scion of David took action against the security of the Emperor or of the Empire? Would you spare him then too, Emperor Domitian, just because he is a scion of David?" The Emperor had listened intently. "You mean, then I could punish him?" he asked. "The crime of being a scion of David," answered Messalinus, "you cannot punish, since it is a crime of the God Jehovah's, with whom you do not wish to quarrel. But every other crime of Joseph's or Matthias's you could punish, for it would be the crime of a human being and would have nothing to do with your fight with the God Jehovah. That is the opinion of a humble mortal," he added respectfully. "It is for the God Domitian to decide whether or not it is conclusive."

"I owe it to Jehovah," Domitian repeated hoarsely, "to let the scions of David live out their lives. But I owe it to Jupiter to punish those who sin against him and against me. You are very wise, my Messalinus. You have expressed what I had already thought to myself."

The blind man held his head bent very far forward to drink in the Emperor's words. An almost voluptuous excitement filled him. He was effecting a master-stroke. One could be blind and yet see exactly what sluices to open to release a great flood. Domitian had absorbed his words. Now a great flood of misfortune would burst upon a number of people, and he in his darkness would rejoice that he had been the one who had caused it all. "I thank the Lord and God Domitian," he said reverently, "that he has let me gaze into the profound and manifold activities of his wise and well-measured thoughts."

"You are as wise as you are loyal, my Messalinus," replied Domitian. "My thoughts find a worthy weapon in you." And he dismissed him in high favour.

When evening approached and it became cooler, the Emperor stood in front of his animal cages. It would be glorious if the boy Matthias committed a crime. It would be glorious if he, Domitian, were provided with a reason for punishing the boy. It would be glorious if the boy no longer existed on earth. The recollection of the boy's deep voice pained the Emperor more greatly than ever had the recollection of his brother Titus's braying.

It would be a heavy blow to the Jew Josephus if he lost that favoured son of his. He would run to Lucia: he would wail and weep. The Emperor pictured to himself how the Jew Joseph would wail and weep; it was not an unpleasant image. It was glorious that skilled hands were engaged in weaving a snare for that handsome and cultivated boy Matthias, the scion of David.

The Emperor noticed that the animals were suffering from the heat, and ordered water brought to them.

SHORTLY thereafter it happened that Lucia entrusted her adjutant Matthias with a mission which gave him much pleasure.

The city of Massilia, whose patroness Lucia was, had sent her an exceptionally beautiful, nobly fashioned piece of coral jewellery, and the Empress wished to give the city a worthy present in return. Matthias was to deliver this present and on that occasion attend to several lesser errands which only a trusted agent could carry out. He was to try to persuade old Charmis, the Empress's eye doctor, who was averse to the trip to Baia because of his great age, to come to Baia after all. Then Matthias was to purchase certain cosmetics for Lucia which Massilia alone manufactured in the quality desired by the Empress. Finally she also gave him a letter which he was to deliver to a trusted man to send on across the Balearic Sea.

Matthias was happy and thought himself very important. Above all he was happy that the trip was to be by sea, and on Lucia's private yacht, the *Blue Gull*. Since Lucia was eager to have her errand executed quickly, Matthias limited himself to bidding his father farewell by letter; Joseph had returned to Rome so as not to attract attention by an overlong stay at Baia. His father's answering letter reached Matthias just before the yacht set out to sea. Joseph asked him to look around in Massilia for the best and most accurate manuscript procurable of the *Navigation* by Pytheas of Massilia, which as a rule could be found only in faulty copies.

Although he had not been able to see his father once more, a kind fate allowed him to bid farewell to the girl Cecilia. Matthias had not seen Cecilia for a long time. To look for her outright would have shamed him in his own eyes; yet he had often lingered near the places where he might have met her; she, incidentally, had done the same. In any case the faces of both lighted up when, the day before he was to leave, they actually happened upon one another.

Cecilia behaved sharply and a little mockingly as always. "So now you have a noble mission, Matthias," she said. "You're to purchase perfumes for Mistress Lucia. But I suppose her personal hairdresser would manage to do that as well and perhaps better than you." Matthias looked amiably into the pretty girl's smooth face and said calmly: "Why do you really talk such nonsense, Cecilia? You know perfectly well that of course I'm not going to Massilia just for the perfumes." "I'd be surprised," Cecilia insisted quarrelsomely, "if it really was something more important. You've learned a few things from your peacocks and you've a habit of being pretty noisy when you've a chance to show off your glory." Matthias, still with the same composure, answered: "Do I really have to show off to you, Cecilia? Do I really have to boast to you that the Empress likes to see me?" He went up closer to her; he looked urgently into her face with his deep, youthful, innocent eyes, and, "if I were the nobody," he said, "that you're so fond of making me out to be, would you yourself be together with me so often? Let's talk seriously, Cecilia. My errand in Massilia, unimportant as it may be, will keep me away from you for some time. Let me take along a picture of Cecilia the way she is in her best moments." And, very close to her, lowering his deep voice yet overflowing with passionate feeling, he burst out: "Cecilia, you're wonderful! What a lovely face you have when you don't twist it up so mockingly and nastily!" Cecilia pretended to be incredulous. "That's all just talk," she said coquettishly. "You really love only her, the Empress." "Who wouldn't love her?" Matthias admitted. "But what has that got to do with us two? I respect the Empress, I love her as I love my father. That is," he corrected himself honestly, "it's not exactly the same. But it's like that. You, Cecilia—" "I know," Cecilia interrupted him jealously, rather foolishly, "you don't respect me. You make fun of me. I'm a silly little girl. You Jews are all so proud and conceited. It's your beggarly pride."

"Let's not talk about Jews and Romans now," pleaded Matthias. "Please, please, Cecilia." He took her hand, a white childish hand, he kissed the hand, kissed her bare arm. She resisted, but he would not stop; he was much taller than she, he put his arms around her, he almost lifted her off her feet; she defended herself, but then, quite suddenly, she went limp and returned his kisses. "Don't go away now, Matthias," she begged in a small, crushed voice. "Let somebody else get the perfumes. Send another Jew." "Oh, Cecilia," was all that Matthias answered, and he embraced her more passionately, more hungrily. At first she let him; then, all at once, she freed herself. "When you're back," she promised, and, "Come back soon," she urged him.

A short time afterward Messalinus again asked to be announced at Albanum. He brought the Emperor a copy of a letter.

The letter ran as follows:

Lucia to Domitilla.

You will have heard, my dear, about the good fortune which has befallen your fine sons. But perhaps the joy you felt about this event was not quite unmixed when you considered that the boys would now live exclusively at the Palatine and at Albanum. I am writing to you to relieve you of that anxiety. I promised you once that your boys would not become too Latin, and I shall do everything I can to prevent their hearts from withering in the severe atmosphere of the Palatine. Moreover, my dear Domitilla, I have reason to hope that after the adoption of your sons you yourself will soon be recalled. Only

one thing I do ask of you: abandon every attempt to influence
the boys' fate from your island. Rather remain completely
quiet, my dear; do not worry about your sons, even though
they are now called Vespasian and Domitian. Trust your Lucia.
Farewell.

The Emperor read the letter slowly and carefully. A tremendous rage seized him. It was not that he was infuriated
because Lucia was intriguing behind his back with Domitilla—
he had not expected anything else; perhaps he had even wished
t. What outraged him far more was that sentence about "hearts
withering in the severe atmosphere of the Palatine." Lucia
dared to write that, she, who knew him! Lucia dared to write
that, after the nights she had spent with him!

He read the letter over several times. "Has the Lord and
God Domitian read the letter?" the blind man finally asked
in his soft, calm voice. The Emperor, in a cold fury, asked:
"Why did you bring me this piece of trash? Do you want to
blacken Lucia in my eyes? Do you dare to affirm that the
words on this dirty scrap of paper are my Lucia's?" "I did not
bring this copy of the letter to Your Majesty," replied Messalinus in his even voice, "because I wanted to cast suspicion
on the person who wrote the original or might have written it.
But from a conversation with which Your Majesty recently honoured me I dared to conclude that the Lord and God Domitian
has a certain interest in the messenger who undertook to smuggle the original of this letter to its addressee."

Domitian impetuously stepped up to Messalinus and looked
into his face with such questioning suspense as if the blind
man could see his gaze. A joyful presentiment elated him.
"Who is the fellow?" he asked, and, "The Empress's youngest adjutant, Flavius Matthias," replied Messalinus.

Domitian breathed deeply, relieved. Yet he made an effort

not to betray his profound, joyful, shameful satisfaction. "What did you do with the original?" he asked Messalinus matter-of-factly. "The original," the other informed him, "remained in our possession but a scant half-hour, just long enough for us to copy it decently. Then, without letting young Matthias notice anything, we slipped it back to him again. The letter has gone on, on the yacht *Blue Gull,* as had been planned; probably the letter is now on its way to the Balearic Islands, perhaps it has already arrived."

Domitian, and this time his voice broke, asked: "And this Matthias? The Empress sent him to Massilia, if I'm rightly informed. Where is he now, this Matthias?" "The young Flavius Matthias," reported Messalinus, "has been honoured by Her Majesty with many small errands. He has to obtain certain cosmetics; he has to find the great eye doctor Charmis and possibly to bring him back with him; he has a lot of things to attend to in Massilia. I believed that the Empress's errands demanded the greatest conscientiousness and circumspection, and I saw to it that Flavius Matthius will have something to do in Massilia for a long time."

"Interesting, my Messalinus, very interesting," said the Emperor; in a rather absent voice, it seemed to Messalinus. "Massilia," Domitian went on to himself; and, still in the same absent voice, he gave a little lecture about the city of Massilia which really had nothing to do with the subject. "An interesting settlement," he declared, "and well suited to hold for some time a young man who is eager for knowledge. It has beautified Gaul, my good city of Massilia; there are beautiful temples there, of the Ephesian Artemis and the Delphic Apollo. It's a pure, unspoiled island of Greek culture in the midst of barbarian surroundings. Also, if I remember rightly, there are interesting ancient customs there," and in that vein he went on babbling for a while quite meaninglessly.

Messalinus, however, did not answer. He knew perfectly that the Emperor did not want any answer; the Emperor wanted only to conceal his thoughts, and those thoughts were certainly not about the peculiar customs of the city of Massilia.

It was true: the Emperor's thoughts, while he gave his lecture, were far from the city of Massilia. "Lucia," he was thinking rather, "Lucia. I sacrificed so much for her sake; I sinned against Jupiter and against my new sons for her sake; I promised her the recall of this Domitilla; and this is how she rewards me. At the Palatine and around me hearts wither, she writes." And suddenly, quite abruptly, he interrupted himself and began to whistle, most unmelodiously and faultily; and Messalinus, surprised and amused, recognized the melody— it was that couplet from the latest comedy:

> Even a bald-head a pretty girl can hold
> If he is willing to pay his weight in gold.

Again Messalinus did not think of disturbing the Emperor's thoughts. The latter, however, suddenly awoke from his musings; he had let himself go, he had let himself sink into thought. It was a good thing at least that the blind man could not read his face. He pulled himself together, and as if nothing had happened, as if there had been no pause and no long silence, he said pertinently: "Are you quite sure of your information?" "I have no eyes to see with," answered Messalinus, "but as far as a blind man can be sure, I am sure."

Surely Messalinus knew how deeply his report had upset him, Domitian; even though he was blind he saw deep into him, much deeper and more dangerously than even Norbanus did; yet oddly enough the Emperor had not the slightest feeling of hatred or inferiority toward Messalinus. No, he was grateful to him, he was honestly grateful to him; and, "You've done very well," he said approvingly, "and I thank you."

Messalinus withdrew, deeply satisfied. Domitian, alone, thought over what he had heard. Strangely, he felt no real anger at Lucia; on the contrary, he was almost grateful to her for what she had done. For now it was no longer possible to determine whether Domitilla would have interfered in the affairs of his young lions, and such a proof of her loyalty was the condition of his promise to revoke her banishment. Actually the letter revealed that Lucia too, although she had befriended Domitilla, credited her with the intention of influencing the boys against his, the Emperor and Censor's, will. But by that he was relieved of his promise, before Lucia, before himself, before the gods. And as far as Lucia was concerned, he would not forget what she had undertaken against him, but he would postpone clearing up the situation. Lucia simply was the way she was; in a certain sense she bore no responsibility. Instead, the consciousness of sparing her, and of having within him a supply of arguments against her at any moment, gave him a certain pleasure. He would keep the whole matter to himself. No one should know how he, the God, had been cheated by those three, by Lucia, by Domitilla, by the boy Matthias, cheated and betrayed—he, the most benevolent, the most generous of rulers. It was enough that the blind man knew. He cared a great deal for the blind man. Actually Lucia and the blind man were the only people for whom he cared. So let Lucia go on having her mistaken, naïve, unfounded pleasure in having tricked him; in reality he would trick her. And let the blind man, to whom as his faithful servant he owed great thanks, warm himself in his darkness with the thought that he shared a secret with the lord of the world.

But what should he do with the other two, with Domitilla and with the young man who had undertaken to smuggle the letter to the Balearic Islands? They must not continue to exist, that was certain, but their punishment must come secretly, out of the dark, and no one must perceive the connexion.

Domitilla. The exile. His father Vespasian had once let himself be talked into recalling an exile from banishment against his will; it was Helvidius the Elder, the father. But Vespasian, lucky and far-seeing, had been lucky there again; before the pardoned man received news of his recall he had died. He too, Domitian, would prove once again that he was a man of luck and foresight. He would pardon Domitilla; he would announce it grandly to Lucia and the whole world. If poor Domitilla did not then learn of her happiness in time, that was her concern, not his.

And as far as young Matthias was concerned, an obscure fate would overtake him also, by no means a punishment. Perhaps he, Domitian, would explain to Joseph why he had to do away with the boy; for the God Jehovah and His servant must not think that he had harmed the boy without reason, and only out of hatred against Jehovah. But nobody else besides the Jew Josephus, Messalinus, and himself was to know about the connexion. For everyone else it was to be an accident that snatched away the beautiful page boy from the Empress.

THE Neptunalia were not a very important festival. Only a prince who gave as much importance to tradition as Domitian did would put himself to the trouble of exchanging his summer residence for the hot city because of the festival.

For three days the Emperor conducted the ceremonies. Then, on the fourth, he summoned Joseph to the Palatine.

The invitation struck Joseph like a thunderbolt. Since the Emperor had taken so long to prepare his revenge for that reading, what a terrible revenge it would be! It would be a bad moment; Joseph would have to scrape together all his courage from the corners of his soul. There had been times when he had longed for his own end, when he had longed ardently to bear witness for his cause by his death. But to be torn away now, in the full bloom of his happiness—he shuddered at the thought.

To begin with, however, the Emperor received him with cheerful calm; he showed neither anger nor that dangerous affability which all who knew him feared more than his fury. Instead he seemed rather absent-mindedly cordial.

"How is your Matthias?" he asked after a while. Joseph told him that the Mistress and Goddess Lucia had sent him to Massilia. "So she did," the Emperor recalled, "on the yacht *Blue Gull*. Massilia—a beautiful city," and he began to talk about the peculiarities of the city again; in fact he could hardly keep from lapsing into senseless garrulity as he had recently done in Messalinus's presence. "In any case, my Josephus," he caught himself up, "I'm glad that your Matthias is getting to see a little of the world. And the errands which he has to do for the Empress there won't press him too hard. He's to buy her perfumes and cosmetics, and he's to entice Doctor Charmis onto the yacht with him. Important errands." Joseph was puzzled that the lord of the world should know in such detail about the unimportant errands which his Matthias had to do in Massilia. "It is a great favour and most amazing," he jested, "that Your Majesty's eyes follow my Matthias with such attention." "Did you see him before his departure?" asked the Emperor. "No," answered Joseph. "He could really have travelled via Rome and embarked at Ostia," said Domitian. "But the Empress obviously thought her errands were important and was in a hurry. By the way, she's very much attached to your Matthias; I saw that myself. And he is a nice boy, with pleasant

manners; he appealed to me. It must be in the family that
we—we Flavians and you—again and again find our fates so
closely bound together."

It really was strange how closely the Flavians were bound
together with Joseph and his family. But he did not know what
to make of the Emperor's remarks; he felt uneasy. "You no
doubt love him very much, your son Matthias?" the Emperor
went on. Joseph replied shortly: "Yes, I love him. I think," he
added, "he's probably already at sea again, on his way back
to Italy. I'm looking forward to seeing him again." "It's a good
thing," said the Emperor slowly, and he looked dreamily into
Joseph's face with his protruding eyes, "that we've celebrated
the Neptunalia just now and that I took part in them myself.
Thus we have done our part that Neptune may grant him a
fair return voyage." Joseph thought that the Emperor was
joking, and he was about to smile; but the Emperor had such
a serious, almost gloomy expression, that his impulse to smile
forsook him.

Yet at table the Emperor again behaved with particular good
humour. He spoke about Joseph's book against Apion. The
book was proof that Joseph had at last freed himself from his
dishonest, fashionably cosmopolitan objectivity toward his own
people. "Of course," he declared. "everything you advance in
favour of your Jews is just as unproven and subjective as what
your hated Greeks and Egyptians advance against those same
Jews. Nevertheless, I congratulate you on your book. Your old
ideas of fusion and cosmopolitanism were a lot of foggy nonsense. I, the Emperor Domitian, like a healthy nationalism."
Although the Emperor's condescending remarks seemed more
like censure than praise, Joseph heard them with joy. He was
relieved that the Emperor spoke to him about his books and
no more about his son.

After dinner also Domitian spoke about literature. He lay

on his couch, lazily, and aired his views. Joseph waited nervously for what the Emperor would want of him; he told himself that now that he had waited so long he would surely be able to wait one hour more, but he became increasingly shaky. At last, unexpectedly, Domitian demanded that Joseph once again recite the "Ode to Courage" to him.

Joseph was deeply alarmed. Now it was plain that the Emperor had summoned him to wreak vengeance upon him for his rash deed. "You understand, Josephus," the Emperor explained, "I wasn't prepared that time for your reading those verses. And the verses are a little strange; I wasn't able to take them in completely the first time. So I'd be obliged to you if I might hear them again." But everything in Joseph rebelled against the idea. Whatever this Roman meant to do with him, he himself, Joseph, was not in the mood to recite those verses. Today he did not feel them, today they seemed alien to him, and he considered it unworthy to play a part in the farce for which this evil man wished to use him. "On that occasion," he replied accordingly, "Your Majesty showed me plainly that my 'Psalm of Courage' did not appeal to you. So why should I once again trouble Your Majesty's ears?" But Domitian insisted. He had determined to hear the insolent words from the lips of this servant of Jehovah once more; it was Jehovah's declaration of war, and he wanted to know exactly how it was phrased. Impatiently, stubbornly, he commanded: "Recite the verses to me."

Joseph could not help but obey. He recited the verses, angrily yet without spirit, and with an unbelieving heart; they were words without content for him.

Therefore I say:
Hail to the man who takes death upon him,
That he may speak as his heart bids him.

Therefore I say:
Hail to the man who says what is so.
Therefore I say:
Hail to the man who cannot be forced
To say what is not.

He saw the Emperor's gaze fixed upon him; it was a searching, thoughtful, malignant gaze; he wanted to evade it, but
then he saw his own face in the mirrors lining the walls;
everywhere he saw his own face and that of the Emperor, the
Emperor's eyes and his own mouth, opening and closing. He
seemed to himself like an actor, and the content of his "Psalm
of Courage" seemed theatrical to him. Why wish to say what
was so to a world that did not really want to hear it? For
thousands of years men had told the world what was so, and
they had changed nothing; they had only brought misfortune
upon themselves.

Domitian listened attentively to the end. He repeated dreamily: " 'Hail to the man who says what is so.' What do you
mean—'hail to the man'? The gods do not reveal that which is
so, except possibly in the mysteries; so they certainly do not wish
one to say it always and to everyone. What you preach in your
verses, my dear fellow, sounds quite beautiful and interesting,
but if one examines it closely it's foolish stuff." He eyed Joseph as if he were one of his captive animals. "Odd," he said
and shook his head, "that someone should hit on such out-
landish ideas. 'Hail to the man who says what is so.' " And
several times again, slowly, he shook his head.

"So you love your Matthias?" he said suddenly, picking up
his earlier subject of conversation. The "Psalm of Courage,"
Matthias—an enormous fear gripped Joseph's heart. "Yes, I
love him," he replied constrainedly. "And of course you've big
things in mind for him?" Domitian went on asking. "You're

ambitious for him? You want to make him into something important?" Joseph answered cautiously: "I know that I have not deserved the evidences of favour with which the Lord and God Domitian and his predecessors have overwhelmed me. But my life has had sharp ups and downs. I want to spare my son that. What I wish to leave my son is security." And so it was; for the dreams of glory and fame which he had dreamed for his son Matthias had left him in that cruel moment, and he wanted him back, right there with him, so that he could take him away from Rome as quickly as possible, to Judæa, to safety and peace. In his innermost being he cried out to his God that He might give him strength in that grave moment to find the right words and save his son.

"Interesting, very interesting," the Emperor was answering meanwhile. "So that's what you want for your son—repose and safety. But do you think that an apprenticeship at court is the best means to that end?"

It touched Joseph to the quick that the enemy had at once found out his weakest point, his sin. For that was precisely where he had sinned: in setting his son on that dangerous path. He groped painfully for an answer. "The Empress liked my boy," was the answer he found at last. "Was I to say no when Mistress Lucia invited me to put him in her service? I should never have dared to show such disrespect." But now Domitian had discovered the weak point of his enemy, the servant of Jehovah, and he would not leave it. "If you hadn't wished it," he declared, raising his finger reproachfully—in the mirrors lining the walls it was many fingers—"you would have found ways and means. You were ambitious for him," he insisted; "be honest, admit it. Why else would you have put him in the Empress's service?" "Certainly a father is ambitious for his son," Joseph admitted, and he felt weak and empty.

"You see," Domitian said with satisfaction, and went on probing the wound. "You once told me, didn't you, that you sprang from the line of David? Since you yourself admit that you're ambitious for your son, did the idea never occur to you that perhaps he, your son, might be the chosen one, your Messiah?" Joseph, his lips very white, his throat dry, answered: "No, I did not think of that."

At first it had seemed to Domitian a wearisome task to argue out the case with the Jew, a burden which he had assumed only to justify himself in the sight of Jehovah. But now, when he saw Joseph's face, his haggard, agonized face, it was no longer a painful effort, but a great, fierce, cruel desire seized him to see what the man would do now, how he would behave, how his face would change, what he would say, when he found out what had happened to his son. The Emperor's eyes longed to see it; his ears longed to hear the outcry of his wounded, hated enemy who had spoken insolent words right into his face and who was liked by his Lucia.

So deliberately, thoughtfully, weighing his words with particular cunning, he went on: "If you never awakened the thought in your son that he might be your Jehovah's chosen one, perhaps you spurred his ambition in some other way, or perhaps he misunderstood you, or perhaps your God endowed him with an extremely ambitious heart from the beginning." Joseph followed the Emperor's words with painful suspense. "I am very stupid," he said, "or perhaps I have a bad day today and a thick head, but I don't know how to interpret Your Majesty's words." Still with the same merciless gentleness Domitian went on: "At any rate, it's a good thing that it's repose and safety in particular that you ask of heaven for your Matthias." Joseph, his heart and voice constricted with pain, implored him: "I should be eternally grateful to Your Majesty if you would speak to a fearful father in words simple enough for him to understand." "You are very impatient," said Domitian reprovingly. "You're so impatient that you offend against the decorum which you owe your imperial friend. But I'm used to having to forgive; to you in particular I have often granted indulgence; let it be so this time again. Listen then, you impatient fellow. This is what happened: your Matthias engaged in an extremely ambitious undertaking. I think, I hope, I can see it in your face, I am convinced—that you do not know about it. I'm glad for your sake. Because it was a very dangerous undertaking, and he did not succeed. Unfortunately it was also a criminal undertaking." "Have pity on me," Joseph implored him, in a low voice, but full of extreme agony. "Have pity on me, my Lord and God Domitian. What has happened to my Matthias? Tell me. I implore you."

Domitian eyed him with the grave, objective curiosity with which he looked at the animals in his cages and the plants in his hothouses. "He did the Empress's errands in Massilia," he said, "as he was told; he did them well, too well." "And has he left Massilia?" Joseph asked breathlessly. "Or where is he?" "He has set sail," answered the Emperor. "And when will he be back?" Joseph pressed. "And when shall I see him again?" And because the Emperor gave only a slow, gentle, pitying smile Joseph forgot all reverence; only one great, senseless fear spoke in him; and, "Then he won't come back?" he asked, his eyes fixed rigidly on the Emperor; and he went up quite close to him; he even touched the imperial robes. Domitian, who ordinarily shunned the touch of every stranger and regarded it as the most shameful offence against all reverence, freed himself gently. "You have more children, haven't you?" he said. "Now, my Jew, show that your poem about courage is more than mere words." "I had only one son, and he is no more," said Joseph, and he repeated senselessly, stubbornly: "Then he won't come back?" He stammered so badly that one could barely understand the words, yet the Emperor understood them and enjoyed the annihilation of his enemy. "He had an accident," he informed him in a friendly, regretful tone. "He fell. He made a boyish wager with one of the cabin boys. They climbed a mast, it appears, and he fell. They couldn't save him. He broke his neck."

Joseph stood there; his eyes were still glued to the Emperor's lips with the same tensely expectant expression. The latter waited for a cry, but there was none; instead Joseph's face slackened suddenly, and his lips began to work strangely; he opened and shut his mouth as if he was trying to speak and could not form the words.

But Domitian enjoyed his triumph to the full. There, opposite him, stood a man whom the gods had vanquished—all the gods, his own also, his Jehovah. Then he, Domitian, had been right: he had won a great battle against the God Jehovah, with the God's own weapons, by cunning and yet by fair, irreproachable means, so that the God could not reprove him or bring any charge against him. In a confidential tone and yet very distinctly, enjoying every one of his words, he went on: "You may know the truth, Josephus. It was not an accident that your son Matthias came to grief. It was a punishment. But I'm not vindictive, I'm merciful, and now that he has departed from this world I no longer bear him any grudge. So no one shall know that it was a crime for which he had to die. The whole world shall think that he had an accident, your beautiful, young, and lovable son Flavius Matthias. And that you may see that I wish you well, listen further: he shall be buried as if he had been the chosen one; it will be a princely burial, as if your King David had been a Roman."

But the Emperor was not granted the chance of seeing what impression his pride and his generosity made on his opponent. For Joseph obviously was no longer absorbing his mild and lofty words. Instead he stared at the Emperor with an empty, idiotic gaze; his lips still worked; and then, abruptly, he collapsed.

Domitian, however, had more to say yet; he could not keep it to himself, and since he could no longer say it to the hearing Joseph, he said it to the unconscious one. "Your Doctors," he said to him, "told me that the day would come. But in my lifetime and in yours, at any rate, my Josephus, that day will not come."

ONE evening soon after the interview with the Emperor, a small, black, solemn procession arrived at Joseph's house. It brought the corpse of Flavius Matthias, who had met his death in the service of the Empress by a fall on board the yacht *Blue Gull*. The art of embalming was highly developed in the city of Rome, and Domitian had engaged the best practitioners of that art. With ointments, spices, and doubtless with paint as well, they had managed to make the body which was delivered at Joseph's house appear beautiful and practically uninjured. His bony head lay there with an air of young manhood, the glossy black hair carefully arranged; it was the same and yet changed, for it had drawn all its life from the eyes, and those eyes were closed. And whereas his son's beautiful head, when Joseph had last seen him, had sat upon a very childlike neck, now the Adam's apple stood out more markedly and like a man's.

With his own hand Joseph overturned the furniture in Matthias's room and arranged the bier for his homecoming son. There he sat in the dim light of a single oil lamp, and on the overturned bed, lay the boy.

Joseph had become an easy-going man in his happiness; a

man who was afraid of his own depths and reluctant to analyse himself. Now all his depths had been torn open; his inmost being cried out against him; no evasions were possible. When his son Simeon-Janiki had died he had wavered between the most varied feelings; there had been grief in him, remorse, self-accusation, but also self-justification and indignation against God and the world. Now, by the body of his son Matthias, he felt only one thing: revulsion, hatred against himself.

He did not hate the Emperor. He had done away with a young man whom he regarded as a pretender; that was his imperial right. He had even behaved considerately. He could have let the corpse disappear; he could have left it to the sea and the fishes; and the picture of his dead son drifting in the restless waters was horrible to Joseph. But the Emperor had been merciful: he had let him have the dead boy; he had even adorned him and filled him with sweet perfumes for him— the merciful, most gracious Emperor. No, there was only one man in this case against whom all hatred, all aversion must be directed, and that was he himself, Joseph Ben Matthias, Flavius Josephus, the fool, the boaster, who had grown old but never wise, and who had thrust his son upon the road to destruction. Joseph's inner collapse was much deeper now than in those days of Simeon-Janiki's death. This time there was nothing to twist and try to explain; this time all causes had their being in himself. If he had not, out of sheer spiritual arrogance confessed to being sprung from the line of David, then Matthias would still be alive. If he had not, out of pure, stupid fatherly pride, kept him from going to Judæa with Mara, Matthias would still be alive. If he had not, out of absolute, external vanity, put him in service to Lucia, Matthias would still be alive. It was his ambition, his vanity, which had killed Matthias.

He had beeen tremendously, insanely presumptuous. He had wanted to make of his Matthias that Cæsarion whom the great Cæsar had failed to make of his son—little imitator of a great man that he was. All that he had ever undertaken in his life he had done out of vanity. Out of vanity he had gone to Rome as a young man; out of vanity he had played the prophet and prophesied the Emperorship to Vespasian; out of vanity he had made himself the historian of the Flavians; out of spiritual arrogance he had confessed to being a scion of David. Out of vanity he had written his lying, fashionably objective *Universal History;* out of vanity his effective, glowing apologia *Apion.* And now out of vanity he had killed his son Matthias.

As Jacob loved the boy Joseph, so had he loved his boy Matthias, with foolish fatherly love. And as Jacob had given the boy Joseph the coat of many colours and thus awakened his brothers' envy against him, so had he wrapped his Matthias in splendour which invited retribution. And as it was announced to Jacob: "Torn, torn to pieces is your son Joseph," so had the enemy informed him: "Dead is your beloved son." But in Jacob, the ancestral father, there had been no sin but his insane love; while he, Joseph Ben Matthias, was covered over and over with sin. And while the boy Joseph had still been alive, even if deserted and deep in a well, his Matthias lay there dead, waxen, and painted, his Adam's apple standing out unmoved by any breath of life; and there was no hope that he would be saved.

The night passed, a short summer night, and with the morning came countless numbers to greet the dead Flavius Matthias once more. It was known that the Emperor was taking a personal interest in the accident which had carried off his Lucia's protégé; romantic stories were current about his life and end; people spoke much about the boy's beauty and brilliance. So an endless procession filed through the room with the overturned furniture where lay the dead Matthias. The sympathetic, the curious, the ambitious. They came so as not to miss the slightest opportunity of making themselves agreeable to the Emperor; they came to see the corpse, to show their sorrow, to express their sympathy. All Rome filed past the body. But Joseph remained absent, locked in the innermost chamber of his house, squatting on the ground, barefooted, with hair grown wild and garments torn.

Marullus and Claudius Reginus came; old, old Caius Barzaarone came, and he thought how soon he would lie there like that; Senator Messalinus came, and he stood by the body for a long time with a politely sympathetic face, and no one could read what was within him; and the peacock-keeper Amphion came also, and burst into loud sobs; and the girl Cecilia came. She too let herself go; she let the tears stream all over her bright, smooth face; she regretted that she had vexed Matthias so foolishly and that she had resisted him and postponed everything until his return.

The two princes came also, Constans and Petronius, or rather Vespasian and Domitian as they were now called. They stood by the body, gravely, with their tutor Quintilian. People had made way for them, but behind them waited countless numbers; the street was choked with people who wanted to see the dead boy. But the twins did not hurry, and even when Quintilian urged them very politely they did not move away. They gazed at the lifeless countenance of their dearly beloved friend. They were accustomed to death; young as they were they had seen many die; and only few of a quiet death in bed. Their father had met with a bloody end, their grandfather and their uncle also, and quietly and peacefully as their friend Matthias lay there, they guessed, and in their hearts they knew, that he too had been brought low by a hand familiar to them. All this they thought over as they stood there by the overturned bed; they did not weep; they looked very mature and grown-up; and except for the fact that they could not be torn away, Quintilian could make no complaint about their behaviour. Only at the very end, before they went, the younger of the two could not keep from making a childish and blameworthy gesture. He drew a peacock feather from the sleeve of his toga and laid it in the dead boy's hand, so that when he was in the lower world he would have something that gave him pleasure.

THE Jews of the city of Rome were horrified by the misfortune which had befallen Joseph; yet a slight sense of satisfaction was mixed with their horror. What had brought Joseph low was a well-earned chastisement from Jehovah. They had warned him; it was not a good thing for a man to reach so high and boast so loud as had this Joseph. He had done them great favours, but he had also done them great harm; he was an equivocal, dangerous man; he was strange and mysterious to them; and with humility they praised the just God who had thus warned him and frightened him back within proper bounds.

They showed him grief and sympathy, as the Law prescribed; they sent him the lentils of mourning in willow baskets. They came to comfort him, but they were glad that he refused to be seen. This too was a punishment from Jehovah—that his pride forbade him to receive comfort.

That whole day while Rome filed past his son's body, Joseph remained locked in and saw no one, neither Jews nor Romans. It was a very long day, and he yearned for the night, when he would have the boy to himself again. But toward evening someone arrived whom he was obliged to see, the

Emperor's First Courier, an official of the highest rank, and he asked to see Joseph in the name of the Emperor.

The Lord and God Domitian wished to provide Flavius Matthias, who had been killed on a journey in the service of the Empress, with a most distinguished funeral. He wished to erect a funeral pyre for him, as if he were a member of the Emperor's own family.

The courier was practised in delivering messages for the Emperor in a suitable manner, but he had no little difficulty in doing so this time, he was so taken aback at the sight of Flavius Josephus. He had seen him a few days before, when the Emperor had summoned him to the Palatine. Then he had been a brilliant man in the prime of life, a person who cut a good figure in the palace. And now a dirty, unshaven, ragged old Jew stood before him.

Yes, Joseph stood there unkempt and aged, nor could he find any words. For he was torn in two directions. What his enemy was doing to him was the most insolent, the most horrible mockery conceivable. At the same time the idea came to Joseph that such a grand funeral was only suitable for Matthias, who had loved splendour, and that his dear son would not forgive him if he refused such an honour. So he was silent a long time, and when at last the official respectfully asked him what answer he should take back to the Emperor, he answered in vague sentences which were neither a yes nor a no. The courier stood there at a loss. What kind of person was this? He had the insolence to think it over, when the Emperor vouchsafed him an honour the like of which had never yet been shown to anyone! Yet just because the Emperor wished to show Joseph that tremendous honour, the courier did not dare to press him, and he withdrew uneasy and full of misgivings lest the Emperor vent on him his anger at this man's curious behaviour.

Joseph, alone, could not find the proper course. His inner voices contradicted each other. At one moment he was determined to accept the Emperor's offer. Then he told himself that it would be an admission that the Roman was in the right and a denial of his own idea. Then again he saw his dead boy's face, and he felt as if Matthias longed for the honour of the great fire which was to light up his image in the eyes of the whole world. He found no solution.

The next day he admitted the most trusted of his friends, Claudius Reginus and John of Gishala. He squatted on the floor, his hair disordered, his feet bare, his garments torn, his mind clouded, his soul crushed; and with him sat his friends. Just as the night before he had been Jacob who mourned his favourite son, so now he was Job whom his friends came to comfort. But it was a good thing that their comfort was restricted to practical advice; he could hardly have borne sympathy, shameless pity.

So they spoke only about the external problem that had to be solved on that same day, the question of the funeral. What should Joseph do? If he accepted the Emperor's offer, he was breaking one of the Doctors' basic laws. Since the time of their ancestral fathers, since Abraham, Isaac, and Jacob had been buried in the cave of Machpelah, the Jews had been forbidden to join their fathers in any other way than through the earth, and it seemed to Joseph an act of defiance against his own people if he let his son be laid away in fire. But if he buried him in the Jewish manner and refused the Emperor's pyre, would he not bring down the Emperor's wrath upon himself, and not upon himself alone?

Claudius Reginus, the realist, spoke up. "A dead man is a dead man," he said, "and he doesn't feel whether you burn or bury him. Fire or earth—one harms him as little as the other, and one or the other gives him as little pleasure as the peacock

feather that nice young prince put in his hand. Nor can I imagine that a soul has eyes or a skin to see or feel how it is buried. But as far as your other misgivings are concerned, they're
sentimentalities. I'm no Jew; perhaps that's just why I can
judge exactly where the advantages and disadvantages for your
people lie. So let me tell you that your people would have to
pay dearly, at the least with a great loss of income, if you gave
consideration to its superstitions and stupidity. It's precisely
your consideration for the true advantage of Jewry which demands that you accept D.D.D.'s offer. For the splendour of
that pyre will light up all Jewry, and Jewry, which has of late
fallen into darkness, has great need of such splendour."

"That it has," said John of Gishala, and fixed his sly grey
eyes on Joseph. "And in respect to your other misgivings, Doctor Joseph, I'm no scholar like you and don't know whether
a person feels anything after death or not. Inwardly I don't
say either yes or no to that. But if your Matthias should feel
anything in the place where he is now, then it certainly would
be agreeable to him if the fire which consumed his body
warmed all Jewry. And, moreover, I believe," and now his
eyes became even slyer and friendlier, "he would enjoy the
splendour of such a great fire; for he loved splendour."

Joseph was moved by what they both said. The glory offered him by the Emperor was to the advantage of Jewry, and
he could not honour his son's memory better than by that
glory. Nevertheless, everything in him revolted against Domitian's pyre. His Matthias simply was not a Roman; only because they had wanted to make him into a Roman had he
perished.

Then a bold idea came to him. The Emperor wished to honour the dead boy; therefore he felt guilty. But if he wanted to
honour the dead, he should not do it his way, but the dead
boy's own way. Matthias should be buried in Jewish earth, as

was fitting for every Jew, and yet his funeral should be surrounded by that splendour which the Emperor had intended
to bestow on it. Joseph himself wished to bring his dead son
to Judæa, and the Emperor should supply him with the means.
He should put one of his swift ships at his disposal for that
purpose, a *liburna,* one of those narrow warships which were
manned by picked oarsmen. That was how Joseph wished to
bring his son to Judæa, and there he wished to bury him.

He told his friends. They looked at him, and they looked at
each other, and they said nothing.

Then Joseph said, and his voice was full of anger and defiance: "You, Claudius Reginus, would be the proper man to
convey my request to the Emperor. Do you want to do it?" "I
don't want to," answered Claudius Reginus. "It's not a pleasant job." But as Joseph bridled up and seemed about to make
answer, he added: "But I'll do it just the same. I've done many
unpleasant jobs in my life, out of friendship. You never were
a comfortable friend, Doctor Joseph," he grumbled.

THE warship *Avenger,* a *liburna,* belonged to the top class
of vessels built for speed. The *Avenger* had three rows of
oarsmen; she was built narrow and low, light and swift, and
with one stroke of the oars she shot forward twice her length.
The imperial navy had ninety-four ships of her type. The
Avenger was not the largest; her displacement was only 110
tons, her length 44 metres, her depth 1.7 metres. One hundred
and ninety-two galley slaves served her.

Everything required for the conveyance of the body had
been prepared in all haste and yet with care; even an em-
balmer had been sent along. But there was no need of his
services. The weather was favourable, the ship sailed before a

good wind, the nights were cool. They could keep the body on the upper deck; in the daytime it was protected by an awning.

Joseph sat beside the body, alone. He liked the nights best. The wind blew, and he shivered in the rush of the ship's motion. The heavens were deep; there was only a slender moon; the water was black with streaks that gleamed faintly. And Joseph sat beside the body, and like the wind and the waves his thoughts came and went.

It was a flight, and his opponent, clever as he was, had given him his fastest ship so that he would flee the quicker. Disgracefully, thrice disgracefully, he was fleeing from the city of Rome which he had entered so insolently and sure of victory more than thirty years ago. He had been in Rome for a generation, he had fought for a generation, and again and again he had thought that now he had victory firmly in his grasp. This, then, was the end. The most ignominious defeat and flight. Fleeing, escaping, retreating, running away, hastily, shamefully, on the ship which the enemy had provided for him with mocking, polite willingness. There beside him lay what he had saved from that generation of battles: a dead boy. He had saved a dead son—that was the price of a generation full of pride, of self-control, of suffering, humiliation, and false glory.

How the ship flew, the ship with the ironical name—*Avenger* —a good ship and a swift one. How it danced over the water. The *Avenger*. So now Matthias had the swift ship he had wanted for the voyage to Judæa, a swifter and more magnificent one that he had ever dreamed of. His son was being honoured, highly honoured, in death as in life. His friend the Emperor was doing him great honour. For him, for his Matthias, these oarsmen moved, chained to their benches, one-two, one-two, unceasingly; for him the officer beat out the rhythm;

for him the ingeniously placed sails bellied in the wind; for him the ship sped across the black waters, the Emperor's best ship, a masterpiece of the shipbuilder's art.

Why all this? Who could interpret it? Matthias too had always asked: Why? In his dear, deep voice he had asked it, childishly; and involuntarily Joseph imitated the dear, deep voice, and into the wind and the night he asked in Matthias's voice: Why?

Was there an answer? Only one, the answer of the Doctors when in days past he had come across a really difficult problem. They discussed it this way and that, and chattered and examined and rejected, and then, when he waited for the solution with the greatest avidity, they answered: It remains a problem, difficult, insoluble, undecided, *kashya*.

Kashya.

And yet it was not so. And yet there was an answer. One man had found the answer, several hundred years ago, and because of that answer they disliked him, and because of that answer they had not wanted to include his writings in the canon of the Holy Book. His answer was not *kashya*. His answer was clear and definite, and it was the right answer. Whenever Joseph was really shaken, he found in the depths of his being the answer of a wise old man, the preacher Koheleth; it had sunk into the depths of his being and there it remained; and it was the right answer.

"I know that, whatsoever God doeth, it shall be for ever: nothing can be put to it, nor any thing taken from it. . . . That which hath been is now; and that which is to be hath already been. . . . And moreover I saw under the sun the place of judgment, that wickedness was there; and the place of righteousness, that iniquity was there. . . . I said in mine heart concerning the estate of the sons of men, that God might manifest them, and that they might see that they themselves are beasts.

For that which befalleth the sons of men befalleth beasts; even one thing befalleth them: as the one dieth, so dieth the other; yea, they have all one breath; so that a man hath no pre-eminence above a beast: for all is vanity. All go unto one place; all are of the dust, and all turn to dust again. Who knoweth the spirit of man that goeth upward, and the spirit of the beast that goeth downward to the earth?"

Thus he had felt himself; thus it had risen up from his own depths, with the same certainty as long ago it must have risen up in Koheleth; thus he had understood it when he had sat beside the corpse of his son Simeon-Janiki. And then, later, he had not wanted to know it any longer, and he had been indignant at the thought and he had forgotten it. But now Jehovah had reminded him of it a second time, harshly, mockingly, grimly, and had chastised him, the forgetful pupil. Now he could inscribe it in his heart, must inscribe it, ten times, twenty times, as the great teacher had commanded him. "All is vanity; all a pursuit of the wind." Write it down, Joseph Ben Matthias, write it with your blood, ten times, twenty times, you who would not perceive it, you who wish to correct Koheleth. You went and sought to refute the wise old man, with your deeds and your works, with your *Jewish War* and your *Universal History* and your *Apion*. And now you squat here, on a ship that sails across a mighty ocean before the swift winds, and all that is left to you, you carry with you: your dead son. Wind, wind, a pursuit of the wind.

The slender moon had climbed higher; a faint, pale radiance shone from Matthias's thin, painted face.

And what should he say to Mara, now that for a second time he would have to stand before her and announce: The son whom you put in my trust is dead?

Softly, barely opening his lips, into the night wind, he spoke his lament:

"Woe to my son Matthias, my blessed, my vanquished, my favourite son. A great radiance surrounded my son, and he was pleasing to all men, and all men loved him, the heathen and the chosen. But I filled him with vanity, and in the end I brought death upon him through vanity. Woe, woe unto me and unto you, my beautiful, beloved, sweet, radiant, blessed, vanquished son Matthias. I gave you a gorgeous coat such as Jacob gave Joseph, and I sent you to your downfall as Jacob sent his son Joseph, whom he loved with a love that was too great, too adoring, too vain. Woe, woe unto me and unto you, my beloved son."

And he thought of the poems he had written, of the "Psalm of the Citizen of the World," and of the "Psalm of Self," and of the "Psalm of the Glass-Blower," and of the "Psalm of Courage." And his poems seemed to him empty, and one thing alone seemed meaningful to him: the wisdom of Koheleth.

But what use was that knowledge to him? It was no use to him; his pain grew no less for it. And he wailed into the wind, and his wailing was louder than the wind.

To the officers, the sailors, and the oarsmen, the man who was taking the corpse across the sea seemed sinister. It was a disagreeable task that the Emperor had given them. They feared that the Jew might be hateful to the gods; they feared that the gods might send down misfortune upon their good ship. They were glad when the coast of Judæa came in sight.

WHEN Lucia heard of the death of her favourite Matthias, she made an effort to remain cool and clear-headed, to resist the suspicion which at once arose in her. First she thought of travelling at once to Rome. But she knew Joseph's lack of restraint; he would surely, without testing and weighing the evidence, believe in treachery and crime, and she did not want to be infected by the violence of his feelings. She wanted to preserve her reason, wanted to form a just opinion before she took any steps. She wrote a letter to Joseph, full of sorrow, sympathy, friendship, and condolence.

Yet the courier who was to take him the missive returned with the news that Joseph was already at sea, conveying the boy's body to Judæa.

Lucia was not offended that in his misfortune, which after all was hers as well, Joseph had not turned to her, that he had not allowed her to share it, that he had not even had a word for her. But suddenly he seemed strange, that man who let himself go so completely, who knew no measure or restraint at all, whose grief was as self-centred as his happiness. She no longer understood how she could have let the extremist come so close to her. What had been between them might still have had a long growth and blossoming; now he had broken it off by the way he had left for Judæa. He was a doomed man, doomed by his own violence; he attracted misfortune by his wildness and by his ideas of sin. She was almost glad that he had broken off their relationship.

Whether Domitian had committed the crime, she did not dare to decide. She was in Baia, he in Rome; she did not want to see him as long as she was torn by doubts; she did not want to speak one unconsidered word to him lest she destroy her chance to see clearly whether or not he was guilty. If he had committed the crime, she would avenge Matthias.

She received a cool, friendly letter from Domitian. Domitilla, he informed her, had now actually left the young princes in peace for a long time. So to his joy he found himself in a position to fulfil Lucia's wish. He had instructed the Governor of Eastern Spain to announce Domitilla's pardon to her. So Lucia would soon be able to welcome her friend back to Rome.

Lucia sighed with relief. She was glad that she had not prematurely accused Vellykins of murdering Matthias.

Two weeks later her secretary informed her, while giving his morning report of the latest news, that the Princess Domitilla had met her death in a pitiful manner. She had been preaching the doctrine of a certain crucified Christ on her island, the faith of the Minæans, a Jewish sect. She had addressed herself in particular to the natives of the island; but these were half-civilized Iberians, who lived in dwellings more like the burrows of wild animals than the habitations of human beings. One day, when she was coming back with her maid from one of these settlements, some members of the cutthroat mob had lain in wait for the two women, attacked them, robbed them, and murdered them. It had happened when the Governor of Eastern Spain had already dispatched the messenger who was to inform her of her pardon. The Emperor had commanded that every tenth man of the tribe to whom the murderers belonged should be crucified.

Lucia's bright, bold face grew dark when she heard the news; two deep, vertical folds cut into her childlike forehead; her cheeks grew mottled with anger. She interrupted the secretary in the middle of a word. Without delay she ordered the preparations for her departure.

She did not yet know what she would do. She knew only that she would hurl her whole fury into Domitian's face. Often as she had become indignant at him, there had always been something like respect in her for his violent, severe personality; the love which his pride, his vehemence, his obsession, his unique quality had kindled in her had never been completely extinguished. Now she saw only his altogether evil side, the ravening beast. As surely as he had murdered Domitilla because he had promised her her pardon, it was his cruel claw that had struck down the boy—young, radiant, innocent. Oh, he would have many big, proud words with which to justify himself again. But this time he would not confuse her with his talk. He had murdered the boy because of the good in him, just because the boy was the way he was; perhaps just because the boy had appealed to her, Lucia. And he had killed Domitilla also just to wound her, Lucia, the way a bad child breaks a toy in which another finds pleasure. She would tell him so to his face; if she did not, the unspoken word would choke her. She would hurl her whole rage, her whole disgust, into his face.

Without delay she set out for Rome.

WHILE he had been speaking to Josephus, Domitian had had a feeling of deep satisfaction. Again when Josephus had rejected his suggestion of providing the boy with a glorious funeral, he had only smiled. He did not take offence at Joseph's insolence; it only proved that he had really wounded his opponent in his most vulnerable spot. Then when Claudius Reginus had brought him the Jew's impudent request, his triumph had perhaps reached its peak. For now, to top everything, he could show himself to be generous and prove that what he had done had not been directed against the God Jehovah. The Emperor Domitian had had to punish the crime of the boy Matthias; to the favourite of Jehovah he paid the highest honour. And he gave his deep smile, glad and sombre, when he learned that of all his swift ships it was the *Avenger* which lay ready, that it was the *Avenger* which would take Josephus and his dead son to Judæa. Set sail, Josephus, my Jew; sail away on my good, swift ship. A favourable wind to you and your son; sail away, sail on. Catiline has fled, has retreated, has run away, has departed in haste.

But the farther the enemy hastened away, and the farther

away the *Avenger* was from Rome, carrying the dead man and the living, the more the Emperor's joy dwindled. He became unusually indolent, disinclined to any activity. He could not even get up the energy to go to Albanum, but remained in the hot city.

Slowly the old doubts reasserted themselves. True, he had done right in putting Flavius Matthias to death; the boy had committed high treason; he, the Emperor, had not only the right but the duty of punishing him. But his opponent, the God Jehovah, was a shrewd, tricky being. Human wit was of no avail against Him. He would find reasons for being offended at the Roman for having snatched away His scion of David, His chosen one. He, Domitian, had many sound arguments to advance in his own favour. But would they seem valid to the hostile God? And everyone knew how revengeful that God Jehovah was and how mysterious, and how His hand smote man from out of the darkness.

For what could He reproach him, that God Jehovah? Jehovah's favourite, Jehovah's messenger, had hurled his contemptible "Ode to Courage" into the Emperor's face in the presence of all Rome. That same messenger of Jehovah had caused Lucia to maintain friendly relations with him and to treat his mission with favour before all eyes in provocative fashion. But it was not the desire to revenge himself against those two which had moved him, Domitian, to do away with Matthias. He had not wanted to strike those two. That he had had to strike them had been one of the usual incidental manifestations of a function with which the gods had unfortunately entrusted him. No, he bore no grudge against Joseph or against Lucia; rather he had an actual feeling of affection toward them. It was by no means he who had brought misfortune upon them; the gods had done it—fate—and he, their friend, had a sincere desire to comfort them.

Yet a secret feeling remained in him that it was a matter of guilt, and in his usual way he tried to unload that guilt onto someone else's shoulders. Where was the first cause of the deed? It had begun with Norbanus's bringing the two scions of David before him. Norbanus had done that with a definite purpose. The Emperor no longer knew what end Norbanus had achieved by doing it, but this much was sure: Norbanus had expressly put into his hand the first link of a chain, a chain whose last link was the death of the boy Matthias. So if a guilt existed, the guilt was Norbanus's.

Domitian, to be sure, was careful not to clarify these thoughts fully or to draw conclusions from them. When he sat at his desk and thought of his Chief of Police, nothing but loops and circles appeared on his writing-tablet, never letters or words, and those loops and circles corresponded to the Emperor's thoughts. But when he spoke directly about Norbanus, to others or to himself, he always said that his Norbanus was the most faithful of men.

WHEN Lucia arrived at the Palatine, Domitian had shut himself into his study and given orders that he was not to be disturbed. But Lucia insisted so vehemently on seeing him at once that Chamberlain Xanthias finally announced her. He was afraid that the Emperor would fly into a rage, but the latter remained calm; he even seemed to be looking forward to the meeting.

Of course Domitian feared that Lucia would guess how Matthias's downfall and Domitilla's death had come about. But his Norbanus had proved his worth again: he had done a good job and there were on hand unexceptionable witnesses to the˙accident which had cost Matthias's life as well as to

Domitilla's murder by the Iberian cave-dwellers. And if Domitian could justify himself externally, he could do so inwardly even better. Matthias had undoubtedly committed high treason, and Domitilla's assassination, especially after the highly treasonable letter, had been necessary if he wished to protect the boys' souls.

Yet when he saw Lucia storm into the room, tall, fierce, indignant down to the very folds of her dress, his confidence deserted him. Again and again he became weak before this woman; today too he felt all his arguments melting away. But that weakness lasted only a fraction of a second. Then he was again the Domitian he had been before, and in soft, courteous words he expressed his grief at the fate which had carried off his two friends and hers.

Lucia, however, did not let him finish. "That fate," she said darkly, "has a name. It's called Domitian. Don't lie; don't speak; don't say anything. You don't have your Senate before you. Don't try to justify yourself. There is no justification. I don't believe anything you say, not a sentence, not a word, not a breath. You can make up some lie for yourself, but not for me. And this time you can't even fool yourself. You've acted like a coward, meanly, contemptibly. Just because the boy pleased you—that was why you put him to death; because you yourself saw how innocent he was and how much purity he radiated, and because you couldn't stand anything like that near you. It was nothing but sheer petty jealousy. And Domitilla! You yourself said that she had done nothing to you. Fie upon you! What a filthy soul you have! Don't come closer to me; don't touch me. I'm disgusted at myself when I think that I let you lie with me."

Domitian had retreated obediently; he was leaning against the desk; he sweated a little. "But you liked it, Lucia," he grinned, "or didn't you? At least pretty often I had the im-

pression that undeniably I appealed to you." But now Lucia's
face showed undeniable revulsion, and slowly the grin faded
from Domitian's darkly flushed face; for a moment he even
became terrifyingly pale. Yet then, not without an effort, he
produced the smile again, and, "The boy must really have been
very close to you," he reflected aloud, with polite, thoughtful irony. "And it's interesting, very interesting in any case,
what you've just revealed to me about the history of our relationship."

"Yes," Lucia answered, much more quietly now, and
through that calm her bitterness sounded even more scornfully, "it's interesting, the history of our relationship. But now
it's over. I let you seduce me; I loved you. Ten times, a hundred times you did things against which my whole being revolted, and again and again I let myself be convinced by you.
But now it's over, Vellykins," and this time her "Vellykins"
did not sound at all humorous, but bitter and scornful. "It is
over," she repeated, with a slight emphasis on the "is." "You've
often talked me around; you're tenacious, I know, and slow
to give up an idea. But I advise you, accustom yourself to the
idea that it's all over between us. My decisions come suddenly
but I hold fast to them, you know that. One can't distort my
words as one can yours. I'm taking leave of you, Domitian.
You disgust me. I'm through with you."

AFTER Lucia had gone, the somewhat embarrassed, artificially
ironical grin behind which Domitian had tried to hide
his rage remained for a while on his flushed face. His near-
sighted eyes stared after her vanished figure; her words still
rang in his ears. Then slowly his face relaxed; mechanically
he whistled to himself the melody of that couplet:

Even a bald-head a pretty girl can hold
If he is willing to pay his weight in gold.

Then he sat down at his desk, picked up the golden stylus, and scribbled on his wax tablet, circles and loops, loops and circles. "H'm, h'm," he said aloud to himself, "interesting, very interesting." So she had scorned him. Many had said that they scorned him, but those had been words, impotent gestures; it was unthinkable that a mortal should scorn him, the Lord and God Domitian. Lucia was the only one among mortals of whom he believed it.

For a moment he let it sink fully into his consciousness: she had gone from him, then, she had made a break between them. The break was painful; the chill of the break entered deep into his soul. But then he resisted it, drew himself up, reflected that her words were final and that therefore there was no sense in mourning for what was over and done with. There were only the consequences to be drawn.

Lucia had declared herself free of him; she had removed herself from his protection. She was no longer his wife who belonged to him, only his enemy, a traitor. She had wanted to move him to recall Domitilla, although no one knew better than she that Domitilla would try to exert a harmful influence over her sons. That alone was high treason. In addition, she had intrigued with Domitilla, had tried to cheat him, to make him believe in Domitilla's good behaviour so that then, from close quarters, the latter might be all the more free to estrange his sons from the State religion. Plain high treason. Lucia was a criminal; he must hurl his lightning.

He remained in Rome.

Lucia too remained in Rome, although August was unusually hot that year. Perhaps she did not return to Baia because the house and garden had become distasteful to her; they were full of memories of Matthias.

Princes Vespasian and Domitian paid her a call, accompanied by their tutor Quintilian. The recent events had given him a good excuse for bringing home to his pupils the Stoic modes of thought. "Preserve a calm spirit in times of affliction." But he did not need to give the boys long lectures; they had become quiet; they did not complain; their faces were reserved, severe. They were more Domitilla's sons than Clemens's; they were true Flavians. They had travelled only a short distance along their road, but that road was lined with dead. Now the place of their father was being taken by a man who had sent their true father and probably their friend as well to the lower world, and their mother into banishment. They had to live at the side of that man, and they could speak to each other only secretly and in half-phrases about what was closest to their hearts. The man who called them sons was the mightiest man in the world; an inconceivable fullness of power awaited them. But they had less power than slaves in a mine pit, for those were allowed to talk of what they would, were allowed to complain, while they, the Emperor's sons, went about in deeper darkness than the miners, and the mocking splendour around them ill concealed that darkness, and even in sleep they might hardly lay off the masks which they were forced to wear.

When they learned that Lucia was in Rome again, it was a great comfort to them. But now that they saw her for the first time, Quintilian's presence hampered them. Lucia was shocked to see how the boys had changed. They had changed so quickly, here at the Palatine. Everything had changed here, or perhaps until now she had seen everything in a false light. She did not really know what she could say to the boys; in embarrassment all three groped for words; skilful Quintilian often had to fill in the agonizing pauses. Finally Lucia could stand it no longer. "Come here," she said, "don't be men. You be Constans and you be Petronius, and weep for Matthias and for your mother." And she embraced them, and they no longer heeded Quintilian's presence but let themselves go in sweet and sad memories of Matthias and in dark words of anger.

After that meeting Quintilian would have liked best to keep his pupils away from the Empress. But the boys defied him. Domitian, who, slow as ever, had not yet decided when he should hurl his lightning against Lucia, did not want things to come to an open break, and so it was agreed that the princes should see Lucia once every six days.

Sullenly and dangerously life went on at the Palatine, and the heavy sultriness of that summer made it harder than ever to bear.

The city too felt that clouds were gathering around Domitian, and much was made of the evil omens which occurred with increasing frequency. Once, in that month full of tempests, lightning struck Domitian's bedroom; once a storm tore down the tablet with the inscription on his triumphal column. The dissatisfied Senators saw to it that much was made of these omens; and a number of reputable astrologers declared that the Emperor would not live to see the next winter.

Domitian had the lightning which had struck his bedroom decently buried, as custom required. He had the inscription on the triumphal column cut into the pedestal, so that no storm could ever blow it down. Norbanus had one of the soothsayers arrested; he confessed under torture that he had let himself be bribed by one of the Senators of the opposition to misuse his art by prophesying untruth. The Senator was banished; the soothsayer executed.

The attachment of the populace to the Emperor did not

lessen because of these evil omens. They felt safe under his rule. His moderate foreign policy was showing favourable results. No expensive war and prestige policy was undermining the well-being of the country; the governors dared to plunder the provinces only on a relatively modest scale; justice was administered in severe and orderly fashion. And people did not forget the great festivals of donation which Domitian had held. So while the populace was content with his rule, he was hated the more by the highest aristocrats and the class of the very rich. They complained of lost liberty and of the arbitrary, despotic regime; and there were people to whom the world went black when they saw the hated, imperious face of the Emperor.

Among these was old Senator Corellus. Since his thirty-third year he had suffered from gout. Abstemiousness had lessened his sufferings for a while, yet in later years the illness had seized his whole body, crippled and distorted it; he suffered unbearable pain. He was a Stoic, known as a courageous man, and his friends wondered why he did not put an end to his sufferings. "Do you know," he once declared in a whisper to his closest friend, Secundus, "do you know why I control myself and endure this horrible existence? I have sworn to outlive that cur Domitian."

Domitian made fun of the evil omens. They were falsely interpreted; they meant nothing; one had only to open one's eyes to see how happy his rule was, and how the well-being and contentment of the people were growing. But he was too much of a realist not to notice that, in spite of this, hatred was also growing around him. And with that hatred grew the Emperor's misanthropy and fear.

He was terribly alone; he was betrayed and sold out on every hand. Now his Minerva had deserted him too, and finally Lucia herself had betrayed him. Who really was left him?

He let the faces of his friends, of his intimates, file past him. There were Marullus and Reginus. But they were doddering old men, and he did not even know whether he could be quite sure of them since the death of Matthias. Then there was Annius Bassus. He was younger. He was absolutely reliable. But the simple soldier, the blockhead, could not be used for involved matters which demanded a subtle understanding. And if he, Domitian, had not been able to make Lucia understand, despite enormous efforts, how could he make that fellow understand him? Then there would be Norbanus. But Norbanus had looked very deep into him, deeper than one was allowed to look into the Lord and God Domitian, too deep. Moreover, it had been Norbanus who had put the first link of that dangerous chain in his hands. Norbanus was the most faithful of men, but all was over between him and Norbanus.

In reality one man was left: Messalinus. What a blessing that the gods had made Messalinus blind! To Messalinus's dead eyes the Lord and God Domitian could show his face without fear, without shame. Blind Messalinus was allowed to know what no other man might know. There was at least one person in the world to whom Domitian could say everything, and he did not have to fear that he would repent it afterward.

Domitian sat in his locked study, but he was not alone; with him, around him, were his misanthropy and his fear. Why was it all thus? Why was he so alone? Why was he surrounded by this hatred? His people were happy; Rome was great and powerful, greater and more powerful than ever. Why was he surrounded by this hatred?

There was only one reason—the enmity of the God Jehovah. He would not let Himself be conciliated, that God. Cleverly as he, the Emperor, had guarded against it, the God Jehovah

with His legalistic Eastern mentality had no doubt found
something in the occurrences surrounding the boy Matthias
which gave Him rights against the Roman Emperor. Surely
it was the vengeance of that God Jehovah which did not let
him find peace.

Was there then no means by which to pacify the wrath of
the God?

There was a means. He would sacrifice to the God the man
who had instigated the murder of the boy Matthias, the man
who had put the first link of the chain in his hand, his Chief
of Police Norbanus. That was a great sacrifice, for Norbanus
was the most faithful of men.

He sat at his desk. But this time it was not loops and circles
which appeared on the writing-tablet; this time it was a list
of names. For if he sent his Norbanus to the lower world, he
would not send him alone on his dark journey; he would send
others along with him.

Slowly he pressed the stylus into the wax; neatly, one below
another, he set down the names. There was a certain Salvius,
who had dared to celebrate the memorial day of his dead uncle,
of the Emperor Otho, the enemy of the Flavians. With enjoyment Domitian's stylus dug the name of Salvius into the wax.
There was the writer Didymus, who, in his renowned history
of Asia Minor, had made many allusions which had not
pleased the Emperor. He put the name on his list, and added
in parentheses: The publisher and scribes also. Then, and
that name he wrote very quickly, Norbanus followed. Then,
after a short hesitation, he let the name Nerva follow. To be
sure, he was an aged gentleman, near seventy, and moderate
and cautious. One could not prove anything against him, but
just because he was so quiet and deliberate the opposition
grouped itself around him. Domitian read over the name; it

looked well on the list. Only then, slowly, carefully, in cunningly shaped letters, he wrote down the name of Lucia. Then, so that the name might not be the last, he put some unimportant people at the bottom of the list.

He had been very much absorbed in his list. Now that he had assembled it he gave a sigh of relief and looked up; he felt as if a victory had been won. He got up, stretched, smiled, and from all sides, in the mirrors lining the walls, Domitian smiled back at him. If the Eastern God had found an excuse for attacking him, the Roman Emperor had twisted that excuse from His grasp. He had sacrificed his Norbanus to the God. Now the God must be content; now the God must leave him in peace.

Late in the afternoon Domitian dined with the two princes. They were alone; not even Quintilian was there; he was at a friend's house attending a reading. During the whole past period the Emperor had been behaving morosely and irritably even to the boys, but today, at this meal, their cousin and father the Lord and God Domitian was in a good humour. He talked cheerfully to the two of them. They had no idea how much they had to thank him for, how much he had done to lighten the rule which awaited them.

The boys sat there with grave faces. But he refused to notice their gravity and depression at all today. Well and good, they had lost their mother in the last weeks. But what a thin, dry, ineffectual, half-mad mother she had been, and what a great, powerful, imperial, divine father they had in him, who spread his glory and riches at their feet! They should not look so gloomy; and he tried to cheer up his youthful, over-silent table companions. He had always had the ability to be scurrilous in a way that was at once sinister and fascinating. He made an effort, he was especially affable, he spoke to them as to children and yet as to men, he made it easy for them to be

polite and respond to him, and they, to be sure, smiled politely
at his jokes.

Yes, he was not at all the god that evening; he was human,
familiar. He asked about their hobbies. Prince Domitian accordingly told about the peacock run at Baia. At first he spoke
with great animation; but at a glance from his brother he too
thought of Matthias, became more taciturn, and fell silent.
The Emperor, however, did not seem to notice this; he made a
note on his writing-tablet, and then told them about his own
little whims and weaknesses. "What I like," he confided to
them, "is to surprise people, with good things as with bad. I
love slow decisions and the act that follows like lightning. I
sometimes permit such surprises to cost me much time and
effort." The boy Vespasian said: "And are your surprises
always a success, my Lord and Father?" "Usually they're a
success," answered Domitian. The boy Domitian said: "You
talk as if you were preparing a new surprise, my Lord and
Father." "Perhaps I am," replied the Emperor, in a good-
humoured and talkative mood.

Both boys looked at him, and in their gaze there were fear,
hate, and curiosity; at the same time they seemed flattered that
the lord of the world should speak to them so familiarly. "You
see," the Emperor went on, enjoying to the full the suspense
on their young faces, "now you're surprised that your father
should tell you so frankly about the surprises he's preparing.
Yet what I'm about to do isn't at all so far-fetched. Once it's
done, everyone will think it was the obvious thing to do. And
yet it will come like a dolphin suddenly jumping out of a calm
sea." At that the older of the two, the boy Vespasian, was
seized by a fit of sullen presumption, and he asked: "Will people have to die from your surprise, my Lord and Father?"
Domitian glanced up suspiciously, astonished at so much boldness. But then he laughed—had he not called forth the ques-

tion by his own familiar talk?—and, half jokingly, he explained: "When we gods jest, it sometimes doesn't agree with
the subject of the jest."

After Domitian had dismissed them, they said to each other:
"He's plotting a new blow, the butcher." "It's to be a surprise,
yet it's obvious." "Who's left for him to murder?" "We ourselves?" "That would neither be a surprise, nor is it obvious."

Domitian had retired to his bedroom. He had a habit of
doing this often now after dinner, and the imperial chambers
were left to the boys. Had not the Emperor as good as challenged them to discover his surprise? They were burning to
find out whom he would murder next. They were Flavians,
they were eager for action, they were eager for vengeance, they
were rash and daring.

They went to the Emperor's study. It was guarded by a
captain and two soldiers. "Let us in," begged Prince Vespasian. "It's for a surprise; it's for a bet with the Emperor. If
the Emperor loses it, he'll only laugh. And if we win the bet,
Captain Corvinus, then we won't forget that it was you who
let us in. So you can only gain by it, Captain Corvinus." The
captain hesitated. He had never liked doing guard duty for
Domitian; what one did and what one did not do were dangerous; the officers of the bodyguard had a habit of joking:
"The man who stands guard for the Emperor does well to
sacrifice to the gods of the underworld beforehand." If he
denied the boys access, it could end badly; if he admitted them,
it could end badly. He did not admit them.

The boys were Flavians, sons of Domitilla, and resistance
made them only more stubborn. They went to the Emperor's
bedroom.

It was guarded by a captain and two soldiers. "Let us in,"
begged Prince Domitian. "It's for a surprise; it's for a bet with
the Emperor. If the Emperor loses, he'll only laugh. And if we

win the bet, Captain Servius, we won't forget that it was you who let us in. So you can only gain by it, Captain Servius." The captain hesitated. If he denied the boys access, it could end badly. He let them in.

Domitian lay on his back and slept, his mouth half open. He breathed slowly, regularly; his head with the very red, wrinkled, veined eyelids looked a little foolish; his stomach was a large, conspicuous bulge. One arm lay limp and lifeless at his side; the other he had bent above his head. The boys approached on tiptoe. If he awoke they would tell the truth: "We wanted to find out your surprise, my Lord and Father Domitian."

Prince Vespasian reached beneath the pillow. He found a writing-tablet; he and his brother read the names. "Have you memorized them?" whispered Prince Vespasian. "A few—the most important," answered Prince Domitian. The sleeping man moved, a faint snore came from his half-open mouth. "Come away," whispered Vespasian. They slipped the writing-tablet under the pillow again, crept away. The officer sighed with relief when he saw them coming out. "I think you have made your fortune, Captain Servius," said Prince Domitian; he spoke genially yet grimly, like a prince.

"Did you see?" asked Vespasian. "At the bottom he's written: 'Peacocks for the Princes.' He didn't want to put us to death; he wanted to give us peacocks." Yet they decided that one of them must go at once to see Lucia. Vespasian undertook it. He found her, told her. She threw her arms around his neck, kissed him, thanked him vehemently. It was the greatest moment of his life.

BEFORE the sun went down, Norbanus was already with Lucia. He was slightly indignant that Lucia had asked him to come with such urgency and secrecy. What could she have to tell him that was important? Probably some silly love affair.

Lucia told him dryly what had happened. The thick-set man did not flinch; throughout her whole narrative he had not taken his brown eyes from her, the eyes of a fierce, faithful watchdog. He still did not take his eyes from her; he was silent; obviously he was thinking it over; he did not trust her.

Then, in place of any answer, he asked her objectively, almost brutally: "You had a quarrel with the Lord and God Domitian?" "Yes," she replied. "I had none with him," he said, and his challenging tone did not disguise his distrust. "You have cause to be my enemy; the Emperor has not." "But perhaps you know too much about him," Lucia guessed. "That's plausible," Norbanus reflected. "But there are many other possibilities. For example, it might be that Prince Vespasian in his youthful imaginings believes that it was not an accident which carried off his playmate Matthias and his mother, but an evil intention of the Emperor's." "It's not impossible," Lucia admitted for her part, "that Vespasian came to see me for such reasons and that he lied. But it's not probable. In your inmost heart, my Norbanus, you know as well as I do that Vespasian is speaking the truth, that your name and mine were on the tablet, and that you and I and the boy interpret rightly what that meant."

"I'd really like to wring that prying Vespasian's neck," Norbanus growled suddenly. The fashionable curls fell untidily, rather grotesquely over the low forehead of his square face; he looked unhappy, like a fierce, faithful dog whose world has fallen to pieces. For all her rage, sorrow, and anxious absorption, Lucia came near laughing at the fierce man's clumsy rage. "Then you're so much attached to Vellykins?" she said. "You're so upset because he wants to make himself safe against you too?" "I'm faithful," Norbanus explained stubbornly. "The Lord and God Domitian is right. The Lord and God Domitian is always right. Even if he wants to have me put to death, the Lord and God Domitian surely has his own good reasons and is right. And I'll make that Vespasian pay for it!" he raged. "Don't talk nonsense, Norbanus," Lucia said, bringing him back to reality. "Look at things the way they are. You don't like me, and I'd be lying if I said that you appealed to me. But the common danger simply makes us allies. We have to take action ahead of Domitian, and we must hurry. The boys don't remember all the names that were on the list, but some they do. Here they are. Get in touch with those among the gentlemen who can be of use to you. I, for my part, will see to it that Domitian sleeps with me tonight. So you take care of the rest."

Norbanus gave her a long, calculating stare out of his brown, watchful, yet lifeless eyes. "I know what you're thinking about now," said Lucia. "You're asking yourself whether you should go and report to the Emperor what I've suggested to you. That would not be advisable, my Norbanus. You would postpone your own execution by that, but only postpone it. For then you'd know even more about the Emperor, and much as it would pain him, the duty of doing away with you would become all the more pressing. Am I right?" "You are right," Norbanus admitted. "That impertinent Prince," he growled, and could not compose himself. "You would prefer to have perished, unknowing," inquired Lucia with interest, "to knowing and anticipating the Emperor as you do now?" "Yes," Norbanus admitted unhappily. "I am very much disappointed," he said, honestly saddened.

"And you're sure," was his last question, impudent and to the point, "that you can get the Emperor to sleep with you in spite of the quarrel?" Lucia was not angered; she was rather amused. "I'm sure," she said.

"MY LORD and God Domitian, Vellykins, D.D.D., I do not know what inimical god inspired me to address such insolent and foolish words to you as I did. The Dog Star must have bewitched me. But I know the Emperor's mercy and generosity. Do you remember our night that time on the ship to Athens? Do you remember our night when you had the kindness of recalling me from exile? Come to me and tell me with your own lips that you forgive me. Come tonight. I shall await you. And if you come, I shall also give you the building materials for your villa in Selinunta at half the price. Your Lucia."

Domitian grinned as he read the letter. He thought of his list; thought of Messalinus, with whom he would talk over the list the next day; but also thought of the two nights which Lucia had recalled to him.

Domitian was glad if those whom he had to put to death saw that their execution was a just punishment, a necessary measure. He was pleased that Lucia admitted that she was in the wrong. He was pleased that she still loved him. To be sure, how should she not love him, since he had honoured her with his affection? And no aspect of the whole affair was thereby altered. Lucia's crime grew no less because the traitress Lucia was at the same time his wife who loved him. He did not waver in his intention; he did not think of crossing her name off his list.

Nevertheless, he would accept her invitation. She was a

magnificent woman. When he thought of the scar beneath her left breast his knees grew weak. The gods were kind to him to let him kiss that scar once more. She was an exuberant woman; she was the woman who was fit for him. Too bad that she was a traitress and would no longer have much opportunity of writing him letters like that.

So the Emperor came to Lucia and slept with her. After their embrace his head lay upon her shoulder, heavily. Yet Lucia did not draw her arm away. She gazed at the sleeping head in the dim light of the oil lamp; she sought, beneath the puffy, slack, tired face, that quality which she had been the first to perceive, at the time when people called him the Sproutling and he was a good-for-nothing of whom nobody except she had any hopes. Now she did not love him and did not hate him; she did not regret her decision, yet she no longer felt any of the grim satisfaction which had filled her when she had won Norbanus for her side and her revenge. She waited, and her heart was heavy and weary, like the arm on which lay his sleeping head.

At last Norbanus and his men arrived. But they did not succeed in forcing their way in as noiselessly as they had hoped; for ever-suspicious Domitian had had himself accompanied by two officers, who stood guard in the hall before the bedroom. So Domitian started from his sleep as the conspirators forced their way in. "Norbanus!" he cried, and: "What is it?"

Norbanus had hoped to surprise his master while sleeping. It upset him that he cried out to him, and he stood still near the door.

The Emperor had awakened fully, he saw the men behind Norbanus, saw the weapons, saw Norbanus's face and posture. Understood. Sprang from the bed, naked as he was, tried to get to the door, threw himself against the men, screamed shrilly for help. One man stabbed at him, but aimed badly. The Emperor defended himself, struggled with the man, went on screaming. "Lucia, you bitch, why don't you help me?" he cried in a breaking voice, and turned his head toward the bed.

Lucia was kneeling on the bed, half naked, and with a heavy, sad, expectant gaze she looked at the man struggling for his life. "It's for Matthias," she said, and her voice sounded strangely calm and objective.

At that he understood that it was the God Jehovah with whom he had to deal, and he defended himself no longer.

BEFORE morning the whole city knew about the Emperor's assassination.

Annius Bassus's first reaction, after he had recovered from tremendous, outraged horror, was to have the murdered man's adopted sons, the Princes Vespasian and Domitian, proclaimed rulers. The officers and the soldiers of the garrison were devoted to the dead man, and with their assistance he would have been able to force the Senate to recognize the princes. Yet he was not unscrupulous and adaptable enough to present his "Emperors" to the Senate without first conferring with Marullus and Reginus.

However, by the time he finally got in touch with the two others, it was already too late. Old Nerva, the leader of the Senatorial opposition, whom Domitian had put on his list, had been informed of the events by Norbanus before they had taken place, and had at once called together the Senate. If the attempt should fail, he had said to himself, he would propose prayers of thanksgiving to the gods for the Emperor's rescue; if it should succeed, he would have himself elected

by his friends as Domitian's successor. So the Conscript
Fathers had assembled very early in the morning, and when
Marullus and Reginus finally appeared—while Annius was
rousing the garrison—the proposal to outlaw the memory of
the dead Emperor had already been made.

Marullus, as soon as he had grasped the situation, indig-
nantly set about opposing the measure. Yet he and the few
Senators loyal to the Emperor were at once shouted down.
Each man outdid the others in ugly invective against their
fallen lord. In furious haste they voted one defamatory measure
after another, to annihilate even the memory of Domitian.
They decreed that in the whole Empire his statues should be
overturned and the tablets which bore inscriptions honouring
him should be destroyed or melted down. And finally Marullus and his party had to witness a spectacle the like of which
the Roman Senate had not afforded since the founding of the
city. Full of enthusiasm over their regained power, full of
grim memories of the disgrace they had suffered, of the sessions when they themselves, assembled here, had condemned
to death their best men, their leaders, the Senators summoned
workmen and slaves that they might execute the outlawing of
his memory at once and in concrete form. They even helped
in the work themselves. They wanted to have a hand in the
destruction, in the extermination of the insolent despot. Awkward in their high shoes, in their gorgeous robes, they seized
crow-bars, axes, and hatchets, climbed up ladders, and rained
blows on their hated enemy's busts and medallions. With de-
light they smashed to the ground the statues which wore the
dead man's haughty face; they maimed and crushed his stone
and metal limbs; amid wild cries they built a bonfire in the
anteroom of the Curia and threw into it the horribly muti-
lated sculptures.

Then, having cleaned away despotism, the rule of the individual, they set about replacing it with the regime of freedom, namely, with the rule of the sixty most powerful Senators; and they elected Nerva as Emperor.

The old gentleman, highly cultivated, a great lawyer, a practised orator, kindly, liberal, affable, had behind him a stormy day, a stormy night, and another stormy half-day. He had been in a state of anxiety for some time, lest, despite all his care, he be put to death by Domitian. Instead he had now, in his seventieth year, not only outlived the forty-five-year-old Emperor but even captured his throne. Yet at this moment, after the strains, the excitements, the upheavals of the last day and a half, he was exhausted; he had a right to be so; and his pleasure at being able to go home now, to bathe, to have breakfast, to go to bed, was almost as great as his pleasure at attaining world dominion.

But he was not to be granted his desired repose so soon. Barely had he arrived at his house when Annius appeared at the head of a great detachment of troops, accompanied by Marullus and Reginus. Annius was indignant over his own sluggish mentality; because of his slowness in thinking he had lost for the adopted sons of his honoured Lord and God the dominion of the world which was theirs by right. He wanted to save what was still to be saved. He forced his way in to Nerva and launched forth on a brutal harangue: the army would not stand for having the Flavians, conquerors of Germany, Britain, Judæa, and Dacia, cheated of their throne. The new Emperor was a man of quiet, refined manner; Annius's loud, coarse speech made him nervous; moreover, he had a number of things to reply to this irrelevant talk from the legal point of view. But he was tired, he did not feel in good form; besides, the other had thirty thousand soldiers behind him, and he only five hundred Senators. So he preferred to disregard the rude general's unfitting behaviour, turned instead to the two others, whom he knew as civilized persons, and asked them affably: "And what do you wish, gentlemen?"

The two gentlemen, realists that they were, knew, to be sure, that the garrison of the capital stood behind them, but they were very doubtful whether the armies of the provinces would remain loyal to the Flavians. On the other hand, the offensive behaviour of the Senators had deeply outraged them. The sight of those elderly men climbing the ladders with their wobbling knees, in their high shoes and purple-bordered togas, to strike in the face the man whose hand they had crowded to kiss only three days before, had turned the stomachs of the two. They wanted to make their own demonstration.

The new Emperor, they declared, was a lawyer. Let him therefore administer justice against those who had murdered Domitian. They spoke to Nerva in civil terms; they did not say emphatically after every third sentence, as the coarse general had, the army stands behind us. What they demanded was not much; it was one thing only, the punishment of the guilty. But this they demanded absolutely and within a short period; on this they insisted. Nerva was forced—and this was the first act of the rightful, decent, even kindly new ruler— at once to hand over to them the main culprit, Norbanus, the man to whom he owed his throne.

After Nerva had been forced to give in on that issue, he saw that he would have to take precautionary measures. No, he might not yet lay his tired old head upon the pillow if, in the end, that old head were not to risk being forcibly severed from the neck on which it belonged. Before he could retire to his bedroom he must write a letter. And the old Emperor, while every limb ached with weariness, dictated his letter. He offered the position of co-regent to his young friend General Trajan, Commander in Chief of the army operating on the German border. Then at last he went to bed.

Marullus and Reginus for their part went to see Lucia. They wanted to save Lucia, and they wanted to punish Lucia.

"I won't talk to you about your motives, Mistress and Goddess Lucia," said Reginus, "but it would have been more considerate and probably also wiser if you had got in touch with us, for example, instead of with Norbanus." "I believe you are my friends—you, my Reginus, and you, my Marullus," replied Lucia, "but be honest: confronted by the choice between saving me or Domitian, would you have decided for me?" "Perhaps there would have been a way out," said Marullus. "There was none," said Lucia somewhat wearily. "Norbanus was my natural ally." "In any case," Reginus summed up, "those two nice boys have lost the throne through your fault, and in addition, my Lucia, you have placed yourself and your brick-works in serious danger." "If I had been in your place, Lucia," said Marullus, "I should have informed such good old friends as we are, at the moment when on the one hand we could no longer have harmed you, but on the other we could have been of use, for example, to the young Princes." Lucia reflected for a moment. "You're right about that," she said then, sensibly.

"It's too bad about him," said Reginus, after a while. "People were often unfair to him." "If those words are supposed to apply to me," answered Lucia, "if you demand that I agree with you, you ask too much of me. No woman whose life has been sought and who has escaped death by a hair's breadth can exhibit such a degree of objectivity. And please think of my Matthias." "And yet people were unfair to him," Reginus insisted stubbornly.

"Let's leave the judgment to the poets and historians," Marullus suggested pacifyingly. "Let us rather occupy ourselves with your immediate future, Lucia. We have reason to believe that you are not overly safe. Our good Annius Bassus and his soldiers do not wish you well." "Have you a summons to convey to me?" said Lucia haughtily. "Is the army behind you?" she went on with scorn. "To be sure, the army is behind us," said Reginus amiably and patiently, "but what we're bringing you is not a summons, but advice." "Then what do you want?" asked Lucia. "We want Domitian's body to be decently buried," Marullus said, formulating their wish. "As you know, the Senate has outlawed his memory. A public funeral would lead to disturbances. We suggest that you erect a pyre for Domitian, as soon as possible, if not in Rome itself then at least close by, say, in your park in Tibur."

Lucia did not hate the dead man any more, but she had always felt an aversion to funerals. That aversion was mirrored on her lively face. "How deeply you can hate," said Marullus. But at that her face relaxed, and, "I don't hate Vellykins," she said, now suddenly very tired, and all at once she looked like an old woman.

"I think it would have been to D.D.D.'s liking," said Marullus, "if you of all people arranged this funeral for him. Remember that it was he who wanted to bury Matthias." "And it would be wise," Reginus added, "if you of all people held the funeral. For then the rumour that you had something to do with unfaithful Norbanus's action would doubtless be silenced." "Unfaithful Norbanus," said Lucia meditatively. "D.D.D. had no man more faithful." "You too of course did not hate him, my dear Lucia," mocked Marullus, emphasizing the "you."

"Very well," said Lucia, giving in. "I shall bury him."

However, it appeared that Domitian's corpse had already been removed from the Palatine. It was his old nurse Phyllis who had had him taken away, secretly and with danger.

They went to Phyllis's house, a simple farmhouse on the outskirts of the city. Yes, that was where the body had been dragged. Phyllis, an enormously fat old woman, had spared no costs: the corpse was indeed already washed, anointed, perfumed, prepared; the most expensive cosmeticians must have attended to it. Now Phyllis sat there, by the coffin; tears ran down her baggy cheeks.

The dead Domitian looked calm and dignified. There was nothing left of the forced grandeur which his countenance had sometimes displayed during his lifetime. His eyebrows, which he had had a habit of drawing together threateningly because of his near-sightedness, were relaxed now; his closed lids hid the eyes which had gazed forth so sombrely and fiercely; of all the exaggerated energy of his countenance only the decided chin remained. A laurel wreath lay on his half-bald skull; to her grief the old woman had not been able to procure any of the other insignia of power. But the dead man had a handsome, virile face, and Marullus and Reginus felt that D.D.D. looked more the Emperor now than many a time when he had made a passionate effort to be the Lord and God.

The old woman had already prepared the pyre. She opposed the idea that Lucia, the murderess, should attend the cremation. The two gentlemen went back to Lucia; they suggested removing the body from Phyllis's home by force and taking it to the Empress's estate. But Lucia was unwilling. Inwardly she was glad to have an excuse to omit the gesture which Marullus and Reginus had demanded of her. She had become the old Lucia again. She had loved Domitian; he had done her good and evil; she had done him good and evil; their accounts were squared. The dead man had nothing to demand of her. She was not afraid of the consequences of her act, of Annius and his soldiers.

So only Marullus, Reginus, and Phyllis were present when the body of the last of the Flavians was laid upon the funeral pyre. They opened the dead man's eyes for him, they kissed him; then with averted faces they lighted the pyre. The perfume with which he was saturated diffused a strong fragrance. "Farewell, Domitian," they cried, "farewell, Lord and God Domitian." But Phyllis shrieked and wailed, tore her clothes and clawed her fat flesh.

Marullus and Reginus watched the pyre burn down. Probably no one, not even Lucia, knew the dead man's weaknesses better than they, but no one knew better his virtues.

Then, when the pyre had burned down, Phyllis extinguished the glowing embers with wine, gathered together the bones, poured milk upon them, dried them with linen, and laid them, mixed with ointments and perfumes, in an urn. She had succeeded, with the help of Marullus and Reginus, in getting admission to the Flavian family temple. There she put away Domitian's remains, but she mixed them with the remains of Julia, whom she had also nursed. For in the opinion of the indignant old creature, Lucia was not the woman who belonged beside Domitian; but beside her eagle, Domitian, belonged her dove, Julia.

THE following day, in the presence of his friend Secundus, old Senator Corellus, who, crippled with gout, had borne his excruciating pains with manly fortitude up to that moment, opened his veins. He had managed it; he had lived to see the death of the accursed Domitian and the re-establishment of liberty. The day had come. He died happy.

The day had come. In his study Senator Cornelius, the historian, sat and thought over what had happened. The heavy furrows in his sombre, earth-coloured face had grown even deeper; he was only in his early forties, but he had the face of an old man. He remembered his dead friends; Senecio, Hel-

vidius, Arulenus; full of sorrow, he thought how often he had
warned them in vain to be reasonable. Yes, that had been the
point: to be reasonable, to be patient, to keep resentment
locked in one's breast until the time came to let it out. Now
the time had come. To survive the era of terror—that had
been the point. He, Cornelius, had survived it.

Reasonableness was a good thing, but it did not make one
happy. Happy he was not, Senator Cornelius. He thought of
the faces of his friends who had gone to their death, of the
women who had gone into exile. They had been grim faces,
yet the faces of people who were resigned. They had been
heroes; he was only a man and a writer. They had only been
heroes; he was a man and a writer.

He was a historian. One had to evaluate things historically.
For the period of the founding of the Empire, for the period
of the Republic, heroes had been necessary; for these centuries,
for the Empire, there was need of reasonable men. The Empire could have been founded only by heroism. It could be
preserved only by reason.

Yet it was a good thing that the type of Helvidius and
Senecio and Arulenus had existed. Every period had need of
heroes, to keep heroism alive for the periods which could not
exist without it. And he was glad that now he might put into
words his unfrozen hatred of the tyrant, and his loving, sor-
rowful memory of his friends. He took up the numerous notes
and memoranda which he had made for himself and set about
composing his introduction, a great picture of the era which
his book was to describe. In powerful, sombre sentences, like
towering blocks of stone, he re-created the horrors and crimes
of the Palatine; and for the heroism of his friends he found
words large and bright as the skies of an early summer day.

III

ON THAT fresh day in early spring, as Joseph walked through John of Gishala's mulberry orchards with him, neither of the two men looked his age. Joseph's seventy years had greyed his beard, and his lean face was somewhat withered, but now in the wind it had fresh colour, and his eyes had a lively glance. And while John's moustache was shining white, his crafty brown face was ruddy and well preserved, and the expression of his sly eyes was actually youthful.

Joseph had been John of Gishala's guest for three days. John knew that Joseph was not much interested in agricultural things, but he could not restrain his peasant's pride, and although he made fun of himself he was once again dragging his friend through his extensive model farm. Joseph had to observe and admire his magnificent oil presses, his wine cellars, his threshing-floors, and above all his mulberry orchards and his silk-works.

He did so mechanically; his thoughts were elsewhere; he was enjoying the pleasure of being in Galilee once more.

He had been settled in Judæa now for almost twelve years, far from Rome, from the new Rome of the Soldier-Emperor Trajan which was very alien to him. No, he did not miss it at all, that militaristic, orderly, magnificently organized, extremely frigid Rome; it revolted him; he was as unable to make anything of the sober, practical, politely unconcerned society of Rome as it was of him.

True, he did not feel at home in Judæa either. Sometimes he tried to persuade himself and his friends that he was content in the quiet of his Be'er Simlai estate. He had been an individual, an exception, long enough, he would declare; now in his old age he would like nothing better than to be absorbed

into the community. He did not want to be anything but a
man in Judæa like other men in Judæa. Yet even if he meant
it sincerely, at bottom he felt uncomfortable in this quiescence.

The Be'er Simlai property, which he had once bought on
John's advice, flourished and prospered. But he, Joseph, was
not needed there: his son Daniel, now twenty-five years old,
had developed into a capable and interested farmer under old
Theodore's instruction; Joseph's presence was more disturbing
than helpful. And the prosperity of the estate was assured according to all human calculation; for everything situated here
in the environment of the capital, Cæsarea, was encouraged by
the Roman government. To be sure, the district was settled
for the most part by Syrians and retired Roman soldiers, and
the scattering of Jews looked upon Joseph unkindly and indulged in gibes at the patronage of the Romans which he enjoyed even under this Emperor Trajan. Mara would have preferred to live in Judæa proper rather than here among the
"heathen"; Daniel too suffered from the suspicion and scorn
of the Jewish settlers. On the other hand, his wife and son
took great pleasure in the thriving of the estate—certainly more
pleasure than he took himself.

Mara had taken the loss of Matthias more calmly than he
had expected; she had not cursed him or made wild speeches.
But the bond between them was broken. Inwardly she had
freed herself from him, as the murderer of two of her sons;
she no longer saw in him the anointed of the Lord, but a defeated man, a bringer of misfortune. However, she was so
detached from him that she did not even remonstrate with
him about that any more. They lived calmly side by side, in
amicable indifference.

Nor were things as they should have been between him and
his son Daniel. Not only was Daniel distressed by the Jewish
settlers' opinion of his father, but in his whole personality he

took more after his mother; he had her composure and her polite reticence. He was an irreproachable son, but he shrank from his violent, incomprehensible father, and Joseph's attempts to win his confidence had been a failure.

So Joseph lived quite alone in the midst of the orderly activity of his estate. He wrote, and spent much time with his books. And now and again he went on a trip to visit friends; he travelled to Jabne, perhaps to see the Grand Doctor, or as now to Gishala, to see John. He had many friends in the country; ever since *Apion* he had enjoyed the respect of the majority of the Jews. Yet it remained a respect without warmth; they had not forgotten his earlier, equivocal position. He lived in Judæa like a stranger among his own people.

Lately he had been seized by a fit of restlessness. He laid the blame on the uncertainty of the political situation. For the great Eastern Campaign which the warlike Emperor Trajan was preparing formed a new threat to Judæa. Yet the causes which drove Joseph away from the peace of his Be'er Simlai estate lay in himself. It was as it had been in his youth; it was as it had been in the period when he had written:

Cast thyself free from thine anchor, saith Jehovah.
I love not them that dally in the harbour.
And an abomination to me are they that rot in sloth.
I have given feet to men to bear them over the earth,
And legs that they might run,
That they might not remain for ever where they are,
 like a tree rooted to its place.

He could not stand it at Be'er Simlai any more. He had set out to travel here and there through Judæa, with no definite destination; only on the evening before the Feast of Passover, thus not for three weeks, would he return to his estate.

So now he was visiting John. John had been in the country

a much shorter time than he. John had remained true to his resolution, and had left Rome and his Roman business only when he could be sure of his control over his ardently patriotic heart. And indeed, during the five years which he had lived in Judæa he had bravely withstood the temptation of aiding the Zealots. He had occupied himself in that period with a costly and imposing reconstruction of his native city, the small and ancient hill town of Gishala, for it had been destroyed first in the great Jewish War and then a second time in the uprising of the Zealots. But above all he had been making his own large estate into a model farm.

The two old gentlemen walked about, and John showed his friend the improvements he had installed in his mulberry and olive fields and his vineyards. The bright, friendly young sun of early spring was shining; the two men enjoyed it; but if one wanted to keep warm one had to keep moving. So they strode forward briskly, Joseph somewhat bent, John, who was shorter, very erect. John was talkative. He noticed that Joseph was not listening, but he did not need an attentive listener; he wanted only to express his joy in what he had made, and he smiled a little himself at the loquacity of his old age. But finally he was tempted to draw Joseph into a real argument, and with humorous contentiousness he began: "You see, Joseph, my property is well kept up; it's what one calls a model farm. Yet this model farm doesn't pay me a profit; on the contrary, I lose money on it, and if I don't give it up it's only because it gives me pleasure. It gives me pleasure to produce very good wine, very good oil, very good silk. And now please consider this question further: if I with all my special advantages can't farm a profit out of my property under this Roman government, how is an ordinary olive-grower to support himself with the sweat of his brow? The new taxes and customs duties that Trajan's Minister of Finance levies on the Eastern provinces are simply murdering the little peasant. And yet of course their alleged purpose isn't being accomplished, since the Italian wines aren't made any better or more saleable thereby. For Judæa the only result is that the unrest in the country increases."

"Is the unrest increasing?" asked Joseph, and now he was far from absent-minded. John gave him a sidelong glance. "If I draw my conclusions for the rest of Judæa from my Galilee," he said, and smiled more with satisfaction than with malice, "then the peasants can't be very well satisfied with the new edicts in any locality. There's no question that the Zealots are gaining ground everywhere. Perhaps that's even the Romans' main purpose in pursuing their peculiar financial policy. For I can imagine that when Trajan begins his planned campaign in the East, certain military elements will first want to put things in order here in Judæa—what they consider order. And what could be more convenient for them than to provoke an uprising here and during it to do away with all the not quite reliable elements once and for all? But it's not merely the financial policy," he went on. "For although I'm still of the opinion"—he smiled as he came to the subject of his eternal dispute with Joseph—"that with sensible wine and oil prices neither the Jewish War nor the later uprising would have occurred, yet I gladly admit to you that it's not just a question of wine prices in our Jewish wars, but of Jehovah as well. Both must become a problem, the market *and* Jehovah. Otherwise the proper state of excitement won't arise."

"So you think," asked Joseph, "that Jehovah too has become a problem again?"

"In that field, Doctor Joseph," answered John, "you're the authority, not I. But if you want to know the opinion of a simple country gentleman, who doesn't look at his Jehovah as a theologian but as a man of common sense, then I'll be glad to tell you. Jochanan Ben Sakkai's idea of replacing the lost State and the lost Temple by Jabne was excellent; there was no other means at the time, after the collapse, to save national unity. And ritual and the Law really have replaced the State. But gradually, as a new generation grew up which no longer had any experience of State and Temple, the meaning of the rites was lost, and today the Law has become a mass of formulas; the rites smother the meaning; Judæa is smothered under the domination of the Doctors; the empty Word cannot permanently replace God. To acquire meaning and life God needs His country. You see, that is what makes Jehovah a problem today. Jehovah can only acquire real new life when Judæa has become the land of His Jews instead of a temporary resort for His Jews. Jehovah needs a body. His body is this landscape, His life these olive groves, vineyards, mountains, lakes, the Jordan, and the sea; and as long as Jehovah and this country remain separated, neither the one nor the other is alive. Forgive me if I become poetical. But naturally a simple old country gentleman can't express himself as clearly as you."

Joseph had something to say about the pagan quality of this conception, but he did not say it. Instead he summed up: "Then, since both problems, Jehovah and the market, are clamouring for a solution, you find the external and internal conditions for an uprising on hand? You think that the Zealots have good reason to say: 'The day has come'? I understand you rightly, don't I?"

"How youthful you are, for all your seventy years," replied John, "and how fiery. But you can't pin me down so easily. True, as long as those two issues, Jehovah and the market, don't become burning, an uprising is impossible. I did say that. But I did not say that those factors were the only prerequisites. If you want my opinion, then the first, the most important, condition is that the military chances of such an uprising are not too bad." "So everything you've been saying remains purely theoretical," said Joseph, disappointed. But, "Now you already want to pin me down again," John reproached him jokingly. "How can we, in our position, see what the military chances of the Zealots are if this Trajan really begins his Eastern Campaign?"

Now Joseph became impatient. "Then do you condemn the tendencies of the Zealots?" he asked. "Yes or no?" Yet, "I'm not active in politics," John said evasively. "As you know, before I left Rome I examined my feelings thoroughly, and only when I had made sure that my heart would not play me any more tricks would I permit myself to return to Judæa."

In annoyed silence Joseph walked along beside him for a while. Until John began again: "My resignation, however, does not keep me from certain dreams. Let us suppose, for example, that the Zealots are not as reasonable as we are, and that they initiate an uprising in spite of a very slight chance of success. Could you then imagine any greater joy for us, Joseph, than to let ourselves be carried away by it? Imagine how two old dodderers like us, who have nothing more to expect from life, would be revivified and rejuvenated by such an uprising. I don't like to use strong words, but to meet one's death in a revolt of that kind—I can't imagine a more magnificent end to my life."

It upset Joseph that the other expressed such feelings so shamelessly. "Aren't you very egotistical, John?" he asked. "Isn't it improper, isn't it simply indecent, for you to behave with such unreasonable youthfulness at our age?" "You've become awfully dry," said John, shaking his head. "You just can't take a joke any more. Because I was only joking, of course. But if you want to be absolutely clear-headed and scrupulously fair, you'll have to admit that it's not pure egotism if the dream of such an uprising warms my heart. Probably a new rebellion of the Zealots will collapse just as quickly as their old one. Nevertheless, it will not have been senseless. I'm thinking of my problem of Jehovah. An uprising like that would be a reminder not to forget Judæa, not to forget the country over the rites and words. And a reminder of that sort is necessary. Human beings forget so terribly fast. It would be a good thing if our Jews were to be reminded of their country again, that it's *their* country. Otherwise a serious danger exists that the Doctors will finally kill Jehovah and Judæa will be smothered by Jabne."

"Tell me," Joseph urged him, "are military preparations under way? Do you know whether the Zealots have definite plans?"

John looked at him with an intimate, cunning, and impudent smile which made his face young again. "Perhaps," he answered, "I know something, and perhaps I don't. I don't want to know anything definite, because I don't occupy myself with practical politics. What I'm saying is idle chatter, such as an old man talks to a friend when a new spring's coming and he falls to gossiping in the kindly sunshine."

But this time Joseph turned away in serious vexation, and had nothing more to say to John. Then the latter nudged him and said slyly: "But even if I don't know anything, I do know my people, and I can sense certain things the way I sense the weather. And for that reason, my Joseph, take a little piece of advice along with you. If you want to travel about the country just now, go first to Cæsarea and there, at the Governor's palace, have them issue to you a detailed passport which will identify you to everyone. I just mean—so that you're prepared for anything."

When Joseph left Gishala the next day, John accompanied him for a good stretch of the road; and when Joseph, riding

away, glanced back after a while, John was still standing there
and gazing after him.

In Cæsarea, where he went to obtain a passport as John had
advised, Joseph paid a call on the Governor. Lucius Quietus,
with that assiduous and distant courtesy which was characteristic of almost all the Emperor Trajan's trusted agents, invited
the Knight Flavius Josephus to dinner.

So there sat Joseph in the midst of the high officials and officers of the province, and felt bitterly alien and uncomfortable.
In spite of the marked amiability of the gentlemen, he felt
once again that they did not take him at his full value. He
did not belong. True, through his past and through his privileges, he was more closely connected with them than anyone
else, but in the last analysis he remained a paid agent.

They spoke about coming events. In all probability, if the
Eastern Campaign was really about to begin, disturbances
would break out all over Syria, Judæa, Mesopotamia. John had
been right. The gentlemen scarcely concealed that such an uprising would be convenient for them. It would provide a welcome excuse for thoroughly cleaning up Judæa—the area to be
used for marshalling troops and bringing up reinforcements—
before the armies set out for the Far East.

Again and again they asked Joseph, as the best expert,
whether the Zealots might not after all abandon the uprising
because of its hopelessness. Joseph explained that the great majority of the Jewish population was thoroughly loyal, and that
the Zealots thought too realistically to initiate a hopeless uprising. Governor Quietus listened attentively, but it seemed to
Joseph that he was not at all convinced.

Moreover, Joseph had not spoken with his usual persuasive power. Instead he was strangely distracted. It was because he had been searching for a certain face since the moment he had entered the Governor's house. The owner of that face, Paulus Bassus, was the man who was best informed about military conditions in the Province of Judæa; the governors changed, but Colonel Paulus stayed; actually he was the man who ruled Judæa, and when the Governor gave a reception one expected to see Paulus. On the other hand, of course, it was out of the question that Paulus should appear here, knowing that he would meet his father. Yet foolish as it was, his father kept looking for him.

The next morning Joseph went to the government building to obtain his passport. A feeling of strangeness and hostility arose in him as he entered the palace, which stood there cold, white, gorgeous, powerful and threatening, a symbol of Trajan's Rome.

The room in which he had his business lay in the left wing of the house. Having quickly disposed of the matter, he was crossing the great hall to leave by the main portal when an officer entered through that portal. The officer, a very slender gentleman with a white, fleshless face, elegant, very erect, turned to the right. No one could have told, as he acknowledged the salute of the guards, whether he had seen the man who came from the left. Nor could anyone have told whether Joseph had recognized the officer. But as Joseph left the building he seemed old and tired; the square in front of the palace, wide and empty as it was, did not contain enough air for the man who fought for breath there; and whoever saw him might wonder why such an easy and unimportant piece of business as the procuring of a passport should have exhausted him to such an extent.

The officer, for his part, as he turned into the right wing of the building, was a shade paler than usual, and his narrow lips were even more tightly compressed. But then, even before he entered his office, he relaxed. Instead, Paulus Bassus—or, as he had formerly been called, Flavius Paulus—seemed rather satisfied. He was. The idea, an idea which he had been seeking for a long time, had come to him.

The very same day he spoke to Governor Lucius Quietus.

JOSEPH had taken a vacation from his Be'er Simlai estate, from his wife and son, until the evening before Passover; until then he could wander across the country, a free man, wherever the wind and his heart might drive him.

On the mountains it was still winter, but in the valleys it was already spring. Joseph travelled about restlessly, now on a mule, now on horseback, sometimes even on foot. The old man remembered the time when he had first journeyed through Galilee, to investigate its inhabitants. This time too he felt happiest as long as he was unknown, and if anyone called him by name he did not stay long.

Yet he sought out friends and men whose type and opinions interested him. Thus he came also to B'ne Berak, to see Doctor Akibah.

Joseph had seen Akibah often, and opposite as the Doctor's personality and teachings were from his own, the two men were not unappreciative of each other's company. Without question Akibah was the most important of the Doctors next to Gamaliel. Yet like Gamaliel he was only in his early fifties. But while everything had been showered on Gamaliel from birth, Akibah had come up from the very bottom; he had been a cowherd; he had had to go throught a bitter struggle to acquire his education and his place in the Council of

Jabne and to establish his teachings in the face of a hundred obstacles. It was a doctrine which isolated everything Jewish from everything non-Jewish with a sullen fierceness and at the same time with a cunning, twisted method of logic; it was a narrow, fanatical doctrine which contradicted everything that Joseph had experienced in his great period and preached in his great books. Nevertheless, Joseph could not escape the fascination which went out from this Doctor Akibah.

He stayed one day at B'ne Berak, and then another and a third. Then, if he wanted to be back at his estate for the Passover, it was time to make his departure. Yet when he took leave of Akibah, the latter held him back. "How would it be, Doctor Joseph?" he asked. "Wouldn't you like to spend the evening of Passover with me for once?"

Joseph glanced up in astonishment, wondering whether Akibah had meant his suggestion seriously. Akibah's large head sat upon a thick, powerful body. His cheeks shone rosy and fresh from out of a silvery-grey beard; his hair grew low on his broad, furrowed, imposing forehead. Thick eyebrows bushed out over his brown eyes. A stern and passionate flame glowed in those eyes and made one forget his flat nose. Today, however, as Akibah suggested to Joseph that he spend the evening of Passover with him, there was a sly little gleam in the eyes which were usually so wild and fierce.

As a matter of fact it was astonishing that the passionately nationalistic Akibah should invite him, Joseph, the compromiser, who all his life had wanted to reconcile Jews and Greeks and Christians, to sit at his table on the evening of Passover, the great national feast of commemoration. It was a challenge and an honour. For a fraction of a second Joseph was so astonished that he did not know what to do. Custom dictated that Joseph, the master of the house, should spend that evening on his estate in the midst of his family and servants, that he

should read the Haggadah aloud to them, the story of the
Jews' deliverance from their bondage in Egypt. But Joseph said
to himself that his wife and son would not miss him very
much; it would more likely be a cause for satisfaction to them
that Joseph, the "traitor," should on this evening in particular
be the guest of Akibah, the most revered of the Doctors, whom
all Jewish patriots regarded as their foremost leader. After his
first astonishment Joseph felt a deep satisfaction. "I thank you,
Doctor Akibah," he said. "I accept your invitation; I shall stay."
And the two men looked at each other; they smiled into each
other's eyes with a smile of recognition, challenge, and friendliness.

So on the evening of the narration, the evening of the
Haggadah, Joseph had the place of honour to the right of the
master of the house, in the home of Doctor Akibah at B'ne
Berak. The blissful amazement with which he had been overcome when Akibah had invited him had still not deserted him;
it had become stronger. He felt elated, exalted; this evening
seemed to him a greater honour than the moment when the
Emperor Titus had had his, Joseph's bust set up in the library
of the Temple of Peace in Rome and had laid the laurel wreath
upon it.

That the evening of the Haggadah was being celebrated
with such fervour and passion only a short time after its introduction, not by the Jews of the Land of Israel alone but everywhere in the world—that was above all to the credit of Doctor
Akibah. It was he who had created the "arrangement" of the
evening, its *seder,* which now more than ever, in the time of
oppression, caused the memory of the bitter trials and miracu-
lous deliverance from bondage to rise up with such force in
every Jewish breast.

From the costly, three-tiered silver bowl which contained all
kinds of food commemorating with a naïve and effective sym-

bolism the period of slavery and deliverance, Akibah took the flat cakes of unleavened bread—a reminder of the haste with which the Jews had once departed from the hostile land of oppression. Akibah distributed the cakes and showed them to the guests. "This," he said, "is the bread of sorrow, which our fathers ate in Egypt. Whosoever is hungry, let him come and partake of it. Whosoever has need, let him come and celebrate the Feast of Passover with us. This year here, next year in Jerusalem. This year slaves, next year free men." Everywhere in the world at that moment the Jews were speaking those simple and confident sentences of Akibah's; and everywhere, Joseph felt, their hearts were uplifted at the sound. Yes, this year is the last of oppression; in the next we shall celebrate the Passover in a Jerusalem miraculously re-erected.

And Akibah went on to tell the story of the deliverance from bondage in the simple and moving formulas which he had established. He lived his own narrative, familiar as it was to him; he obeyed his own command: "On this evening let every Jew feel as if he had himself been freed from bondage in Egypt."

Joseph listened to the voice of Akibah. It was a deep, rough, unmusical voice, yet its passionate, imperious confidence carried him away. The words of Akibah intoxicated everyone at the table as if the words were wine. Some of Akibah's guests had seen the glory of the great celebration of the Passover at the Temple in Jerusalem. Yet in this time of misery and oppression, the memory of the pilgrimage, the memory of the solemn splendour of the priests, did not make them downcast; on the contrary, the grim relation of their pitiful, fervent rites to the present day only served to make their pride in their people and their mighty God all the more intoxicating.

Joseph recalled the evening that he had spent shortly before at the house of the Governor in Cæsarea. He remembered the officers and officials who, sure of their power, looked down with cold realistic arrogance upon the barbarian idealists who were eternally throwing themselves into a hopeless battle for their country and their God. No, ten times rather was he here, at the side and in the circle of the vanquished, than with those who were the conquerors.

And the vanquished went on intoxicating themselves with the memory of their victories in the past and the anticipation of their victories in the future. They prepared a cup of wine for the prophet Elijah, the greatest prophet of ancient times. Assuredly he, the forerunner of the Messiah, the messenger of the avenging Jehovah, would appear on this solemn night, and he should find the drink of welcome waiting for him. No one doubted it.

And they sang the lines of the great Hillel, the ecstatic psalm of jubilation which celebrated the deliverance from Egypt and the might of the Jewish God who had inspired them. "The sea saw it and fled," they sang, "Jordan was driven back. The mountains skipped like rams, and the little hills like lambs. What ailed thee, O thou sea, that thou fleddest? thou, Jordan, that thou wast driven back?" Their imaginations were already savouring the destruction of the Romans by the God Jehovah. The waters would come upon the Emperor Trajan and his legions and swallow them, as once the waves of the Red Sea had swallowed the host of the Egyptian Pharaoh and the chariots and the horses. Hallelujah!

The rites had been performed, the prayers spoken. As the night wore on, the guests took their leave. Joseph too wanted to retire. But Akibah held him back, again and again, until in the end there were only five left; Akibah, Joseph, and three others.

Akibah's art consisted in being able, through a method worked out to the last detail, to find in the words of the Book an interpretation for everything that happened on earth. In the

Book everything had been foreseen, everything that was and ever would be, and whoever was able rightly to interpret the Book had a key to the meaning of all earthly occurrences. The bygone events in Egypt and those of today under the Emperor Trajan were one and the same, and their end also would be the same, and there were good reasons if today more than ever the Feast of Passover was celebrated with such wrathful jubilation. The holy frenzy of that evening's intoxication was nothing else than a fierce anticipation of the triumph over Rome.

Now Akibah turned directly to Joseph himself, challenging him. Moses as well as the prophet Elijah had simply forced God, without much ceremony, to do their will and to work miracles. And thus God wished it. He wished one to force Him. He expected one to help Him. Whoever declared that the time had not yet come, for him it would never come. Instead one should believe, believe fanatically, that the Messiah, a Messiah of flesh and blood, would come tomorrow. This night he would come, the prophet Elijah, the forerunner, and he would drain the cup. Whoever believed that, whoever believed it as firmly as the multiplication table, forced God to send the Messiah tomorrow.

Akibah liked to behave as a man of the people. A gigantic peasant, settled immovably in his faith, he sat before Joseph; he let coarse and vulgar expressions slip into his speech; and finally he attacked Joseph rudely: "If everyone behaved the way you do, if everyone limited himself to folding his hands in his lap and showing patience, we could wait till the grass grew out of our mouths and the Messiah still wouldn't be here." Scornfully and threateningly the words rolled from his lips; with a violent gesture he brushed some crumbs of unleavened bread from his silvery-grey beard. Joseph sat before him, a slim, refined aristocrat; but he was not offended; he did not want to spoil this great evening for himself. He postponed what he had to

say to a later time, and immersed himself completely in the
pleasure of letting himself be fired by the other's fanatical faith.

For with more and more abandon they surrendered themselves to their beautiful dreams. But were they only dreams?
No, they were much more, they were plans, detailed plans.
When they spoke about the next seven weeks, the weeks of
Atonement, the weeks between the Feasts of Passover and Pentecost, the youngest of the group around the table, handsome
young Doctor Eleazer, looked about him with an ecstatic
glance and asked: "Where, my elders, where, my Doctors and
friends, will we celebrate this Pentecost?" Doctor Tarfon, with
a half-nod toward Joseph, gave the rash speaker an admonish-
ing glance. But Akibah, as if he himself had not just rudely
attacked Joseph, said: "Are you by any chance afraid, my
friends, of the man who has written *Apion?*"

Joseph had been horrified when he heard young Doctor
Eleazer's words; his intelligence told him that he should wax
indignant at the foolhardy, hopeless undertaking which these
men were obviously planning for the very next weeks. But there
was much sweetness mingled with his horror, and when he
actually heard words of confidence from Akibah's lips, a great
joy flared up in him. More and more vigorously the old temptations rose up in him, a man of near seventy; he was swept
along with the others in their divine drunkenness. Now he too
was absolutely sure that the prophet Elijah would drain the
cup on the very same night.

As never before he savoured fully that night of refuge when
the Lord takes the people of Israel under His especial protection. With the others he listened believingly to the wild, wise
speeches of Akibah, the crude magician; with the others he indulged in fierce and magnificent fantasies about the downfall
of the enemy and the re-erection of the new Jerusalem.

Thus with the others he sat the whole night. And with the

others he was sorry when the pupils arrived and reminded the Doctors that the time for prayer was at hand. The morning had come.

Two days later, when he was alone with him, Joseph asked Akibah point-blank: "Why did you invite me to stay for the Feast of Passover?" Gigantic Akibah sat there quietly, with his ankles crossed; his right hand lay relaxed on his thigh; he leaned his left elbow on the arm of his chair, and his head in his left hand. Reflectively, with his brown, rather small eyes, he scrutinized Joseph's gaunt face. Then he said calmly right into his face: "I wanted to have a chance to get a close look at a traitor."

Joseph recoiled at this unexpected affront. Akibah noticed this with satisfaction. "I have always," he went on, "sought to teach my pupils respect for old age. So with all due respect to a grey head, I repeat: you are a traitor. I admit that by your services you later made up for many of the injuries which you had done. Today you're a traitor above all to yourself and to your own soul." Akibah sat there uncouthly; the restraint with which he tried to speak emphasized his peasant's pronunciation.

"What you say, Doctor Akibah," replied Joseph, and without being conscious of it he spoke especially politely and with the accent of a man who in his day had won the great title of Doctor at Jerusalem, "what you say sounds general. Won't you explain the application to me?"

Akibah snorted, blew into his hands, rubbed them together as if he were about to lift a heavy weight. Then he said: "Jehovah destined you to be a fighter for His cause, for Israel. But as soon as the task began to demand effort and courage you dropped it. You took refuge in literature and your cosmopolitan rigmarole. After a while that bored you, and you went back to the fight. Then it got to be stale, and you evaporated again, back into your comfortable writing which didn't commit you to anything. A man of the people like myself calls that treachery. I say what is so, with all due respect to a grey head."

"Isn't your attack still very general?" returned Joseph, even more politely. "Though perhaps it's because of my old head that I can't grasp the actual application." "I'll try to translate my simple opinion into your cultured Aramaic," replied Akibah. "You see perfectly, Doctor Joseph, what this day and hour demand. But you don't want to see it, you prefer to shut your eyes and to 'fight' for an ideal which you know perfectly well is unattainable. You flee from the difficulties of the attainable into the comfortable dream of a completely unattainable ideal. You betray today and tomorrow for the sake of a nebulous future. You betray the Messiah of flesh and blood, who may already be walking among us, for the sake of a foggy, spiritual Messiah. You betray the Jewish State for the sake of a cosmopolitan Utopia." The educated phrases came awkwardly from the clumsy man.

"What do you really expect to accomplish," asked Joseph very calmly, "by telling me these unpleasant things?"

Akibah was impressed that Joseph remained so calm, but it also annoyed him. "We don't know what to do with you," he said at last angrily, and ran his fingers through his silvery-grey beard. "Which of your books is the one that counts? The *Jewish War?* The *Universal History? Apion?* A great writer," he growled, "should at least be able to express himself so unambiguously that the people can understand him. I'm no great writer," he finished boorishly, "but the people understand me."

"I don't understand you, Doctor Akibah," Joseph answered affably, with a slight emphasis on the "I." "I don't understand why you speak in favor of the Zealots. You know that under the Emperor Trajan the number of legions has been strengthened, that the Eastern legions are full, that the military roads, the military equipment, have been brought to a peak never reached before. Who saddles a lion must know how to ride him. You as a man of judgment know that you cannot ride him. So why do you favour an uprising? The day will come, very well. But it's up to you to decide when it has come. And if you arouse the people at the wrong time, won't you ruin the day and take a heavy burden of guilt upon yourself?"

"The God who commanded me to saddle the lion," said Akibah, "will also teach me how to ride him." Then, recognizing that this was a sentence suitable for a public assembly but not for the writer Joseph Ben Matthias, he allowed him to look deeper into his being. "Not reason," he said grimly, "can decide whether the day has come; only instinct can do that. Again and again reason comes to naught before God. I do not say that because I've avoided reason and its temptations. I know the joys of logic and learning. I have studied the Book and the Law with every available means, and I have wrestled with the philosophy of the heathen. But everything I have learned is that when it's a question of something serious, inner knowledge alone helps one out—the belief in the God of Israel who is above all reason—and not logic and not the belief in a constant cause and effect. I believe in Moses and the prophets and not in Trajan and his legions. I want to be prepared when the change comes, when the day comes. And the day is coming, I tell you. Laws and rites are good and God is gracious, but they remain idle talk if they are not a preparation for an independent State with a police force and an army and a sovereign system of justice. Only the re-erection of the Temple can help us, of the real Temple of stone and gold, and the re-erection of the true Jerusalem, a city of stone and wood with unassailable walls. You see, my Master and Doctor, the masses understand that. One has to be very learned in Greek wisdom not to understand it."

It would have been senseless to attack the man's fanaticism with rational arguments. It was not that Akibah lacked reason. On the contrary, his power of reasoning was probably no less than his, Joseph's. But Akibah's faith was simply strong enough to overwhelm his reason.

That knowledge made Joseph fall silent. And indeed he now felt completely dwarfed. For Akibah arose; he came toward him like a giant; he bent down his great head to him, intimately; the little eyes, sly yet fanatical beneath the broad furrowed forehead and the bushy eyebrows, looked very close into his own. And mysteriously lowering his rough voice, he announced: "Do you know why I supported Gamaliel so strongly when he included the Song of Songs in the canon of the Holy Book? Because the Song of Songs is a parable, a duet between the bridegroom God and the bride Israel. But if Jehovah is the bridegroom, He must fight for His bride Israel, He must pay. How harshly and bitterly He made Jacob serve for his bride. God must fight for Israel. He must earn His people. Jehovah has given Israel a difficult mission; Israel will fulfil it. But Jehovah too must fulfil the terms of the contract; He must give Israel back its power, its State. And not at some indefinite time, but in the immediate future, now. You, Joseph Ben Matthias, want to make things too easy for God. You want to give Israel away cheaply. I'm not so refined. I'm a peasant and I'm suspicious. I demand payment when I've fulfilled a part of my work. I demand of Jehovah—understand me rightly, I don't ask, I demand—that He give back to Israel its State and its Temple."

Joseph was shocked at the fierceness with which the man stated his sly and presumptuous demand; he was obviously convinced of its justice to the very core of his being. "You create Jehovah in your own image," Joseph said softly, embarrassed. "Yes," Akibah admitted candidly and in a tone of challenge. "Why should I not create Jehovah in my image, since He created me in His?" But then he returned from the realm of mysticism to reality. "But don't be afraid," he comforted Joseph; he smiled, and suddenly, in spite of his huge, silvery-grey beard, he looked very young. "I've given my word to the Grand Doctor," he confessed, "that I would not support any Jewish uprising so long as Edom, so long as the Romans, don't commit a new outrage." His smile became sly and made him unexpectedly like John of Gishala. "To be sure," he said, "I could freely give the Grand Doctor that promise. For I'm certain that we won't have long to wait for a new Roman outrage. The Roman cleverness is a stupid cleverness, a short-sighted cleverness, without God or grace. The Romans will commit an outrage, I and the Zealots will be freed from our promise, and God will help us, not the Romans."

JOSEPH, disturbed by this conversation, went to Jabne to talk over the political situation with the Grand Doctor.

Not only was Gamaliel not jealous of Akibah, but with wise foresight he had done his best to increase the latter's prestige. For Gamaliel could not have kept his domination over the Jews if he had not had Akibah, the passionate agitator, at his side. While Gamaliel taught: "Be patient, yield to the Romans," Akibah complemented him by preaching: "But only for a short time; then you may rise up and fall upon the insolent enemy." So both their interests were served, the Grand Doctor's because the people could not have stood the eternal, nerve-racking waiting which he demanded of them if it had not been for Akibah and his encouragement, Akibah's because his reason recoiled from the adventure which his heart desired, and fundamentally he was glad that Gamaliel's prudence again and again prevented and postponed it. The two men, different as they were—tolerant, polished Gamaliel and fanatical, boorish Akibah—loved, honoured, and respected each other.

Joseph was soon forced to note that the Grand Doctor was much better informed about the political situation than he himself, who had but recently been to see the Governor and Akibah.

The Emperor Trajan, Gamaliel explained to Joseph, was by no means anti-Semitic. However, to get under way effectively, his gigantic war-machine required the land of the Jews as a base of operations. So the Jews were a nuisance to him, to him and to his Governor Lucius Quietus. Yet the Governor was not actually an enemy of the Jews either; as he did not want to destroy the prosperity of the province he wanted to avoid excessively dangerous measures. But unfortunately there was a man in his immediate circle who longed for just such measures. And now, according to reliable reports, that man had cleverly exploited the atmosphere of patriotic violence which had been created by the preparations for the Eastern Campaign, and had converted the Governor to his point of view.

It cost Joseph an effort to follow Gamaliel with full attention. For he knew that the Grand Doctor referred to the dangerous man in the Governor's circle in such vague terms out of consideration for him, Joseph; for that dangerous, nameless man was none other than Paulus Bassus, Joseph's son.

Gamaliel, however, went on talking, and Joseph listened despite the tempest in his heart. For truly the grand Doctor's report deserved an attentive ear. The nameless one had hatched a really fiendish idea; the Governor had given his consent, although half-heartedly; and now they were waiting only for the agreement of Rome before putting the unlucky plan into effect. The plan was as follows: so that they might better be able to separate the reliable from the unreliable elements, they wanted to reintroduce the poll-tax in Judæa.

The poll-tax. The two drachmas. Among all the oppressive measures which the Romans had invented, the most disgraceful. If that special tax, after having been abolished by the rightful Emperor Nerva, was really going to be reintroduced, it would be the signal for the uprising which Rome desired and the Zealots unfortunately wanted also. Probably Akibah too had heard about the projected introduction of the tax, and probably that was the "outrage" to which he had alluded.

Joseph listened to Gamaliel's report as if paralysed. What paralysed him, who was usually so full of animation, was the thought that it was the nameless one, that it was his Paulus, whom the Deity had chosen to bring this new disaster upon Judæa. What a creature of misfortune he was, Joseph. How misfortune sprang from everything he had created, again and again, from his sons, from his books. He sat without moving, as if stunned.

Finally he became conscious that Gamaliel had long since ceased speaking. He sought Gamaliel's eye, hesitantly. The Doctor returned his glance and Joseph saw that the other knew perfectly what was going on inside him. "I thank you," said Joseph.

"If Cæsarea decrees the poll-tax," Gamaliel went on, as if there had been no silent interchange, "Akibah will be released from the promise he gave me. Nevertheless, it is possible that he will remain quiet. He knows as well as I do that the 'outrage' from Cæsarea doesn't in any way alter the relative strengths of Rome and Judæa. He has a powerful intelligence. It remains a question whether that powerful intelligence will withstand his even more powerful heart." He gazed sadly before him. Up to

that moment he had always seemed a young man to Joseph.
Now the old Joseph saw that Gamaliel too had not remained
young. His once reddish-brown beard was almost completely
grey; the eyes beneath the arched eyebrows were dull; body
and countenance had lost their imposing erectness.

Yet unexpectedly the Grand Doctor straightened up and was
his old self again. "I want to ask a favour of you, Joseph," he
said warmly, yet in the tone of one used to command. "Go to
the North. Speak to John of Gishala once more. If I don't succeed in holding back Akibah, perhaps you'll succeed in restrain-
ing John, so that at least the North remains quiet. You're his
friend; he listens to you. He has such a clear mind. Persuade
him to use it."

"Very well," replied Joseph, "I'll go to Gishala again."

Since he had left his estate Joseph had been restless. Now he
became even more unquiet. In haste he departed, and he
travelled in ever-greater haste. Yet he did not take the shortest
route but travelled to and fro across the country. So he once
more traversed the greater part of the Land of Judæa and the
Land of Samaria, hurriedly, as if he might miss something, as
if he might never again see what he did not now see and ab-
sorb once more.

Then in Samaria he learned that the Governor had issued an
edict reintroducing the poll-tax for the Jewish inhabitants of
the province. And the very next day, in the little town of Esdraela, people were saying that serious disturbances had broken
out in Upper Galilee. They could not give him any exact information. But this much was certain: in several Galilean lo-
calities with a mixed population the Jews had attacked the
Romans, Greeks, and Syrians. In the meantime, the story went,

Roman fighting forces had already set out from Cæsarea to restore order. The leader of the uprising, one had heard, was John of Gishala.

According to all this, the events had obviously relieved Joseph of his mission, and he had no further errand in the North. The wisest course was to return to Be'er Simlai as quickly as possible and there to look after his interests, after Mara, after Daniel.

But while he was telling himself that, he already knew that he would not do it. From the first moment, the horror with which he had heard the news had been mingled with a great sweetness. With pride and shame he noted that he felt light, free, happy. It came to him that through all the years in Judæa he had been waiting only for this uprising. Now those years in Judæa had acquired meaning and justification. For if he had received the news of the uprising in Rome, late and far from the actual events, he would have missed the most important occurrence of his life.

Madness, it was sheer madness to want to take part in the uprising. In the beginning there would be a few victories, full of enthusiasm and exhilaration; then a bitter and final defeat would follow. The Romans would accomplish what they wanted; they would bloodily trample underfoot all the manliness, youth, and fighting spirit left in the Jews. It was insane and criminal to have a hand in it.

Thus, by summoning all his powers of reason, he could drive away the intoxication which had overcome him at the news of the revolt. But only for moments.

In the night, upon the poor couch that the little town offered him, the intoxication gained full control of him; there was no longer any defence against it; and voluptuously he abandoned himself to his dangerous happiness. He felt as he had in the days of the first war, when as a young man he had been in command of the Galilean militia against the Romans—uplifted, exalted. Oh, to feel it again, the glowing joyousness with which they had gone forth to battle in those days. That melting of one into the other. That thousandfold, overflowing aliveness, because that very day might be the last. That great ecstasy, compounded of piety, violence, fear, confidence, and boundless rapture.

He tossed from side to side on his couch, ground his teeth, cursed himself. Do not grow insane again in your last days, Joseph. If a young man let himself be seized by such insanity, it could be divine, it could be noble. But if it happened to a person like himself, an old man, there was nothing noble about such a drunken old man; he was ridiculous, nothing else.

He was not ridiculous. If after so many years, if after so many experiences, the voice within him still spoke with such power, that voice was right. And if it should be the voice of madness, that madness came from God. Akibah was right. Who dared to declare that Jehovah was identical with logic and arid reason? Had reason spoken out of the mouths of the prophets? Or something else? If you, with brazen pedantry, want to call that other element madness, then blessed be it, that madness.

And old Joseph drew himself blissfully into his madness. Yes, John of Gishala was right, and Akibah was right, and the Book of Judith and Joseph Ben Matthias's book against Apion; and the Grand Doctor and the *Universal History* of Flavius Josephus were wrong.

Once he had decided to be mad, he set out that very night to fight his way through to John of Gishala.

He found a mule-driver who took him as far as the little village of Atabyr, which lay half-way up the mountain of the same name. The man did not dare to go along with him any further. The inhabitants of the little village also advised him not to press forward. For here began the area of military operations.

So Joseph, after he had bought a few provisions, continued his journey alone. He avoided the highroads and chose lonely, out-of-the-way paths used by the shepherds, along the ravines and ridges of the mountains. In this region he had once fought; he had fortified the mountain; he knew the district well. Silently, evenly, cautiously, in discreet haste he walked onward.

A radiant spring day was breaking. The winter had lasted a long time that year; the snow still lay on the mountains of Upper Galilee; it fed the swollen brooks so that they babbled merrily. The air had an exhilarating purity; distant objects were distinct and close. Joseph climbed deeper into the mountains; he called on his memory; it obeyed him, and every height, every valley, was familiar to him.

There was the overhanging ridge. From there he must be able to see the lake, his lake, the Lake of Tiberias, the Lake of Gennesaret. Look, there it gleamed already! Minute dots moved on its mirrored surface; Joseph's memory transformed them into the reddish-brown sails of the fishing-boats.

He climbed over the ridge, looked for a crevice which might shelter him, found it, crouched down. That restlessness which had been torturing him all the time had left him at last. He could rest. He settled himself more comfortably, ate some of his provisions—fruits, a little meat, bread—and drank some of his wine.

A merry little breeze was blowing. Joseph's chest expanded. In an atmosphere of magical clarity the Land of Galilee lay before him, below him, a true garden of God, fruitful and manifold with its valleys, hills, mountains, with its Lake of Gennesaret, its River Jordan, its sea-coast, with its two hundred towns. What Joseph could not see, he guessed; he knew it from memory.

He drank in the view. The rocks were reddish grey, juicy green the locusts, silvery the olive trees, black the cypresses, brown the earth. In the plain the peasants, tiny little figures, squatted on the ground and smelt the earth to forecast the weather. Beautiful, rich, colourful, fruitful land. Now, in the spring, even its deserts were covered by grey-green and lavender blossoms.

But they begrudged the land its fruitfulness. Perhaps it was too fruitful. Perhaps the earlier John of Gishala had been right, and it was the price of wine and oil after all which started the endless wars that raged over this land. At any rate it was fertilized with blood. Perhaps the Deity wished it to be fertilized with blood.

Joseph rested in his mountain crevice. All sense of oppression and inner division had fallen away from him. His thoughts ebbed and flowed, and he liked it to be so.

On them, the Jews, the Deity had bestowed this land flowing with milk and honey. It had bestowed more on them.

> The Kingdom that I promise you, its name is not Zion,
> Its name is the earth.

But the dominion of the world was a vague, distant affair. If at least once he had been allowed to see it from afar, the land of his hopes, the land of the Messiah, of justice, of reason! But, "Then you can wait till the grass grows out of your mouth." Joseph laughed, thinking of Akibah's coarse words. A magnificent man, that Akibah.

Again he gazed forth, enjoying the view. At least Galilee existed. He had been forced to let so many things slip from his grasp, hopes and beliefs; Galilee he would not let slip; he clung to it now, he held it fast.

He had wanted to preach reason, the kingdom of reason, of

the Messiah. Such a prophetic calling comes too dear, my good fellow. Who takes the part of that prophet must pay with too much self-denial. But it is sweet and honourable to preach nothing but the cause of one's people, of one's nation. A prophetic calling of that kind sustains a person, inwardly and outwardly. It gives one fame and inner satisfaction.

From the distance, from below, came a noise. Joseph knew that far below his feet, invisible to him, there was a road; the noise seemed to be the trot of horses. Involuntarily he ducked deeper into the rocky fissure which sheltered him.

Why really was he here? What was his business here, in Galilee, in the midst of insurrection, in the midst of war, he, an old man? Here he could only ruin himself; he could help no one.

Nonsense. As if he had ever wanted to help anyone. He had had to grow so old before he understood that he had never wanted to help anyone else, always only himself. He had wanted to be "I," always only "I," and of all that he had thought and written and told himself, the "Psalm of Self" had been the only true thing.

> I will be I myself; I will be Joseph
> As I was born out of my mother's body,
> And not a pawn between peoples
> Forced to declare myself of the one side or the other.

Justus had really wanted to help, help the others, the distant peoples. Poor, great, knightly Justus. Too soon were you born, too soon did you labour, a forerunner, a prophet of an unfashionable truth. Bitter and unhappy you lived your life, bitter and unhappy you died; your work is forgotten. The reward of the just.

The Messianic hope must exist, true; otherwise one could

not live. And there must be people who proclaim the true Messiah, not Akibah's, but Justus's. They were elect, those people, but they were elected to misfortune.

I, Joseph Ben Matthias, have experienced this. I have felt it, the true Messianic idea, the whole truth, and I was unhappy. Only when I gave it up did things become better. And I was at one with myself, happy, only when I acted against my reason. Beautiful period, glorious period, when I followed my impulse completely, when I wrote the book against Apion, the stupidest and the best I have written. And perhaps, in spite of everything, the one most pleasing to God. For who is to decide which is the good impulse and which the bad? And even if it sprang from the bad, does not the Book say you should serve God even with your evil impulse?

His chest expanded. He felt light and refreshed; lightly his breath came from his mouth; he felt quite young. About his old lips there was a smile absolutely foolish with happiness. He had had to reach almost seventy before he became so wise as to be unwise. Praise unto you, O Jehovah, our God, who hast let me come this far, and hast let me breathe once more the pure, sweet air of Galilee and the wild tang of war.

In his inmost being he knew that this happiness would not last long, that he would have only a few days more or perhaps only a few hours or perhaps only a few miserable minutes. No, not miserable minutes, but rather very good and happy ones.

HE STARTED on, climbing down. He had heard noises and was wary. He avoided every wider path, ducked wherever he might be seen, set his feet down carefully. But once he made a clumsy step. A stone came loose and fell awkwardly, so that it was heard on the road below. The men riding along the road, Roman horsemen, stopped and began to search the slope of the mountain.

Joseph's vision was no longer as good as his hearing; for a while he did not know whether people from his side or the Romans were searching the slope. Then they came nearer, and he recognized them as Romans.

For a moment a wild panic flooded him and washed away all his strength. He had gone a good distance that day, up and downhill, on rough paths, and suddenly his whole freshness was gone. He was an old man; his heart, which had been so light up to that moment, suddenly lay like a heavy, painful growth in his breast; his knees gave way; he had to crouch down.

Yet gradually the weakness passed, and again he was overcome with his earlier sense of great resignation, of something even like joy that now he had reached his goal. He should have fallen in the days of the first war, in the bloom of youth, in Galilee. He had evaded that; instead he had led a life of great agitation, and brought children and books into the world, good and bad ones, and some still lived and some had vanished; and he had brought about a great deal that was bad, but also some good; and now, very late, he was being given a chance to make up for what he had once criminally failed to do: to die in the war, in Galilee.

So he sat in the light clear air and looked at the men who came toward him, weak in body, but free from fear and filled with expectancy.

The soldiers approached and found an old Jew. They looked at him, undecidedly, and he looked at them, curiously. "Give the password, Jew," their leader demanded finally. "I don't know it," answered Joseph. "What are you doing here?" asked the soldiers. "I have many friends in Galilee," replied Joseph,

"and I was worried about them and wanted to find them."
"So you slink around on hidden paths and don't take the imperial highway?" they asked. And he answered: "I thought
the imperial highway was full of imperial soldiers. So an old
man does better to keep to the side paths." The soldiers laughed.
"That was clever of you," said the leader, "but now you will
probably have to make an even bigger detour than by way of
your mountain paths. And who are you, anyway? You're not
a peasant, and you're not from Galilee either." "I am Flavius
Josephus, of the second rank," said Joseph, and he showed
them his golden ring, and now he spoke Latin, whereas before
they had been speaking Aramaic. "Is that so?" laughed the
soldiers. "You're a member of the second Roman rank? That's
just how we always imagined a Roman Knight." "Well, now
you see," said Joseph amiably, "that reality sometimes looks
different from what you think. Incidentally, I have a valid
passport." And he produced his identification which had been
issued to him at the Governor's headquarters in Cæsarea.

The soldiers did not spend much time looking at the document. "We can't do anything with this scrap of paper," they
said. "Only one signature counts around here, Paulus Bassus's."
Joseph gazed thoughtfully before him and said: "I know your
Paulus Bassus very well, and he knows me very well." At that
the soldiers guffawed at the old wag of a Jew, who claimed to
be a friend of their commander, Paulus Bassus. "Then," they
replied, "you really should have your friend tell you the regulations which he set up. If a Jew or a circumcised man is found on
a Galilean road and he is not a native of a neighbouring locality,
and doesn't know the password, then he's to be regarded as a
spy. Are you a Jew? Are you circumcised?" "I am," said the
old man. The leader was silent for a moment, then he slowly
raised his shoulders and let them fall again; it was almost an
apology. "Well, then," he said. "You seem intelligent; surely

you'll understand that if we make short work of this it isn't out of ill-will, but a rule of the service." "Thank your friend Paulus Bassus," one of them added. Joseph looked at them attentively, one after another. "That I should like to do," he said quietly, "and you would do well to make it possible for me. For I really am a member of the second Roman rank, and I really know your Paulus Bassus very well."

His voice, his eyes, his quiet manner made an impression on the soldiers. And the man did not seem to be a spy; for that job surely they would not have picked such an old, conspicuous Jew. But orders were orders. Besides, they were late; the scouting expedition had taken more time than they had expected. If they loaded themselves down with this fellow and so reached their destination even later, they would get a dressing down; if they did away with him, they were unquestionably in the right.

But the soldiers were not ill-natured. They belonged to the group who had been quartered in the district for a long time; now and again they had had contact with the Jews, and they did not regard them only as enemies. "The regulations say," one of them reflected aloud, " 'Be humane as far as military considerations permit.' " "War is war," said another. "Listen, old man," the leader suggested to Joseph, "we have to get to Tabara, and we haven't much time. We'll try to drag you along. We won't gallop, but we won't walk either. We're late already. It's like in the arena—some survive. We'll give you a chance. We'll tie you to a horse, and if you make it, then you've made it. Is that a good suggestion?" "I think it's a good suggestion," said the one who had spoken first, "and it's in the spirit of the regulations. What do you say, Jew?" he challenged Joseph. The old man looked at him long and thoughtfully. "You're right, my boy," he said. "It's in the spirit of the regulations."

They examined him. He had a few coins on him, a little of the provisions, the identification from the Governor's head-quarters, and on his finger the ring of the second rank. "That could be stolen," they said, and took it from him. Then they climbed down to the road and tied him to one of the horses. The rider was a certain Philippus, a good-natured person. "I won't ride too fast, old boy," he promised, and gave Joseph some wine to drink so that he might be strengthened. Then they rode off.

The wind blew, the air was fresh and aromatic, the trot was not too fast, and for the first few minutes it seemed really not quite impossible that the man would make it. His old feet ran, he breathed evenly, and they said: "Well, now, you see, the main thing is not to give up." But then he began to pant, and then he stumbled and fell. His gown was torn, he bled, but only from scratches, nothing serious. He soon got to his feet and ran on. Then he fell again, this time more seriously, yet it was only his arms and face. Philippus stopped his horse, gave his prisoner another drink, and granted him a minute before he rode on. But then Joseph fell a third time and this time he was dragged awhile along the road. In spite of the spring there was thick dust on the road, which was fortunate for Joseph; but of course there were stones as well, and when Philippus finally drew rein the old Jew was befouled from head to foot with blood, his eyes were closed, and from his chest came a rattle that was unpleasant to hear.

Philippus called out something to the others, and they gathered around Joseph. "What shall we do with you?" they said. "Obviously you've lost the game. Shall we do away with him," they debated, "or shall we let him lie?" And, "Shall we do away with you, old man, or shall we let you lie?" they said addressing themselves directly to him. "We stuck to the regulations," the leader declared again, apologetically.

Joseph heard them talking, but he did not understand them. They spoke Latin, yet he, the linguist, could understand only the language of his country now, and he was unable to speak. "I think," one of them finally suggested, "we'll leave him to himself. He won't do much harm any more." And they did so. They lifted him up and laid him at the edge of the road, under a yellow bush, so that his face was in the shade. Then they rode away.

Now the region in which this happened was a high plateau, barren, covered with only a few bushes; but in the spring those bushes bore yellow blossoms. So Joseph lay in the mild, bright sunshine, and with blurring senses he absorbed the yellow-speckled desert and the mild, cheerful sun.

The Joseph who had come to Rome to impregnate Rome and the world with the Jewish spirit;

The Joseph who had hailed General Vespasian as the Messiah;

The Joseph who had married the prisoner of war, Vespasian's concubine, Mara; and later the Græco-Egyptian, Dorion;

The Joseph who had fought in Galilee as a Jewish leader, and then from the camp of the Romans had watched the burning of the Temple and Jerusalem;

The Joseph who had been witness of Titus's triumph and who had bowed beneath the yoke of his triumphal arch;

The Joseph who had written the warlike book of the *Maccabees,* and the politely conciliatory *Jewish War,* and the cosmopolitan, lukewarm *Universal History,* and the patriotically ardent *Apion;*

The Joseph who had struggled in vain for his son Paulus, and who had caused the deaths of his sons Simeon and Matthias;

The Joseph who had sat at the table of three Emperors and of the Princess Berenice and of the Grand Doctor Gamaliel and of the violent Akibah;

The Joseph who had studied the wisdom of the Jewish

Scriptures, of the Doctors, of the Greeks and Romans; who had come back always to Koheleth's final conclusion that all was vanity, and yet who had never acted on that principle;

That Joseph Ben Matthias, priest of the first rank, known to the world as Flavius Josephus, lay now upon the slope, his face and his white beard befouled with blood, dust, muck, and spittle, breathing his last. All the bare, yellow-speckled surrounding uplands and the bright sky belonged now to him alone; the mountains, the valleys, the distant lake, the pure horizon with the solitary bird of prey, were there for him alone and were nothing but the frame of his being. The whole land was filled with his ebbing life, and he was one with the land. The land came to get him, and he sought it. He had sought the world, but he had found only his land; for he had sought the world too soon. The day had come. It was a different day than he had imagined, but he was content.

As WEEKS passed without any news of Joseph, Mara addressed herself to the Governor in Cæsarea and the Grand Doctor in Jabne.

The Roman officials made a serious effort; it was a question of a member of the second rank, who was known to Rome and the court. And Gamaliel, horrified, did everything to find Joseph. High rewards were offered to those who brought him in dead or alive. Yet they could discover only that he had last been seen in Esdraela; from there on all trace vanished. It was difficult to find a lost man in the territory ravaged by the war; there were tens of thousands of corpses after that uprising.

A month passed; Pentecost came, the Pentecost of which the men around Doctor Akibah's table had dreamed, but it was a bloody Pentecost for Judæa. And the hot month of Tammuz came, and the anniversary of the day when the siege of Jerusalem had begun, and the month of Ab came, and the anniversary of the day when Jerusalem and the Temple had been burned. And still no trace was found of Joseph Ben Matthias, whom the Romans called Flavius Josephus. It appeared that they would have to give him up for lost, and Gamaliel had to abandon hope of holding a worthy funeral for the greatest writer the Jews of that century had possessed.

Then the Doctors said: "As it is written of Moses, our teacher, 'But no man knoweth of his sepulchre to this very day.'" And all recognized that it was Joseph's work which was destined to be his memorial, and nothing else.